NO OBVIOUS CAUSE

VALERIE KEOGH

ALSO BY VALERIE KEOGH

No Simple Death

For Robert

An Garda Síochána: the police service of the Republic of Ireland.

Garda, or gardaí in the plural.

Commonly referred to as *the guards* or *the gardaí.*

Direct translation: "the Guardian of the Peace."

1

The old house was set back off the road, down a long, curved driveway lined with maple trees. Their autumn display, glorious the week before, had been blown to smithereens by a storm that had battered the Dublin suburb of Foxrock for two days. The wind had dropped in the early hours and now fat grey clouds sat waiting for their turn to wreak havoc. But the maple trees had already given in. Their autumn finery shed, they settled down to wait for the spring.

Detective Garda Sergeant Mike West murmured 'nice' as he navigated the entrance between two stone pillars and drove slowly towards the house. He and his partner, Garda Peter Andrews, were responding to a call for assistance from uniformed gardaí who had earlier answered an emergency call from a panicked family. West, staring in appreciation at the beautiful home that appeared in front of him, thought it was an unsuitable place to find a dead body.

On the short journey from Foxrock Garda Station, neither man had bothered to speculate on what they might discover, they'd know soon enough. There was plenty of time to begin the long round of speculation and investigation when they decided it warranted it. Suspicious deaths didn't always mean murder, but standard procedure meant they treated it as such until told otherwise.

West parked on the paved semicircle in front of the imposing house between an old, but perfect BMW, a fairly new Ford Fiesta, a battered Renault and an ambulance whose crew were sitting in the front, their eyes shut, their services currently redundant.

'That's Doc's,' Andrews said, nodding towards the Renault and referring to Dr O'Halloran, who, along with his occasional work for the gardaí, had a small practice in the village. 'We were lucky he was available.'

West stepped out of the car, his eyes drawn to the beautiful house, its classic lines and mellow brickwork drawing a sigh of appreciation.

Andrews, however, was staring up at the ominous clouds with distrustful interest. 'It's going to chuck it down, look at that sky,' he complained, with a grumble to equal the distant sound of thunder.

Grey eyes narrowed in impatience. 'You're standing in front of an amazing piece of architecture and all you can do is to complain about the weather – you're a philistine, Pete.'

'Joyce has organised a fifth birthday party for Petey,' Andrews said glumly. 'On Saturday, twenty of his friends will be descending on our very small house. If this blasted, dreadful weather keeps up, they will have to stay indoors. That's not being a philistine, that's being a realist, or maybe...' he added, reconsidering, '...a survivalist.'

The two men, each with their own thoughts and concerns, headed up the worn, stone steps to the front door where a uniformed garda greeted them and directed them to the hub of the more immediate matter.

Not that there was anything pressing about a dead body; it

wasn't going to get any more dead. No last-minute reprieve, but for West, there was a certain urgency in getting to the scene. The sooner they saw the body and the crime scene, if crime it was, the sooner they could find some clues, some evidence, the proof they needed to put whoever it was that *done it* away.

They'd pick up all the pieces, arrange them, struggle to get them to fit and finally, with luck, hard work and a bit more luck, they'd have the jigsaw complete, and would show the finished picture to the powers that be and the bad guy would get banged up.

Simple.

If only, West thought, his footsteps loud on the wide, oak floorboards of the entrance hall. A stunning, stone, cantilevered stairway dominated the space, bringing him to an abrupt halt. 'Wow,' he said, almost reverently, staring up to where the stairway curved out of sight. 'Isn't that just amazing.'

'Amazing,' Andrews said sarcastically, and with a none-too-gentle thump on West's arm, they moved on.

Murmurs, as they approached the back of the house, separated gradually into individual voices, one calm and measured, the other raised in the high-pitched pain of someone struggling to understand death's unexpected arrival.

A short corridor from the entrance hall finished in front of two doors. A uniformed garda stood between them, a slightly anxious look appearing on his face as the two men approached.

West recognised the nineteen-year-old, as Garda Anthony Mackin, recently transferred from Waterford. He was also familiar with the slightly shocked look on the young officer's face. His first dead body, he guessed. 'Well, fill us in,' he said without preamble, officialdom being a better response than sympathy. He hid a smile when the report came in clear, concise terms, without elaboration, exaggeration or extraneous details, recognising ambition when he saw it. Mackin, he decided, was determined to make his mark, to be remembered when the time came for the promotion he obviously craved.

'Garda Cosgrave and I answered a 999 call at ten this morning,' Mackin said. 'We arrived at the same time as the ambulance. The paramedics ascertained, almost immediately, that the victim, a Gerard Roberts, was deceased. Garda Cosgrave and I considered the circumstances to be suspicious—'

West interrupted the smooth flow abruptly. 'Why?'

The young garda, intent on getting his report out without a hiccup, was momentarily nonplussed by the question. 'W-why?' he stuttered.

Andrews, seeing his confusion, took pity. 'Why did you think it was suspicious?'

Sweat prickling his brow, Mackin took a deep breath and refocused. 'I looked at the dead man's face, sir. There was blood around his mouth, and it looked as if he'd chewed off part of his tongue. I thought, maybe, he'd been poisoned.'

West frowned at him. 'It sounds like he may have had a seizure. Maybe he was allergic to something?'

'His wife insisted he wasn't,' Mackin said. He drew a breath and, since no one made further comment, he continued. 'Present at the time of our arrival was his wife, Clare, his daughter Emma, and son, James. We asked them to stay in this room' – he indicated one of the rooms behind him – 'and they have been there since. A few minutes ago, a lady came from the victim support group, *Offer*, and she is sitting with Mrs Roberts.'

Garda Mackin closed and pocketed his notebook with a look of relief on his face.

It was short-lived as Andrews quickly queried the last sentence. 'A lady from where?'

'From *Offer*,' Mackin said, his voice quavering at the sharp tone. 'You know? The victim support group that started up recently?'

'How'd she hear of this so quickly?' West asked. 'She was here before us.'

'I think she was in the station when I rang back,' Mackin explained.

'You rang back after you spoke to us?'

The garda took a breath and explained. 'The lady, Mrs Roberts, I mean, was hysterical. I asked them to send a female garda.' He blushed, the colour spreading out to his rather protuberant ears. 'I thought it would be better, you know... a woman... but there were none available so they asked if a victim support person would be of assistance.' He shrugged helplessly. 'Mrs Roberts was shrieking, Sergeant, I didn't know what to do with her. The ambulance crew and the doc were busy with Mr Roberts, so I said yes. She arrived only a minute or so before you.' He looked worried. 'I thought it was okay to let her be with the family.'

Neither West nor Andrews thought it was okay. If Gerard Roberts had been murdered, and they had yet to establish that fact, there was a statistically high chance that it had been done by someone he knew. His family would all be under suspicion. This soon after the murder, if murder it was, guilt might be seen in the shiftiness of eyes, nervous garrulousness, a tremor, an uncertain laugh, a reticence – all the nuances and signs that experienced detectives would be looking for. They didn't need those first signs diluted and adulterated by an outsider who would be unaware of them, someone who would console and offer a shoulder to cry on. Who would listen without hearing at all.

West was about to enlighten Mackin, when the door behind him opened and Dr O'Halloran appeared. His narrow face, topped with a thick mop of greying hair, looked grimmer than he had ever seen it.

'I thought I heard your voice,' the doctor said, extending a hand. 'A bad one this. Gerard was a patient of mine. His whole family were.' Shaking his head sadly, he heaved a sigh. 'A very bad one, Sergeant, but I suppose we'd best get on with it.' He stepped back and waved West and Andrews into a bright, high-ceilinged, well-appointed kitchen.

Free-standing bespoke furniture, lined two out of the four walls; the third held two floor-to-ceiling windows overlooking the garden, and the fourth, a connecting double door into the other room where the grieving family sat.

Stopping in the doorway, West and Andrews stood silently, observing the scene, taking mental photographs of the position of the body, the layout of the room. They would have a multitude of photographs, true, but both men found this initial evaluation to be a critical step in what would be, more than likely, a long winding stairway. Or perhaps, more like an escalator, moving up, stopping on every floor, and breaking down if they weren't careful.

Apart from the dead body, it didn't look like a crime scene. There were no overturned chairs or broken dishes, no signs of a struggle. In fact, it appeared quite peaceful; light from the big windows combining with the pale-yellow walls to make the room bright, even on this grey day. A big, antique pine table surrounded by mismatched chairs, took centre stage. At the head of it, Gerard Roberts was seated, leaning forward, his head resting on arms crossed in front of him. He could have been sleeping or having a well-deserved rest, his head turned as if to look through the windows and out across the garden.

Andrews muttered to himself and then, at a questioning glance from West, he spoke aloud. 'It doesn't look suspicious, Mike. A heart attack or stroke, I'll bet. It's too quiet and orderly for a murder.'

West silently agreed, but then smiled suddenly. 'What is it you're always saying about Petey when he's quiet?'

Remembering drew a grimace from Andrews who had spent the previous weekend repainting their lounge after Petey, unusually quiet, was found drawing on the walls with his crayons. He had succeeded in covering three walls before being discovered. When later questioned by an irate father, he had innocently said he was copying cave paintings Andrews had shown him in a National Geographic magazine the previous week.

Quiet, then, both men knew, didn't necessarily mean innocent.

Dr O'Halloran had crossed the room to stand beside the body. He waited until they joined him before saying, 'A fifty-five-year-old man, who suddenly collapses and dies. When I was called, despite knowing Gerard to be a healthy man, I suspected a heart attack, aneurysm or even a massive stroke. You'd have thought the same, wouldn't you?' He waited, briefly, for an acknowledgement from the two men, before shaking his head, his face grim. 'Well, you would be wrong. None of these things, I am almost positive, killed poor Gerard. Well, except he did eventually die of a heart attack, I suppose, but cause of death was, almost certainly, poisoning.'

'Garda Mackin was correct,' murmured Andrews, causing the doctor to raise his eyebrows.

West and Andrews moved to stand beside him. From this angle, the peaceful scene that both men had noticed when they had stood in the kitchen door, changed radically. They were used to death, had seen their fair share over the years, but neither had developed the impermeable carapace that allowed them to examine the last death throes of Gerard Roberts without a twinge of sympathetic horror.

Because the man had not died a comfortable death. His mouth was locked in a bloody rictus of agony, and his staring eyes reflected terror. Hanging from his mouth, barely attached, was the mangled remains of his tongue. The resemblance to West's favourite coarse liver pâté with cranberry sauce, was stomach-churning. He'd never order it again.

O'Halloran spoke softly. 'From the way his tongue has been bitten almost completely through, I'm assuming he had a seizure prior to death. Since I know Gerard, I was able to discount an allergic reaction. It only leaves poison.'

Whether it was accidental or deliberate was, at this stage, immaterial. It wasn't a natural death. West and Andrews exchanged glances. It was time to set the ball rolling.

'Thank you, Dr O'Halloran,' West said, 'we'll take it from here.'

The doctor looked towards the double doors into the other room. 'I'd like to pay my respects to Clare and the children. I'll come back after you've spoke to them.' He picked up a cumbersome bag, and took a last glance at the dead man. 'I'll do the necessary paperwork, of course.'

West waited until O'Halloran had left the room before taking out his mobile. 'It's a suspicious death,' he informed Inspector Morrison when he was put through. 'The garda doc thinks he was poisoned.' It was a short conversation. He slipped his mobile back into his pocket. 'Right,' he said to Andrews. 'The pathologist, and Garda Technical Bureau, will be on their way soon. Let's go speak to the family.'

2

They retreated back into the hallway and stood in silence, listening to the murmur of voices from the adjoining room. West glanced at Mackin who still wore a worried expression, and was unconsciously shuffling from one foot to the other. 'At least, Mrs Roberts doesn't sound hysterical anymore, but in future keep everyone away till we get here, and that includes victim support workers.'

'Yes, sir,' Mackin replied promptly, glad to be escaping lightly.

'Okay, go, take Garda Cosgrave and monitor the gates. The Garda Tech Bureau and pathologist are on their way. The press might descend on us yet, keep them at bay.'

At the mention of the technical bureau, the garda's eyes lit up. 'It's murder?'

'A suspicious death,' West said quellingly, 'let's keep our minds open, and our mouths shut.'

Taking him literally, Mackin pressed his lips together and headed back down the corridor to the front door.

'He'll learn,' Andrews said dismissively, and looked towards the room where the family were sitting. 'Should we go in?'

'We may as well hear what they've got to say,' West agreed and followed him through. He'd expected a dining room, or maybe a living room, but the room they entered was more akin to a conservatory with huge windows, pale wood and numerous skylights. Huge exotic plants, many taller than the two detectives, had been cleverly positioned by some well-meaning if incredibly optimistic designer to provide shade from the sun; today, in the gloom of the stormy sky, the room was more like the lower reaches of a tropical jungle.

The large plants also served to divide the room into a number of smaller seating areas. Both men stood silently as they looked through the fronds of a plant to where the family sat around a table, the mother weeping quietly, her son and daughter on either side, each with an arm around her. Opposite and speaking quietly, holding their attention, was the victim support person.

It was instant recognition. West wasn't sure if his gasp was audible, but he felt Andrews' eyes on him as he continued to stare across the room. She hadn't been a victim support person when he'd met her in the course of a case, what was it, five months ago? He remembered her name without hesitation: Edel Johnson.

Five months ago, he'd watched as the lift doors closed behind her in a Cork hotel. He hadn't seen her since, had lost count of the times he'd picked up the phone, a casual *just checking to see if you're okay* on the tip of his tongue. Each time, pulling his hand away, biting his lip and swallowing words he knew were pointless.

Five months.

He had dragged his reluctant body around Dublin's social scene, renewing old acquaintances, remembering quickly why he had dropped out, but persevering, jumping in and out of several, intensely sexual, but ultimately unsatisfying entanglements, only to wake every morning knowing he had failed yet again. But he continued the sequence, determined to convince himself that his attraction for Edel was due to the simple fact of proximity; they'd been thrown together by circumstances not of their making, nothing more.

Five months... they may as well have been five seconds. He straightened his shoulders, tried to remember where his backbone was, and straightened that. This wasn't the time or place. His focus had to be on the dead man slumped over the table in the next room. He listened to the soft murmur of voices, unable to make out the conversation, his gaze sweeping lightly over the bereft family to linger on the speaker. Her words may not have been audible, but whatever she was saying seemed to be having a calming effect.

She had put on some weight since he'd seen her last, a healthy glow replacing the pallor he remembered. He took a deep breath; she looked stunning.

A gravelly harrumph from beside him, brought his attention quickly around to Andrews, who was doing innocent as only he could. 'You wanted to say something?' he asked, a note of warning in his voice.

'Nothing, just clearing my throat. Must be all these plants,' Andrews observed, nodding to the overgrown greenery touching his shoulders.

West shook his head, his eyes still taking in the sight of Edel sitting there, his brain playing catch-up. Then, firmly putting her to one, ever-increasing, corner of his mind, he turned to face Andrews. 'On second thoughts, let's wait to see what the pathologist says before we speak to them. After all, it might be accidental.' West had never hoped for the outcome so much – it would mean he was superfluous, and he'd happily choose to be so, rather than have to face Edel. He knew Andrews' sharp eyes were on him; he'd tried to hide his attraction to the woman when she'd been a murder suspect, but hadn't done a very good job. Or maybe, Andrews just knew him too well.

Now here she was again, like a bad penny, at what could be another murder scene.

Another cough, and muttered complaint about plants, brought his attention back to Andrews. 'Let's get out of here,' he said.

Back in the hallway, he checked the time. It would have made sense to have spoken to the family while they waited. He could feel assessing eyes on him and reached into his pocket for his phone. 'I've a few calls to make,' he said, nodding towards the entrance hall. 'I'll go and make them in my car, hopefully by the time I'm done, the pathologist will be here.' He headed off without another word and sat in his car, a dead phone held to his cheek.

Twenty minutes later, just as he saw Andrews coming out with an expression on his face that said he was both bored and fed up, a car rolled up the driveway. Recognising the pathologist, West got out and gave him a wave as he pulled up alongside.

Dr Niall Kennedy was not only quick and efficient, generous with information when it came, and willing to offer speculative theory if requested, but also a man who knew when to shut up and butt out. A combination, in West's opinion, that was rare if not unique.

'Hi,' Kennedy said, climbing from his car with a grin. 'Well, if it isn't Mike and Peter, Batman and Robin, The Lone Ranger and Tonto.'

'Just don't get to Dumb and Dumber, please,' West quipped.

The pathologist chuckled. 'Would I?'

It would have been on the list. West had been the recipient of his sarcastic sense of humour on many occasions. Humour helped them keep afloat when they appeared to be drowning in a sea of grime and crime, but sometimes, just sometimes, the cure wasn't worth it.

He gave him a quick rundown of the situation as Kennedy opened his boot and took out his scene of crimes kit.

'Right,' he said, pulling on a disposable jumpsuit. 'I know you'll want to know everything, as soon as, but try to give me a few minutes.'

West and Andrews walked with him to the door of the kitchen, neither surprised when the pathologist shut it firmly after him. They were about to return to the entrance hall when the other door opened slowly and they turned, as one, to see Edel Johnson silhouetted against the dark greenery of the plants behind. She was dressed simply in T-shirt, trousers and jacket but the clothes were well-cut and expensive, the overall impression being one of restrained elegance. Her auburn hair was tied back in some kind of knot, tendrils escaping to caress her cheek and throat.

West's breath caught sharply. His feelings hadn't changed. It was pointless to deny it. She had taken up residence in a part of his brain he kept tightly locked. Only in the early hours of the morning, that hour of wakefulness when everything seemed to him impossible, when there was a need for succour, for something simply to hold on to and keep the screams at bay, did he unlock that door and allow himself to think about her.

And in those wakeful moments, he rehearsed, over and over again, what he would say if he ever bumped into her. The scenario was always set in some shop, restaurant or theatre; some social setting where they would meet as equals, two ordinary people who would exchange polite small talk, who would look at one another, and think *maybe*. And he would, perhaps, suggest they meet for a drink. And, of course, she would smile and say *yes*.

And it would be ordinary, and delightful and, just maybe, a little romantic and magical.

That was the way his dreams went. That's how he hoped their next meeting would be, if it ever happened.

Not at another damn crime scene.

This wasn't what he envisaged at all. This wasn't ordinary. You couldn't have polite small talk over a corpse. She was going to see him as a policeman… again.

Andrews, moving to break the prolonged silence, stepped forward with his hand outstretched. 'Mrs Johnson, good to see you. You appear to have changed career.'

She returned the smile and took his hand. 'Hello, Garda Andrews. No, not a career change exactly. I do some volunteer work for *Offer* and happened to be in the station when the call came through. It's a relatively new group, not everyone is aware of us as yet.' She indicated the room behind with a nod of her head. 'Mrs Roberts was hysterical when I arrived. She's calmer now, but I don't think it would take much to set her off again. I did ask if she wanted her doctor, but she refused. Her daughter's not much help, she appears to be in shock, and the son just keeps saying, "he can't be dead".'

West saw her eyes flick to him, and then back to Andrews. 'I thought, if you were finished, I could make the usual panacea,' she said, and then, when neither man answered, she clarified. 'Tea. I thought I could make some tea.' She reached up and brushed a strand of hair behind her ear, the gesture easy, relaxed, poised.

'I'm afraid that won't be possible just yet,' West said. This wasn't the anxious, distraught woman he had met five months ago. He realised, with a start, that he resented her poise. Why wasn't she as disturbed at seeing him, as he was at seeing her? He kept his voice clipped and cool, an instinctive reaction to the heat this woman generated. 'It would've been better, if you'd waited until after we'd interviewed the family before offering support, you know, in case you inadvertently say the wrong thing, or they made a confession.'

Edel's friendly smile froze at his tone, and at the dismissive expression on his handsome face. Then it faded away completely, along with the slight frisson she had felt at seeing him again.

At her lowest, abandoned in a remote cottage in Cornwall months before, it was to this man she had turned, and he had been there for her. The last time she had seen him was in Cork, where she had been hiding from the man who had murdered her husband. He'd gone to tell her it was all over. That she was safe. She had thought he might keep in touch, ring her to check that she was doing all right. But he hadn't.

The realisation that she had been stupid, came with a pang. He'd just been doing his job. Why had she expected something more? She should have learned by now.

She'd come through a hell of a lot. Abandoned, betrayed, molested. But she *had* come through it. The counsellor this man had recommended had really helped, and nowadays she felt good about herself. When she looked in the mirror, she could smile at the face that looked back.

She had picked up the strings and ties of old friendships too; rang old girlfriends, apologised for not keeping in touch, arranged meetings for lunch, for coffee. She'd started to enjoy living in Foxrock Village, getting to know people, faces to greet in the shops, and on the street. And if she still felt lonely, she didn't feel quite so alone.

West had been there when she needed help, but she didn't need help anymore. His or anyone else's. And, if there had been that little frisson when she saw him, it was definitely gone now.

Fixing him with a glacier gaze, she said, '*Offer* is the first victim support group to be available in this area. It is our policy to immediately inform the person or persons we are here to support, that they must not discuss the case until given permission to do so by the gardaí.

'As to my, inadvertently, saying something wrong, you will be relieved to know that the most dangerous statement I made, was to encourage Mrs Roberts to take deep breaths to control her hysteria. When I arrived, she would have been incapable of answering even the most innocuous of questions; you should be grateful that she is now completely coherent and calm. Unless, of course, you prefer to question people when they are shrieking in misery?'

Having given him a large and pointed piece of her mind, she watched a tide of red creeping over his face. It might be embarrassment, it also might be anger. She didn't care either way. Turning her back on him, she reached for the doorknob.

Anger flushed his face. 'Just a moment,' he said. 'I am aware, Mrs Johnson, that you have experience both as a witness and' – he reminded her acidly – 'as a suspect. However, you are not a member of the Garda Síochána. If Mrs Roberts, in the middle of her hysteria, had confessed to murdering her husband, what would you have done? Told her to take a deep breath? To think again?

'Shortly,' he said to her rigid back. 'We will be interviewing everyone. We are going to do so, one by one. You may wait with the other members of the family, and continue your inoffensive consolation, or come with the person being interviewed, but I caution you, if you come to the interview, you don't open your mouth. Understood?'

She turned and glared at him. He had to be honest with

himself, and admit that he preferred this version of Edel Johnson to the wan, pathetic victim who had hidden out in the Cork hotel. But he'd known, even then, that her wretched look was hung on a rod of steel. The same steel that was in her stance now as she faced up to him.

'Perfectly, Garda Sergeant West,' she said, a sharp platinum edge to her voice. Without another word, she pushed open the door, shutting it with a decided snap behind her.

Andrews coughed. 'Well, that went well, didn't it?'

'You know I was right,' West said, in a voice that was tightly controlled, and laced with justification. 'Mrs Roberts could have confessed to poisoning her husband. Hell, any of them could have confessed. And what would she have done. Eh?'

'Of course, you were right,' Andrews agreed soothingly, 'though perhaps you needn't have been quite so obnoxious.'

Obnoxious? Yes, West supposed he had been. Attempting to avoid the fall from the tightrope of emotional complications, he had opted, for the safety net of officialdom and dogma. He rubbed a weary hand over his eyes, wishing for a rewind button. If it were only that easy.

But it wasn't. Settling the mantle of Garda Síochána firmly on his shoulders, he concentrated on the job he was paid to do.

3

He heard the pathologist's call with a sense of relief and, ignoring Andrews' critical eyes, opened the door into the kitchen. 'That was quicker than we'd expected. What have you got for us?'

Kennedy was peeling off disposable gloves. 'Obviously, I can't be sure until I have done tests,' he said, with the air of a man who knew he was going to impart some unusual information, 'but I am 99.9 per cent sure it's cyanide poisoning.'

Both men looked startled, West recovering his voice first. 'Cyanide. But not cyanide gas?'

'Correct. Had it been gas, the whole family would be dead. I'd say he ingested it. Again, I am speculating,' he said, holding his hands up, 'which, of course, as a scientist I shouldn't do. I'll be able to give you a more definitive answer later, but the signs are pretty clear.' He pointed towards the dead man. 'See how red his face is?'

'Isn't that an indicator of carbon monoxide poisoning?'

'Yes, but death from carbon monoxide poisoning is not normally preceded by a seizure. Plus, in a kitchen this size, it would be impossible to contain enough carbon monoxide to kill so quickly, and this man died within a few minutes. It's less commonly known that cyanide poisoning also leaves its victims with a red face. It's due, if you're interested in the science bit, to cyanide-haemoglobin complexes.'

West looked around the kitchen with its assortment of jars, packets and boxes. Poison. The technical bureau was going to have its hands full. 'Could it have been an accident?' he asked, delving into his limited knowledge of poisoning and finding next to nothing on cyanide.

Dr Kennedy considered a moment. 'I think it highly unlikely. I couldn't imagine where you would get your hands on it, for one thing, but it's not impossible. There are some vegetables that naturally contain the cyanogenic glycoside toxin. Cassava, for instance, a vegetable that's poisonous when raw, but can be safely eaten when cooked. There are well-documented cases of accidental cyanide poisoning, especially in parts of Africa where it's widely eaten. It's available in the UK, but I've never heard of an incident here. Apricot stones also contain the toxin, but it's unlikely that our friend here was chewing on many of those.'

'So, he ate something that contained this cyanogenic glycoside toxin. Accidently or not.'

Kennedy, never a man for doing something simply when it could be done with a flourish, shrugged elaborately. 'Looks that way. The stomach contents should give us more detail. I'll be able to tell you the concentration in his body and that might also be an indicator of how he took it. The lethal dose of cyanide ranges from zero point five to three milligrams per kilogram body weight.' He ran an experienced eye over the dead man and quickly calculated. 'He's a slightly-built man, probably doesn't weigh more than seventy kilograms, so you are looking at between thirty-five and two hundred and ten milligrams of cyanide.'

'That doesn't seem much,' Andrews said, looking again at the dead body.

'It doesn't take much. Cyanide is a quick, effective killer.' With a final nod and wave, the pathologist departed, promising to let them know the results of the autopsy as soon as possible.

The Garda Technical Bureau arrived just as Kennedy was leaving and, with a quick exchange of information with him, the officer in charge moved to join West and Andrews.

'Detective Sergeant Maddison, Garda Technical Bureau,' he said with a friendly nod to each. 'If you're happy to let us carry on, we'll start packing and tagging, but first we'll get Mr Roberts sorted and ready to be moved.'

West resisted the temptation to ask how long it was going to take. 'Yes, that's fine, you carry on,' he said. 'We're going to speak to the family.'

It was easier, in the end, to interview the softly sobbing Mrs Roberts where she sat at the conservatory room table. The siblings, Emma and James, were brought to another downstairs room, accompanied by Garda Mackin who stayed with them as they sat, hand in hand.

Mrs Roberts was a little woman, no more than five feet tall, and slightly built. Fine, delicate hands rested on the arms of the chair, the nails neatly manicured but unpolished. Small, ornate gold earrings and a diamond engagement ring next to a narrow band of gold on her ring finger, were her only adornments. Her clothes were unremarkable, but well-cut and obviously expensive. She was probably usually described as a neat, pretty woman. Today wasn't usual, however, and her face had a grey, harried expression; eyes that normally viewed the world from under mocha-coloured lids, were puffy and swollen with tears. The eyeshadow and attendant mascara had long since washed off onto the countless tissues that littered the floor around her chair. She reached, mechanically, for a fresh one and blew her nose gently as the two detectives sat opposite.

They introduced themselves and made the standard expressions of sympathy. She looked at them, eyes as wide as her swollen lids would allow, and whimpered. 'I don't understand, what happened to Gerard? How can he possibly be dead?'

'That's what we're going to find out, Mrs Roberts,' West replied gently. 'We need you to tell us exactly what happened this morning. Everything you can remember, no matter how irrelevant it may seem to you, okay?'

Taking yet another tissue, Mrs Roberts dabbed her eyes, blew her nose and dropped the tissue onto the growing hillock on the floor. She took a shuddering breath and started to speak, slowly and so quietly that both men leaned forward to hear.

'Gerard got up before me. That's normal really, but we had a late night, so I stayed in bed a little later than usual. He went for a cycle. It's something he usually does at the weekends, but he'd taken a few days off work because the children are back to university next week and he was making the most of it. He came in and kissed me goodbye, and went... I don't know where he went, probably down by Marley Park and up to Two Rock. I don't know definitely but that's where he usually went, he liked the variety. I got up about nine thirty and he was just coming back.' She frowned. 'Actually, he was gone longer than usual, now that I think about it. He usually went for an hour, at the most, but it must have been at least an hour and a half this morning.'

'Did he say why he was delayed?'

A solitary tear plopped to her blouse and shimmered there for a second before soaking in. 'I didn't really speak to him much, you know,' her voice quavered, 'but he was definitely later than usual. He didn't say why, and I was too busy bustling about to ask. I'd planned to do a big fried breakfast for the children. You know, sausages, bacon, eggs. A treat for the end of their holidays.

'Gerard is... was... a bit of a health fanatic, and faddy eater. He didn't eat meat very often, and wouldn't ever eat a fry-up. He was happiest really with a big plate of vegetables; not over-cooked either, they had to be crunchy, almost verging on raw. He'd been to that vegetable shop in the village while he was out and bought some stuff. But that wouldn't have delayed him,' she added quickly, anticipating their interruption. 'He often did pop in there, when out for a ride. He said he'd bought some interesting vegetables and would do his own breakfast.' She looked at West. 'I was barely listening. To be honest, he was always trying new things, experimenting... he had some odd ideas.' A smile tried to materialise but drooped under the weight of sorrow. 'He had some odd ideas,' she repeated, 'but he wasn't an odd man. He was a very good man. And I wished I had listened to him.' The sobbing she tried hard to control took over again, and she wept uncontrollably.

West saw Edel look from the crying woman to him, her head tilted in a question. Their eyes met, and it was as if the last five months had never been. He raised the corner of his mouth in a slight smile, and gave an almost imperceptible nod, watching as she quickly moved to sit closer to Mrs Roberts, taking her hand and speaking soothingly into her ear.

With a glance at Andrews, West stood and both men walked to a far corner of the room separated by the fronds of a giant fern. They listened to the murmurs from the table, the wailing slowing then ceasing, the restoration of calm.

Five minutes passed without a sound before they heard a firm 'Sergeant West' called from the table. They returned to their seats and Mrs Roberts continued her description of an unexceptional morning in the Roberts' household. 'I had everything ready to start cooking the breakfast, but the children still weren't out of bed, so I decided to wait. Gerard went ahead with his, because he was hungry after his cycle and wanted to get some work done in the garden afterward.

'I went into the garden. There were some plants that needed repotting, and I was busy with this when I heard a shout from the kitchen.' Her eyes closed on the memory, a tear squeezing out to run down her cheek. 'I thought he had dropped something, or maybe cut his finger, or something equally trivial. He did tend to make a fuss at minor incidents.' Her breath caught on a sob, and she reached for Edel's hand again. She pinched her trembling lips together for several minutes, and then took a deep breath. 'I was used to him making a fuss about nothing. So, I ignored him.'

She looked around at them, eyes shimmering, lips trembling once more, a stricken look on her face. When she spoke, it was in a whisper they all strained to hear. 'My husband was dying,' she said, 'he called out, probably for help and I... ignored him.' She sat unmoving, the tears now drying on her pale cheeks, and when she spoke again her voice was a barely audible breath. 'When I came in, he was leaning over the table.' Her eyes darted from one to the other as if, on one of their faces, she would find something that would make sense of it all. 'I thought he was resting.' Her eyes glazed over. 'To be honest, I didn't think much of it. I wanted to get the breakfast started.' She looked stricken. 'I went to the drawer to take out the frying pan, turned the ring on, threw on some mushrooms, then looked for the salt. Gerard had taken the salt cellar to the table. I could see it and went to fetch it. And then... ' She held a hand over her mouth and shook her head.

Remembering his own horror when they'd seen the man's face, West felt a tug of sympathy for this neat little lady. He reached across and took her free hand. 'I know it's very difficult for you, Mrs Roberts, thank you. We're going to have a word with Emma and James now, and leave you with Mrs Johnson. A family liaison officer will be assigned to you, and they will keep you informed of what is happening in the investigation. As soon as we know what happened to your husband, we will inform you either through the liaison officer or, more than likely, in person. Do you have any questions?'

There was one, he could tell, and it was one he had heard so many times he had the answer primed before she asked. 'If I had gone to him when he shouted, would I have saved him?'

At least, this time he could be honest, not bend the truth or lie outright as he had done so many times to too many people. 'I spoke to the pathologist before I came through, Mrs Roberts; he thinks death was almost instantaneous. Had you come straight away, the outcome wouldn't have changed.'

She gave a small nod of acknowledgement as her hand reached for a tissue.

Neither of the siblings had anything to add. They had run down the stairs on hearing their mother's scream, and had immediately called an ambulance, although they had known from the start there was no hope. 'I've done a first aid course,' James offered in a colourless voice. 'I could see he was dead before I tried for a pulse. His eyes... he looked terrified.' His voice broke on a sob that he tried hard to cover with a cough. 'I can't believe he's dead. He was the healthiest man, you know, didn't smoke or drink. Rarely ate red meat. All the things you are supposed to do to live forever, that's what my dad did, and he's dead anyway.'

West repeated the information about the family liaison officer. 'At the moment, there's a volunteer from a victim support group sitting with your mother. She is not linked to the gardaí, and is not privy to information about the investigation, but she seems to be helping your mother cope. Is there anybody you would like me to call, anybody who can help you through all this?'

'We're going to ring my aunt, Mum's sister. She doesn't live far away. She'll come when we ring; and her husband, he'll be able to help too,' James said, relief in his twenty-year-old voice; knowing he wasn't quite grown up enough yet to face organising his father's funeral.

'Good. Meanwhile, if you have any questions or if there is anything you want to discuss, please, either talk to the family liaison, or' – he handed him one of his cards – 'you can contact me directly.'

James put the card in his pocket and moved closer to his sister, both of them looking dazed. As West watched, he put his arm around her and she laid her head on his shoulder. He wished he could assure them he'd find out what happened. But he was too experienced a copper to make promises he couldn't guarantee to keep. He could promise he'd do his best. But he doubted it would be of any consolation.

Back in the hall, he rubbed a hand over his face. 'Let's see if they've found anything of interest in the kitchen, Pete. Mrs Roberts mentioned her husband had bought some vegetables this morning. It would be nice to find he had bought some of that... what was it that Dr Kennedy said contained cyanide?'

'Cassata?' Andrews guessed, reaching for his notebook where he had written it down.

'Isn't that a type of ice cream?' West asked.

'No idea, but anyway, not cassata, cassava.'

'Cassava,' West repeated, 'never heard of it. Let's see if they found any indication he used that for his breakfast. His wife said he didn't like his vegetables well-done. Maybe he used this cassava stuff, and didn't cook it properly.'

When they opened the kitchen door, they saw Sergeant Maddison deep in conversation with one of his team, so they stood in the doorway and waited, neither of them patient by nature but both knowing when it was necessary. Nothing could be achieved by bullying their way in, all intimidation and loud noise, full of their own importance. Vital rapport would be lost, perhaps forever, and so much of their job depended on a free and fluid exchange of information. The most frustrating part of their job was finding out that an essential piece of information had been held back for self-advancement by some ambitious, ladder-climbing colleague.

So, they waited. West mentally rewound the tape of what he had said to Edel, rewound it, deleted and started over. If only life could be that easy. Trying to put her out of his head, he glanced at Andrews, seeing a frown on his normally placid face. Petey's birthday, he guessed with a slight smile.

Finally, Maddison came over to them, a ready apology on his lips. 'Sorry to keep you waiting, guys. Was there something specific you wanted to know?'

'It seems the victim ate a meal of lightly-cooked vegetables shortly before he died. Dr Kennedy said that cassava contains cyanide and we wanted to know if you found any, or remnants of any. To be honest, I haven't a clue what cassava looks like, neither does Pete here, so we're grasping a bit.'

'Cassava,' Maddison muttered. 'I don't think I know that one. Hang on though, I have someone who might.' He called one of his team over, a tall, serious-looking man with thick glasses. 'This is Samir, he cooks a mean curry and uses ingredients I have never heard of. He may know about your cassava.' He looked questioningly at the younger man.

'Sure, I do,' Samir said. 'Cassava, it's a root vegetable, tastes a bit like potato, but it looks like a long, fat, brown parsnip. You peel the rind and cook the flesh really well. It can be eaten in a variety of ways, on its own, or added to a curry. I've used it once or twice, but it's not that common to find in the shops here.'

'Have we found rind from it here?' West asked.

'I don't know, sir. The family have a small food-waste recy-cling bin. It and its contents are going back to the lab for exami-nation. I could have a quick look, if you like, and if that's okay with Sean.' He looked at Maddison for permission, and then headed to where a small green bin had been put to one side. A label attached to the handle identified where the bin had been found. It had been sealed shut, and both men initialled the seal which they would replace and sign again when they had finished their examination of the contents.

Samir peered inside, using a gloved hand to move the contents around, concentrating on looking for a specific discard. 'Here we go,' he said, pulling out a piece of what looked like wood. 'This is the rind of a cassava root.' He held it up for them to see. 'There is some more, not much. Perhaps enough for one small cassava root, no more.'

They all peered at the harmless-looking piece of rind. Andrews sniffed. 'This is our murderer?'

'I don't think so,' Samir said. 'He might have been very sick, he may have suffered from a form of paralysis, but even if he had eaten it raw, I don't think it would have killed him.'

'Paralysis?' West said, taken aback. He leaned closer to peer at the cassava rind and sniff it curiously. 'It looks so... so nothing.'

'I did some voluntary work, some years ago in central Africa, where cassava is commonly eaten,' Samir explained. 'There had been some tribal unrest and, as a result, villagers from isolated regions were cooking it in a hurry without the proper preparation. These were people who already suffered from malnutrition, and several weeks of eating nothing but this under-cooked cassava resulted in cyanide poisoning. It didn't kill them, but left many with a form of paralysis called Konzo which is irreversible. Whole villages were affected because they ate the same thing. It was pretty horrendous, believe me.'

He took the rind back, returned it to the bin, closing it and resealing it. 'I have read research since, which suggests Konzo is caused by the combination of protein malnutrition and high dietary exposure to cyanide. I can't see that as being a factor here, somehow, even if he were paralysed rather than dead.'

'Well, it's about the only thing we are sure of yet, he is definitely dead,' Maddison said, and with a nod dismissed Samir and his recycling bin.

'It's too much of a coincidence, though, isn't it?' West asked, as they walked together from the room. 'Here we have a guy, who we believe died from cyanide poisoning, and a vegetable that contains cyanide is found in his recycling bin. Tell me there isn't a connection?'

'If there is, we'll find it,' Maddison said. 'But you heard Samir, and believe me, this is not a guy who talks about things if he doesn't know what he's talking about. One cassava root would not have killed Gerard Roberts.' With a wave he left them and returned to organise the removal of the specimens to the laboratory.

West had great respect for the forensic process, but more of a respect for his knowledge and experience, and in his experience, coincidences that resulted in a dead body just didn't happen. How many people eat cassava root, and how many people died from cyanide poisoning in Ireland?

He put the questions to Andrews.

'Few and none,' came the brief answer as Andrews, stepping through the front door, spied the dark cloud overhead.

'Exactly,' West replied, opening the car door. He drove slowly down the drive, admiring the well-kept flower beds and lawn, wondering when he had last cut his own grass. He'd make time soon, he promised himself, knowing as he did so that this case might very well run into the weekend. So, what was new. When did he last have one free? Worse, when did he last care? He loved his job, but it was starting to be his social life and, he glanced at Andrews, his family as well.

He hadn't gone to see his parents for weeks, he realised with a twinge of guilt. Another thing he would do when he had time. He knew his mother would understand. She'd stood by him when he turned his back on his law career to join the gardaí. Unquestioning support, in the face of loudly-voiced criticism from friends and colleagues. The support didn't falter. She'd understand, she always did. His father would look at him, as *he* always did, as if he'd just left the room – he'd continue conversations where they'd left off at their last meeting, almost to the word. Unquestioning acceptance. Hard to beat.

He drove through the impressive entrance, stopping for a brief word with Garda Cosgrave who was holding off photographers, the press and the plain nosy. Reporters, recognising both the car and the occupants, surged forward as soon as the car stopped. West, in turn, recognised a reporter from a small local paper, The Foxrock Weekly, and one from a larger national. West believed in using the press, when it suited him, and considered the use as being one of the tools at his disposal. To this extent, he fed them information when it was expedient to do so, but this wasn't one of those times and he gave them the standard 'no comment at this point' dismissal and headed back to the station three miles away. He'd leave, issuing press releases to the press office, or to Inspector Morrison who, freshly returned from extended sick leave, was delving into everybody's work with the zeal of a chocoholic recently introduced to Lily O'Brien's.

A muttering from the passenger seat drew his attention to Andrews who was gazing balefully out the window.

'For goodness sake, you're not still obsessing about the weather, are you?' he asked, half amused, half irritated. 'Tell you

what. Why don't you preempt the weather? Give that kid's club...
what's it called... Clang Clang, Cling Cling?'

'*Bang Bang!*' Andrews said with a grin. 'With an exclamation
mark.'

'Very appropriate, by all accounts,' West replied. 'Anyway,
give them a call, see if they have a vacancy for Saturday.'

Bang Bang! was a newly-opened children's club with a
number of individually designed rooms providing facilities for
play, parties or events. There was one large, well-equipped playroom, that was used on a pay-as-you-play basis, and other rooms
which were rented for parties where games, entertainment and
food came as a package. It was increasingly popular, especially
for the five to ten age group. But it cost. A lot. It wasn't a venue
West would normally have known about, but the law firm he
had worked for had handled some business for the owner.
When they had opened a few weeks before, he had read about
the development with interest.

Andrews looked at him askance. 'Have you any idea what
that would cost for twenty-one kids? Give me a break.'

'Give them a ring. I was wondering what to buy Petey for a
birthday present; I'll pay for the day.'

West had been born into a comfortably well-to-do family,
and had earned a good salary as a solicitor before joining the
gardaí several years before. While in law, he had bought an
apartment in the city for a reasonable amount of money, and
had seen the price soar in the boom years. He'd sold at the top
of the market, but with the houses he wanted out of his league,
he'd banked the money and waited, renting an apartment in
Blackrock that was small but convenient. When the housing
market crashed, not many months later, he was in a good position to pounce and pick up a house in Greystones – spotted by
his eagle-eyed and adoring mother – not precisely for a song,
but certainly for a lot less than the vendors had hoped for.

'It's a steal,' the agent had said, before remembering West was a garda and quickly changing his expression. 'A song. An absolute song.'

West, walking around the beautiful Edwardian semi-detached house on a quiet, leafy road, thought the agent's first words were correct. It was a steal. Even the necessary decorating and refurbishing – the big extension to the back of the house and glass folding doors opening onto the garden – hadn't damaged his finances. His only current expense was the little chihuahua, Tyler, left in his care by an old friend who, last he had heard, was in Japan.

He looked at money as a means to an end. Not something to worry about from one pay cheque to the next. Paying for Petey's birthday party was an easy outlay for him, and would serve to stop Andrews' incessant comments about the weather which were starting to bore him.

His offer hung in the air for a moment, before descending and developing rabid tentacles of pride and offence that hung from Andrews, dragging his face and shoulders down, making him look suddenly older. Used to a comfortable silence, since Andrews wasn't an overly talkative man, it took a few minutes for the tension to become obvious to West. It caught him by surprise before it punched him in the gut. He didn't need to glance at the suddenly severe face to know the damage his unthinking offer had caused, and felt genuine regret for having inadvertently offended a man who he had come to regard as a friend. What could he do? Withdraw the offer? Tell him it wasn't *charity*, and not to be so bloody oversensitive?

Damage repair was definitely required. West had been an exceptional solicitor before deciding his future lay in catching criminals. His quick thinking and adeptness had marked him out for the partnership that had, ironically, been the impetus he had needed to leave. He'd given his notice on the same day the partnership had been offered. The years in law had, however, honed his thinking to a needle-sharp quickness and he employed this now to mend the hole that gaped like the jaws of hell before him.

He continued, casually, as if as an afterthought to his offer. 'The owner, Manuel Armando, was a client of the law firm I worked for, did I tell you? He's Portuguese,' he said, keeping his voice light and chatty. 'He'd originally wanted to call all the clubs *Crianças*, it means children in English. His general manager persuaded him that using a name children couldn't pronounce and parents couldn't spell, would be bad for business. It was he who suggested using the more onomatopoeic *Bang Bang!* It's a very successful business; they've opened five to date around the country. All called *Bang Bang!* but the group as a whole is still registered as a business under the name *Crianças*.' He gave a short laugh. 'Every time he came into the office, he'd tell us to bring our children to his club. When we'd tell him we didn't have any to bring, he'd say loudly, "Bring your sister's, Bring your friend's!" He's one of those men you meet in business who feel they owe you a favour, and are never happy till they have it paid.

'When I left the firm and moved to Greystones, I never thought I'd see him again. Turns out he's a neighbour. Well, not a neighbour exactly, he lives about halfway between my house and the parents'.' He had a quick look to his left. Andrews' face hadn't softened but he could tell he was listening. 'Every time I see him, he asks me the same thing: "When are you going to bring children to my club?" It's become a standing joke with him, and he laughs uproariously each time. It's got to the stage where I avoid walking that way to steer clear of seeing him, and take a long rambling detour instead. It will be a great relief to actually take him up on his offer. Maybe that will be the end of it. I don't know why I didn't think to bring Petey before.'

Passing through the barrier to the station car park, he risked another look at the still silent man beside him. The carved-ice look had thawed slightly, and the tightness had gone from his mouth.

'He'd hardly expect you to bring twenty-one children though, would he?'

'From what I remember, we saved him just over two million euro, Peter, so I doubt very much if he is going to care how many I take.' The legal company West had worked for had indeed saved Manuel Armando a lot of money, and the man had seemed genuine with his invitation, but twenty-one children was possibly pushing it. Maybe he wasn't being completely honest, but he salved his conscience by considering it a version of the truth, rather than an out and out lie.

He had one last weapon in his arsenal. Sneaking a surreptitious look at Andrews' face he decided it was worth using. 'Of course, I don't want to be in the way. You probably want to keep it in the family.'

A perfect shot.

'Don't be daft,' Andrews said quickly, 'you know Petey loves when you come to visit. And Joyce considers you family. You know that damned well.'

'So, you'll let me organise it then?' He watched him from the corner of his eyes, saw him relenting, deciding perhaps that he'd been too quick to see the offer as charity. As it had been, West thought, with a lash of guilt.

'Well, okay then, that would be great. If you're sure?'

West, parking the car in his designated spot, smothered a sigh of relief. 'I'll give him a ring as soon as I get into the office, make sure they have availability, and let you know.'

They walked into the station, as they had walked into the house earlier that morning, lost in thought.

4

It took West twenty minutes of phones calls, and a lot of patience and determination, to get through to Manuel Armando, but only five minutes to apprise the successful businessman of the situation.

'It's very short notice Senhor Armando,' he said, 'and, despite your frequent generous offer, I don't expect to bring such a large party of children for free, but if you could fit us in on Saturday that would be a great favour.'

'Mr West, I insist that *Crianças* would be delighted to accommodate your party, and there will be no charge.'

'No, really, I–'

'I insist. Your law company saved me so much money. It is a small return.'

West laughed shortly. 'Accommodating twenty-one children is a very big return, Senhor Armando. And I no longer work for that law firm, you remember. Even when I did, when your case was dealt with, I was a very junior associate. This is a gift for the son of a friend. I would be happy to pay, or at least to make a contribution.'

'Please, I must insist,' Armando said. 'You have been kind enough to have accepted my invitation. Please be so kind as to accept the terms. As it happens, Saturday is a quiet day because of two cancellations, and it will be no problem whatsoever to accommodate your party. Unfortunately, due to prior commitments, I will not be there myself to welcome you to what I regard as *Crianças'* flagship. But I will impress upon my manager, Ian, that you are an old and valued friend. He will treat you, your friends and the children accordingly.'

A further exchange of civilities and West hung up with a 'phew.' He looked at his watch in frustration, next time he'd just let Andrews moan about the weather and not offer any advice. He'd dug himself a very big hole, he just hoped it wouldn't fill with water and drown him.

Twenty irritating minutes were spent updating Inspector Morrison on the death of Gerard Roberts; twenty, not because there was much to say, but because the Inspector had a comment on every detail, several anecdotes from his past that had little, if any bearing on the case, and advice as to how the sergeant should organise the inquiry, all of which West listened to intently, as a good subordinate should, and proceeded to ignore before he had left the room.

Making his way back to the general detective's office, he saw Andrews at his desk, a phone attached to his ear by an uncomfortably scrunched shoulder. He headed to the coffee percolator in the corner and filled two mugs, adding sugar to one and milk to both. Putting the sugared one in front of Andrews, he perched on the side of the desk.

When he was finished, Andrews put the phone down, picked the coffee up and drank deeply. 'I needed that. That was the vegetable shop in Foxrock. I was trying to find out what Gerard Roberts bought there this morning. I may as well have saved my breath. The young one I was talking to shouldn't be left in charge of a puddle, she might fall in and drown. The owner is on an extended lunch break, and should be back in about an hour. Do you want me to go talk to him?'

West took a sip of the overbrewed coffee and grimaced at the bitterness. 'Bloody hell, this stuff gets worse.' He looked at his watch. 'Let's get something to eat, we've had no lunch and I'm starving. Then we can both go and talk to him. I've just spent twenty minutes with Mother Morrison and need to get out of here.'

'You never got to know him before he went on extended sick leave, did you? He was the scourge of the division, honestly. Tough as the canteen beef. You know what the motor mouths are saying?'

As a garda sergeant, West was less in the way of station gossip than Andrews, but it got to him eventually, usually elaborated and exaggerated. He always listened and usually managed to winkle out the kernel of truth that lay at the heart of it, and discarded the rest. People who said they never listened to gossip missed out on one of the oldest and quickest forms of communication there was. He hadn't heard anything about Morrison, however, and said so.

'They're saying he joined one of those weird religious sects, and that's why he has become all interested, helpful and creepy.'

West laughed. 'He can be as creepy as he likes as long as he stays in his office and doesn't interfere. Okay, where do you fancy for lunch?'

'Let's go to the Lep Inn. Food's always good and we should get parking easily at this time of the day. Plus, they do a good pint of Guinness, by all accounts.'

'Ah,' West sighed dramatically. 'You've said the magic word.'

West drove, listening to Andrews' recounting various titbits of gossip he had heard that morning. He listened to the tone of his voice more than the words, relieved to hear no lingering trace of annoyance at his earlier blunder, thinking, not for the first time, how much he regarded Andrews and valued their partnership. He'd put his foot in it there, thank goodness for *Bang Bang!* Now that was something he never thought he'd be thinking.

They weren't the only ones having a late lunch and they found parking by luck, a car pulling out just as they drove in. The Lep Inn was busy with the flotsam and jetsam of the many and varied offices in the vicinity. There were a few empty seats, but the highly-prized nooks and crannies that gave a modicum of privacy all seemed to be occupied.

Andrews was a veteran and he left West without a word, seconds later his arm appearing from a corner nook to wave the sergeant over.

'How on earth did you spot this?' West asked in admiration, as he settled himself into an elaborate chair of vast proportions.

'Because it's behind this wall, it's often the last to be spotted. Except by regulars like me,' Andrews said smugly. 'Thought I'd head straight for it and hope for the best, and bingo.'

'Well done,' West said, picking up the menu card. 'That conversation with Mother has given me an appetite. Think I'll go for a burger and all the trimmings.'

'Yeah, me too,' Andrews agreed, putting down his card and looking around for one of the serving staff, waving to one as she passed.

The order given, the men sat quietly until a pint was before each. West sat a moment, admiring the black and cream before lifting the glass and taking a mouthful of what was, he decided with pleasure, a really good pint. Andrews, to his disgust, sipped a Heineken with evident relish and no shame.

'A bit of a surprise, wasn't it, seeing Edel Johnson today?' Andrews said, putting his glass down.

'A bit,' came the blunt answer, and then with a quick, decisive change of direction, West asked, 'Have you got someone doing a background check on Gerard Roberts?'

'Yes, Edwards is doing it. We should have some information by the time we get back.'

West checked his watch and frowned. 'Okay. The day is pushing on. Hopefully that will get us somewhere.' He took a mouthful of his Guinness and continued, keeping his voice casual. 'Oh, by the way, I sorted Saturday. No problems, Senhor Armando was delighted I was taking him up on his offer at last. He won't be there himself, but said his manager Ian would look after it all. So, you can let Joyce know.'

Andrew's face lit with pleasure. 'Hey, that's great. Joyce will be pleased and Petey will be over the moon. You sure you won't be bored?'

West almost choked on his mouthful of Guinness. By the time he'd stopped coughing, he was able to put a brave face on and say, 'No, of course not.' He'd forgotten his part in the story and, now, he could hardly back out. He'd have to rely on the demands of the Roberts' case to keep him from spending a free Saturday afternoon with twenty-one screaming five-year- olds. The day after tomorrow. Surely, something would turn up to throw a spanner in the works.

Their burgers arrived with a generous helping of fries. 'This looks good,' West said, using two hands to lift and hold the whole concoction together, sinking his teeth in and letting out a small groan of pleasure.

'Perfect,' Andrews said, before lifting his own burger and tucking in.

Conversation was limited to guttural appreciation of good food until every mouthful was gone and the two men sat before empty plates.

'A glass of red wine would wash that down nicely,' West said.

'Shame we have a case to solve, isn't it?' Andrews replied. 'We should get a job in a nice office, eat like this every lunchtime, drink wine and beer, float back to sit behind our desks till five.'

'Been there, done that,' West said. 'You'd hate it. Come on, let's see what the vegetable shop has to add to the equation.'

A few minutes' drive took them to the centre of Foxrock Village. It wasn't difficult to locate the shop; it was called, without any claims to pretension, The Vegetable Shop.

'At least they didn't stoop to adding a *pe* to the end of shop,' West murmured as they parked on the road outside.

'If they had, they'd have had to add an *olde* and that would make it *The Olde Vegetable Shoppe*. And who wants to buy old vegetables.'

West raised his eyes to heaven as Andrews cackled at his own joke.

The shop was laid out in the tradition of vegetable shops the world over. Trays of vegetables and fruit sat on tables outside the shop, green plastic baskets and paper bags handily set at both ends of the table for customers to help themselves. A multitude of signs gave prices. Per pound and per kilo, West noticed, impressed by their marketing, remembering his mother complaining that kilos made no sense to her whatsoever.

'They're catering to their demographic,' West said to Andrews, with a nod to the signs.

'I was just thanking my lucky stars we don't have to shop here,' Andrews said, pointing to a tray of apples. 'Have you seen the prices? Can we charge them with theft?' Both men, with their wildly different view on the pricing, headed into the shop.

Inside, it was poorly lit and cool. As in many other shops, a number of sidelines had been introduced to increase turnover. Eggs, sauces, condiments, and a variety of utensils neither man could decide a use for, were set on a display table in the centre of the shop.

Andrews reached for one metal object. 'What's this for do you think?'

West took it, turned it over. 'Not a clue.' He put it down and walked around the shelves, surprised to see no staff. Finding a door at the back of the shop, he gave two smart raps of his knuckles. Seconds passed without reaction; he knocked again. This had the desired reaction and a short, thin man opened the door with profuse apologies.

Their identification as the gardaí didn't change his manner, and he immediately asked what he could do for them with a surprising lack of curiosity, as if the gardaí arriving at his shop was a daily occurrence. Red flags went up in both men's minds almost at the same time; someone this free and easy with the gardaí usually had had dealings with them. Someone this willing to be of help often had something to hide.

His instincts heightened, West introduced himself and Andrews. 'We've just a few questions we'd like to ask you, Mr...?'

'Beans, Bernard J. Beans,' the man said.

'Mr Beans,' West started, ignoring a muffled snort from Andrews, 'do you know a customer by the name of Gerard Roberts?'

A mild curiosity swam into Mr Beans' colourless face. 'Certainly, Sergeant. He was here, in fact, just this morning.' He screwed up his nose as he spoke, making him look like an inquisitive rabbit. 'He is a regular customer, one of our best.'

'What did he buy this morning?'

A frown drew Mr Beans' eyebrows together and a bony finger reached up to rub his nose before he answered. 'Well, let me see now... carrots, broccoli, red onions, mushrooms, green beans, figs, a cantaloupe, or was it two?' He considered. 'No, just one. And he also bought some manihot esculenta and a bunch of parsley. He likes to stop here on the start of his cycle, he says the extra weight makes him burn more calories.'

Both men had been listening for cassava, when they didn't hear it, they fixed on the one item they didn't recognise. 'What was that second last one?' Andrews asked.

'Manihot esculenta,' Mr Beans repeated cautiously. 'At least, I think that's how it's pronounced.' He gave a little titter.

'Can we see some, please?' West asked.

Mr Beans rubbed his hands together and tittered again, the sound irritatingly unattractive. 'Well, of course. If we have any left that is. We didn't get an awful lot of it in.' He led them to a corner of the shop, to an area supporting smaller baskets holding fewer items. 'This is where we keep what I like to call the exotic products, and as you can see, I'm afraid we are all out of manihot esculenta.' He indicated a small, empty basket.

West made a *tch* sound of annoyance. 'Can you describe it, please?'

'Describe it? Well I can try. It comes in roots,' Bernard Beans said, using long bony fingers to draw the shape in the air, the fingers fluttering to a halt, giving neither man a clearer picture of the shape. Seeing their blank looks, the man tried to elaborate. 'It's a bit like a big parsnip. It has a hard rind that is peeled away, and then it is cooked much like a potato.'

'Is it the same as cassava?' West asked bluntly, recognising the description of the vegetable as the one they'd heard earlier from the crime scene technician.

The little man squirmed. 'Well, I don't know. I've sold cassava the odd time, and it has been much thinner and shorter. Maybe it's a different variety? I really don't know, I'm afraid. It was sold to me as manihot esculenta, so that's what I sold it on as. It was the name that appealed, actually, that's why I bought it. My customers, at least some of them, like to try the exotic and unusual, you know, a bit of variety. But the appearance let it down. Didn't look the least bit exotic. To be honest, I didn't think it would sell at all.'

'Who is your supplier, Mr Beans? Perhaps we can get more information about this vegetable from them.'

The squirming increased, accompanied now by a shiftiness of expression. 'Supplier? Well, you know, I'm not too sure... you'll have to come back when I can... I use a number of different sources and...'

West interrupted his ramblings with a curt, 'The name of your supplier or suppliers, Mr Beans. Or do I need to go and get a court order?'

A heavy sigh deflated the already thin man so that he seemed to shrink to half his size. 'I don't always get my supplies from the usual source, you see. Sometimes, especially with the more unusual items, I have to go to other sources...'

Reaching the end of his patience, West's voice was sharp. 'Mr Beans, I want to know where you got that manihot escu-whatever.'

'Manihot esculenta,' Beans repeated with a sniff. 'I got it from a woman who'd brought it back from a holiday to her homeland. Her family had given it to her, and she hadn't the heart to tell them she hated the sight of the stuff.'

'From where?'

'Guyana.'

'You do know it is illegal to import raw vegetables from abroad without a licence, don't you, Mr Beans?'

'I didn't,' he said, shaking his head. 'I didn't import them. I was just doing the woman a favour.'

A favour! West glared at him. 'You knew they were illegally brought in, you sold them to your customers, and now one of them is dead.'

If the man had been pale before, now every notion of colour

drained from his face and he grasped the table behind him in shock. 'Dead? Gerard Roberts is dead?'

'And the last thing he ate were the vegetables he bought here. In *your* shop. So, it's time to be very, very helpful, Mr Beans. Now, tell me how much of this stuff you bought, how much you sold to Mr Roberts, and where the rest went.'

Pale, but galvanised by fear, Beans went to the till and pulled a ledger from the cupboard underneath. 'I have it written down, Sergeant. See here, this is the amount of manihot esculenta I bought from Louisa Persaud, the lady from Guyana. Ten roots.' He closed the ledger. 'Mr Roberts bought just one root. I don't know who bought the rest. After I served Mr Roberts, I left for a meeting, leaving my assistant Pat in charge. She must have sold the rest.'

'Is she still here?'

'Just having a cup of tea, I'll call her.' With a look of relief, he went to the doorway and shouted hoarsely for his assistant.

She came without haste, a big-boned, well-padded girl/woman of uncertain years, who looked blankly at the two detectives when they asked her about the exotic vegetable.

'You know the brown one, like a cross between a turnip and a potato,' Beans said, simplifying the matter. Then, with an eye-roll to whatever gods had made him employ a woman he referred to as his sister's daughter, rather than his niece, as if it kept the connection more distant, he tried again. 'The one you said looked like a turd, Pat, remember?'

There was a sigh of relief as the men heard the penny drop with a loud reverberating clunk. 'Oh aye, them things. I remember them.'

'What happened to them, Pat, can you remember?' West asked, keeping his voice gentle in the face of her vacuous half-smile.

'A woman, she bought all o' them.'

'All of them? All nine roots?'

Her face, which would cause more wrinkles than it would ever earn, took on a slightly puzzled air. 'I didn't count 'em.'

More used to the vagaries of Pat's thought processes than the detectives, Beans gave her elbow a prod with a skeletal finger and asked bluntly, 'Did anybody buy one before that lady?'

She shook her head, plump cheeks wobbling.

'Do you know who she was?' Andrews asked hopefully, but Pat looked blankly at him.

'What time was it, can you remember?' West tried, needing to pin the time down at least, but was rewarded with a shrug of her big shoulders. He looked to Beans for help. 'Do you have any way of finding out who bought them?'

'No. People generally pay cash, Sergeant,' Mr Beans added in self-defence. 'You're talking about a few euros mostly, sometimes cents.'

Pat stood silently while the men spoke; she was used to being ignored and sidelined, and wasn't insulted by their unthinking dismissal. Being big and broad, people had tended to avoid her rather than denigrate, thus she had missed the worst that people frequently offered those who were in any way different; she had no expectation of cruelty or abuse and took people as she found them. She was slow, but in no way stupid, managing to run the shop fairly well during her uncle's many absences. Most of the transactions were, as her uncle had admitted, for euros and cents, and people generally needed little help, picking and packing their own fruit and vegetables from the trays. She put the money they gave her into the till and never worried whether it was right or not. Truth was, the till was rarely wrong. Pat was an *honesty box* in human form; people were too kind to cheat her.

She stood and waited, as was her way, her eyes flicking backward and forward between the men, until a space opened up for her to speak. It didn't come until the two detectives were taking their leave, with a final warning for Mr Beans that they would have further questions for him, and that there may be charges brought. His speechless shock gave Pat the gap she was waiting for.

'She was talking to that man outside,' she said, with no inflection in her voice.

Andrews heard her first and turned with curiosity. 'What did you say?'

'She was talking to that man outside,' she repeated in the same tone.

West returned to Andrews' side. 'What man?'

'The man with the bike. She was talking to him outside.'

The two men exchanged surprised glances and moved closer to the woman, who backed away in alarm, frightened, not of their size, but of the sudden intensity of their gaze.

'What man?' Andrews asked, fighting to keep his tone gentle.

She looked at him patiently and repeated slowly for his benefit. 'The man with the bike.'

And then, to general relief, she elaborated. 'The man with the bike who bought all them vegetables off him this morning.' She pointed at Mr Beans.

It took fifteen minutes, and more patience than either man realised they possessed, to prise the remainder of the information from the assistant. Finally, they were left with the bones of the tale. Gerard Roberts had bought one piece of manihot esculenta, but before cycling away he had spent a few minutes speaking to a lady who had then come into the shop and bought the remainder of the vegetables. Although most of their customers were local, this woman was not known to the assistant.

'And you didn't see her?' West asked the shop owner, puzzled. 'But you served Mr Roberts, so it can't have been too long afterwards.'

'I was already late for my meeting,' Beans said. 'As soon as Mr Roberts left, I headed off.' He pointed through the door at the back of the shop. 'We have a back exit, it leads into a small car park which has an exit onto The Hedgerows,' he explained, referring to the narrow laneway that would take him back onto the road. 'I was heading to Stillorgan, so I didn't go past the front of the shop. I never saw her.

West, frustrated, turned back to Pat and asked her to describe the woman.

'Just a woman,' Pat replied.

Mr Beans shoved her, none too gently. 'They want to know what she looked like.'

'Just like an ordinary woman,' Pat said, struggling to say more.

West, used to fishing for information, asked her a series of questions relating to the description of people around her. Thus, they learned that the woman was taller than Pat and Mr Beans, but smaller than the two detectives; her hair was the same colour as Sergeant West's; she was fatter than Mr Beans but slimmer than either of the two detectives and, said with a slight quiver of lip, she was pretty.

'And she talked funny,' Pat offered finally.

But none of their many and varied questions could figure out why she thought so, or what she meant by *funny*.

'Did you see her leave?' West asked, reaching for the very last drop of his patience.

Pat nodded and smiled.

'Did she walk away or have a car?'

Another nod.

'Which?' West asked, frustration finally leaking into his voice.

Pat didn't notice. She beamed. 'She had a car. Parked across the road.' Her smile switched off and was replaced by a serious frown. 'She's not supposed to do that.'

'Do you know what kind of car it was?' West asked, knowing it was a waste of time, but also knowing that sometimes people knew the strangest things.

Not this time.

'A small one,' Pat said, smiling again.

'What colour was it?' Andrews asked, seeing West bite his lip.

Pat made an effort to concentrate. Screwing her eyes shut, she took a breath, held it and then let it out in a puff. 'Black, or green. Or maybe blue.'

'Back in their car, a few minutes later, West dropped his head back against the headrest with a groan. 'A blonde, pretty woman around five-six, who drives a small car that may be green, blue or black? No problem then, we'll find her easily enough.' He grinned suddenly. 'I know about eight women who fit that description, Peter.'

'I doubt if many of the blondes you know, would know one end of a manihot doodah from the other, Mike.'

West laughed before putting memories of former girlfriends, blonde and otherwise, firmly to the back of his mind. 'Seriously though,' he said, 'there are too many unknowns here for my liking.' Pulling out his mobile, he did a quick internet search. 'Well, it's definite, manihot esculenta is cassava.'

'Should we issue an alert?' Worry lines creased Andrews' forehead. 'The woman bought them this morning, but she may not eat them till tonight, tomorrow, even the day after.'

West drummed his fingers on the steering wheel. 'It's difficult. We haven't, as yet, any proof that this manihot stuff is what killed Roberts. Let's get back to the station. Maybe they'll have some results for us.'

As they drove in silence, the same thought occupied both men. If the manihot esculenta was so poisonous that Roberts died from eating one, they could have more dead bodies on their hands before the day was out.

5

D r Kennedy's legendary good humour withstood his being asked for the results of the autopsy before he could possibly have finished.

'Nothing for you yet,' he said.

West's frustration bounced off the pathologist and returned to aggravate him tenfold. 'When will we know?' he asked, gritting his teeth, knowing that unless the answer was *straight away* he was going to have to make a difficult decision.

'I'll be finished the autopsy in about an hour,' Kennedy replied. 'Barring further interruptions, of course,' he added smoothly. 'But based on my gross examination, I don't expect to find anything else of interest. You may get some results from forensics; I sent the stomach contents over an hour ago. The lab should be able to give you cyanide levels tomorrow but the remaining toxicology will take a little longer.'

West banged the phone down, and then, glancing at the clock on the wall, picked it up again and rang the inspector. He summarised the situation quickly and then added, 'I may have more information once I have spoken to forensics, sir, but I'm concerned that time is pushing on. This unknown lady may use this vegetable for an evening meal. And if it's the cause of Gerard Roberts' death, well...' He left the sentence hanging.

'We're still speculating, Sergeant West,' Inspector Morrison said. 'We can't issue an alert based on speculation, you know that as well as I do. Your priority now is to confirm facts. Keep me informed, I'll stay here in my office until I hear from you.'

West hung up with a sigh, and headed back into the general office where Andrews sat writing up reports. 'Leave that, Pete. Mother Morrison says we're to confirm facts and not keep speculating. Let's get over to the Park and see what we can find out.'

The Phoenix Park, one of Europe's largest walled parks covering almost three square miles, contains the headquarters of An Garda Síochána and the Garda Forensic Laboratory. It also contains the official residence of the Irish president.

And Dublin Zoo.

Needless to say, both West and Andrews had heard all the jokes about the interchangeability of the inmates of each.

West drove, using his siren to cut through the usual after-school rush, strobe lights flashing on front and back windows. Luck was with them, and traffic on the M50 was surprisingly light. They turned in the main gate and arrived at the forensic lab car park just as administrative staff were closing the front doors for the day.

'Lucky them,' Andrews quipped, checking his watch. 'Five on the dot, and off they go.'

'You'd hate a nine-to-five job, Pete. Stuck in an office all day.'

'Weekends off, evenings off, time for the kids, time for the wife.'

West looked at him, saw he was joking and smiled to himself as they got out of the car and headed to the entrance. Administration staff having gone for the day, a small notice asked them to use the intercom to gain admission.

It was a minute before a tinny voice answered.

'Stephen Doyle,' West said, when asked whom he wanted to see.

'Sorry?'

He moved his mouth closer to the intercom. 'Stephen Doyle,' he repeated loudly.

Several frustrating minutes of silence followed, both men shuffling restlessly. West was just about to press the intercom button again when the sound of locks being turned alerted them to someone's arrival. The door opened. Doyle raised a hand in greeting and waved them inside. 'Hope you're not here looking for results,' he said tiredly, 'we've barely got started. Have you any idea of the amount of stuff they brought back?'

'I know,' West said, 'and we wouldn't bother you so soon if it weren't important.'

'Do you know how many times, in the course of one day, I hear that sentence?' Doyle replied, his lips narrowed in annoyance. 'Everyone thinks their case is more important than anyone else's. Well, I'll tell you what I tell them. Every case is important to us. Every single one. That's the way we approach our work.'

Tense silence ensued. Then all three men began to speak at the same time, apologies, justifications, more apologies, before Doyle gave a rueful laugh. 'I'm sorry, really. It has been the shittiest day imaginable. And I do mean shitty.'

'We too are sorry,' West said. 'And really, we wouldn't come barging in demanding results, if it weren't for the circumstances. We need to know if the one manihot esculenta Gerard Roberts ate was the cause of death, because if it were, we may have more.'

'I don't understand,' Doyle said, rubbing a rough hand over the grey stubble that covered his head, making a sandpaper sound that was loud in the quiet corridor.

West explained, his voice grim. 'There were ten of these roots; Roberts bought one, and an unknown woman bought the remainder. If the one he bought killed Gerard Roberts, and she uses the other nine to feed family, friends, whoever...' He broke off as he saw the forensic scientist nod.

'I get the picture,' he said, 'and I think that qualifies as very important, maybe even enough to bump you to the top of the list.' He pointed to the end of the corridor. 'Follow me.'

Pushing open a door at the end, Doyle motioned the two men inside and indicated a window at the other side of the large, well-lit room. It gave a view over a neat, square laboratory where, moving closer, they could see a mob-capped, white-coated woman standing in front of a work surface almost completely covered with Petri dishes.

'That's Nora,' Doyle said, 'she's been identifying and labelling the stomach contents sent over from Dr Kennedy.' They watched silently until the woman finished labelling an item before Doyle used an intercom to speak to her. 'I've two gardaí here,' he said, not bothering with names. He filled her in with a precis of their predicament. 'We need to find out if the cause of death is there among the contents.'

'Okay,' Nora replied slowly. 'I've started, as you can see,' she said, indicating the array of labelled items in front of her.

West and Andrews stared through the window, fascinated at the smorgasbord of Petri dishes. As with most work, the technician had started with the easier options and she pointed out dishes labelled as carrots, broccoli, onions, mushrooms, green beans and bean sprouts.

Nora indicated two unlabelled dishes. 'I've separated the rest into two items that I've yet to identify.'

Only two unidentified. West and Andrews stared at one another. Maybe they'd get lucky. Identifying two vegetables couldn't take too long.

'They think one of them may be a vegetable called manihot

esculenta, Nora. Cassava, in other words, and we know Samir found the peeling from one at the scene.'

She gave a wave in acknowledgement and turned back to her work.

'Right,' Doyle said. 'I'd better get in and give her a hand.' He pointed to the far corner of the room. 'Help yourselves to coffee, this could take a while.'

Moments later, West and Andrews saw him appear on the other side of the window, mob-capped, white-coated. A total transformation. He gave them a wave and then proceeded to ignore them.

For a while, both men stood watching, hoping for one of those eureka moments that would give them the information they wanted. But like their job, forensic work seemed to be a slow plod. The technicians moved from one piece of equipment to the other, staring into each with more patience than either garda possessed, even on a good day. It quickly became boring to watch.

West poured two mugs of coffee, found sugar, and milk that was just this side of turning, handed one to Andrews and sat with the other to wait. He'd almost finished his second coffee before he saw both forensic scientists straighten and look at one another. Standing, he moved closer to the window. He couldn't hear what they were saying, but he could read the expression on their faces. Maybe it was wishful thinking on his part, but it looked as if they'd made some kind of breakthrough. He watched as Doyle crossed the lab to a phone, his forehead furrowing as he picked up the handset.

'Something's happening,' West threw back to Andrews, who was flicking through a magazine he'd found.

'Results?' Andrews asked, joining him.

'Something. They'll let us know, I suppose. Eventually.'

Just when West was reaching the tearing-your-hair-out

point, Doyle walked to the window and pressed a switch on an intercom. Nora stood slightly behind him; they shared the same grim expression.

'My results are irrefutable,' he said. 'I have checked, double-checked and the conclusion is the same. Cassava, or manihot esculenta if you prefer, is generally divided into two basic types called simply, sweet and bitter. Sweet cassava has a concentration of cyanogenic glycoside less than fifty milligrams per kilogram, which requires basic cooking to render it non-toxic. Bitter cassava, on the other hand, has a concentration greater than fifty milligrams. To render bitter cassava safe to eat, it needs to be grated; the gratings are then soaked for a period of days, with the water being discarded several times during this period, then it is safe to cook well and eat.'

West pressed the button on the intercom and asked, 'Which did Gerard Roberts eat?'

'I tested the cassava from the stomach, and also the rind from the cassava we collected from the Roberts' house. Both have a concentration of sixty-five milligrams of cyanogenic glycoside. It appears that the concentration is often affected by weather conditions where it is grown. Periods of drought concentrate the levels.'

He returned to where the Petri dishes sat, his voice fading slightly as he moved away from the intercom. 'You mentioned that the victim bought one cassava root. Are you certain it was only one?'

'Yes, pretty sure. We spoke to the man who served him in the shop. He said one. Why?'

'We found the chewed remnants of approximately one small, cooked cassava root, which gels with what you say he bought,' Nora explained. 'Badly prepared, as it was, he may have been extremely unwell, possibly would have had some neuropathy following its ingestion, but it wouldn't have killed him.' She picked up a dish and brought it to the window. 'This is the chewed cassava.'

West and Andrews peered at it and said nothing.

Nora put the dish down, picked up another, came back and held it up. 'See the difference?' she asked.

'That looks smoother,' West offered.

'This is raw, bitter cassava,' she explained. 'It appears to have been finely grated, maybe even liquidised, rather than chopped like the cooked one. We found quite a lot of this in Gerard Roberts' stomach.'

West met Andrews' startled eyes. 'How much, do you think?' he asked.

'Using the weight of the one cooked root, we can extrapolate – and this is a rough approximate because we are comparing cooked with non-cooked – somewhere between six and eight roots.'

'Or maybe nine?' West asked.

Nora shrugged. 'Could be, Sergeant. We could be talking about nine small roots or five big ones. We've no way of knowing exactly.'

'You said there was sixty-five milligrams of cyanogenic glycoside per kilo of cassava,' West said, trying to do mental arithmetic. 'Would he have eaten a kilo?'

'Each cassava weighs a few grams so, in theory, yes,' Nora said. 'But I'm not saying he necessarily ate them. I can't imagine why he would have; it would be the equivalent of you eating grated raw potato.'

'But you found it in his stomach,' Andrews said, puzzled.

'Yes, but he may have drunk it, rather than eaten it.' Nora put the Petri dish down and crossed her arms. 'It's very finely grated, and could have been mixed into something. Or I suppose it could have been added to his food, like parmesan cheese, for instance. I've no idea what raw cassava tastes like, whether it would be noticeable or not. We've no way of telling, I'm afraid. We've done the science bit, I'm afraid the *why* bit is your department.'

If that was a dismissal, West wasn't listening, he had one more question to ask. 'It was definitely enough to kill him, yes?'

Nora looked directly at them through the glass. 'Forty milligrams would kill a cow. At the least computation, he ate almost a kilo containing sixty-five milligrams per kilo. More than enough to kill him. We'll get the exact concentration in his blood from the lab, probably tomorrow.' With that, Nora gave a nod and disappeared out a door on the other side of the lab.

Doyle raised an index finger. 'Hang on there a sec.' But it was slightly longer before he appeared. He'd shed his white coat and gloves, but had forgotten to remove the mob cap. 'Have we helped your dilemma or made it worse?'

West ran a hand through his hair. 'Changed it almost completely, Stephen. It looks like we have probably accounted for all the cassava that was bought, so at least we won't have to issue an alert. But, if Roberts bought one, and the mystery lady bought nine, how did he end up with all ten in his stomach? As your colleague said so succinctly, it's time we did our bit.' Turning to leave, he remembered something. 'Was there a grater or liquidiser in the Roberts' kitchen?'

Doyle moved to a nearby computer and, moments later, had an inventory of the Roberts' kitchen on screen. He hummed under his breath as he quickly scanned the data, scrolling through pages of items that had been recorded earlier. 'Yes, both. One stainless steel box grater, and one liquidiser. I would guess from where they were found though, that Mr Roberts didn't use them to prepare his meal this morning. Everything he used was either on the counter or in the sink, whereas the grater was in the back of a cupboard and the liquidiser was on a high shelf. However, I'll have both tested to make certain. Unfortunately, they're not items we have looked at yet.' He went to rub a hand over his head, found the mob cap and pulled it off with a tired grin. 'If you desperately need to know, I suppose I could do them now.'

'Thanks, but no, it'll keep until tomorrow. Let me know as soon as, okay.'

'Sure.' He looked thoughtful. 'I'm expecting the results will be negative based on where they were stored. If you find a suspect, look for a grater or liquidiser in their home. They'll have washed them, but people never clean these pieces of equipment properly. We may be able to find traces of cassava in the teeth or the mechanics. Keep that in mind.'

With a nod of thanks, both men left and headed back to the station where they sat and went over the series of events, looking at the limited information they had from every angle, identifying the gaps, planning a strategy for the following day. Edwards had left notes on West's desk regarding Gerard Roberts. 'He was a partner in a public relations business – Roberts and McMahon,' West told Andrews, reading from the report. 'We'll have to look into it.' They'd poke into every part of Roberts' life, into every dark shady corner trying to find the reason someone wanted him dead.

Andrews was stuck on their first puzzle. 'How did Roberts end up with all the manihot esculenta? Pat said he cycled away as the woman came into the shop. It doesn't make sense. And when he did, somehow, end up with all of it, why would he have cooked one piece and eaten the rest raw?'

West, sipping bitter coffee with a grimace, didn't reply. He stood holding his mug and moved to the window where raindrops played follow the leader to a puddle on the flat roof outside. He turned with a frown. 'He peeled, chopped and cooked the one he had bought himself. The rest of the manihot esculenta was grated, and he took it raw. I don't think he knew it was the same, Peter.'

Andrews looked puzzled. 'So, where did he get it?'

'The woman. It has to have been the woman. She bought the rest, grated it and somehow gave it to him.' Something Mrs Roberts said during her interview came back to him. 'Do you remember what his wife said,' he asked, 'something about her husband taking longer for his cycle than usual. She said he was usually gone about an hour, but this morning he was gone almost an hour and a half. Why?'

'You think he met the woman and she gave him the grated manihot stuff?' Andrews didn't even try to hide the scepticism. 'Why?'

'She bought nine roots which would have weighed nearly a kilo, just about what they found in his stomach. He had to have got it from her. He was talking to her outside the shop. Maybe they arranged to meet later.'

'And she gave it to him?' Andrews raised an eyebrow.

'His wife said he was a fitness addict. Perhaps she told him it was some kind of health food.' Becoming more certain he was on the right track, he said, 'Maybe she told him he had to mix it with water and drink it, or sprinkle it on his breakfast. Why would he have been suspicious?'

Andrews, looking dubious, threw question after question at West's theory. 'Who was this woman then? Someone he knew? Why did she give it to him? Was it an accident or a deliberate act? Did she know it was poison? Isn't it all a bit far-fetched?'

West sat back, tilting his chair onto its back legs, causing a creak of protest and Andrews to raise his eyes to heaven.

'Far-fetched? I suppose it is, but can you think of a better explanation?' At Andrews' shrug, he brought the front legs of the chair down with a bang and leaned forward over his desk. 'If we go with what we know, Pete. Gerard Roberts died from cyanide poisoning after eating raw manihot esculenta. Although he bought only one root, more than one was found in his stomach contents. He was seen talking to a woman who bought nine roots of the stuff, and took almost half an hour longer than usual on his cycle ride. I think my theory fits quite well. We just need to find out who that woman is, and why she wanted Gerard Roberts dead.'

6

There was nothing more to be achieved that night, no point in mulling over and over the few facts they had, and nothing to be gained from sitting there getting hungry and tired. It was almost dark when they left the station, autumn licking the final edges of summer away.

'I'll see you in the morning, Peter.'

'I'll be here, Mike, see you at seven.'

West, who had refrained from stating his intention to start so early, raised his eyes to heaven, provoking a knowing smile from Andrews who waved and drove from the car park with his customary speed, barely waiting for the barrier to rise before scraping under it. He shook his head, the smile lurking on his lips to soften the hard lines that accumulated, some days faster and deeper than others.

Not for the first time, he thanked whatever gods there were that partnered him with Andrews. The mutual respect and rapport that had developed between them was, frequently, the only thing that kept him sane. He couldn't believe he'd almost blown it with his careless offer earlier. Luckily, he'd covered his tracks.

He drove at a more sedate pace from the car park and, a short while later, pulled up in front of his house. Climbing wearily out, he breathed a sigh of relief to be home. Even if it was only for a few hours.

He opened the front door, expecting his usual greeting from the little chihuahua who would normally pitter-patter across the wooden floor of the hallway to greet him. When Tyler didn't come running, he hung his jacket on the coat stand and opened the door into the living room.

It had been two smaller rooms divided by double doors when he had bought the house. Removing the double doors and knocking the partition walls down was the first thing West had done, opening the now single room up to light from both ends. He had furnished it with a comfortable, eclectic mix of styles, colours and patterns, adding to the pieces he had brought with him from his apartment, items he picked up in local antique shops, car boot sales, charity shops. He had a good eye and picked up the unusual or the odd, and it all fitted. Wooden floors were strewn with a mix of old and new rugs of varying shades. A large but exceedingly comfortable sofa, bought for a song in auction rooms in Dublin because it was too big for most people, and too worn for others, took up most of the space along one wall. On the other, fitting neatly under the window, sat a smaller, horrendously-expensive sofa whose jewel-coloured tapestry glowed in the firelight.

Tyler had chosen the older sofa to curl up on. Half buried under a cushion, his only response to the door opening was to cock a small velvet ear.

West dropped his keys on a side table and looked at him. 'Is that the only greeting I'm getting?' he asked, amused. 'What have I done this time, bought the wrong brand of food again?'

He had experimented in buying different brands of dog food a number of times, mainly for convenience, but the damn dog made up for its small stature by being incredibly fussy and insisting on eating a very epicurean diet. He had finally settled on buying three different brands of dry foods, but was stuck with having to buy an unusual, expensive and, more annoying, a hard-to-get brand of tinned food. The only place that sold it was a small shop in a little lane off Grafton Street and when he went to get it, he bought it in bulk. There was no parking outside the shop, of course, and he had to lug the heavy weight, arms aching, to the nearest car park, cursing his stupidity with every step. One of these days, he'd search online and find someone who could deliver it. When he had several hours to spare.

'You're not even my damned dog,' West said. 'One of these days, your owner will stop mucking about, get his ass home and take you off my hands,' he threatened, with a final glance at the little dog who glared at him with prominent eyes.

It didn't take long to sort out the cause of Tyler's umbrage. West had forgotten to fill one of his automatic feeding machines. Unfortunately, it was the dog's favourite one, so he was having a sulk. He corrected his omission and Tyler had his nose in the food before he'd finished saying his name.

Laughing, West got up, washed his hands and investigated the fridge for something to eat. When it came to his own meals, he was much less organised, and there wasn't much in it apart from beer and a piece of lasagne he'd bought recently. He peered at the label but couldn't make out the date. When had he bought it? He couldn't remember. A quick sniff – it smelled okay. It would be fine; extra time in the microwave would heat it, and blast any bugs. A cold Guinness from the fridge and his notes would be good dinner companions.

He could sit at the table, he supposed, looking around the room. When he had bought the house, the kitchen was small with a narrow window and a single door into the garden. He'd had it extended; more than tripling its size. He'd gone for classic cream for the kitchen cabinets and a granite worktop called Silk which lived up to its name. There was a double oven, integrated microwave, and dishwasher. Everything you could possibly need. And none of which, apart from the microwave, he had ever used.

The small door to the garden had been replaced by a set of bifolding doors that could open back against the wall on a sunny day, allowing access to a decked area he'd had made at the same time. He'd never sat on it, and had only opened the doors the day they were installed. There hadn't been the need to do so since.

A huge walnut table dominated the dining area, the rich colour a nice contrast to the cream kitchen cabinets. Rather than buying the matching chairs, which were incredibly uncomfortable to sit on, he had opted for six Phillip Starck, Ghost chairs. The contrast between the solidness of the table and the ethereal appearance of the seating appealed to him. They added a touch of modern glamour but, more importantly, they were extremely comfortable.

He had envisaged frequent dinner parties; old friends, family, new friends. Convivial conversation, good food, excellent wine.

But he had yet to have one.

With its view over the pretty garden, the table would have been a nice place for a solitary meal. But to sit surrounded by five Ghost chairs seemed a bit too ironic.

So, he never ate there.

What a sad creature he was to be sure, he said to himself with mock seriousness. Looking around the room again, he smiled. He'd use it all someday. If a snapshot of Edel Johnson's face popped into his head, he ignored it, returning to the fridge instead to remove both the lasagne and the Guinness.

When the microwave pinged, he brought everything to the

living room, switched on the TV and sat into the comfortable sofa with a sigh of contentment.

The news of the day muttered on as he picked at the lasagne. It didn't taste very good; maybe the use-by date had passed more than a day or two ago. He put the plate down on the sofa beside him. Tyler, having finished his meal, had curled up in the corner. Uncurling, he approached it. Fussy as he was, if it took his fancy, he sometimes deigned to eat human food. He took a sniff of the lasagne and backed away, raising big brown eyes to West, as if to say, *you eat this?* before returning to his corner.

West laughed. 'I should let you sniff all my food before I eat it, to make sure it's okay.' He picked up his pint glass from the floor. The Guinness, at least, was good and he drank it as he half-listened to the news, and thought about the day. Yawning, he laid his head back against the sofa and closed his eyes.

He didn't like what he saw there. Not going there. Not thinking about her.

His eyes flicked open. He stayed like that, staring at the ceiling before lifting his head and taking another mouthful of Guinness. To give his mind something else to focus on, he picked up his notes and started to read the information gathered during the course of the day.

Why would anyone want to murder Gerard Roberts? True, they didn't know much about him yet, and God alone knew what they would discover when they turned over a few stones. The most normal-looking of people, the most respectable of families, could have all kinds of aberrations and sinister goings-on behind the carefully constructed facade that society insisted upon.

Families like the one in Glasnevin. And with that one word, came the sound of Brian Dunphy's laughter, seconds before a bullet tore through him, the terrible smell of blood and death, and the memory of the woman and the three small, dead bodies in that upstairs room. A tough time. With help from his family, and a counsellor he had seen on and off for months, he'd come through it and learned to deal with the survivor's guilt, with the *what ifs* that kept him in a destructive loop for a while.

He wondered how Edel had managed to survive what she had been through, what coping mechanism she had used.

Dammit, he thought, draining the pint, does every thought have to lead back to her? Resolutely putting her out of his over-full mind, he considered his empty glass and weighed up the pros and cons of getting another Guinness. Another might help, he decided. He dumped the lasagne into the bin and, grabbing another can, sat back into the sofa, picked up his notes and gave them his full attention.

He had told Andrews that it had to be the woman Roberts was seen speaking to outside The Vegetable Shop. *Cherchez la femme.* The oldest motive in the book. A woman scorned. Maybe, but it was a very odd way to murder somebody. And would Roberts have accepted the manihot esculenta from her, in any shape or form, if they had been in a relationship that had ended acrimoniously?

If it wasn't sex, was it money? They'd have to look long and hard at Roberts' finances and his business partner's too. It would be nice if they had a secretary who fitted the blonde woman's description. But it was rarely that easy. Not in any case he had ever worked on, anyway.

Restless, he closed the file and leaned back, linking his hands behind his head and gazing across the room.

And there she was again.

He had refused to think about her all afternoon but now... well, now she just kept popping into his head. Why did he have to be such a pompous jerk? Couldn't he have been sophisticated, cool, suave? Now, not only would she always associate him with dead bodies, but she'd remember him as an obnoxious boor as well. He stood up and walked to the window where the night sky reflected him back.

'Idiot,' West addressed his mirror image. He stood a long time, feeling the room cool around him, waiting for the self-directed anger to abate. It did, eventually, but its distant cousin regret replaced it, and it was with its bitter taste in his mouth that he headed to bed.

7

Morning brought West's focus firmly back to the case. He was at his desk at seven, quickly followed by Andrews, and they sat and organised the day. At seven forty-five, they had things planned to their satisfaction.

When his desk phone rang, West answered it and listened a moment, a frown appearing between his eyes. 'Shouldn't you be talking to Sergeant Clark?' he asked, annoyance obvious in his voice, but he continued to listen while the explanation was given. 'All right, I understand. Yes, I'll be there. Give me fifteen minutes, okay?' He put the phone down on a groan of annoyance. 'That was Garda Foley. He's at a house burglary, and he thinks there's something off about it. He wants me to go out there.'

Andrews looked resigned. 'Don't tell me, they can't contact Sergeant Clark.'

'Clark's a liability, he seems to be in charge of the robbery division in name only, but if Foley is worried, it'll be for a good reason. You know him, level-headed and doesn't panic unnecessarily.' West stood, stretched then slipped on the jacket suit he'd hung on the back of his chair. 'You carry on here as planned, I won't be long. If the inspector asks where I am, tell him I'm doing Clark's work for him.'

The address he'd been given was only ten minutes' drive from the station, but traffic had started to build and it was almost twenty minutes before he pulled up behind Foley's Fiesta. The front door opened immediately. Foley stepped out and came to meet him, a worried look pinching his face.

'Well, what's the problem?' West asked as he approached.

'Thank you for coming, sir. I did try to get Sergeant Clark but...' He shrugged. Garda Foley, looking slightly embarrassed, proceeded to explain. 'Maybe I'm imagining it,' he said, 'but it does look so staged.'

'Staged?' This wasn't what he'd expected to hear. 'An insurance scam, maybe? Could it be the owner?'

'I don't think so. That's Mrs Lee; she was hysterical when I arrived, still is, in fact. She's an elderly lady, lives alone. I wanted to call an ambulance, have her taken to hospital. But she refused. Wanted to stay where she was. I called in for assistance, but you know the way staffing is now, there's never anyone free. But luckily, there was someone from *Offer* in the station who came and sat with her.'

Feeling an instant heart-sink, West frowned. 'From *Offer*? A woman?'

Thrown by the question, Foley stammered a reply. 'Y-y-yes. She has calmed the poor old lady down a bit. They're up in her bedroom.'

The fates were conspiring against him. With a grunt of resignation, West headed into the house to see if he agreed with the younger detective's take on the situation. A few minutes, however, was all it took. A broken window in the kitchen door at the back of the house, showed the point of entry, glass scattered across the tiled floor. Cupboards and drawers had been opened, but, unusually, the drawers hadn't been hauled out and upturned. Some of the contents from each had been pulled out... no, he reconsidered... not pulled out, taken out and dropped on the floor. He squatted to look at a fine china cup, it was on its side but unbroken. His eyes narrowed as he glanced at the other items, none were damaged. Not thrown down, placed, almost with care. It looked staged, just as Foley had suggested.

'Is this the only room disturbed?' he asked him.

'No, Sergeant, there's more.' Foley led the way down the hallway to the sitting room door. The sound of crying and soft murmurs of reassurance drifted down the stairs and West glanced upward trying to decide if it were Edel's voice he heard.

It was Foley's noisy deep breath that focused his attention, and he put Edel out of his head as he concentrated on the worried face that looked at him.

'This is what upset her the most,' Foley said, pushing open the door.

It was an old lady's room. Old-fashioned, three-piece suite, heavy mahogany furniture filling every space, photographs on every surface. The only picture on the wall was a very poor Constable reproduction that made West shudder. Over the fireplace, a mirror had been hung that was far too large for the room. Positioned directly opposite the door, it gave anyone entering the room a startling view of their own reflection. Not today though, today the reflection was shattered by the message written across it, in what looked like blood.

West noticed the same ordered chaos that was apparent in the kitchen; cushions tossed, photo frames lying on the floor but not smashed. The message on the mirror was the worst part; one word, clear and succinct. *DIE*. No ambiguity there. Closer, he was almost sure it wasn't blood, but he would leave it for the experts to decide. Turning around, he had the same feeling he had in the kitchen; it was all too staged, almost too perfectly done. He met the eye of the young detective standing in the doorway. 'Your instincts haven't let you down, Garda Foley. Have you called in the forensic technical team?'

'I haven't. I didn't want to –'

'Make a fool of yourself? Trust your judgement, it's good. Give them a call now; we need to find out what that message is written with.' He looked around the cluttered room. 'Is anything actually missing?'

'The lady has been too hysterical to answer any questions.'

'Right. Make that call, and let's see if she's calmed down any.' He stood staring at the message on the mirror while Foley contacted the nearest minor crimes Garda Technical Team which was based in the nearby suburb of Shankill.

'They'll be here in fifteen,' Foley said, hanging up.

They headed up the stairs together, West trying to compose his thoughts, and his expression. Opening the bedroom door, expecting to see Edel, he was relieved and disappointed in equal parts to see, not her strikingly attractive face, but an older one. The volunteer was hunkered down on the floor beside the chair where Mrs Lee sat.

Leaving Foley standing by the door, he approached, quietly introduced himself and sat on the side of the bed facing both women.

'Is there anybody we can call for you, Mrs Lee, family or friends?' he asked, hoping there was someone who cared enough to come to her, relieved to see her nod. She was one of the lucky ones.

'My daughter is on her way,' she said, her voice trembling, 'this lady rang her for me.' She gave a grateful glance to the volunteer, who continued to hold her hand, and then looked back at West. 'She's probably stuck in traffic, but she'll be here.'

West continued carefully. 'Is there anything missing, money or other valuables?'

'I don't keep anything valuable in the house,' Mrs Lee said. 'Well, nothing valuable to anyone but me – my photographs and things. But no money – Karen, my daughter, is very strict about that. She collects my pension for me, you know, and puts it safely away. The most I would ever have in the house is ten pounds, and that's in my purse over there.' She pointed to an oak dresser in the corner of the room.

'Have you had any trouble with neighbours, anyone in the village?'

Tears fell and she hiccupped. 'No, nothing. I've lived here for years, never had a day's trouble. There are young people living both sides, and they are so good. They shop for me, if I run out. Bring me in home-made cakes, and invite me to parties and celebrations. Nothing bad happens here. Not usually.'

West gave her a moment to dry her eyes. 'Have you noticed anyone hanging around? Someone you haven't seen before?'

'It's quiet around here; you don't see many people walking about.' She looked at him apologetically. 'I'm not being much of a help, am I? But I really don't remember seeing anybody out of the ordinary.'

There was nothing to be gained by pointing out that criminals were frequently masters of appearing *ordinary*; that, contrary to the current vogue for the supernatural, bad guys didn't have a predilection for becoming vampires or werewolves once the sun went down.

A panicked call of 'Mum!' heralded the arrival of an anxious daughter. West yielded his place in the small room to the woman who burst through the door, arms outstretched to enfold the older woman, to offer comfort and to be comforted in return. He caught the eye of the victim support volunteer, and with a tilt of his head indicated that she follow him from the room.

Downstairs, Foley headed out front to await the Garda Technical Team while West turned to the quiet lady at his side and introduced himself.

'My name is Liz, Liz Goodbody,' she said in turn. 'I'm a volunteer with *Offer*.'

'You were in the station this morning when the call came through from Garda Foley?' he asked curiously. Foley had called the station for help with the old lady when he had arrived at seven fifteen. That was early for a volunteer to be about.

The aptly-named Liz Goodbody smiled sweetly. 'It appears we need to do more advertising and education, if you are not aware that we provide a twenty-four-hour service. Unless we are with a survivor, you will find one of us in the station at any hour – day or night. I was there because that's the time slot I have volunteered for, 6am to 10am. It suits me best, I'm an early bird.'

Survivor, not *victim*. *Offer* was obviously determined to be politically correct. 'Did you notice anybody around when you got here?' he asked.

'No. Nobody.'

'Did Mrs Lee say she was worried about anything?'

'No, Sergeant, she was too upset to say anything. She is terribly shaken about the message.' She looked at him intently, small, beady eyes in a pretty but faded face. 'It was an evil thing to do, pure evil. Why would anyone do such a thing? What can it achieve, to frighten a little old lady like that?'

Did she think he would have an answer? West wondered, meeting her gaze. He'd seen evil in many forms, many guises, it didn't need reason or rhyme. It lurked maliciously, catching the wary as much as the unwary, and there was no answer to it. Or, if there was, he certainly didn't know it.

Liz Goodbody opened a capacious bag and searched inside. 'I'll leave you my card, Sergeant West,' she said, pulling a handful out. 'In fact, I'll leave a few for you. Just in case you need our services. And if you would pass one to Mrs Lee's daughter, please. If Mrs Lee would like someone to talk to, I can come back, or one of the team can. Or if her daughter would like to speak to someone. We have to remember,' she said seriously, 'there is always more than one survivor. We're available anytime. She just has to call.'

West watched from the front door as she walked down the road and climbed into a small Nissan. *We have to remember there is always more than one survivor.* She probably meant well, but the last thing he needed was to be told about the repercussions of crime. He knew them only too well.

Putting her out of his mind, he turned on his heel and headed back into the kitchen. He looked around and took in the carefully orchestrated disarray before going back into the claustrophobically furnished sitting room. Here, he was struck even more with the feeling that he had walked onto a stage set for a low-budget horror movie. He could see how it would have been terrifying for the elderly woman, to have come upon this in the early hours of the morning, but now, in the chilly light of day, the message verged on the silly rather than scary. It was hackneyed horror at its worst. He looked closely at the message. Someone had taken care in writing it; just enough blood, dye, or whatever had been used, so that each letter ran a little without dripping onto the mantelpiece. As in the kitchen, drawers had been opened and some of the contents taken out and placed on the floor, but again nothing was broken or damaged in any way. It was all very strange.

A clatter in the hallway announced the arrival of the Garda Technical Team and, with a few words to Foley, who promised to keep him apprised, he made his departure.

Back at the station, the detective unit was empty apart from Garda Jarvis who was busy on the phone, one hand writing at speed whatever it was he was hearing. West poured a mug of coffee and headed to his office. Taking a sip, he picked up his phone to speak to Inspector Morrison and apprise him of the burglary and the elements that caused both Garda Foley and himself concern.

'You think it was faked?' the inspector asked.

'I've seen fake burglaries,' he replied. 'They tend to go over the top, smashing and breaking things to cover up the fact that nothing was taken. This wasn't like that. It was staged to look the part, but too perfectly. Whoever did it wasn't interested in causing chaos, they appeared to be more interested in causing effect.'

'Is Garda Foley capable of running the case?'

'He's extremely competent, sir, but inexperienced. He does, however, know his limitations, witness his calling for assistance this morning, for example.'

'Hmmm,' was the reply and West waited. 'You'd better supervise. It sounds like an odd one.'

He struggled to keep an even tone to his voice. 'With all due respect, sir, Sergeant Clark is supposed to be handling burglaries. I have my hands full with this Roberts' case.'

'Hmmm,' Inspector Morrison murmured again. 'Unfortunately, Sergeant Clark will be on sick leave for some time. It appears he has strained his back, and has to have intensive physiotherapy before he can return to work. For the moment, you'll be covering his cases as well as your own. Hopefully, he'll be back on his feet within a couple of weeks.'

Without more ado, the inspector hung up, leaving West holding the handset and seething impotently. He was still muttering imprecations against him and Sergeant Clark when Andrews walked in five minutes later.

'Don't tell me,' Andrews said, 'let me guess. Mother Morrison doesn't like your theory about the manihot doodah stuff.'

'No, he thinks I have something there. It's this burglary I was called out to.' He gave Andrews a brief rundown. 'Now, because Clark is out sick,' he said, rolling his eyes, 'we have to cover his cases too.'

'Garda Foley does most of the work there, everyone but Mother knows that. Sergeant Clark's been skiving for years.'

West ran a hand through his hair. 'Well, I'm not worrying about his cases this morning. Let's concentrate on the Roberts' case and get it sorted.'

'I've arranged a meeting with the team at four. They're all out following up on what we discussed yesterday. I'm heading to talk to that lady from Guyana, the one who brought in that vegetable in the first place. Do you want to come?'

West looked at his watch. 'No, I'll leave her to your tender mercies. I want to talk to Gerard Roberts' business partner, get the details on his financial status, and see if there's a money angle to this. I'll see you at four.'

When Andrews left, West stared into space, lost in thought. He'd have liked to put Clark's cases out of his mind, but it wasn't easy. Getting to his feet, he grabbed his car keys and headed out, stopping at the front desk on his way to have a word with the desk sergeant.

Sergeant Blunt was well-named. A large, big-boned man with unusually short, stubby fingers, he was renowned for his inability to use two words when one would do. It had the effect of stopping agitated members of the public in their tracks. Station legend had it that a very irate father came in to complain about his son being arrested on a drunk and disorderly charge. He stood at the desk complaining, and promising retribution, railing at the sergeant about his son's treatment, threatening to call his local politician, and throwing in names of various important people. Getting no answer, he eventually asked the stony-faced sergeant if he'd been listening.

Sergeant Blunt had stared him straight in the eye and said, 'No,' as cool and calm as you please. The deflated man had to start all over again, but couldn't work up the same ire second time around.

When West approached him, he greeted him cordially and put his pen down, waiting to see how he could help.

'This victim support group, *Offer*, what can you tell me about it?' West asked him.

Blunt didn't reply immediately, but cast an eye over his shoulder at a young man who sat on a chair in the public area. He tilted his head toward the back office, and without waiting for a response, led the way.

Sitting behind the desk, and waving West to a chair, Blunt started without preliminaries. 'It began four months ago. A woman called Viveka Larsson came to visit Inspector Morrison and introduced this volunteer group she'd started. She brought all the required papers for six volunteers. Mother Morrison was very taken with the idea, thought it was a good community support. So, they started arriving and sitting there, day and night.' His grim expression said he didn't approve. 'At first, Mike, there wasn't much of a need for their services. In fact, I would go so far as to say we never needed them. Then, about a month ago, we had a number of cases with... ' Blunt searched for the appropriate word, '... needy victims. You know how we are for staff these days, rarely anybody available to sit and hold a hand. The volunteers proved very useful.'

'You don't like them though?' West guessed.

'They're always around. They hang around the front desk, reminding us that they are available, spouting dogma about victim's needs, no let me rephrase that, *survivor's needs*.' He raised his eyes to the ceiling. 'That young man out there, he's been sitting in that seat for about three hours. He's only about twenty-five. It's not normal, in my opinion.'

'Remember that case in May, the dead body in the grave-yard?' West asked. 'The woman who found the body, Edel Johnson, she's one of the volunteers, have you met her?'

Blunt tapped his fingers on the desk top. 'She was here yesterday when the call came for assistance with Mrs Roberts. I don't think she's been with them that long. She certainly wasn't one of the original six volunteers. But I think, they've had another seven or eight join since then.'

'That many?' West said, surprised. 'That's a lot of volunteers.'

Blunt sniffed. 'People like to be involved in the gory lives of others, as long as it's on the periphery. *Living vicariously,* isn't that what those psychology people call it? Some of the volunteers seem genuine; they really want to help people get through bad times. But some, like that man outside, seem to get their kicks from hearing about the cruelty and hardship people go through. A bit like someone who picks out and rereads the violent parts of a novel, or who rewinds and rewatches the gruesome parts of a movie.' His dislike of the volunteers was making him unusually garrulous. 'And you know, Mike, no matter how many checks we do, it doesn't keep the weirdos away.'

'The checks only tell us if the person has a criminal record,' West said, 'not if he or she is a bit odd or has unusual proclivities.'

'Inspector Morrison wants us to use these people. He was quite taken with that Larsson woman, I gather, and thinks the volunteers are a valuable tool when we are short-handed.'

'Has there been any feedback?'

'None negative. I'd've heard. Some positive feedback from our lot,' Blunt admitted reluctantly. 'It's convenient to be able to call on a volunteer to sit with a victim.' He rubbed a hand over his face and grimaced. 'I s'pose I'll have to get used to them, what Mother wants, Mother gets, eh?'

West smiled. 'It makes our life easier,' he said, standing and moving to the door. 'Let me know if you hear anything iffy about them, will you?'

Blunt looked as if he wanted to ask why, but without another word he followed him from the room.

8

Gerard Roberts' business partner, Alistair McMahon, was as helpful as it was possible to be. He printed out details of their current customers, their accounts, various companies they did business with and every person, place or thing the small company had had dealings with in the previous ten years. West would have been suspicious of this unusual helpfulness in the normal course of events. The most law-abiding of people weren't willing, generally, to divulge business data, citing confidentiality, data protection etc, ad nauseam.

But McMahon's grief was obviously genuine, as was his desire to do anything and everything to assist in solving the mystery of Gerard Roberts' death.

'We've known each other since junior school, Sergeant West,' he said, making no effort to hide the tremble in his lower lip. 'Since we were five. We've been friends that long. I was his best man, he was mine. He is... was... godfather to my first child, and I am to his.'

Reaching into his pocket, he took out a handkerchief, one already soft from mopping previous tears, wiped his face and blew his nose.

Most men would have apologised for their tears, but this man didn't, as if the death of such a close friend was deserving of this outpouring of grief. West admired him for it, and felt a tinge of regret for never having met the man who inspired such affection.

With a final snuffle, McMahon continued. 'We started this business together, you know?' He smiled then, looking across the room at a photograph that West recognised as being the two men at a younger age. 'It was a struggle in the early days. We'd stay up till two or three in the morning to meet deadlines. Then it got easier. Success came, slowly at first and then building up speed. And it was fun. Always.' He struggled to control his voice, the reality of his loss, the enormity of it, sinking in with every word. He looked angrily at West. 'How could something like this have happened? You say you suspect poison? Who would have done something so awful to such a good man?'

'We don't know, Mr McMahon, but we will find out. Can you think of anyone who would have held a grudge against him?'

'No, no, definitely not,' McMahon said. 'He was so easy-going, so genuinely decent. A bit eccentric, he did go on about his diet, and he was a nightmare to go for a meal with, but he was a brilliant business partner. We have... had... equal shares in the company, but most of our success was down to him. He had this amazing ability to communicate both professional compe-tence and trust, and as a result our customers are incredibly loyal. In a field like public relations it's unusual, believe me.'

'So business is good?'

'Well, it was until Gerard died,' he said cuttingly, and then held a hand up. 'I'm sorry, yes, it's good, we're right on target. As I said, we have very loyal customers. That's a great cushion in the current climate.'

West phrased his next question carefully. 'Mr Roberts' share of the company, what happens to that now?'

'The money as motive theory?' McMahon said, raising an eyebrow. 'I'm going to have to shoot that down, I'm afraid. Gerard and I drew up our wills several years ago; his share of the business goes to his wife. If she decides to sell, I have first refusal to purchase at market value.' He frowned as he considered the catastrophic loss in business terms, a tremble in his voice as he spoke. 'To be honest, I don't know if I can carry on, on my own. Ger was more than a partner and friend; he was the heart of this business. It sounds melodramatic to say it, I know, but we happily marched to the beat of his drum.'

He sat straighter, sniffed, and with a stronger voice said, 'If that's all, I really must get home. Patricia, my wife, is waiting for me. We're going over to the Roberts' now. I only came in this morning to get the information for you; the office will be closed until next week.' He rose as he spoke, anxious to be gone.

'Just a couple more questions,' said West, anxious in turn to get the information he needed. 'Is there any possibility Mr Roberts was having an affair?'

A look of genuine amusement crossed McMahon's face, superimposing the stricken look for a brief moment. 'Of course, you never met Ger, did you? Believe me; he never looked at another woman once he met Clare. He used to say it was such a relief not having to worry about dating, and all the second-guessing and mind games that was expected in a new relationship. I think he was a little scared of women in a personal way. Business, now that was a different bowl of bananas, he had no problem there, but there was never a sexual element in his dealings.'

'Mr Roberts was seen speaking to a woman on the morning he died; about five-foot-six, blonde hair, attractive. Any idea who she may be?'

'Doesn't ring a bell, I'm afraid, but it's a very general description, isn't it? Could be any number of women.'

He was right, of course. West stood, and then remembering his earlier hopes, asked, 'I don't suppose your secretary comes any way close to fitting the description?'

McMahon gave a short laugh. 'Welcome to the twenty-first century, Sergeant West, our secretary is called a personal assistant and *he* is five-foot-eleven or thereabouts.'

9

Louisa Persaud was enjoying her first day off after working six days of twelve-hour shifts. She didn't mind the long days; her meals were included and that saved her a lot of money on food. And every penny counted. Two more years, maybe three, she would have enough money to go home permanently and buy a house in a decent area of Georgetown. Once she had that, she would have no problem finding a handsome man to marry. It was how it worked, and she had it all planned.

She was only half-awake when the doorbell rang, and answered it while belting her robe tightly. The man who stood there looked harmless enough, but the identification he held up for her attention made her eyes shoot fully open.

'Are you Louisa Persaud?' the man asked, and she wanted to deny it, to take off and run because in Guyana, when the police came calling, that's what you did. She took a deep breath, this wasn't Guyana, and she hadn't done anything wrong. As far as she knew.

Andrews waited patiently, seeing the hesitation, doubt, mistrust in her eyes. He hoped she wasn't a poker player because he could read every emotion that flitted across her face as if they were subtitled. They were all there; shock, fear, guilt, resentment, anger, and now, just coming, curiosity.

Curiosity won out. 'I'm Louisa Persaud, yes, can I help you?'

'My name is Detective Garda Peter Andrews. I'm a policeman,' he explained. 'I have a few questions I'd like to ask you.' He waited a moment for a reaction and when he got none he asked, 'May I come in?'

She stepped back, without replying, and waved him in, indicating the living room where she offered him a seat. 'Would you like a coffee?' she asked, and when he declined, she sat in a seat opposite.

Andrews began. 'We were talking to the owner of The Vegetable Shop in Foxrock Village. Mr Beans says he bought some vegetables from you. Is that correct, Ms Persaud?' He watched her expression change and begin to relax at the seeming innocence of the question.

She gave a quick jerk of her head. 'Yes.'

'Can you tell me about them?'

'It was some manihot esculenta my mother gave me before I left Guyana. She gives it to me, to remind me of home. I don't have the heart to tell her I hate the stuff, always have done, only ever ate it to keep her happy. Usually, as soon as I come home, into the bin it goes and good riddance. But I was buying vegetables one day, and mentioned it to Bernie. He said, next time I brought some back, he'd be interested in buying it, that some of his clients liked to try different things. Exotic, Bernie called them.' She gave an amused snort. 'They're not so at home. Cheap food. But he was willing to pay me for them, so I said okay. I'm saving to go home permanently, so every little helps.'

'How much of the vegetable did you give him?'

'Ten roots. He gave me five euro for it. It was a fair price.' She started to look a little nervous and shuffled in her seat. 'Why are you asking about it, I don't understand.'

'Are you aware it is illegal to bring vegetables into the country without a licence, Ms Persaud?'

A worried frown appeared on her brow and she gave a nervous laugh. 'It was a gift from my mother, one I didn't want. It's not illegal to give away a gift.'

'Didn't you see the signs in the airport? I'm amazed you were never stopped. It's illegal to bring vegetables into the country like that,' Andrews said patiently. 'Especially,' he added, 'a vegetable that is poisonous.'

Her frown deepened. 'What are you saying? Manihot esculenta is not poisonous.'

Andrews looked at her. There was no guile on her face. Did she really not know? 'How do you prepare it, Ms Persaud, do you know?'

Irritation on her face, she replied crisply. 'Of course, I am not stupid. This is the bitter not the sweet variety, so it is a bit more of a fuss. You have to grate it and soak it in water for a few days, changing the water every day, and then it must be very well cooked.'

'And you gave these instructions to Mr Beans, did you?' he asked, knowing in advance what the answer would be.

'I asked him if he knew how to prepare the bitter variety. He said he did, and brushed me off.'

'But you didn't point out that it is poisonous unless it's cooked properly, did you?' Andrews persisted.

Puzzlement creased her brow. 'It's not poisonous,' she insisted. 'My family eat it all the time.'

Yes, thought Andrews, understanding now. Her family ate it all the time, and wouldn't have dreamt of eating it without the grating, soaking and water change that was essential. They would as soon as eat it without preparation, as he would eat raw potato.

All this for a miserable five euro. He broke the news to her. 'It's very poisonous when eaten uncooked though, Ms Persaud, and unfortunately, a man died from doing so.'

She paled and gasped. 'But I asked Bernie. He said he knew.'

Andrews remembered being amused by Mr Beans. He didn't find him quite so amusing anymore. 'Unfortunately, there may be charges brought for your part in supplying the vegetable. For the moment, you must remain available for questioning if needed, understood?'

Her eyes wide with shock, she said shakily, 'I didn't mean... ' and then faltered to a stop.

He stood and looked down on her. 'People rarely do,' he said kindly, and took his leave.

10

F our o'clock, and most of the team were perched on desks or slouched in chairs waiting for the meeting to start, their voices melding into a loud hum; information being shared and dissected; gossip being made and disseminated. A case board had been set up with a photo of their victim, Gerard Roberts, in central position. It dominated the room and possibly should have set the tone.

But the focus of interest for most of those present, was Sergeant Clark's strained back. Conjecture as to how the strain occurred was colourful and wildly, almost slanderously, speculative. Sergeant Clark managed to lower the tone even in his absence.

West and Andrews, returning at the same time, had to shout to be heard over the hoots of raucous laughter as the speculation became more and more defamatory.

'Okay, okay,' Andrews tried again, flapping his hands.

West took a quicker way of getting attention. He slapped the photo of Gerard Roberts loudly with the palm of his hand and asked in the ensuing silence, 'Who killed this man?'

All attention now focused on the case board. West took another photo from his file and pinned it beside the other. It graphically showed Gerard Roberts' death throes and drew a collective indrawn breath from the assembled team.

'Whoever did must have hated him,' West continued quietly, 'because he did not die painlessly.' He waited a beat while they considered his remark.

'To have hated him that much, they must have known him pretty well, mustn't they?' Jarvis asked.

'To hate someone that much, they must have had a good reason. We should be able to find out what that reason is, shouldn't we?' Edwards suggested.

West was pleased with their quick take. 'Good point, both of you. Problem is, we can't find anyone to say a bad word about this guy.' He quickly filled them in on his interview with Alistair McMahon. 'So, no money problems, no personal problems, no mistress lurking in the background. Ergo, no motive. Yet, dead he is.' He paced the floor in front of the team tossing a pen from hand to hand. He tossed it towards Andrews who caught it deftly and taking his cue, summarised his meeting with Louisa Persaud.

'It was just as our Mr Beans said, she'd been given the vegetables as a parting gift from her mother, hated them and was only too willing to sell them to him, for the paltry sum of five euro. She did ask Mr Beans if he knew how to prepare them, and he said he did, so she thought no more of it. She confirmed there were ten roots in total which also gels with what he said.'

With a quick flick of his wrist, Andrews threw the pen to Edwards who fumbled and dropped it, sending it skittering under the desk from whence he fished it covered in dust bunnies. He wiped it on the sleeve of his jacket before filling the team in on his fruitless canvassing of Gerard Roberts' assumed journey on the day he died.

'We followed the route his wife said he normally took. But there are so many cyclists that it was impossible for anyone to remember one particular person. We took photos of what he looked like, a description of what he was wearing. But, although a few said, *maybe*, nobody was sure.'

'Concentrate on the roads between The Vegetable Shop and his house. Try and find anyone who saw him coming back. We need to find out where he was for that missing thirty minutes.'

Edwards nodded.

'Baxter, what about Gerard Roberts' financial status?' West asked, moving on, eager to get some positive feedback from their days trawling.

It wasn't going to happen though. He could tell from the tired, downward slump of Seamus Baxter's shoulders. Nothing was as enervating as getting nowhere, as debilitating as searching and finding nothing; and equally, nothing was as regenerating as finding some crucial link, some focus. It was his job to keep them going when they felt themselves floundering.

Baxter gave his account; it didn't take long or add anything to their knowledge. 'His finances are in impeccable order, nothing out of the ordinary, nothing shady. Some money invested but nothing radical or unusual. He was obviously big into transparency – every i was dotted and t crossed.'

'The transparency wasn't a clever act?' West asked. After all, shiny apples frequently hid rotten cores.

'No,' Baxter said. 'It did cross my mind when I first saw his accounts, but I checked and double-checked, he wasn't hiding anything, I'd swear to it. His wife and both kids have credit cards with healthy balances. This is a very financially secure family.'

'Okay, so we can probably rule out money as a motive,' West said. He searched through a file in front of him, pulled out a sheet of paper and pinned it to the case board under the photo of Gerard Roberts. 'Sergeant Blunt was kind enough to find this map for me.' With a marker, he put an x where The Vegetable Shop stood, and another x on the Roberts' house.

'Mr Beans said Roberts always went there first to collect his veg and then went for a cycle.' He drew a line indicating the route he would have taken. 'We know he stopped outside the shop to speak to our mystery lady before continuing his ride. He didn't get the manihot esculenta–' He was interrupted by a whoop as he pronounced the vegetable's name. 'Manihot esculenta,' he repeated. 'You'll all be able to pronounce it as easily when you've said it a thousand times. We know he had to have gotten it from her, but we also know he didn't get it from her then.'

Baxter interrupted, raising a hand. 'How do we know that?'

'The shop assistant says that Roberts was speaking to the woman before he cycled away. It was at this stage that she went into the shop and bought the rest of the vegetables. The assistant wouldn't be the most reliable of witnesses,' he continued, ignoring a snort from Andrews, 'but we found the peelings of only one manihot esculenta in the Roberts' bin. He didn't cook it properly, didn't do the grating and soaking that is essential. But he did cook it. It probably wouldn't have killed him; he'd have been in a fairly sorry state, but he certainly wouldn't have ended up like this.' He pointed to the photo on the board.

'Someone else,' he said, 'had to have peeled and grated the rest of the vegetables and given them back to him, and this time he ate or maybe drank them, raw. Another piece of proof that Roberts didn't grate the vegetables himself came from the forensic team. They've tested the grater and liquidiser found in the Roberts' kitchen; they definitely hadn't been used. So,' he said, walking across the room, 'it means that Roberts had to have met the woman later. She had to have gone somewhere to peel and grate nine roots, put them in some sort of container, and give them to him.'

He pointed back to the map. 'Roberts would probably have used this route to Marlay Park after The Vegetable Shop' – he continued the line along the route – 'and he would have returned to his home along this road.' His line ended back on the x that was the Roberts' home.

'What if,' Jarvis asked hesitatingly, 'he didn't go to Marlay Park? He was out thirty minutes longer than usual, what if the woman asked him to go somewhere else, and that's where he got the grated mani... vegetable thing?'

They all looked at the map.

'The shop is what... a ten-minute cycle from the house? We're talking about a thirty-five-minute cycle.' West looked at his team. 'How far can you cycle in thirty-five minutes, remembering Roberts was an experienced cyclist with a very slick bike?'

'I've cycled a bit; I'd guess around eight, maybe nine miles,' Baxter offered.

West looked carefully at the map and then, tentatively, drew a circle in pencil with the shop as a central point. With a collective groan they realised it took in a huge area. 'Okay,' West said. 'Jarvis has made a very good point. We'll need to see if we can put Roberts anywhere. If we can place him, it might give us somewhere to look for this mystery blonde.' He tapped the map. 'There is a traffic camera at the crossroads in the village. Get onto Traffic, give them our time frame and ask them to check. If he went through, we might be able to see which direction he was heading. The Vegetable Shop doesn't have CCTV but the neighbouring shops might so call to them too. Stop and question cyclists, dog walkers, mothers with children, on every route away from the shop, someone may remember him.'

He looked around at the attentive faces and smiled. 'Yes, I know it's a needle in a haystack situation, but give it your best shot. Jarvis, you and Baxter start; Edwards can join you when he's finished the shop to home canvass. Ask Sergeant Blunt if he can spare any uniforms to help out too.' He waited for the nods of agreement.

'I'll be helping to celebrate young Petey Andrews' fifth birthday in *Bang Bangs!* tomorrow,' West said. 'We'll be there from two till four, so we'd prefer not to be interrupted unless absolutely necessary, okay?'

Jarvis, Edwards and Baxter nodded obligingly, each of them, in turn, having difficulty in picturing the debonair sergeant with a gang of five-year olds.

West was having much the same problem. Wasn't paying for the damn thing enough? The grin on Peter Andrews' face told him it wasn't, and he couldn't, wouldn't, ignore it. He'd go to *Bang Bangs!* and he would smile, and nobody would know from his face that it was the last place on earth he wished to be.

The arrival of a harassed-looking Garda Foley gave his thoughts a new direction to drift. He waved him into his office, where the young detective collapsed rather than sat into a chair.

'It's not going too well,' Foley began.

'Fill me in, Declan, and we'll see where we go,' West replied calmly.

'I checked into Mrs Lee's finances, and her daughter's too. Nothing untoward there. Daughter is married to a very successful architect, a very *wealthy*, successful architect. So, there is no financial incentive for trying to frighten the old dear to death.

'I questioned all the neighbours. Nobody saw anything strange, or anyone behaving in a suspicious manner. It's a very quiet, peaceful area. A stranger would stand out. Mrs Lee hasn't fallen out with anyone, hasn't met anyone new in the last few months, and hasn't been anywhere recently where she might have come across someone who would do such a thing. She's an inoffensive lady, minds her own business, potters about the village with a walking stick. I've questioned everyone I can think of, called on a couple of locals who've been in trouble a few times, and nobody knows anything. I can't think of anything else to do.' He ended on a plaintive note.

Without a doubt, it was a strange case. 'Have a word with local estate agents,' West said. 'See if anyone has shown an interest in buying a house in the village, maybe someone is desperate enough to frighten an old lady into leaving. It's a long shot,' he said, 'but one worth checking out.

'Then, I'm afraid you're going to have to put it into storage.' West held his hand up to stop the argument he saw poised on the young detective's lips. 'I know, I know. You'd like to get it cleared up, but you've done everything you could. If the estate agents don't throw up anything, you'll have exhausted every possibility, and you have to move on. Nothing was stolen, nobody was injured; we can't spend more man-hours on this.' He watched the play of emotions on Foley's face and sympathised. It was never easy to let a case go, there was always the lingering guilt that you could have done one more thing. But time was a constraint and there were other cases that needed looking at.

'Right,' Foley said, getting to his feet. 'Those *Offer* people have been very supportive, by the way, Sergeant. They sat with Mrs Lee when the daughter had to go away. I thought I might ask them to keep their eyes open and report any suspicious activity. That's okay, isn't it?'

Almost reluctantly, West agreed, and watched him leave before leaning back in his chair and groaning. He didn't want to hear one more comment, good or bad, about *Offer*. The group was firmly linked in his mind with Edel, and he didn't need the constant reminder. If only he had something substantial to go on in the Roberts' case to focus his thoughts. Without that outlet, his choices were Edel, or the exciting prospect of a party for a five-year-old.

11

S aturday dawned, a glorious autumnal day harking more to the summer it was leaving than to the winter it grudgingly faced. West woke with equal reluctance and groaned. Please, please ring, he pleaded to the silent phone by his bed. It would when he was exhausted, and desperately in need of a sleep, why not now when he sorely needed it to?

Throwing back the bedclothes, he headed for the shower, and stayed there for a long time. A firm believer in the restorative power of running water, he always felt particularly energised after a shower. His mood was certainly more positive afterwards. He towelled dry, pulled on boxers, jeans and T-shirt and headed to the kitchen for breakfast, checking Tyler's food on the way. Despite his determination to be positive about the upcoming party, he heaved a weighty sigh of relief when the phone rang and he heard Jarvis on the line.

'Just to let you know, Sergeant, that we've turned up nothing so far. There are too many people cycling these days for anyone to notice one unremarkable cyclist. Edwards finished the canvass of the roads between the shop and the house, and it was the same there. We're going to keep at it though, just on the off-chance we get lucky. Just thought I'd let you know before you headed off to *Bang Bangs!*'

There was no getting out of it, was there? He thanked Jarvis and hung up. A pot of coffee sufficed for breakfast, especially since, once again, the cupboards were bare, shopping being on the very short list of things he had planned to do that morning.

Dusting, vacuuming and ironing, he left to a very pleasant and obliging woman called Beth who came every Monday for three hours. He just had to get the stuff washed. That or buy more shirts and underwear which he had done before, on more than one occasion, so that he now had in excess of eighty shirts. Ridiculous, his sister had said, on one of her infrequent sleepovers. She was right, he supposed. It was ridiculous to buy more clothes, when all he had to do was put his dirty laundry into the washing machine. He'd been better since he came to Greystones. How much was due to better organisation and the wonderful Beth, or to the fact there was nowhere local to buy the shirts he liked, he wasn't sure.

Supermarket shopping was on the list of things he hated, and he only went when his need outweighed his reluctance. Today was definitely one of those days. List in hand, he arrived at Dunnes with the intent of getting the deed done as quickly as possible. He would have been in and out in fifteen minutes, if he hadn't spied Edel at the end of an aisle pushing a shopping trolley. He stopped under the guise of examining some fruit and watched her.

Her hair was loose; it fell forward when she bent to look at something on a shelf, then she straightened and tossed it back over her shoulder. She wasn't wearing jeans today, instead, she wore knee-high boots, a jewel-coloured short dress and navy coat, and she looked...

A woman cleared her throat, disrupting his thoughts. Apologising, he put the large bunch of bananas he'd been holding into his trolley, and pushed it forward as Edel vanished from sight.

He threw the odd item he needed into his trolley, but was far more intent on watching Edel as she walked slowly through the shop. *Stalking her.* The idea gave him pause as he picked up a loaf of bread, uncaring as to whether it was brown or white, sliced or not, and threw it into the trolley. He was being ridiculous and pathetic, but when he saw her heading down another aisle, he changed direction, walked quickly back down the aisle he had come up, and joined hers from the other end. She was examining something, so he made his way toward her, stopped and picked a packet off the shelf, put it into his trolley and moved away too quickly, accidently-on-purpose bumping his trolley into hers.

'Sorry,' he said, and then with feigned surprise. 'Ms Johnson, hello.'

'Hello,' she replied with a cool nod, dropping an item into her trolley and preparing to move off, but trapped by two trolleys blocking her way.

'It's a bit crazy in here today, isn't it?' West tried. As a smooth sophisticated conversational gambit, it was up there with *What's up Doc?* But to his relief she smiled.

'You shopping for your girlfriend?' she asked.

The question surprised him. 'No, no, I'm just getting a few things for home. There's no girlfriend.'

'Sister?'

This conversation wasn't going the way he wanted. Puzzled by her insistence that he was shopping for a woman, he tried again. 'No, there's just me and Tyler, the dog.'

She smiled again and, as the two trolleys in front of her finally moved out of her way, she started to head off, stopping beside him to say, 'I'm not a detective, Sergeant West, so perhaps I'm wrong, but your trolley is contradicting you.'

He looked into his trolley as she walked away, and felt the blush begin at his toes and work its way quickly to his cheeks where it lingered. With a quick look around to make sure nobody was watching, he picked up the large box of tampons and replaced them on the shelf. Keeping his head down, he made his way to the checkout, paid for his shopping and left without seeing her again.

At home, he unpacked the stuff he'd bought. He'd no idea what he was going to do with the jar of pickled onions, the tin of custard powder and the large bunch of bananas. The first two he put on the shelf of an empty kitchen cupboard. The bananas he put in a bowl in the middle of the walnut table. He'd try to remember to eat them. At least he hadn't bought the blasted box of tampons. He squeezed his eyes shut. What must she have thought?

Trying, once again, to put all thoughts of her out of his mind, he headed out, resigned to a few noisy and wearisome hours in the company of a pack of small boys.

He'd arranged to meet Andrews and his family in *Bang Bangs!* at two. He arrived just before the hour, to see him surrounded by what seemed like hundreds of very small, incredibly noisy children. Joyce, spotting him first, headed in his direction dragging an obviously reluctant Petey by one hand.

'Michael,' she called over the clamour of voices, 'this was so kind of you. Wasn't it Petey?'

Young Petey, well-primed, trotted out his thanks before disappearing back into the melee from whence he had come.

Joyce laughed, her eyes following him fondly. 'The social niceties are beyond a five-year-old, but he is so delighted with this. He'll be the envy of his class for a long time.'

'It's hard for me to know what to buy him, Joyce. Organising this was an easy way out, honestly.'

'It was very kind. And even kinder of you to come yourself.

Pete will be glad of the company and, to be honest, the help. Keeping twenty-one five-year-olds under control isn't an easy task.'

West smiled. He liked Joyce a lot. For the first time, he was honestly pleased he had come. His friendship with the Andrews' family had become important to him. He gained a lot from it, and it was rare he had a chance to do something in return. He just wished he had thought of it before, and didn't have the lingering sting of guilt irritating the hell out of him.

The manager, Ian, said all the right things and the gang of boys and girls were let loose in the playroom. The two hours flew by and, if West didn't exactly enjoy himself, it wasn't as bad as he'd expected either. All the children appeared to enjoy themselves, if their screams of pleasure were any indication. The play hour was followed by an hour of eating party food, most of which West had never seen before, and couldn't bring himself to try. If the variety of colours was anything to go by, he guessed every letter of the alphabet was in the ingredients.

'Won't they throw up if they eat all that?' he asked Andrews who stood nearby, eyeing his son with pride.

'Without a doubt, but hopefully not until they are on their way home and someone else has to mop it up.'

'Don't worry,' Joyce added with a grin, 'the parents will come equipped with plastic bags and towels. We warned them.'

The arrival of the respective parents sent the noise level stratospheric as each child, in increasingly high-pitched squeals, regaled them with the adventures they'd had during the afternoon. Some of the children, looking more than a little green, were wrapped up in their coats and quickly taken away.

West stood to one side and breathed a sigh of relief; it was almost over. He was exhausted and felt a headache start between his eyes. Where did parents get their energy? He looked over at Andrews with a new respect.

The noise level dropped gradually, as each child was claimed and taken away. West, deciding he had more than played his part, was about to make his own farewells when a voice, laced with worry, rose above the clamour.

'Max? Max?' The call was loud, causing each adult present to look toward the source. The tone was recognisable. The terror of loss.

A harried-looking woman ran forward. 'Have you seen Max?' she cried, her eyes darting, assessing every child, dismissing each in turn. 'I can't find him.' She spun on her heels, ran towards a staff member, and grabbed him frantically. 'My son, Max, I can't find him.'

West didn't waste time asking if she was sure. Grabbing Andrews by the arm, they sprang into recommended protocol; shut the place down, keep everyone inside until the child is found. If the child had been taken, the faster they acted, the better the chance they had of recovery. A member of staff was sent to each exit, to shut and guard the doors, another sent for the manager.

Ian arrived, on the run, and with a nod of gratitude to the two detectives, he organised other staff to search the building. 'There are other play rooms occupied. He may have just wandered into one,' he explained to the tearful mother. 'Some children just don't want to go home.' He patted her arm gently. 'It's happened before. I'm sure we'll find him safe, don't worry.'

'Where did you see him last?' West asked her.

'I was chatting to Alice Bradley, and Max was talking to his friend Ben, Alice's son. When they left, a couple of the other mothers came over for a chat. We were going to leave together but, when I turned round, he was gone.'

'You're sure he didn't leave with his friend?'

She looked at him expectantly, a glimmer of hope appearing. 'You think he might have?' And then, a tightening of her mouth.

'No, Alice would never have done that without telling me, she's very careful.'

The staff began returning from their varied searches. West, seeing the look of concern on Ian's face grow, knew it had become a police matter. Meeting Andrews' worried eyes, he tilted his head in the manager's direction and together they headed over.

'There's no sign of him,' Ian said, keeping his voice low, his eyes glancing to where Ann Saunders, the mother, sat sobbing, one of the other mothers trying vainly to console her.

'Okay,' West said. 'We'd better take over, Ian.'

The relief on the young manager's face was almost comical. 'What do you want me to do?' he asked, ready to be of assistance now that someone else bore the brunt of the responsibility.

Speed was necessary. 'A complete list of everyone who was here today, phone numbers and addresses if you have them. A list of all staff who were here, and a separate list of staff who work here, but weren't on duty. A floor plan of the building, if you have one, would be helpful.'

'I'll get all that, quick as I can.'

West waited until he had gone before turning to Andrews, frowning when he saw his pallor. 'You okay, Peter?'

Andrews looked at him without speaking.

'We'll find him,' West said, reaching out to grip his partner's arm tightly. 'I'll ring it in. We need more people. Try to contact that Alice Bradley, double-check that the boy hasn't gone with her. If not, ask her did she see him with anyone, or if she saw anyone suspicious.'

Andrews headed off, stopping to give his wife a reassuring hug in passing.

West rang the station. The short conversation resulted in the arrival, several minutes later, of all the available staff including Jarvis and Baxter who had returned to the station.

Armed with a copy of the floor plan provided by Ian, they quickly organised a complete search of the building. Two gardaí interviewed all the remaining parents and children. The questions were the standard: 'Did you see Max Saunders?' 'When did you see him last?' 'Did you see anyone you didn't recognise?' 'Did you see anyone suspicious?'

Nobody had seen anything.

Other gardaí contacted the parents who had already left, but none had anything to add.

Parents were allowed to leave with their children as soon as their interview was over and, as they did, each child was held just that little bit tighter.

Joyce Andrews, her own arm tight around Petey, sat with Ann Saunders until raised voices at the door announced the arrival of her husband.

'What kind of a place is this?' he shouted angrily as he arrived. 'How can my son just disappear? Where were all the staff? What kind of security system has this place got? And you' – he rounded on Andrews – 'you were supposed to be looking after him.' Andrews held his gaze, and reached out to grasp his arm.

'We'll find him, Joe, I promise.'

Fear that had gripped Joe Saunders since the phone call informing him of his son's disappearance, bubbled to the surface, anger dissipating to leave him pale and shaking. He turned, looking for his wife and, as if in a trance, crossed the room and sat beside her, pulling her to him. They stayed wrapped around one another, their faces contorting with shock and distress.

West and Andrews coordinated the search, receiving reports from the teams as they searched the premises and then the outlying buildings. A makeshift incident board was set up, and to this they pinned the reports as they came in, intent on covering every base, knowing how easy it would be to miss the crucial detail that could find the child safe and well.

'Edwards is checking the CCTV tapes, Mike. It's a short window, it won't take long,' Andrews said, as West checked a map of the surrounding area to coordinate the next wider search.

'This building is surrounded by dozens of small businesses, with garages, outhouses, and sheds of all sorts,' West said, tapping the map. 'We're going to need a lot more people.'

'Some of the parents who were here are coming back to help after they've dropped off their children,' Andrews replied, the strain becoming evident in his voice, a grim look on his face. 'They can cover the roads and lanes, leaving our lads to search the buildings. Sergeant Blunt is contacting off-duty officers to come in, they should be here soon. We'll get the area covered.'

'We'll find him, Pete,' West said again, with as much conviction as he could manage, trying to ignore the pain of knowledge in the other man's eyes. He saw it in almost every garda who reported to help; they had seen too much, knew the horrible truth. If they hadn't found Max by now...

He couldn't get the idea out of his head that a gift made with the wrong intention was doomed from the start. He'd thought he'd got away with it, hadn't he? Was even priding himself on his great idea. Well, it didn't seem such a great idea now. Next time he was being an idiot, he'd just apologise and leave it at that.

Just when he thought the day couldn't get worse, the door opened and in walked someone he definitely didn't want to see. He closed his eyes. Maybe he was seeing things.

He wasn't.

Edel walked towards him, a set look on her face, her eyes flitting between him and the parents of the missing boy seated behind him. 'Sergeant West,' she said. 'I'm–'

'Let me guess,' he interrupted her brusquely. 'You're here from *Offer*?'

She nodded slightly, and moved past him to introduce herself to Joe and Ann Saunders, pulling up a chair to sit in front of them.

'That is all I bloody need,' West bit out.

Edwards, approaching to fill him in on the CCTV footage, was taken aback. 'I'm s-sorry,' he stuttered. 'I thought you'd want the results of the CCTV as soon as possible.'

West looked at him, confused. 'What? Oh, sorry,' he said, 'I didn't mean you.' He shook his head. 'Something else. Never mind.' He indicated the back of the room, further away from the distraught parents, further from Edel bloody Johnson too.

'Well?' he asked, seeing barely contained excitement in the younger man's face.

'It didn't take long,' he said. 'Ian recognised Max. You can clearly see someone take him by the hand. She pointed toward a door, and he went with her without hesitation.'

'A woman? Are you sure?'

'She wore a shawl or scarf, or something, over her head, and was wearing trousers, but it's a woman. I'd swear it is.'

'Not a man dressed up?' West said.

Edwards took a breath and considered what West had asked. 'No,' he said, 'definitely a woman. It's not any one thing. Her hand when she reaches for the boy's, her shape, her height.'

'Let's look at it together,' West said. 'I don't doubt you, but another viewing and two sets of eyes might see more.' Spotting Andrews coming through the door, he gave him a wave. Three sets of eyes would be even better.

Back in the manager's office they ran the footage, and then ran it again. They froze frames, peered, moved on, froze again. West swore quietly. There was no clear shot of her face.

'I think you're probably right though,' West said after the

second viewing. 'Most likely a woman. She's keeping herself well covered.'

'Judging from the height difference with young Max, I'd put her at about five-five,' Andrews said.

West agreed. 'Right, contact all the search-party teams. Tell them that Max may be with a beshawled woman of medium height. Make sure everyone is updated. It's not much. But we have to go with what we have.'

Leaving Edwards to sort that out, he headed back to where the parents sat, Edel holding a hand of each. She was speaking quietly, both parents listening intently. Maybe there was something in this victim support group after all. Certainly, he could ill-afford to take someone off the search to sit with them.

Looking up to the skylight, he knew the light would soon start to fade. Too early in the year for frost, and the rain, thankfully, had stopped, but it would get cold. Very cold for a little boy. He took a deep breath and approached the parents. Maybe there was a woman within their family or circle of friends who would have taken Max.

Edel was still speaking, their eyes were on her, but they switched to him as he approached and the look of terror returned. Sometimes, he wished he didn't have to see that look in the faces of those he was trying to help. He shouldn't take it personally, it wasn't directed at him or caused by him. But still...

As he neared, Edel stood and waved him into her chair so that he sat facing the parents. He could feel her behind him, and decided to take comfort from the fact and concentrate on the anguished faces before him.

'We've looked over the CCTV footage, Mr and Mrs Saunders. It shows, very clearly, someone taking Max by the hand and walking through the door with him.' He stopped at a cry of anguish from the mother. Joe Saunders, tears rolling down his face, tried to console her but she pushed him away.

'It's all my fault,' she cried. 'Max... my baby.' She started tearing at the skin on her face, her nails leaving gouges that stood out against her pallor.

West, unsure what to do for the best, looked around for Edel. She'd kept them calm, maybe she could do so again. He didn't have to ask. Hearing the woman's cries, seeing her self-mutilation, Edel quickly went to her, took her hands, pulled her close and rocked her, as you would an upset child.

Getting to his feet, West indicated to the father that he should follow and led him to the far side of the room.

'Ann is very highly strung,' Joe explained, as they stood looking back at the two women.

'You don't have to make excuses for her, Mr Saunders. Any mother going through this would be equally distraught.' He pointed towards the manager's office. 'Do you feel up to looking at the CCTV footage? Just in case the woman looks in any way familiar.'

Unfortunately, apart from obvious distress when he saw his son being led away, Saunders could throw no light on her identity. 'He is going with her willingly though,' he commented, 'so she must have offered him something irresistible. He has been told over and over, he must never go with strangers.' He looked closely at the frozen screen, the woman with her hand held out; his son's face raised to hers, a smile glowing. 'She must look kind,' he added. 'Max isn't used to other people. We don't get babysitters or that. He wouldn't have gone with her if she looked cross or anything.' He caught West's eye. 'That means she'll probably look out for him. Right?'

Unable to pierce that faint bubble of hope, West agreed.

12

Reports came in from the various teams over the next hour. Nobody had seen a little boy matching Max's description. Joe Saunders had driven home to pick up a recent photo of his son and that had been copied and distributed. The CCTV footage from the car park was looked at several times by whoever was available, but led nowhere. Every car on it was identified as was each adult and child.

Darkness fell, and the temperature slowly dropped. 'He's wearing a warm coat,' Joe Saunders told everybody, 'he'll be warm enough. He'll be fine.'

Everybody nodded in return. Nobody willing to enlighten the worried man. Nobody willing to tell him that being cold might be the least of Max's problems.

All train stations, airports and ferry terminals had been notified, of course, but a five-year-old boy was easy to hide. The boot of a car, a large enough box. If there was a will, there would be a way.

Too easy to hide, Andrews knew, remembering how Petey had disappeared for hours only to be found fast asleep under the duvet on their bed. They hadn't thought to look there, had searched every cupboard, every hidey-hole in the house they could think of. Then they had searched behind every tree and bush in the garden. Andrews had been about to ring the station to report him missing, would have done so, hours before, only Joyce was convinced he hadn't left the house. It was she, going back to their room to change her shoes into sturdier ones for a longer search, who noticed the bump under the duvet and, pulling it back, found Petey fast asleep, curled up like a dormouse.

It wasn't going to be so simple for young Max.

The search teams had been warned to search every corner of every shed and outhouse, and they did. Every wheelie-bin in the area was opened and checked; full ones emptied – just in case. As night fell, torches were collected, extra batteries taken. Nobody was going home until they found the boy.

Ann Saunders sat hand in hand with Edel who, now and then, would whisper in her ear. Ann would nod but said nothing, her eyes following whatever person came in or out of the room, searching their faces for news, her eyes dropping to the floor at each failure to see what she wanted.

Occasionally, Joe Saunders would sit on the other side and attempt to take his wife's hand. She allowed him to, but it was obvious she took no comfort from the gesture. It seemed neither did he, as he stopped trying, walking up and down instead, and finally leaving to go to the manager's office which had become the headquarters of the search. He replayed the CCTV footage showing his son. Again and again.

An IT technician from Garda Headquarters had come to clean up the footage as much as possible and take a screen shot of the result. It would appear on the nine o'clock news along with the photograph of Max. Nine o'clock. An hour away. The boy had been missing four hours.

Andrews wanted to go out and join the search team, but West kept him in the office to coordinate the search. He could see the strain on his face, knew the guilt trip he was on.

The ring of the phone caught them off-guard, startling them, so that for a second nobody moved. First to recover, and nearest anyway to the phone, Andrews picked it up.

West didn't have to hear to know the news was good. It flitted across Andrews' face, relaxing the tension, smoothing the taut lines. His mouth, fixed in a compressed line for hours, softened, the corners moving back to their habitual upward tilt. As he continued to listen, anxious to pass the good news on, he punched the air with his fist.

Saunders, his face pale, looked first at Andrews and then over to where West had begun to smile. 'He's okay?' he asked, his voice a tremulous whisper. 'Are you sure? He's really okay?'

Andrews put his hand over the mouthpiece. 'He's been found. Unhurt. They're on their way back with him now.'

Saunders started to smile, then laugh. 'He's okay. My God, he's okay.' His laughter turned to tears, then he was sobbing. West went to him, put an arm around his shoulder and let him sob a moment more.

'Do you want to come and tell Ann?' he said gently as the sobs eased back to tears.

Wiping his face with the arm of his shirt, Saunders took a deep breath. 'He's really okay?' he said again.

'Yes. We'll get the full story soon, but you need to go and tell your wife before the car gets here.'

They headed out to where the two women sat. Words were redundant. As soon as Ann saw their faces, she jumped to her feet. 'He's all right?' she cried, grabbing her husband's arm.

'He's on his way back,' he assured her, taking her into his arms and holding her tightly as they both cried their relief.

Edel moved close to where West stood. 'Where did they find him?' she asked.

'I don't know,' he said with a faint smile. 'Pete took the call. They're on their way with him now. I wanted Mrs Saunders to know so she could calm down before he arrived. Pete will come and tell us everything in a moment.'

As he spoke, Andrews came from the office, a bounce in his step as he crossed the room toward them. 'He should be here any moment,' he said. 'He was found wandering around Stillorgan Shopping Centre. The security man there picked him up and rang the local station.'

'And he's okay? He's not been hurt?' Joe Saunders asked quickly.

'He was munching on a huge bar of chocolate when the security man noticed him,' Andrews said. 'He appears unhurt. But I have arranged for a paediatrician to give him the once-over in Temple Street. The car will take you straight there.'

Seeing Saunders was about to argue, West stepped in. 'It will be best to ensure he is completely unharmed, as soon as possible. There's a specialist team in the National Children's Hospital,' he said, giving the hospital its formal name. 'They know what to look for, and they're good at what they do. Max will be safe in their hands. I promise.

'We'll also take some of his clothes for our forensic people to have a look at. See if we can find any evidence of who took your son. We want to make sure this person can't put any other parent through what you've gone through this evening.'

Joe and Ann looked at one another.

West smiled reassuringly. 'It'll be done before you know it. If you give me your car keys,' he said to Joe, 'I'll have someone take your car home. Garda transport to the hospital will be faster.'

The Saunders nodded agreement to this, happy to have someone telling them what to do at this stage, unable to think past their son's safe return.

Edel stepped forward and put a hand on Ann's arm. 'I'll go now. I'm so glad everything turned out okay.'

'Oh no,' she cried, grabbing her hand, holding on tightly. 'Please don't go.'

'If you could stay a little longer,' Joe asked. 'Just till Max gets here?'

Edel squeezed the hand she held. 'Yes, of course, I'll stay as long as I'm needed.'

The sound of a car pulling up drew their attention to the entrance and the distinct sound of running feet was heard before Max tumbled headlong through the door. A smile split his chocolate-smeared face from ear to ear; his hair was tousled and his hands dirty but there was never such a wonderful sight.

'Mummy, Daddy,' he shouted happily. 'I've had a ride in a police car. And they put the siren on for me.'

'Just for a couple of seconds,' the uniformed garda who followed him in, hastened to add.

The boy was held tightly by his anxious parents before they pulled back to examine him, hugging him again when they saw he was unharmed. Max, tiring of the fuss, pulled away to return to the embarrassed uniformed garda. 'Can we go again? Catch some bad guys?'

His parents looked on with relief tempered by anxiety. He *seemed* all right, but was he?

West knew the priority was getting the child checked by the medical team, but it was also important to prevent this happening again. If Max could provide information about the person who took him, and where she took him, well, that was information he needed. 'You must be thirsty after all that chocolate,' he said to him, 'come and have a drink.' He indicated the table where coffee and juice had been placed earlier. Filling a glass, he handed it to the boy, offering him a chair. He indicated to the garda that he should sit alongside. 'Did you have a fun afternoon?' he asked as the boy drank, adding an orange moustache to the array of stains on his face.

'Uh-huh,' Max replied, happily.

Glancing up, West caught Andrews' eyes. He had no idea how to approach a five-year-old. He'd give way to someone who did. They quickly exchanged places.

'Petey was tired after all the games today,' Andrews said, 'he went home to bed when it was all over. You must have a lot more energy.'

'Petey's a baby,' Max said. 'I'm nearly six.'

'A big lad,' he agreed.

'Uh-huh.'

'Did you go with the lady to play more games?'

Max looked at his parents, and then back to Andrews. He cupped his hands around his mouth and leaned closer to him. 'I'm not supposed to go with strangers,' he said through his hands. 'But the nice lady said there were more exciting games in the other room. She said she'd show me.'

'So were the games in the other room better?'

Max cupped his hands again. 'The other room was a long way away. We had to go in her car. When we got there, it was only bumper cars. Daddy took me there before. I don't like them; people shout and say rude words.' He took his hands away and said, clearly intending his parents to hear how good he had been. 'I'm not allowed to say rude words.'

'Bumper cars?' West asked, looking questioningly at Joe Saunders.

'Yes, in Bray. I took Max there during the summer. He didn't like them at all.'

'How long does a ride last?'

'Fifteen minutes, maybe. No longer, I would have thought. Max wanted to get out after two.'

'The drive to Bray, finding parking, the bumper ride. An hour, max. So, where has he been until now?' West said.

Andrews looked at the rapidly tiring boy. 'Where did you go then?' he asked and then, thinking of Petey, said, 'Did you go for something to eat?'

Max nodded but said nothing.

'Was it nice?' he persevered.

'She got it from a window, just asked for it and they gave it to her.' He looked accusingly at his parents. 'We never do that.'

There was a moment's silence, as everyone tried to puzzle it out and the penny dropped collectively as, almost as one, they said, 'A drive-through.' Where was the nearest?

'McDonald's have drive-through places,' Edel said.

To be certain, Andrews asked the boy what he'd had to eat. 'Did you have a Big Mac?'

A tired smile appeared. 'A Big Mac, and fries, and ice-cream, and a big Coke. I'm not allowed Coke. There was an awful lot. Then I had to pee and the lady was cross.' His smile vanished.

'What happened?' Andrews asked.

'She made me be bad,' Max said, his chin trembling. He looked over to his parents. 'I didn't want to, but she told me I had to. And I didn't want to pee in my pants.' He turned and whispered into the young garda's ear.

'Is it okay if I tell them?' the garda asked him, receiving a nod in reply. 'Max said she made him pee into his empty Coke cup.'

'That's okay, much better than peeing your pants, after all,' Andrews said. 'And you didn't want to upset the lady. Was she a pretty lady?'

Max looked at him. 'She had a thing,' he said, waving a hand across his face.

'A shawl,' he queried, 'or scarf?' The boy shrugged. The

vagaries of women's dress were beyond the interest of a five-year-old.

Edel pulled a scarf from her bag, wrapped it around her head and pulled it over her mouth. 'Was she wearing something like this?' she asked.

Max nodded.

West looked at Andrews and shook his head. They weren't going to get any more information from him. He was wilting and his parents were getting restless, wanting to help but more importantly, wanting to have him checked out, take him home and put his ordeal behind them. He didn't think they'd have too difficult a task. If the boy were hurt in any way, he'd be very surprised. But still, they had to get this person, had to stop her. Next time they may not be so lucky.

'Just one last question,' he pleaded, pre-empting their request to leave. 'Where did you go next, Max?' There were still so many hours unaccounted for.

The child dropped his head to one shoulder, obviously and worriedly embarrassed by whatever it was that had happened next.

At a nod from West, the young garda told him, 'You can tell me, and I'll tell them for you, if you like.'

Max was happy to confide in the young man who had made the highlight of his day by putting the siren on, so he turned and whispered into his ear.

The garda smiled and gave him a manly, gentle punch on the shoulder. 'That's okay, mate,' he said, 'I often have a snooze in the afternoon after a big meal myself.'

That's what happened. Max, tired after an exciting day, swayed to the rhythm of the car as it drove around and fell asleep. 'When I woke, I was sitting on a seat beside lots of shops, there was a big bar of chocolate beside me, and the nice lady was gone.'

'It's all very strange,' Joe Saunders said, putting a hand on his son's head. 'But he's back now and he seems okay. Do you think we need to go–?'

West interrupted him before he finished. 'You will always wonder. It's better to be sure. Another hour and this will all be over.'

Saunders bent to pick up his sleepy son. 'Come on, Tiger, just one more stop and we can go home.' The boy curled into his father and was asleep before they left the room.

There was an uneasy silence after they left. Both men wanted to discuss what Max had said, but were conscious of Edel standing there, unmoving.

'You were of great help there, Ms Johnson,' Andrews said.

She smiled at him but looked perturbed. 'Isn't it all a bit odd?' she said.

'Like many of our cases,' West replied shortly, and added, 'we won't keep you any longer.' He watched her eyes flash at this blatant dismissal.

'I'll just go then, shall I?' she said, cuttingly. Without glancing his way again, she picked up her bag and, chin held high, walked from the room.

'You two,' Andrews said, after her steps died away, 'you'll be the death of me.'

Ignoring him, West headed back to the manager's office.

The two gardaí on the phones straightened when he appeared, giving him a nod by way of acknowledgement. He perched on the corner of the desk until they'd finished.

'All done?' he asked.

'Yes, sir,' one said, answering for them both. 'That was the last search team told. The Press Office has been informed too.'

'Okay, lads,' Andrews said to the two men, 'you can head off.'

Ian arrived, looking pale and exhausted. 'I've just been on the phone to Senhor Armando. He is extremely upset about what has happened. He asked me to tell you that if he weren't in Portugal he would have been here to assist. It was with great relief that he received the news of young Max's safe return. Senhor Armando has asked me to convey his deepest apologies and has given me instructions to offer each child in your party a year's free admission to *Bang Bangs!* And Max is to be offered free admission for life.'

'That's a very generous offer, Ian,' West said. 'I'm sure the parents and children will appreciate it.'

'Senhor Armando asked me to check with you if there was anything we could have done differently. I told him that we'd followed protocol to the letter and the place was locked down within minutes.' There was strain in his voice when he asked, 'There wasn't anything we could have done better, was there?'

'You did everything you should have done, everything you could have done,' West reassured him. 'Problem is, Ian, if someone really wants to take a child, there are too many ways to do so. At least, this time, there was a happy ending. It doesn't always work that way.'

Ian smiled, his relief obvious.

'We're going to head back to the station now,' West said. 'We'll leave you to lock up.'

They headed to the door, turning at the last minute when they heard the word 'joyride' and looked back at him quizzically.

'Sorry,' Ian said. 'I was just thinking out loud.' He looked embarrassed to have been caught out. 'It just seems all a bit odd, doesn't it? She took Max on the bumper cars, then to McDonalds for a slap-up meal. Finally, she leaves him on a seat in a public place, where he was sure to have been spotted pretty quickly, and in case he got peckish she left him a bar of chocolate. Why? It's like she took him for a joyride.'

13

E del jumped into her car and took off at speed, leaving rubber on the concrete surface of the car park. To say she was annoyed would be doing her emotions an injustice. She was, as her mother used to say, spitting feathers.

How dare he? She overtook a parked car, hitting its wing mirror with hers, hearing a clunk as both bounced. Garda West would no doubt have said she was driving *without due care and attention*. She swore, stopped and checked, but both mirrors were unscathed. Driving on, she tried not to take her annoyance out on the world around her.

She felt she'd done a good job with the Saunders. After all, both Ann and Joe had pleaded with her to stay.

Her thoughts turned back to West. He'd dismissed her like she was some kind of servant. The utter cheek. Annoyance flared again and she swung her car across the lane and into Wilton Road, ignoring the flash of an irate driver who had to brake suddenly to avoid running into her. Parking outside her house, she got out and slammed the door, the sound reverberating around the quiet cul-de-sac.

Her nosy neighbour would complain about the noise. She

looked across the drive to where the man in question lived and stood waiting, hoping he'd appear. He wasn't West. But he would have done as a stand-in; she could have vented some of her annoyance on him. Typically, just when she could have made use of his interfering ways, his door remained steadfastly shut.

'Bloody typical,' she muttered, opening her front door and shutting it quietly behind her. She dropped her bag in the hallway, headed to the kitchen and filled the kettle. She hadn't seen West in five months, and now she'd met him three times in quick succession and each time he'd been horrible to her. Undeservedly so. She swallowed the lump in her throat. It seemed so unfair when all she was trying to do was help. And she had helped. She knew she had.

She'd spent so much time with him all those months ago. In Cornwall. In Cork. Days when she was so messed up she couldn't think straight. If she were honest with herself, she'd thought he'd quite liked her, and even in the middle of the chaos, she'd been buoyed by the idea.

And then she had returned from Cork. Widowed, but not widowed, never, in truth, wed. She'd struggled to come to terms with the fact that Simon, the man she'd loved, was really Cyril Pratt, another woman's husband. And in all the legal manoeuvring, the meetings, solicitors, letters, and explanation upon explanation, West had drifted to the back of her mind. But she hadn't forgotten him.

Now here he was, back and obnoxious.

Maybe he preferred women needy and frail. Five months ago, she'd been pale, thin and pathetic, but she'd gained the weight she'd lost, and felt better than she had done in a long time. A week in Malta had given her skin a boost, turning it from milky to honey-gold. She'd treated herself to an expensive salon treatment too, and the stylist had worked wonders adding subtle highlights to make her auburn hair glow. She looked good. She *was* good. Most days. She certainly wasn't either needy or frail. Not anymore.

It had taken months to get ownership of her lovely house sorted but, finally, it was hers. Now, she had to decide if she wanted to stay in it. The counsellor she'd seen for a few months, advised against making any life-changing decisions for a year.

'You may not want to believe it, Edel,' he'd said, 'but you're going through a grieving process, whether you want to think of it like that, or not. In your heart, in your mind, you were married. In fact, not only are you grieving for your husband, but for the loss of a dream and,' he'd hesitated slightly before adding, 'for the loss of innocence.'

Edel had broken down and cried then, as she hadn't cried for several weeks. She'd thought she was coping. Adapting to her new situation. She'd been fooling herself.

So, she would make no decision about the house for the moment. She loved it, but it was a huge, spacious Victorian house designed for a large family. Unsuitable for a lone woman.

She sighed and turned to make a mug of herbal tea, taking it with her as she went upstairs. Wired from the day and from her altercation with West, she decided to do some work rather than trying to sleep. Anyway, she liked this time of night, the quiet, the calm. It was a time for loners. A time when she didn't feel out of place.

In the room she had designated her office, she switched on her laptop. Waiting patiently for it to power up, she wondered about Max Saunders. Why take the boy? He looked fine – he'd had a nice afternoon apart from having to pee into an empty Coke container. Innocent child, thinking that was the worst that could possibly happen.

Of course, it may turn out that something more sinister had occurred. But she didn't think so. It was all very odd.

Her laptop signalled it was good to go, as it had done every time she'd switched it on in the months since Simon had vanished. She hadn't been able to write then with the spectre of a missing husband haunting her days. His death, the deception and all the damned lies had prevented her writing since.

Her publisher showed concerned understanding for the first few months. An understanding that was wearing increasingly thin, as they waited for her to make up her mind about signing a contract to write further children's books. The last few phone calls had hovered nearer the, *we've all got problems, get over it,* category.

The glow from her laptop screen was the only light in the room as her fingers rested on the keyboard. It would be easy to churn out another children's story, but she knew she couldn't do it. She wasn't the woman she'd been the year before; dead bodies, lies and cheating weren't conducive to writing for children. She'd tell her publisher tomorrow. He'd not be happy, but perhaps not surprised either.

Over a year ago, she'd started to write the novel that had been in her head for years, and had finished a first draft before Simon disappeared. For adults this time; a family saga. She clicked on the icon and brought the book up, filling the screen with her words. It was only a first draft; it needed a lot of work. It was time she knuckled down to it. She'd no longer have space in her days for the voluntary work with *Offer;* anyway, hadn't she known, almost from the beginning, it wasn't what she wanted.

'It will take your mind off your troubles,' an acquaintance had told her, handing her an application form.

Had she been a friend or family, Edel wouldn't have found it necessary to bite her tongue, but Liz Goodbody was a friendly, pleasant woman she'd got into the habit of nodding a hello to when she met her in the shops. She'd felt obliged to be polite and swallow the retort she'd wanted to give... that the woman didn't know a thing about her troubles.

She'd pocketed the form and, at home later, pulled it out to throw away. But instead, she'd looked at it and wondered if perhaps she was right. Maybe someone else's problems, someone else's earth-shattering heartache would put hers into second place.

Filling out the form, she'd posted it before she could change her mind, and then forgot all about it, so that when the phone rang three days later, she'd no idea what they were talking about when they said they were phoning from *Offer*. Confused explanations on both sides ensued, and Edel was so flustered and embarrassed, she found she'd agreed to go for training the following week without meaning to at all.

When the day came, she'd considered not bothering to turn up. It was a crazy idea. But with nothing else to do, she found herself walking down the road to the community hall in Foxrock Village where the training was being done. The hall seemed so quiet when she arrived, she wondered if she had the day or time wrong. But then the door opened, and Liz Goodbody's cheerful face had appeared. 'I thought I heard footsteps,' she said. 'How wonderful to see you, come in, come in.'

Too late to run away, Edel had pasted on a smile and forced her feet to carry her over the threshold.

The door had been closed and locked, startling her. 'That's everyone,' Liz said. 'We always lock the door for security when we're all here.'

Only partially relieved, Edel had felt her smile waver. She definitely couldn't run away now. Instead, she'd taken the last empty chair around a scarred and not very clean table, and was introduced to three other new recruits whose names she automatically forgot.

'Thank you all so much for coming to our training evening for volunteer recruits,' Liz had started, a serious, almost stern expression on her face as she looked around the table. '*Offer* is providing a very important service to our local community, supporting those who have been through some form of trauma. It was set up, earlier this year, by our founder Viveka Larsson who will be with us later this evening. Ms Larsson ran a similar and very successful group in Helsinki. When she moved to Ireland, she discovered we didn't have anything equivalent, so she decided to give her time and energy to setting up *Offer*.'

Her set speech over, Liz had smiled again. 'Before we get down to the formal training, does anyone have any questions?'

'How much training do we get?' a smartly-dressed, middle-aged woman had asked, using her hands as she spoke, diamonds on the ring finger of each hand catching the light.

They'd distracted Edel; she wondered if the woman used her hands deliberately to show them off, or if she were oblivious to their effect. Her own hands were bare, rings consigned to a drawer on her return from Cork. One day, she'd sell them or maybe give them to charity.

Liz was answering, she tuned back in to what she was saying.

'... three hours this evening will give the foundation. Over the next few weeks, you'll be assigned to a mentor and go with them to see how things work. As soon as you feel able, you can choose to go out by yourself. Viveka knows, from her experience, that some people take to this more quickly than others. Remember everyone,' she said, looking around the crowd of four, 'we are not a counselling service. Our function is to be a hand to hold, a shoulder to cry on. We listen, fetch and carry, do whatever we can to make it easier for the person or family to get on with their lives. Our services can be required for an hour, a day, a week or longer. For as long as we are needed, *Offer* volunteers are there.'

It was well said, and Edel could see the others were impressed. Maybe she was more cynical now, but it took a lot more to impress her than fine speeches.

'Why *Offer*?' she had asked.

Liz, lost in the glory of her speech-making looked puzzled. 'I'm sorry?'

'Why the name? *Offer*?'

'Oh, I see,' she'd said. 'Well, Viveka's original group, in Helsinki, was called *Tarjous* which translates, quite nicely as it happens, to *Offer*. And if you think about it, it's exactly what we do. Offer our services. I would go so far as to say,' she'd smiled, looking at each of them in turn, 'we offer ourselves.'

Was it only her who'd found that a bit nauseating? Looking at the faces of the other three volunteers, Edel realised it was. It was just her. Maybe she was more damaged than she had realised. More cynical, certainly. But, really? *Offering ourselves*? That was going just a little over the top.

A door to the side of the hall opened, and a woman entered, pushing a trolley laden with mugs, biscuits and jugs.

'Wonderful, Imelda,' Liz sang out, 'we'll have a tea or coffee and get down to it.'

Resigning herself to three hours of boredom, Edel had sat back. But, actually, it hadn't been too bad. Some of the information, perhaps brought from the original group, was interesting. Most of it was related to the art of listening and to the use of reassuring, if meaningless, words. Having heard so many over the last few months, she agreed with what Liz said – they may be meaningless, but something about the formulaic nature of the words and phrases restored a natural order, and anyone who had their world turned upside down, for whatever reason, longed for that.

The three hours, to her surprise, had flown by.

'You've all been wonderful,' Liz had gushed at the end. 'That's the formal foundation done. Now, I'd like to introduce our founder, Viveka Larsson.' She'd turned with raised hands, and started clapping as the door opened and an attractive woman came through. Liz turned to them, still clapping, raising her hands toward them. Edel had thought, at first, she was applauding them but quickly realised it was a hint. They were to join in with the applause. Reluctantly she did, unwilling to be the only abstainer.

Anyway, there'd been something so dramatic about Viveka Larsson it seemed warranted. She'd worn a flowing silk kaftan in a riot of shimmering reds and blues. If she'd been trying to evoke the image of an exotic butterfly, she'd succeeded. The image had been heightened when she lifted her arms in response to their applause, stretching them out towards them and then bringing them back, her hands finally resting, one atop the other, on her chest.

'Bloody hell,' Edel had muttered under her breath, even as she continued to clap.

Finally, Liz had stopped and, as if she had pulled a switch, so did the four volunteers.

Rather than sitting, Viveka had glided backwards and forwards before them, telling them of her plans for *Offer*. How it was going to grow. 'At first,' she'd said, her voice only slightly accented, 'they said they didn't need us. That we were surplus to requirements. But we have proven them wrong. Have we not, my dear Liz?' She hadn't waited for Liz's enthusiastic and emphatic nod but sailed away again, butterfly arms creating a slight breeze as she passed. 'They need us more and more. And soon, we will provide our service not only from police stations, but from hospitals, doctor's surgeries, wherever, in fact, there is human drama and tragedy. And the name *Offer* will be synonymous with support and care.'

Charisma. Buckets of it, Edel had thought, as once again Liz led them in a round of applause.

Viveka Larsson's perambulations had brought her to a full stop directly in front of Edel and, under the harsh light that hung directly overhead, she could see that the woman wasn't as young as she'd first thought. Mid-sixties, maybe even more. Makeup was artful, but heavy. A silk turban which covered her hair, emphasised high cheekbones and beautiful, almost navy-blue eyes. But the costume, the drama, the butterfly arms, couldn't hide the sagging skin under her jaw, or the fine lines that radiated from her mouth and the outer corner of her eyes.

As if aware of her regard, the woman looked down, caught Edel's eye and smiled. 'Welcome,' she'd said directly to her, and then lifted her gaze and her arms to the rest. 'Welcome, all of you.'

And there and then, Edel, who'd already decided she wanted nothing more to do with the group, had changed her mind.

14

C harisma was like suntan lotion, Edel decided, five weeks later. You had to apply it every day, otherwise it just didn't work.

She hadn't met Viveka Larsson since that first day. She'd been out with a couple of veteran volunteers, and it turned out they'd never seen her again either. Edel had also learned the truth about *Offer*. Mostly, they weren't either wanted or needed, and were most definitely considered surplus to requirements. Only the blessing of Inspector Morrison, it appeared, enabled them to sit hour after hour in the waiting room.

Doing just that. Waiting for a call for help that never came.

By her third shift, she was heartily sick of it. Bored with making small talk to the other volunteers. Bored with sitting on hard, uncomfortable seats in a chilly room where the smell of urine was barely held at bay by the astringent smell of detergent.

And she hated the look of derision on the stocky desk sergeant's face.

She'd told Liz after her second night, that not only were they not wanted "more and more" as Viveka had said, but it looked as if they weren't wanted at all. Liz had looked aggrieved and assured her that they were providing a very important service. But when Edel asked when, and who with, she'd hesitated, spun some unbelievable tale about confidentiality and then rushed away before Edel could tell her that she didn't want to continue.

Never again, she decided, leaving the station after her third shift. Enough was enough. She had tried it. It most definitely wasn't for her.

Despite the fact she'd never had a chance to prove she could do it, she felt a failure. She was angry with Liz for dragging her into it. Angry with Viveka Larsson for making it seem so important, so life-affirming. And really angry with herself for... for what? Her counsellor had warned her that anger would come. 'It's all about the grieving/healing process,' he'd told her. 'You will be angry at the world for letting terrible things happen to you, and angry at yourself for being the victim. For being the woman Simon lied to, and cheated.'

He'd left out anger for having been a fool. But she guessed it all went together.'

Restless following her boring evening, she pulled on some leggings and spent an hour on her exercise bike. Finally, tired, she headed to bed refusing to dwell on *Offer*.

Early next morning her phone had rung. Startled, she answered it, fear pumping. 'Hello?'

'Edel, I am so sorry to call you, and I wouldn't, only we're really stuck. We're supposed to cover the station this morning, but Trish has gone down with a bug and there's nobody else to send. I'd go myself but I'm rostered for this evening.' Liz's voice managed to combine equal measures of panic and manipulation. 'It's so important that we keep our presence up. I know you haven't really had an induction yet; your three shifts have, unfortunately for you, been very quiet. But if you could do the shift this morning, Viveka would be extremely grateful.'

Evoking the name of the great lady, it seemed, was Liz's

trump card. Edel wanted to tell her that the charismatic appeal had worn off. Wanted to tell her, no way. Instead, she found herself agreeing. After all, she really had nothing else to do.

And that was why she was in the station when the call came through for help at the Roberts' house. She had been the only one available.

And since that day she'd been busy. She'd been out with Mrs Roberts and her family a number of times. Making tea and listening. She'd also been out to that sweet Mrs Lee, sitting with her and listening to her stories. The woman hadn't yet recovered from the break-in. There was a marked tremble in her hands that Edel would bet money wasn't there before it.

It was the writing on the mirror that had done the damage. A simple burglary would have been bad enough, but the mindless evil of that one word, *DIE*, struck a cold fear into the elderly woman. Several times during her visits, Mrs Lee would say, 'Who would do such a thing? Who would do such an awful thing?'

And Edel would reassure her as best as she could. But she had no answers, just the usual platitudes that offered momentary comfort. She guessed her daughter would get her way and Mrs Lee would move in with her, and she hoped it would work out for both of them.

Catching the person who did it would give her a lot of comfort, but when Edel asked in the station, she was told simply that it was still under investigation. Which she took to be short-hand for, *they didn't have a clue.*

She stared at the words on her laptop screen without seeing them. All she could think about was little Max Saunders, and how distressed Ann had been. It was such a pointless and cruel crime.

The gardaí really needed to get their act together and catch the people responsible for these crimes. *Police incompetence.* She practised the phrase in a derogatory tone, hoping she'd get the chance to use it when in earshot of Garda Sergeant West.

15

W est was standing staring at the case board when Andrews arrived in the station on Monday morning.

'Hey, Pete,' West said, turning to greet him. 'Was Petey okay, after Saturday's drama?'

Andrews smiled. 'He said it was the most exciting party he's ever had. He didn't seem to take it in that Max might have been in danger. I didn't want to rub it in too much, but it concerns me, you know. We tell them, time and time again, not to go off with strangers, and all that woman had to do was promise to show the lad a game he hadn't tried, and off he went.'

'The report from the paediatric abuse unit came in. As we guessed. No interference.' West rubbed his chin. 'She may have noticed the extra garda presence, I suppose, and panicked. Although we didn't have any extra on the ground in Bray, did we?'

'There didn't seem any need. We'd concentrated available staff at the ferry terminals, both in Dún Laoghaire and North Wall.'

'There was a snippet on the news about it this morning,'

West said. 'Maybe it will make people more aware, and they'll keep a closer eye on their kids.'

Andrews shrugged. 'People may for a while, and then things will go back to the way they were. Our abductor will just lay low, bide their time.'

'You're hedging there. You're not convinced it's a woman?'

Andrews poured a coffee, took a sip and grimaced. 'A weekend of decent coffee and then we have to get used to this crap every Monday.' He perched on the side of a desk. 'It may be a woman. But we have no description, and young Max couldn't tell us one way or the other.' He took a thoughtful sip. 'She spoke in a whisper, he said. It's one way to disguise your voice. You or I might be able to tell the difference, but I'm not sure a child as young as Max could.'

'What about the bumper car ride? Did we get any feedback from there?'

'A couple of uniforms called in to have a word. The place was jammed. The bumper-car operator, who was on duty at the time, told them, and I'm quoting here... that he "wouldn't remember one stupid brat from the other." He didn't remember any woman dressed the way we described either, but he pointed out that Bray has quite a high proportion of observant Muslims wearing the full garb.'

'Probably why she chose to go there,' West said.

'Or he,' Andrews countered.

He conceded the point. 'For now, we can't do anything else with it. We need to get back to our murder enquiry.'

Andrews stood, went to move to his desk and then, hesitating, turned and asked, 'Before we get onto that, what are we doing about this burglary? Mrs Lee?'

'Officially, the burglary case isn't mine.'

'Sergeant Clark would say the same if he were here, you

know. Nothing was stolen,' Andrews pointed out, 'so officially it isn't a burglary.'

'A break-in, then. Same difference,' West said.

'We don't have anywhere to log break-ins,' Andrews said, moving to his desk and switching on the computer. 'If we log it as a burglary, we have to fill in what was taken. Nothing was taken, so...'

West raised his eyes to the ceiling. He detested form-filling, the red tape and mindless stupidity of it all. 'I don't know why you're bothering with this, where's young Foley gone?'

'He asked me about it. I didn't have an answer, so I told him I'd speak to you and finish it up. I don't mind helping him. He's a good worker. Diligent too,' Andrews said, staring at his computer screen as if willing it to come alive.

'I agree, he's one of the good ones. Okay, log it as a burglary. Under what was stolen, put down her piece of mind. The computer won't know any difference and you can finish the damn thing.'

'Clever,' Andrews said, his fingers moving slowly, steadily over the keys. He swore softly, deleted, tapped again.

West stood watching, his mind elsewhere.

Andrews finished and glanced up. 'You look... what's that nice word you use... ah, yes, *perturbed*. You look perturbed.'

West smiled and leaned back against the desk behind. 'I'm puzzled over this Roberts' case. So far, we haven't been able to find a motive. We've cherchezed la femme, the money and anything else I could think of cherchezing. Nothing. Nada.'

'Yet, murdered he was,' Andrews muttered.

'Murdered, he most definitely was,' West agreed. 'Reports of his death on the news and in the papers have been accompanied with an appeal for the unknown blonde lady to come forward. She hasn't so we have to look on her as a person of interest. We certainly don't have any other leads.'

Andrews stood. 'The funeral's tomorrow. You think we should go?'

'I've never yet spotted a potential suspect at the funeral of a victim,' he said. 'But conventional theory suggests it does happen. Maybe we'll get lucky, and an unknown blonde woman will turn up looking shifty.'

'Something has to go our way, Mike. We're having a bit of a bad spell.' Andrews turned to deal with the other routine, day-to-day work that needed to be done in any Garda station.

West headed back to his office and sat. He just couldn't get a handle on this one. Decent, upstanding, law-abiding men weren't usually murdered. Restless, he went back out to the case board. There were the usual crime-scene photos, and laboratory reports detailing the results from analysing the stomach contents and foodstuffs found in the Roberts' kitchen. He glanced over the autopsy report for the millionth time – the details of the death made gruesome reading. Gerard Roberts had not shuffled off his mortal coil without a lot of anguish.

There was a report into his finances and an overview of the finances of every member of the family. That was the sum of their investigations.

A motiveless crime? It wasn't unheard of, but looking at the crime-scene photographs and seeing the victim's agonised face, he knew it was something more. To kill a man in this way. To cause such pain. There had to be a reason. It was there. Somewhere. They'd just have to dig a bit deeper.

He just wasn't sure where to stick his spade.

16

The funeral was a colour-coordinated affair. Huge brooding rain clouds in a grim grey sky, black-garbed attendees, the wet greyness of the church.

People gathered in small groups in the churchyard, and muttered sad words. They broke apart only to form almost immediately into other groups, said the same sombre words, separated and formed again and again in a wave of gentle movement. They caught up with distant relatives and vague acquaintances; the myriad people who float in the outer circles of everyone's life, gathering only for weddings and funerals. Heads nodded in sadness, and shook in incredulity. A crowd in constant motion.

West and Andrews, conventionally dressed in dark suits and black ties, stood to the other side of the church grounds, keen eyes scanning the group, watching for something or someone out of the ordinary. So far, all the two men had seen was genuine grief, all they heard were the usual platitudes, the empty meaningless words exchanged between people who didn't really know each other, but who felt obliged to say something.

Voices fell silent as the hearse came into view; faces, like flowers in the sun, turning to follow its progress through the church gates. They moved back to give it room, staring in various degrees of horror, sadness and grief at the wooden box containing the remains of their friend, relation, colleague.

Their victim?

But there was nothing suspicious on any of the faces; no signs of guilt, no shifty glances.

Following immediately behind the hearse, the black limousine carrying the family stopped closer to the church door. It sat for a moment, as if the occupants needed that extra time to compose themselves for the ordeal ahead. James Roberts, gangly in an ill-fitting black suit, climbed out first, then turned to offer a hand to his mother. She moved slowly, clumsily, tripping on the first step to the church door, her small frame, doll-like in a tight-fitting black coat, her face obscured by the brim of a matching hat.

A silhouette, West thought, staring after her, remembering a cameo brooch his mother used to wear. A softly muttered 'oh dear' brought his wandering attention back to the limo. Following Mrs Roberts from the car were a couple West took to be her sister and brother-in-law. But what had caused Andrews' mutterings were the two women who followed close behind. Emma Roberts, of course, he expected, but with her, arm-in-arm, was the bane of his life, Edel Johnson.

He was spared the necessity of commenting as, just then, James Roberts returned to the hearse with his uncle. Four men West didn't know, moved forward to join them. The hearse door was opened and the men hoisted the coffin shoulder high, and moved slowly into the church. West didn't think James was going to make it, his face was pale, his body visibly trembling with the effort. But then he noticed the undertaker keeping a close eye, obviously ready to step in if needed, so he relaxed and fell into step with the crowd who followed behind.

A determination to do his father proud kept James Roberts' pace steady as the funeral cortège moved down the long aisle of the Church of All Saints. Tears were already being shed, the panda-eyed look on many of the women's faces showing they weren't the first of the day. Reaching the altar, the men lowered the coffin to the stand and stepped back, bowed their heads to the altar, and then slid into the pews. James joined his mother who was sobbing quietly, his face stoic, his hand, as he placed it on his mother's shoulder, still trembling.

Friends, family, mere acquaintances and serial funeral-goers shuffled into pews and sat. There was a quiet air of anticipation. They were all there. Even the dead man, the guest-of-honour. And yet they waited.

Then into the silence a voice soared on two words, *Ave Maria*. Heads turned and necks stretched, people contorting themselves to see the woman who stood on the balcony. But as the first two words faded, and the voice climbed through the hymn, effortlessly singing Schubert's notes, they sat back and listened, feeling the hairs rise on the back of their necks, goosebumps appear on their arms, eyes welling, tears beginning to fall, sobs catching.

On the final note, the priest appeared on the altar and the congregation rose to their feet. West hadn't been to a church since a friend's wedding, several years before, but he fell into the way of it, the routine hammered in during childhood and never really forgotten. He stood and knelt with the rest, joined in with the prayers, finding the words on his lips without thinking.

When the mass and the funeral service were over, the congregation filed past the family to offer condolences and there were more tears, shaking of hands, routine platitudes, words designed to be comforting, but remaining meaningless in the face of the family's loss.

From the back of the church, West and Andrews watched

and saw nothing to cause the slightest suspicion. There were, however, some suspicious looks cast their way. It was a damned if they did, damned if they didn't situation, West knew, seeing the looks, knowing they were thinking, *Why aren't they out there looking for the person who did this awful act?* The same people who would just as quickly criticise their absence. The same people who would never believe the killer might be one of them.

This time they were probably right. He didn't think the killer *was* one of them.

The men who had carried the coffin into the church lined up once more to start Gerard Roberts on his final journey. An old Gaelic song, one West hadn't heard since he was a boy, drifted softly from the balcony. *Trasna na dTonnta* – Across the Waves – a sailor's song about returning home after a long voyage. Suddenly, the congregation started singing along, softly at first, and then louder as the coffin passed by. Remembering the chorus, West joined in, startling Andrews who looked at him in amazement. West shrugged and sang louder, the words coming back to him, plucked from boyhood days barely remembered. He was still singing when the family passed in the wake of the coffin, but stopped abruptly, mid-word when Edel Johnson passed, an arm around Emma, her face turned so that their eyes met. He held her gaze unblinkingly for the long seconds it took her to pass.

Outside, people mingled for a while before leaving; some to go back to work or other commitments, others to get their cars to follow the funeral cortège to Glasnevin cemetery. West and Andrews waited till the last person left before heading to their car.

'There's probably not much point going to the cemetery,' West muttered, 'but we'd better.'

Andrews manoeuvred the car into traffic and drove in silence for a moment before throwing a quick glance at his passenger. 'Doesn't seem that long since we found the body in the church graveyard, does it?' he said.

Simon Johnson. West wouldn't forget him in a hurry. Finding his body was what had brought Edel into his life. 'At least we solved that one. Over and done with,' he said, not being subtle with the message. He knew subtlety was absolutely wasted on Andrews.

'What's that saying, something about protesting too much.'

'We're not having much luck with this one, are we?' West said, ignoring his comment. 'No motive, no suspects. Nothing.'

'Luck didn't solve the Simon Johnson murder. It was hard work and attention to detail. Okay, and a sprinkling of luck,' Andrews conceded.

They followed the cortege, found parking on the road outside the cemetery and drifted in with others who had parked nearby. Rain had kept off, but big ominous clouds continued to lurk and threaten. Glasnevin cemetery, with its tall Celtic crosses, towers and leaning tombstones was an eerie place at the best of times, but now with the backdrop of the dark sky it was full of otherworldly atmosphere that made those gathered around the coffin of Gerard Roberts shiver.

The Roberts' family had a plot at the back of the cemetery and the cortège moved off again down the narrow avenues, the coffin transported on a gurney that rattled and shook as it moved. The plot was under a huge pine tree and the ground was soft with damp pine needles, a fresh smell wafting as they were crushed underfoot. The grave had already been opened and the coffin was set down on wooden slats laid across the gaping hole.

They gathered around, some forced to stand on other graves, eyes reading automatically of other deaths at other times. The priest, his robes replaced by a dark suit, said the ritual prayers and then it was over.

Clare Roberts sobbed as her husband's body was lowered and she clung onto James. Slightly removed from the mother and son sculpt, Emma Roberts, her tears falling gently, soundlessly, held fast to Edel's hand.

One by one, those who had gone to the graveyard dispersed. Clare's brother-in-law, Greg, issued invitations to everyone for lunch in a small hotel not far from the cemetery. 'It's just across from the Botanic Gardens,' he said.

He approached the two gardaí and held out his hand. 'Greg McGrath. Susan's husband. This is a terrible business, isn't it? Can I ask? Have you any idea who did this?'

West trotted out the old reliable, 'We're still following up inquiries, Mr McGrath.'

Nodding, he asked again, 'But you have no idea who it might be, do you? I mean...' He hesitated. 'You're going to be looking at everyone, aren't you?'

For the first time today, West saw shiftiness in someone's eyes. 'It's a murder investigation, Mr McGrath. We will be looking at everyone connected to Mr Roberts.' Curious; they had done a superficial check on all of Gerard Roberts' family. Nothing out of the ordinary had turned up. It looked like it might be worth taking a closer look at Greg McGrath. 'Is there something you know that could help us?'

McGrath looked horrified. 'Me? No. I don't know anything. Honestly. Susan is worried, you know, about her sister. Clare isn't coping at all. If you need to know anything, perhaps you would contact me. You know, leave the ladies out of it.' His eyes flicked to West's face and quickly away. Reaching into the inside pocket of his jacket, he pulled out a business card and handed it to him. 'These are my numbers. You can contact me anytime.' There was an infinitesimal quaver in his voice that probably neither West nor Andrews would have noticed, if he hadn't put himself so firmly in the spotlight.

'And of course, you'll join us for lunch, won't you,' he added, his eyes telling a different story.

'We have to get back, but, thank you,' West declined for both of them.

McGrath's relief was obvious. 'Of course. Pressures of work and all that. Well, I must get back to my wife.' He hesitated as if there was something else he wanted to say, but then just walked away.

'Interesting,' Andrews said.

'Hmm,' West murmured noncommittally. He stood watching McGrath as he rejoined his family, noticing how carefully he kept his back to them. Like a child, if he can't see us, we're not here. If we're not here, we can't hurt him.

But West *could* see him. And whatever he'd done. He'd see that too.

17

Turning to leave, West saw Emma Roberts surrounded by a group of young people West assumed were her college friends. To give them space, Edel had moved away and was standing alone under the branches of a huge oak tree.

'I'll meet you back at the car,' he said to Andrews.

'What? Why? Oh,' Andrews replied, answering his own questions when he spotted where the sergeant's gaze was fixed. 'Okay,' he said with a grin, 'good luck.'

Edel didn't see West approach, but as it happened, she was thinking about him. She'd seen Greg McGrath speak to him earlier and assumed, half-rightly, that he did so to extend an invitation to lunch. Part of her hoped he would say no. But there was a larger part, barely acknowledged, that hoped he would say yes. They had locked horns at every encounter recently, but she remembered a different man, one who had been kind when she'd really needed kindness.

Lost in her thoughts, she didn't hear when West said her name quietly, yelping when he put his hand on her arm to attract her attention. A number of people automatically turned around to look. Edel did what seemed best, she looked around too.

'For goodness sake,' she whispered to him when people lost interest and returned to their own concerns. 'You nearly gave me a heart attack. Has nobody ever told you that creeping up on people, especially in a graveyard, is a really, really bad idea?'

'I did speak but you mustn't have heard, I'm sorry,' he said. 'Can you spare a minute? I wanted to have a word with you.'

With a final glance towards where Emma was still surrounded by her friends, she started walking, stopping several feet away, and turning to him with a quizzical raise of her eyebrow.

He smiled. 'You haven't changed, Edel.'

She didn't return the smile, annoyance sweeping through her. 'You don't know anything about me,' she snapped, 'so you can't know I haven't changed. You helped me through some tough times earlier this year. But that woman wasn't me.' She took a deep breath and said more calmly, 'A victim. That isn't who I am.'

West's smile faded. 'That wasn't what I meant, I never saw you as a victim, Edel. Well, perhaps initially,' he conceded. 'But I certainly didn't when I was chasing you around Cornwall. You led me a ruddy awful dance. *That's* what I meant by saying you haven't changed. You still seem to be leading me on a dance.'

'Oh,' she said, colour flushing her cheeks.

'I came over to apologise for Saturday,' West continued, his face grim. 'I'm sorry I bothered.' With that, he turned on his heels.

. . .

Andrews started the engine when he saw West crossing the road. He didn't have to ask how his conversation went. Storm clouds were writ large across his face. And if he were so obtuse that he couldn't read those signs, the slam of the car door and the muttered imprecations would have given the game away.

He decided on the wiser course of action and kept his comments to himself, but couldn't help the shake of his head that drew a glare but no comment. Edel gave West the runaround five months ago. It looked like round two had just begun.

It made life interesting. Gave him something to tell his wife.

Stuck in traffic, with a swift glance in West's direction, he decided it was safe to speak. 'What did you make of Greg McGrath? Funny carry-on, eh?'

'Too much funny carry-on around these days,' West muttered, bad-temperedly.

'You think there's anything in it?' Andrews persisted, knowing the sergeant's bad moods never lasted.

'There's something,' he said, his voice more even. 'Something he wants kept from his wife.'

'Cherchez la femme?'

'I just can't see him for his brother-in-law's murder, Pete. But we'll go through the motions. Find out what the stupid man is up to. We could do without red herrings popping up all over the place. I'm not in the mood.'

They rode in silence back to the station. Normally, they'd've had lunch en route, but West didn't suggest it, and looking at his glum face Andrews decided he'd be better off eating in the station, bad as the food there was.

West went straight to his office, closing the door after him, an occurrence rare enough to draw glances of surprise from Edwards and Baxter who were sitting writing reports.

'Say nothing,' Andrews advised them when he returned

from lunch, and the door was still shut. He filled them in on their strange conversation with Greg McGrath. 'Find out where he works, call around and see if you can pick up anything. But be discreet. The sergeant thinks it might be a case of *cherchez la femme*,' he said, practising the phrase he had learnt from West, hoping it sounded vaguely correct.

'What's that mean?' Baxter said blankly.

Andrews thumped him on the arm. 'Cherchez la femme. Find the woman.'

Baxter didn't look enlightened.

Andrews raised his eyes to heaven. 'I'll spell it out, in words you'll understand. The sergeant thinks McGrath might be having it off. With a woman.'

Enlightenment. 'Why didn't you just say that, and never mind the French stuff,' Baxter said, reaching for the phone. 'We have his address. I'll ring a mate of mine in the tax office, find out where he works.'

Knowing it was a waste of time to ask him to go through official channels, channels that were clogged with buckets of bureaucracy, Andrews ignored what he'd heard. Expediency. That was the name of the game. He'd just make sure West didn't hear about it. Unless of course, he questioned the speed with which they got the information. Andrews sighed. He'd cross that shaky bridge, if and when they got to it.

Friends in useful places, Baxter smiled as he hung up and waved a piece of scrap paper in the air. 'There we go,' he said cheerfully. 'C'mon Mark, let's go see what this guy's been up to, eh?'

Edwards stood and grabbed his jacket from the back of the chair. 'Where're we off to then?' he asked, squinting at the piece of paper in Baxter's waving hand.

'Where does he work?' Andrews asked, wondering if he should, perhaps, go with them.

'Mary's College in Marino,' Baxter replied.

'He's a teacher?'

'Yep. An English teacher. In a girl's school.'

Andrews hesitated. There was cherchez la femme, and there was cherchez la schoolgirl. There was probably nothing to it. Probably. He groaned. He really didn't want to cross the city on a wild goose chase. But... 'Edwards, stay here. Finish whatever it was you were doing. I'll go.'

Andrews opened West's office door. 'McGrath's a teacher. In a girl's school. Mary's College, over in Marino. I'm going to go over with Baxter. See if we can suss out how the land lies, okay?'

West frowned, dropped the pen he was using onto the document in front of him and ran his hands tiredly over his face. 'He wouldn't be that stupid, would he?'

Andrews didn't answer. He didn't need to. They both knew the truth. People could be very, very stupid.

'If he's involved with a pupil, or with a member of the staff, we might get a feel for it, Mike. It's hard to keep these things secret. Someone always sees something. Don't worry,' he added, 'I'll be the soul of discretion.'

The cross-city journey took a long time, Andrews refusing to allow Baxter to use the bus lanes, telling him off for even suggesting it. 'They're called bus lanes for a reason, Seamus,' Andrews said sharply. 'If it was an emergency, we might have had just cause. But it's not, so stick in the traffic, like a good law-abiding citizen should.'

Mary's College, red-bricked and tall-chimneyed, stood surrounded by green playing fields. Elegant stone steps led up to a massive wooden door. Baxter, who never stayed cowed for long, gave a long whistle of admiration. 'Posh this, isn't it?'

They climbed the steps together and approached the door looking for a handle or bell. Instead, what they found was a small, inconspicuous sign: *Please use side entrance.*

'Oh, for goodness sake,' Andrews said, exasperated.

The two men took themselves back down the steps and then scanned from right to left wondering which side the sign referred to. Or was there an entrance on both sides?

'How about I go that way, and you go this way?' Baxter said, indicating with a wave of his hand, one way and then the other.

'You look like a bloody windmill,' Andrews said, before heading off to the right. 'C'mon. We'll try this way.'

It was the right choice. The side door opened into a small hallway from which another door opened into the bend of a wide corridor. To their left, the corridor vanished around another bend. Straight ahead, it appeared to run the length of the building, doors along one side, tall windows on the other, framing glimpses of a central courtyard. It was quiet, but a low hum of voices ebbing and flowing told them classes were being held behind the doors.

'What now?' Baxter asked in a hushed whisper.

'We go cherchez someone in charge,' Andrews said, and headed down the corridor, his eyes drawn to the photographs that dotted the walls, searching for Greg McGrath.

'There he is,' Baxter said quietly, pointing to one.

It was a group photograph. An old one, innocent of anything apart from bad haircuts, broad-shouldered jackets and wide ties.

Halfway down the corridor it opened out into a small hall, a set of double doors on each side. One set bore the designation *Assembly Hall*, but the opposite doors had the men nod in satisfaction. *Administration*. Baxter, pushing open one of the doors, held it as Andrews followed.

The first thing they noticed was the back of the front door they had approached minutes before. 'This must have been an entrance hallway, originally,' Andrews muttered. 'Shame really, it must've been nice.'

The large hallway, over the years, had been sectioned into

offices for the increasing needs of the school. Three had been squeezed in, filling the space between the double doors and the almost redundant front door which served now, according to the posted red signs, as a fire exit.

The two men heard voices coming from one of the offices, the sound drawing them nearer. A small sign gave limited information. *Head*, it read. No name.

'Maybe they go through a lot of Heads and it saves money,' Baxter said with a grin.

Andrews gave him a grin-withering look, and knocked.

Voices within went quiet, followed by audible mutterings before steps approached and the door was opened. A tall, thin man, who immediately reminded classic movie fan Andrews of Fred Astaire, looked down his bony nose as if a naughty pupil had dared to intrude on teacher time. When he saw the two men, his regard changed only slightly. 'Can I help you?' he asked.

Andrews took out his identification, and held it up. 'My name is Detective Garda Peter Andrews. This is Detective Garda Seamus Baxter. We're making inquiries into the murder of a relation of one of your staff.'

Pulling the door closed behind him, the Head stepped out of the room, a frown appearing between brown eyes that looked them up and down. Then he sighed and asked, 'Greg McGrath, is it?'

Andrews had been a garda for twenty years. Being suspicious was part of his nature. He'd learnt over the years to evaluate what was said, and what was left unsaid. Sometimes it was the contrast between the words, and the facial expression that was important. It was often simply, like now, an inappropriate sentence. After all, how many staff had had a relation murdered in the last week? He saw it for what it was. Classic delaying technique. Giving himself time to think. And why did he need that?

It was times like this that he loved what he did. Unpicking the nitty-gritty of what people thought they could hide. Because they couldn't. Not really. Somebody always found out. And whatever it was this man was trying to hide, whatever connection there was between him and Greg McGrath, he wasn't leaving until he found it. He'd had enough of mysteries recently.

'Perhaps we could talk inside?' Andrews said. 'Can I assume you are the Head?'

The man hesitated, his hand now on the door knob, keeping it shut tight. 'Yes. Thomas... Tom... Reilly. I'm just in a meeting at the moment. A parent of one of my girls.' He pointed to a door on the other side of the small hallway. 'If you would take a seat in the secretary's office, she's off today. I'll join you in about five minutes.' He waited until the two men had done as he asked before opening his door.

'Just in case his precious darling's parent is contaminated by our presence,' said Baxter as they opened the office door and went in. 'He reminds me of the headmaster we had in school. I hated that guy.'

Andrews took the secretary's seat, one that faced the door. Tom Reilly would expect him to have sat in one of the other chairs in the room. He hoped it would unsettle him a little. It would certainly put him on the back step. Andrews was determined to keep him there, keep him unsettled. Much more likely to spill whatever beans he had. He sat back in the comfortable swivel chair and waited.

It was nearer to fifteen minutes before they heard a murmur of voices, a firm footstep and then the door opened. As Andrews had hoped, the Head was taken aback to see him sitting facing him.

Tom Reilly quickly rearranged his features, put a mask firmly in place and with a condescending nod, took one of the other chairs. 'How can I help you, gentlemen?' he asked, his voice slightly warmer than it had been, as if he were trying very hard to show a spirit of helpfulness.

Andrews wasn't fooled and prepared to go straight for the jugular. He was tired of being messed around, and there had been a lot of that recently. West would have pushed for discretion but... 'As you are aware, Greg McGrath's brother-in-law was murdered last week. As yet,' he admitted, 'we have no suspect and we have been unable to find a motive for this quite gruesome murder.' He watched the Head wince, wondered if he knew the details. 'We have interviewed those nearest to Gerard Roberts and are now looking further afield, and asking a few more questions.' He hesitated for effect. 'Digging a little deeper.'

Tom Reilly raised his chin and met Andrews' gaze. 'In my experience, if you dig deep enough there is always something to be found. But it's rarely what you are looking for.'

West, had he been there, would have said *touché*. Andrews smiled in acknowledgement of a worthy opponent. 'You can dig, find a penny, put that penny in a slot machine and win the jackpot, Mr Reilly.'

Standoff.

Baxter, too young and inexperienced to have learnt the art of verbal duelling, looked puzzled.

It was the Head's turn to smile, and when he did so his whole face changed. He looked younger, less strict-disciplinarian, more approachable. The smile faded quickly and the severe look was back. 'So how can I help you? My relationship with Mr McGrath is purely professional; I know nothing about his family. I met his wife, once, at a staff Christmas do. But that is the sum total of our dealings.'

'How long has Mr McGrath worked here?'

'Fifteen years.'

'No problems? Arguments with colleagues?'

The Head raised his eyes to the ceiling. 'Garda Andrews, I

am sure it is the same in any organisation. There are always arguments.'

'I mean out of the ordinary, Mr Reilly. There are arguments that pass, and ones that turn bitter and rancid. They're the ones we're interested in.'

Reilly shrugged. 'Not that I'm aware of. And I generally get to hear everything. Eventually.'

'What about with a student or a student's family?'

'Absolutely not,' Reilly said emphatically. 'That would certainly have come to my attention. And quickly.' He gave a half-smile. 'Anyway, we have very little interaction with parents. Parent-teacher meetings aren't what they used to be. Everyone is too busy. And when they do occur, it's a manic round of short conversations. Very little time for acrimony, I assure you.'

Andrews was clutching and he knew it. And yet. There was *something*. Something in Reilly's eyes. 'What about you?' he asked. 'What was your relationship with Mr McGrath like?'

And there it was. Something ineffable. It was there in the sudden tightening of the man's mouth, a dilation of his pupils so that what were brown were now black and empty. Andrews, throwing caution into the whirling wind, risked it and said gently, 'What is it, Mr Reilly?'

The man sat, hands clenched, knuckles whitening. He dropped his gaze and hung his head. And then he sighed, a long hiss of breath that seemed to come from his very soul. His voice was a whisper, and held none of its previous coldness, none of its arrogance.

'Three weeks ago,' he said slowly, 'I came over to this office. Mary, the secretary was off. She generally only works three days a week. Anyway, I was looking for a letter, so came over thinking she might have a copy in her filing cabinet. I wasn't trying to be quiet, it's just the way I am. I'm always telling the pupils to be quiet, you know, so I suppose I try to lead by example.' He sighed again. 'I opened the door and Greg was sitting where you are sitting, right in that chair.' He looked up and met Andrews' gaze. 'He had his eyes shut, so engrossed in what he was doing that he didn't hear me.' Disgust laced his voice. 'He was watching a pornographic movie and wanking. In my school. In that chair. He hadn't even had the common sense to lock the damn door.

'Of course, he was horrified. Tried to say it was a one-off, and it would never happen again. But, of course, it's not something I could close my eyes to. I told him he was suspended. That I would make sure he would never work in a school again.'

Reilly fell silent. He dropped his gaze once more, his voice fading to a whisper so that Andrews, on the other side of the desk, struggled to hear.

'I've been the Head for only two months. My probationary period is three. Mr McGrath told me that if I didn't turn a blind eye he would make sure the Board found out I was a homosexual.' He lifted his chin and smiled sardonically. 'People say it's all changed. That it's totally acceptable now. Try telling that to the board of a Catholic girl's school.' He rubbed his eyes and wiped a hand over his face. 'I've worked here for nearly twenty years, given blood, sweat and tears, I deserve this position.'

'How did he find out?' Andrews asked.

Reilly's smile was bittersweet. 'My partner, George, and I decided we were going to get married. Properly, you know. We'd been for a meal and when we came outside, George turned and kissed me. It was a very romantic moment. And then I saw him... across the street... looking straight at us. I thought he'd say something the next time we met, but, apart from a knowing look, which I ignored, he said nothing, until...'

'Until you caught him here?'

'Yes. He promised me he wouldn't do it again, on school property anyway. I remember he smirked when he said that.

Then he pulled the old *you scratch my back and I'll scratch yours* and gave me a knowing wink. A wink. As if we were in some club for perverts.' An ugly look came over Reilly's face. 'I hated him then,' he said bitterly. 'Hated him for comparing his grubby little habit to my relationship with George, for making something precious feel dirty.' His face softened, the bitterness fading to be replaced with a look of determination. 'My relationship with George. Something so precious isn't worth wasting. Isn't worth hiding. I will make an appointment with the board and tell them. If they don't offer me the permanent appointment after my probationary period,' he sighed sadly, 'well, so be it.'

'Are you a good headmaster?' Andrews asked.

Reilly raised his eyes, and looked at him. 'Yes, and I'm not being arrogant when I say that. In the two months I've been in charge, there is more positive energy, better morale among the staff and, thanks to a number of initiatives I've started, the pupils are better behaved. Parents are complimentary, interested. The attendance at parent-teacher meetings has risen. And I have plans...' His voice, infused with enthusiasm, faded quickly and he became silent.

'Homosexuality isn't against the law, Mr Reilly,' Andrews said quietly. 'Blackmail is. I think you *should* tell the board. There will always be somebody to see, somebody to tell a tale. And you're right, something so precious *isn't* worth wasting.' He waited a moment, allowing his words to sink in. 'But wait, Mr Reilly. Wait until your probationary period is over. Wait, more importantly, for them to realise the asset you are to the school. You leave Mr McGrath to us. He will be way too busy to bother with you.'

Relief mixed with disbelief and the resultant look on Reilly's face was pure confusion. 'You are a strange policeman, Garda Andrews. Do you mean what you say?'

'Strange? No, Mr Reilly. I'm just doing my job. Dealing with the bad guys, protecting the good.'

For the first time, the head's smile was genuine and relaxed. Relief sparkled in his eyes and softened the lines around his mouth. 'Good isn't generally a word used to describe me, at least not in the context you are using it.' He stood and held out his hand. 'I've not had many dealings with the Garda Síochána. I must admit, it has been an unexpected pleasure.'

'We'll keep you apprised of the situation. If you have any problems with Mr McGrath, give me a ring.'

Another nod, and he and Baxter left the office leaving a bemused Tom Reilly still smiling.

18

'So that's the story,' Andrews finished. 'Our Mr McGrath is a piece of work.'

West sat in his usual position, chair balanced on its back legs, rocking pensively back and forth. 'Blackmail is a nasty business, Peter.'

'Yes, I think we'll have to look very closely at McGrath. He has secrets. Maybe Roberts found them out.'

'And he killed him, his own brother-in-law?' West didn't sound convinced. 'I don't know, Pete. It sounds like this blackmail business was reactive. He panicked when he was caught in a compromising situation, used what he knew to redress the balance.'

'You make it sound perfectly acceptable.'

'Just the reaction of a stupid man. You saw McGrath in the graveyard. If he hadn't come to us, we'd never have thought to look closer at him. It was an idiotic thing to do. But Gerard Roberts' murder is a different story. Cleverly planned and vicious.' He dropped his chair onto its four legs with a bang. 'But let's not rule him out. Have a look at his finances. If he could blackmail the school head, maybe he's done it before, and you'll find regular deposits from some nefarious character. Roberts found out, threatened to expose him and McGrath had him killed. We'll arrest him, and that will be that.'

'It happens that way in films,' Andrews said with a shrug.

'And in the best novels,' West added.

'McGrath is a nasty piece of work,' Andrews said, rubbing a hand over his head.

West cocked an eyebrow. He heard the tone of voice, Andrews wanted something done. 'You liked this Tom Reilly?'

'He's a decent man who loves his job, and his partner,' he said. 'The likes of Greg McGrath shouldn't be allowed to wreck any of that.'

Life wasn't usually that simple. Andrews tended to be a bit black and white, but there were a lot of grey shades in between. Blackmail, however, was a foul game – time to call a halt to it. 'I think we should seize his home computer,' West said, seeing an immediate look of satisfaction cross Andrews' face. 'We need to find out precisely what kind of porn he's into. We'll have no problem getting a warrant, all we have to do is put the words pornography and school in the same sentence.'

'Tomorrow?' Andrews asked.

'We need to be considerate of the family's grief. Mrs Robert's sister looked distraught. It might be best to contact McGrath directly, once you have the warrant.' West reached into his jacket pocket and pulled out a card. 'He was kind enough to give us his number, after all, let's use it.'

Next morning, Andrews, determined not to get snarled up in rush-hour traffic that would have made the journey unbearable, picked Baxter up from his Rathmines apartment at six am.

The McGrath's lived in Clontarf, a mid-twentieth century, semi-detached house near St Anne's Park. It was still dark as they drove along the seafront, passing Dollymount where Baxter told Andrews he used to go swimming when he was a child.

'We used to run up and down the sand dunes, get sand everywhere,' he reminisced. 'We'd walk out to find the sea; you had to walk forever and it would be too shallow to do more than paddle. Not that any of us could swim, you know. We'd just mess around, splash water over one another. Dad would pick up pieces of seaweed and chase the sisters, making them squeal. Mum used to say she could hear us from the beach. When we got back, she'd have this great picnic ready. There'd be sand in everything, but we never minded.'

'And I bet the sun always shone,' Andrews said with a smile.

Baxter snorted. 'There were nine of us, my mum didn't care if it rained or shined. She just wanted a bit of peace. It was hard to get that in a three-bedded semi.'

Andrews had never heard the younger man speak about his family. Curious now, he asked, 'You came from around here?'

'Yeah, not too far away. Raheny.'

'Parents still live there?'

There was an uncomfortable silence. Stopping at traffic lights that were giving green lights to an empty crossroads, Andrews glanced over at his passenger, his head turned to look out the car window. 'Baxter?'

The young garda looked back at him. 'Sorry, lost in thought. No, my parents were killed. A car crash. Several years ago. We were going to keep the house till our youngest sister finished college, but she didn't want to stay there. Said she kept hearing mum call her name. We sold it, divvied up the money, and we all bought something small. Funny though, nobody stayed around here. Too many memories, I guess.'

The lights had obviously been green for a while because the car behind, having flashed its lights a number of times, gave up and overtook the stationary car, sending a look of annoyance their way as he passed, the middle finger of his left hand raised in salute.

'I don't come this way often,' Baxter said apologetically. 'Strange how memories come flooding back, isn't it?'

Minutes later, they drew up across the road from the McGrath house. Curtains in an upstairs window were edged with light so somebody was awake. As they watched, glass panels on either side of the wooden front door lit up as someone switched a hall or landing light on. The household was rising.

Andrews took out his phone and the card Greg McGrath had given them. 'Time to get to work,' he said and quickly tapped the numbers.

It was answered immediately, as though the man had been waiting with the phone pressed to his ear. His voice was hushed, conspiratorial. 'Hello, Greg here.'

'Mr McGrath, it's Garda Andrews. You spoke with me and my colleague, Sergeant West yesterday. I'm parked outside your house at the moment. Is it possible to have a quick word? We don't want to disturb anybody.' Andrews hoped McGrath understood the light stress he had put on the word *want*. They didn't want to disturb anybody, but they would unless he cooperated.

McGrath was stupid but not *that* stupid. After the slightest hesitation, when Andrews pictured him looking around to see who was in earshot, he replied, 'Yes, of course. I can come out to you. Okay?'

That would do for starters. Five minutes later, the front door opened and McGrath appeared, trying ridiculously and almost pathetically to appear nonchalant. As if crossing the road before seven in the morning, and getting into the back of a parked car to talk to two men were a normal event. Up close and personal, his demeanour was anything but relaxed. Beads of sweat peppered the brow and top lip of a pale face. He chewed his bottom lip, smiled ingratiatingly and said, 'Well, gentlemen, how can I help you this morning?'

Just as if he were selling used cars, Andrews thought, and swivelled round a bit more in his seat the better to give the man a sharp look. 'As you are aware, Mr McGrath,' he began, 'we are investigating the murder of your brother-in-law. In the course of our enquiries, a number of issues have come to light.' He stopped and let his words sink in whatever way they would.

They had parked their car under a streetlight, and in its dim glow McGrath's face went a more sickly shade of pale. Andrews told West later that he could almost see the man's brain spinning, wondering what they knew, how they had found out, what he could do. Damage limitations.

'Issues?' he said, trying for firm, in control. Failing miserably.

'On the basis of which, we applied for and were granted a warrant to seize your computer.' Andrews reached into his pocket, took out the document and handed it to McGrath, watching as the man unfolded it and read, his jaw hanging loose.

Shutting his mouth with a snap, McGrath turned the document around and stared again. 'I don't understand,' he said quietly, 'it says here, you have reason to believe I am involved in activities which may impact on the welfare of a minor. What am I being accused of? For God's sake, I'm a married man. I have children. I'm a teacher.'

His voice rose with every word, loud in the small car. Andrews held his hand up. 'For the moment, you are not being accused of anything, Mr McGrath. There are issues we need to clear up. We have been as circumspect as possible, which is why we have arrived at this early hour. Garda Baxter will go with you now and take your computer. Discreetly. We will do our investigations; bring it back when they are complete.'

The words *circumspect* and *discreetly*, deliberately used by

Andrews, seemed to have hit the mark. McGrath calmed down. 'I can bring my laptop out to you. You don't need to come in.'

A pair of shaking heads told him this wasn't acceptable. Not that they were afraid of his wiping any data, their technicians would quickly find out, but there could be more than one laptop in the house. They didn't want him pulling a quick switch.

Baxter followed him into the house, and minutes later reappeared with the laptop in his hands.

'Any problems?' Andrews asked, starting the engine and indicating to pull out.

'No, he had it in a satchel. There were documents with his name on them so it was definitely his bag. He wasn't too impressed that I checked.' Baxter smirked. 'He told me to get on with it. And that was it. Didn't see anyone else.'

'Okay, get it to our IT guys,' Andrews said, 'see what, if anything, is on it.'

Traffic had increased in the short time they were stopped and was already starting to tailback from lights and junctions. 'Idiot,' Andrews muttered as a car pulled out of a driveway causing him to break suddenly.

Baxter waited until they were once again stuck in traffic before asking, 'You really think he might have had something to do with Gerard Roberts' murder?'

'He's such a piece of work, I want it to be him but... I dunno. It's not really adding up. Somebody really had to have hated Roberts to have killed him like that. I don't think McGrath has that level of emotion.'

By late that evening, they had even less reason to suspect McGrath. Their warrant covered any information on his computer and, as luck sometimes has it, he banked online and it didn't take their IT people long to access his finances.

'The idiot uses the same password for everything,' Oisin, one of the technicians, told West. 'Anybody with a bit of skill could have accessed his accounts. People just don't learn, do they?'

West hid a smile. He too had the same password for virtually everything. Including online banking. Just because he was an intelligent man who should know better, didn't mean he didn't fall into the trap that millions of others did, and took the easy way out. He'd think of a new password when he had a minute. 'Did you find anything of interest?' he asked the still muttering Oisin.

'Salary in, bills out, one pretty much balancing out t'other. A bit of money put by, but the rainy day better not last too long. A possibly less than healthy interest in pornography, but nothing that rang great big warning bells. No underage stuff. Actually, he seems to have a thing for the older ladies.' He handed West a sheaf of papers. 'I printed all the data out for you.'

West dumped it on his desk. 'Thanks, Oisin. And the laptop?'

'Gave it to Baxter. He's waiting outside.'

'Okay,' West said. 'Thanks again.'

Oisin left with a wave, leaving the door open after him so West could see Baxter's face peering around the doorframe. 'Come in,' he called, and picked up the sheaf of papers. 'I have great faith in Oisin and the rest of the IT crew, but it never hurts to double-check. These are the printouts of all McGrath's financial transactions, and all the internet sites he has ever looked at. Go through them with a fine-tooth comb; make sure we aren't missing something.'

Baxter took the heavy sheaf of papers with a look of dismay.

'Get someone to help you,' West said kindly. 'It shouldn't take you more than a few hours.'

. . .

Baxter looked at the clock. It was just hitting five. He'd been thinking about going for a pint for the last hour. Damn it, he'd been up with *Early-bird Andrews* since cockcrow. He caught West's eye and gave a nod of compliance. 'We'll get it done, Sarge.'

Turning around, he caught sight of Edwards in the early stages of packing up to head off. He approached him with a predatory smile.

He wasn't going to be the only one hanging around for a few hours more.

19

'They found nothing of interest,' West said to Andrews a short while later. 'An unhealthy interest in porn, Oisin said, but nothing else. And an interest in porn isn't a criminal activity.'

'He's a teacher.'

'Still not a crime. Masturbating in the secretary's office while watching it, also isn't a crime. Incredibly stupid, it would certainly warrant being suspended and, more than likely, fired. But it isn't a crime.'

'Blackmail is a crime.'

West bit back a groan. When Andrews got on his high-horse about something he knew from experience he could be difficult to pacify. 'Okay, so we arrest him for blackmail. We'd have to drag Tom Reilly into it. Do you think that's wise?'

Andrews remained mulishly silent.

'What we could do,' West continued, 'is to ask Mr McGrath in. Have a discussion with him about his excessive use of porn, and the danger to his career if his proclivities become known. Tell him we'll be keeping an eye on him, and the slightest whisper of irregularity and we will swoop down on him.'

'Blackmail is a big irregularity.'

'He's not going to do it again. I think we're going to have to close on this. We've taken it as far as is wise.' He was pulling the *I'm the boss card*, something he rarely did, and saw the acknowledgement on Andrews' face, the mulish look fading. 'Go home, Pete. Have your talk with McGrath tomorrow. Put the frighteners on him. Reilly will be okay.'

And on that final word, West headed out into the fading day. Climbing into his car, he sat a moment. Home, he supposed without enthusiasm, and without much persuading, his mind wandered to Edel Johnson. He wondered what she was doing. Her *Offer* work maybe. That group still irritated him. How on earth had she got involved with them?

There was one way to find out. He took out his mobile and dialled a number he knew by heart.

'Hello?'

He was tempted to hang up, but she might have recognised his number. 'Hello,' he said, not the most erudite of greetings, but all he could manage. 'It's Mike West here.'

'Oh?'

A less than encouraging reply. 'I was wondering if you were free for a drink,' he rushed out, afraid she would hang up. There was a lingering silence. 'Hello?' he said, hoping he didn't sound pathetic.

'I'm still here,' she said. 'I'm trying to decide if I should say yes or no.'

'I can't really offer you objective advice,' he said, resisting the temptation to say, *please say yes*.

'No, I don't suppose you can. Where are you thinking of?'

Where? He'd no idea. He hadn't planned this. He tried to think of somewhere smart to bring her, somewhere they could talk without being deafened by music. Somewhere...

'How about The Orchard?' she suggested when he didn't reply.

'Yes. Perfect. What time suits you?'

'I'm not doing anything. I could be there in twenty minutes.'

'Perfect,' West said again, wishing he'd used a different word. Wishing he could think of one.

Hanging up, he wondered if he had time to go home and change. He looked like a policeman. There wasn't enough time, so he did what he could; removed his tie, opened the top two buttons of his shirt, mussed his hair a little. Despite the chilly evening, he removed his jacket and rolled his sleeves up. That would have to do.

It was slightly more than twenty minutes before he pushed open the door into the pub she'd suggested. His eyes adjusting to the dim interior, he scanned the room. He spotted her in the corner, and with an automatic smile of pleasure and relief, he moved over to where she sat. She had taken a corner seat, so he had a choice. Take the banquette seat beside her, or sit on one of the stools opposite. He knew from experience the stools were uncomfortable for any long period of time, so tossing caution to the wind, he sat beside her.

'I ordered you a pint of Guinness, Sergeant,' she said with a smile, moving away ever so slightly.

'You remembered,' he said, inordinately pleased she had remembered this small fact about his likes.

'And that Garda Andrews likes Heineken. It's funny the things that stick in your brain.'

'And you like white wine and blowsy tulips,' West said, turning in the seat to look at her.

The tulips remark was unfortunate, and as soon as the words were out of his mouth, he regretted them. It immediately triggered a memory of the garden of the inn in Come-to-Good, Cornwall, a place that would always be linked to the man she had married. He'd been trying to show her he'd remembered something she liked, but the context came too late. He held his breath, but after an infinitesimal tightening of her features, she relaxed and smiled, and he knew it was going to be all right.

'Unfortunately,' Edel said, 'it's the wrong time of the year for tulips of any kind.'

Relieved, West rambled on. 'No, it's asters and suchlike now, isn't it? I'm very lucky, I have the most amazing roses that flower on and on. Last year, I had one in bloom over Christmas. It's to do with the road I live on being in a hollow or something.' He stopped. 'Sorry, I'm babbling.'

Edel laughed. 'Maybe a little,' she said, and they both smiled.

Their drinks arrived and West, suddenly hungry, asked, 'Would you like something to eat?' He hoped she'd say yes, that it wasn't just going to be a quick drink for form's sake, and then *bye bye, see you around*. He caught her gaze, and knew she was thinking the same.

Their eyes locked and both took a breath and held it, as if it were a moment of enlightenment almost too fragile to survive. When it did, a smile tugged at their lips.

West was first to break the silence. 'Hello,' he said softly, 'my name is Mike. It's nice to meet you.'

'Edel,' she replied with a little laugh.

'Will you have dinner with me, Edel?'

'I'd love to, Mike.'

The timing was right and the circumstances were different. For now, they were simply a man and a woman who liked one another.

Later, when each of them looked back over the evening, they couldn't remember what they had talked about, they'd hopped from this to that and back to this. A meandering nothing that allowed them to just *be* in one another's company. And if they both had a hundred questions they wanted to ask, neither wanted to break the spell to ask them.

West insisted on paying. 'After all, it was my invitation.'

'Next time, it will be my treat then,' she replied.

He smiled, and jumping in, said, 'What about Saturday night?'

Her suddenly downturned mouth told West she wasn't free, before she said the words. He wanted to ask her what she was doing, who she was doing it with, but, instead, he told himself to get a grip and asked if she were free on Sunday. This time her lips curved in a smile, and she nodded.

'Would you like to go to Dún Laoghaire in the afternoon, walk along the pier? We could get something to eat there, or in Blackrock?'

'Perfect,' she said.

They'd both parked in the small car park behind the pub. 'I'm just over there,' Edel said, indicating a red Fiesta near the road. West walked with her, a companionable silence between them until they got to her car, when she turned to say goodbye. With an uncertain laugh, she held out her hand.

He took it and kept hold of it, and there was no longer anything companionable about the silence. It fizzed and crackled. If there weren't sparks flying around, there should have been. And the romantic music they both heard, was probably coming from the pub behind them.

With her hand held tightly in his, he moved closer and pressed a kiss to her cheek, keeping his lips there a fraction too long for convention. He inhaled her scent, resisting the temptation to move his mouth two inches to the left and feel her lips. The moment passed, he stepped back and released her hand.

'Goodbye, Mike,' Edel said.

He watched as she climbed into the car, belted up and with a wave drove slowly out onto the road. Feeling lighter than he had done in months, he walked to his car. Sitting inside, he remembered Saturday night and felt a pang of jealous irritation. What was she doing? Why hadn't she said, *I can't go out with you because I am doing…?* That would have been normal, wouldn't it? Unless, of course, she had a date with somebody. Hell, he didn't know if she was in a relationship with someone or not. They'd not spoken about anything personal. In fact, West realised, he knew no more about her now than he did this afternoon. What the hell had they talked about?

His comfortable mood effectively ruined, he headed home trying to console himself by thinking of Sunday. A walk down Dún Laoghaire pier. It was traditional courting stuff.

It would be a good start.

20

W est had persuaded himself into a happier frame of mind by the time he arrived at the station on Wednesday morning. By dint of concentrating on the positive – she was going out with him on Sunday, and last night had gone pretty well – he was able to put the unknown Saturday night more or less out of his mind.

Five minutes after arriving, he had more to think about. Inspector Morrison wasn't happy about their lack of progress in the Roberts' case and called him to his office to tell him so. No point in telling Mother Morrison he wasn't too happy himself. Adding salt to wounds was always a painful exercise.

'And what's all this malarkey about Greg McGrath? So, he watches pornography, so do half the men in the country,' the inspector said.

'Half the men in the country don't teach in schools though. Plus, there is the issue of blackmail.'

Inspector Morrison shifted papers around, picked up one report and quickly scanned it. 'The head, this Tom Reilly, he hasn't made an official complaint, has he?'

'No, he hasn't,' West said and before the inspector could say more, he added, 'We've almost closed this matter. Andrews has an interview with Mr McGrath today. Just to ensure that we have done our best to secure the moral safety of the girls he teaches. We don't want this matter to come back and bite us. Do we, sir?'

Perfectly phrased, West knew, to remind the inspector, very subtly, that protecting the general public, especially the more vulnerable section, was an important part of their job. That not everything could grind to a halt because a person or persons unknown had killed Gerard Roberts. 'Is there any sign of Sergeant Clark returning to duty?'

Inspector Morrison shot him a scathing glance. 'If that's a subtle dig that you're working short, perhaps it would be more appropriate to leave social work to the social workers, and concentrate on fighting crime.'

Fighting crime? West wondered if the inspector were a Marvel comic aficionado. Certainly sounded like it. It grated on him, however, that he had a point. They'd wasted far too much time on McGrath already, and Andrews still had the interview with him later.

Now returned to his office, he sat and leaned back in his chair. He'd brought the case board in from the main office, and it stood against the wall taunting him. For the first time in his career as a garda he knew he didn't have a clue where to go. He dropped his chair down, stood up, and went through their scant data, scanning down the list of names involved in the slightest way with Roberts – all of whom had been ruled out – and wondered what they were missing. Because there had to be something. Three things they knew for a fact: Gerard Roberts was dead. He'd been poisoned. And the source of the poisoning was this damn vegetable. Four things, he corrected himself, they knew four things. The remainder of the vegetables was bought by a mystery blonde, who had never come forward despite numerous requests.

If they concluded that this mystery woman killed Roberts, they had to find out who she was, and why she killed him. So far, they had failed on both counts. There were no mystery women in his life – or, at least, none that anyone knew about. And there appeared to be no reason to kill him.

And if it were accidental? If the woman who bought the rest of the vegetables somehow gave it to Roberts and he ate it – well then, why wouldn't this woman have come forward? They'd never released the cause of death.

No, they could rule out accidental, he decided. It was just too much of a stretch.

He'd just have to face the bottom line; Roberts was dead, this woman poisoned him and they had no idea why.

They might never find out. It wouldn't be the first murder on their books unsolved. But it would be the only one on his. And he didn't like it.

Was there a stone left unturned? Resting his head in his palm, he rubbed his eyes as if to clear his vision, to see what the hell he should be doing. It resulted in one idea that he almost discounted as worthless, and then reconsidered. They couldn't afford to pass up the slightest opportunity.

Andrews came in holding the sheaf of papers Baxter had been left with the evening before. 'Nothing in these,' he said, waving the papers in disgust. 'Still, I'll take them with me when I speak to Mr McGrath this afternoon. It will look impressive.'

West agreed without much enthusiasm. The sooner they got past McGrath and his shenanigans, the better. 'Getting back to the Roberts' case,' he said firmly. 'I've had an idea. On the off-chance Mr Bean's assistant Pat might recognise our mystery woman, I thought we'd get a photograph of every woman connected to the case, bring them along, and see if she recognises anyone.'

He watched as Andrews' face said it as clear as if he had said it aloud, this was definitely a case of grasping at straws. Annoyed, despite the fact that he had said nothing, or maybe because of it, he snapped, 'Of course, if you've got any better ideas, feel free to mention them.'

Andrews perched on the side of his desk. 'Mother Morrison not too happy with you, is he? How could you not have solved this case, it happened almost a week ago. Almost a whole week. What have you been doing, Sergeant? And why are you wasting your time on this school business?'

'Listening at the door, were you?' West said, and dredged up a reluctant smile.

'He hasn't changed that much. Helpful and creepy, but still unrealistic and demanding.'

'We've nothing to lose by trying my idea with the assistant. We need to interview her again, anyway. She's the only one, after all, who's seen this woman.'

'No problem,' Andrews said. 'We've most of the photos on file; I'll get Jarvis to dig out any we don't have. As soon as we have them, we'll head out, see what she has to say. Worse case, she doesn't recognise anyone.'

'Or recognises them all,' West said. 'Anyway, you'll be tied up with McGrath. I don't want that dragging on. Tell Jarvis to come get me when he's ready, and I'll go. I want to call to see Mrs Roberts anyway. See if she has thought of anything new.'

Paperwork kept West busy until a knock on the door got his attention. It was Jarvis waving a folder. 'Got them all. Ready to go whenever you want.'

'Give me a sec to sign these very important papers, and we'll head,' West said, scrawling his name across the end of first one, and then another document. Tossing both into his out tray he stood, stretched, and grabbed his jacket from the back of his chair. 'Right,' he said, 'let's see if we can achieve something positive today, eh?'

West chose to drive, preferring to do so when he could, never a man who liked being driven about. He hoped Jarvis wouldn't feel he had to make small talk. He really wasn't in the mood. But, luckily for him, the newest recruit to their team was still too much in awe of the sergeant to talk at all, unless spoken to. So, there was silence for the short trip to The Vegetable Shop.

Only when they were parked outside did Jarvis venture a question. 'When did Louisa Persaud bring the...' He struggled to remember the name of the vegetable, and gave up. 'The poisonous stuff in?'

'Two days before Gerard Roberts and our mystery lady bought it. It's not something they normally stock, but Mr Beans said some of his customers liked to try unusual things.'

'Not supposed to kill them, though, are they? Supposed to be the healthy alternative. Think I'll stick to burgers 'n' chips.' He glanced at West, hesitated a moment and then asked, 'If she had planned to kill Roberts, she'd surely have come up with a better plan than waiting for a poisonous vegetable to come into stock, wouldn't she?'

'But she was seen speaking to him, and she bought the manihot esculenta that killed him.' Frustrated, West muttered, 'It keeps coming back to that.'

Jarvis tilted his head in thought. 'Maybe they got chatting, like people do. He mentioned, in passing, that he'd bought something new and showed it to her. She recognised it and knew it was poisonous...'

'It's not. Well, not necessarily,' West interrupted. 'If it's cooked properly, there's no problem with it at all; if it's not, it can have some kind of paralytic effect. But the stuff he took was raw, and it killed him.'

'And we have no idea how she got him to eat it,' Jarvis said, not asking, just speaking aloud, but it drew a sharp look from West.

'Let's go,' he said, opening the car door.

Jarvis had the folder of photographs under his arm. They walked into the shop and, as before, it was empty. Neither was interested in looking around, although West's keen gaze noticed the absence of any unusual vegetables or fruit. Mr Beans had learned something. He wondered vaguely what was happening to Louisa Persaud. It wasn't their problem; they'd handed the case over to the Customs Department.

Jarvis knocked on the door at the back of the shop and when there was no answer, he pushed it open and shouted, 'Hello.'

'Coming,' echoed from the depths of the hallway and, sure enough, it was followed by the sound of shuffling steps and Pat's round smiling face appeared in the doorway. There was no recognition from her, West realised with a sinking feeling, knowing they hadn't a hope of getting anything more from her. But they were there, they had the photos. They might as well give it a go.

West kept his voice low and gentle. 'Do you remember, I was here a few days ago, asking about the manihot esculenta?' He was met by a blank look. 'The funny brown vegetable Mr Beans bought from the foreign lady, Louisa. Remember?' Still blank. 'The one you said looked like a turd,' he tried again, ignoring Jarvis' stifled snort. 'D'you remember? The man with the bike bought one, and a lady bought the rest.'

'The man with the bike,' Pat said, suddenly alert as if someone, somewhere had pulled a switch. And then her face fell, and to both men's horror, a fat tear appeared at the corner of first one eye, and then the other. They seemed to sit and shimmer for a millisecond before running down her plump cheeks, flowing into a crease on either side of her mouth and then dripping off her chin. 'He died,' she said and then sobbed, her large body heaving, jelly-like. Sounds emerged and ricocheted around the small shop. Glancing at Jarvis, West knew he was thinking the same as him – *help.*

'Oh, for goodness sake, what now?' came an exasperated voice from inside. Mr Beans came bustling out, saw the commotion in the shop, and gave Pat a none-too-gentle shove. 'Stop your nonsense,' he said sharply.

To the amazement of West and Jarvis, Pat immediately stopped crying. Using the sleeve of her rather grubby jumper, she dried her eyes, face and nose.

'What is it this time?' Beans asked ungraciously. 'You can't keep coming here, upsetting my staff. Frightening away the customers.'

There was no point arguing that they had done nothing of the sort. West quickly explained about the photographs.

Beans laughed, a shrill noise lacking any element of humour. 'You have two chances. And they'd be called Slim and None. But fire ahead. You obviously have time to spare.'

At a nod from West, Jarvis laid the photographs out on the shop counter. He'd done his best to get clear shots. Every woman who had any contact with Gerard Roberts, in even the slightest way, was here.

West smiled gently at Pat, who smiled back. 'You remember the man on the bike,' he said, praying to whatever gods may be that she wouldn't start crying again. There was a quiver of her full lower lip, but this time, with a wary look at her uncle, she just nodded.

'Do you remember the lady he was talking to outside? The lady who came in, and bought the rest of those funny vegetables.' He watched her mind process his question, every little tick and tock. 'Do you think you could look at the photographs that we have put on the counter, see if you can point out the lady?'

Eager to please, Pat moved to the counter and gazed at the

photographs. West told her to take her time, so she picked up each one, stared at it, put it down, picked up the next.

Behind, Mr Beans was making grunts of disbelief. Then came sneered mutterings, the words 'taxpayer's money' and 'incompetence' standing out from the rest.

West had had enough. 'Have the Custom's Office been out to see you yet, Mr Beans?' he said quietly, not wanting to disturb Pat in her slow progress through the photographs. 'I'm sure they're interviewing Louisa Persaud. After all a man *did* die, after eating vegetables *you* sold him. Someone needs to be held accountable.'

Mr Beans spluttered helplessly.

Jarvis grinned.

West frowned.

Pat picked up another photograph. Studied it intently. Held it so close to her face that West wondered if she was visually impaired. Just as he was about to call a halt to proceedings that were never really anything else but straw-grasping, Pat turned and with a look of delight on her face opened her mouth to speak.

All three men held their breath.

Pat smiled at them, held out the photograph and said, 'I'd like my hair done this way. It's pretty.'

21

M r Beans' laughter followed them to the car. One look at the sergeant's face, and Jarvis decided it would not be wise to follow suit but he couldn't prevent a grin escaping, and quickly developed a cough, moving his hand over his mouth like the well-brought-up young man he was.

West wasn't fooled but didn't blame him. After all, it was funny. Suddenly he was chuckling. He looked over at Jarvis, his chuckle turning into a full-blown belly laugh. Then they were both at it, tears running down Jarvis' face.

Still chuckling, West started the engine and Jarvis, more relaxed now as if the sharing of laughter made them, somehow, more equal, spoke his thoughts aloud. 'We're no wiser, are we? Pat seems to have forgotten all about the woman, like she never existed. We're going to have to go with her original description, aren't we? A blonde, about five-six, who speaks funny.'

'So far, that's got us nothing.'

With the enthusiasm of his years, Jarvis said cheerfully, 'Just going to take a little longer. Perseverance, and all that.'

West thought he might try that line on the inspector when he next asked for a case update. Stalled in traffic, he looked over to where Jarvis was surreptitiously sending a text. In no doubt as to what he was texting, he said, 'I'll drop you back at the station. I don't want to overpower Mrs Roberts. It's really only a catch-up call, anyway. It's unlikely she will have anything new to contribute.'

They pulled into the station car park a few minutes later. 'Write up a report of this morning's meeting with Mr Beans and Pat,' West said, as Jarvis climbed from the car. 'And please, try to keep the comedic element to a minimum.' Jarvis made a mock salute and headed into the station. West would have bet money on him telling Sergeant Blunt all about the morning's work. No doubt Blunt would make a comment later. Not one to let the opportunity to poke fun pass him by.

It started to rain as he drove the narrow roads to the Roberts' house. Within minutes, visibility had dropped and the windscreen wipers, on their fastest setting, struggled to clear the water. Traffic slowed, puddles formed, umbrellas appeared. Switching the radio off, West listened to the rain, feeling cocooned. Comfortable. It would be just fine to stay there all day. Forget about dead bodies, blondes with funny voices, grieving widows. Edel Johnson.

Edel Johnson. He didn't want to forget about her but nor did he want to obsess about what she was doing on Saturday. Maybe he'd find out when they met, after all, walking the pier was the perfect opportunity to talk. And if it rained, he knew a few nice pubs with open fires and cosy nooks. He had thought it all through.

The traffic started moving again, and as fast as the rain had started, it stopped; sun reappearing, umbrellas and puddles disappearing. He put Edel, once more, to the back of his mind and negotiated the turn into the Roberts' driveway, gearing himself up for his potentially awkward meeting with Gerard Roberts' widow. She was bound to ask how the investigation was going. He'd have to be honest, wouldn't he? It wasn't going anywhere. They had exhausted every damn avenue and got absolutely nowhere. And had no plans to go anywhere. No, he couldn't say that. He'd trot out the usual line. *Ongoing investigation. Following all leads. Blah, blah, blah.*

Mrs Roberts greeted him with wide-eyed surprise. 'I was just about to ring you,' she said. 'Come in, I'll make us some coffee.'

Moments later, sitting in the Roberts' comfortable sitting room, sipping very good coffee, he avoided meeting her eyes when she asked him about the progress of the case. 'We're following several lines of enquiry, Mrs Roberts.'

She may have been a little woman; she may have been grieving, but her eyes were sharp. West felt himself pinned and did his best not to squirm. He tried even harder not to look guilty or embarrassed when she said quietly, 'I assume that is as meaningless as it sounds, Sergeant West.' She sat a little straighter. 'It is impossible to live in today's world, without gaining a certain amount of knowledge about things you would rather not. So, I know the first thing you looked for is a motive. What I know, more clearly and more definitively than you, is that nobody had a motive to kill my husband. No motive, no suspects. No suspects, no arrest for the person who took Ger away from me.'

What could he do, but nod? After all she was right. He sighed. 'You want the truth, Mrs Roberts? Yes, you are right. We generally look for a motive, and then we can narrow down a list of suspects. And in your husband's case, we have been unable, as you have pointed out, to find any motive whatsoever.' He too sat straighter. 'There is no such thing as a motiveless crime. It's just that the motive is generally less obvious, sometimes downright bizarre. So that's why we'll keep looking. We won't give up.'

There was a long uncomfortable silence. Mrs Roberts stared at him as though trying to read behind his words, looking for something to hold on to, something to believe in. Then, as if she felt able to trust him, she let out a long sigh and seemed to deflate before his eyes. 'Thank you,' she said softly, her voice catching.

'Is there anything that has come to you over the last few days? Any little thing, no matter how inconsequential it may seem to you?'

To West's surprise, she gently inclined her head. 'That's why I was going to ring you. There is something. I found it this morning, just a few minutes ago, actually. Your visit was fortuitous, Sergeant West, I think it may be quite important.' She stood. 'Wait a moment. I'll get it.'

He heard her footsteps recede, fade, and then slowly, hesitantly return, a piece of paper clutched to her chest. 'It's the last thing he ever wrote.' With a final look at it, she handed it over.

It was a page from a lined jotter, torn roughly, the top edge jagged. He handled it gingerly by the edges, just in case, and frowned as he read it. 'It's a recipe,' he said, puzzled at first, enlightenment dawning when he read one of the ingredients. *Manihot esculenta*. 'Where did you get this?'

'In one of the cookery books. I was packing them away this morning. They're a very painful reminder, you see. They all belonged to Gerard. He was addicted to buying them. Especially fad, healthy diet ones.' She leaned closer and pointed to the date. 'Ger was always copying recipes from magazines, or getting them from people he met. He was very methodical; he'd date it, and if he actually went ahead and made it, he'd rate it one to ten.'

'He wrote the date and this comment. But the rest, that's someone else's writing?'

'The person who gave him this drink,' she said, 'the person who murdered my husband.'

There probably wasn't any point in dusting it for fingerprints but, just in case, West asked Mrs Roberts for some cling film and wrapped the paper carefully.

'You will keep it safe,' she said.

It was an easy promise to make. It was an important piece of evidence, providing as it did, irrefutable proof that Gerard Roberts was deliberately given the manihot esculenta by the woman he met outside The Vegetable Shop. No longer was it speculation. And if it didn't give them a suspect, at least, he told Andrews when he arrived back in his office an hour later, they could stop wasting their time looking at other people.

'And yes, I do know that stopping Greg McGrath and his nasty little habit was important, but we need to focus on the cases we have. Not go looking for others.'

Andrews frowned and opened his mouth to speak.

West held up a hand to stop any argument. 'Yes, I know it was important to Tom Reilly too. And I am pleased you sorted that out. Really, I am. But I'd be happier if we got the Roberts' case sorted.'

Andrews smiled. 'I just wanted to ask you what Roberts had written. The comment. You haven't told me what it was.'

'You set me up for that,' West complained.

Nobody could do innocent like Andrews. 'Don't know what you're talking about.'

Sometimes, you had to know when to quit. 'Right,' he said, deciding that fencing with Andrews was a waste of time, 'the note. I gave it in to fingerprints to see if they can pull anything off it, but I photocopied it first.' He took the copy from his pocket and spread it out on the desk. Andrews leaned in to have a look, peering at the unknown woman's spidery writing.

West read it aloud. 'Twenty grams red onion, grated finely. 50 grams broccoli. 50 grams beetroot. Place into a pot with one pint of water and heat until soft. Sprinkle 500 grams finely grated manihot esculenta on top and drink as soon as possible.'

Underneath, Gerard Roberts had written in small, neat, precise writing, the day's date and the comment: *I met a very nice lady outside The Vegetable Shop who recognised the vegetable I was putting in my carrier basket. She said she knew a recipe for a healthy soup using it and promised to give it to me if I called to her house. I called on my way home, and not only did she give me the recipe, but she'd gone to the trouble of preparing some manihot esculenta for me. She said I could chop the root I had bought and add it to the soup. She explained that the grated root lost some of its nutritious properties if not used straight away so I made it when I came home. It looks disgusting, but she said it has beneficial properties so I'll drink it. Maybe I'll be filled with energy and look ten years younger afterwards.*

'The poor fool,' Andrews said. 'If only he'd written down her address.'

'He was on a bike; he wouldn't have had a pen and paper on him. Anyway, she probably gave him directions rather than an address.'

'The yellow house with the green garage that's around the corner from the pub and across the road from the undertakers?' Andrews said with a smile.

'Something like that,' West said absently, rereading the note. 'Pat's description of the woman isn't going to help, I'm afraid. She didn't appear to remember her at all so we're stuck with what she told us on the day, a blonde around five-six, who talks funny.' He told Andrews about the morning's meeting with The Vegetable Shop duo, and was surprised when he didn't laugh. 'Perhaps you had to be there,' he muttered to himself. Looking down at the page, he read it through yet again. 'Definitely a woman though. Pat might be fooled by a man dressed as a woman–'

'I don't think there's any *might* about it, Mike.'

West smiled. 'True. But leaving Pat aside, I don't think

Roberts would have been fooled. And another thing, I don't think he'd have gone, let alone take some dodgy-sounding stuff, from someone looking a bit iffy.'

Andrews reply was an unconvinced, 'Hmmm.'

'Pat couldn't give us an age range for the woman she saw, but read this again,' West said, tapping the page. 'Roberts writes that he met a very nice *lady*. Not a girl or a woman. Who would you normally use the word *lady* to describe?'

Andrews perched on the side of the desk, looking suddenly interested. 'An older woman.'

'Exactly,' West agreed, and Roberts was... how old?'

Andrews stood, walked to the case board and quickly found the information he wanted. 'He was fifty-five.'

'So, a blonde woman, around five-six, who speaks funny, and who's at least that age.' West caught Andrews' eye and this time both of them laughed. 'Bloody Hell, Peter, this case will drive me to an early grave.'

'If we go with that age range, there is a slight problem,' Andrews said, skimming through other information on the board.

'Please, don't I have enough? What now?'

'We've eliminated every woman on our list.'

22

E del woke on Wednesday, puzzled. It was bright. Rolling over, she stretched out and grabbed her mobile phone, fingers seeking for the right button as she moved it in front of her face. What she saw stunned her. It was nine o'clock. She had slept all night long.

Contrarily, she felt a sudden loss for all the nights when she had woken and grieved, when she had lain there in the dark wondering what she was going to do. Some mornings, she'd been too tired to function, bleary-eyed and dull-minded. If someone had told her she was wallowing in, and almost relishing the tiredness, she would have told them they were wrong. Her happy, solid world had proven not to be, and she had done a Humpty Dumpty, fallen off and broken into a million jagged never-to-be-put-together-again pieces.

But now she'd slept the whole night through so maybe the pieces weren't irretrievably broken. And maybe the world wasn't so scary after all. She curled up on her side. 'Come on Edel,' she admonished in a whisper, 'be honest. You had sweet dreams about the nice Garda West, didn't you? Big, strong Garda Sergeant Mike West chased all your fears away.'

With a squeal, she pushed off the duvet and jumped out of bed, refusing to think about him. Anyway, wasn't it silly to see the one night's good sleep as more than it was? She probably wouldn't sleep for the rest of the week. If she was going to start seeing Mike as the glue needed to stick poor old Humpty Dumpty back together, she was in more trouble than she knew.

A quick shower, toast and coffee and she was ready for the day, sitting in her office, computer powered up. She had told her publisher there would be no more children's books. If he wasn't thrilled, he hid it well, and by the end of the conversation she had promised to give him the first look at the novel she'd started.

'I'm not promising anything,' he had said, 'but if your adult work is as good as your children's, perhaps we could do business.'

She opened the first draft of the novel she'd written months before, and read the first page. It was okay, just a couple of minor changes needed. She kept working on it, trying to put any thoughts of West firmly out of her head, knowing she was losing the battle when she typed the words *jeans or dress,* instead of what she was supposed to have written. She sat back and dropped her hands to her lap. Maybe if she went and decided what she was going to wear on Sunday, she could concentrate on her writing. That decision made, she saved her work and went back to her bedroom to search for something suitable.

The out of the blue phone call had surprised her. He had sounded like the man she remembered, the one she'd found attractive and, when they'd met, it was as if the last few meetings, the ones where he was rude and dismissive, had never taken place. So now, she was completely confused. Which man was he really? Maybe it was worth trying to find out.

Opening her wardrobe, eyes flicking along the hangers, she decided to keep it simple. It was a walk down the pier, followed by something to eat. She took jeans from a hanger and a baby-blue, round-necked cashmere jumper from a shelf. Perfect, simple but stylish. A navy jacket would complete the outfit. Looking to the other side of the wardrobe, she saw it hanging next to the yellow one Simon had loved, one she couldn't bear to wear, but hadn't been able to bring herself to give away. She had been wearing it on the day he vanished.

She ran her hands down its sleeve and thought of Simon with a shiver of regret. A shiver, she realised with a return of the morning's sadness, not the deep regret of the last few months, not the searing sadness of loss. Just a shiver of regret for the *what-might-have-been*, for all the *what ifs*, and *if onlys* that had started her sentences for so long. But not any longer. It was, she realised for the second time in a day, time to move on.

She gave the sleeve one last stroke, pulled the coat off its hanger and folded it in on itself, hiding the memorable yellow in its lining of grey. She would give it to the charity shop sometime. Meanwhile, she put it into a bag and shoved it up onto a shelf.

She felt energised. Almost elated. And hungry. Checking the time, she saw it was after one. Damn, she'd planned to have written a few chapters by this time. She made herself a sandwich and a mug of tea and took it back up to her office, ate while her computer woke up again, read a few pages, munched a bit, read some more. And then the rest of the sandwich was forgotten as she immersed herself in her story. She became the heroine of her tale, lived her life of drama and excitement, remembering why she loved to write. The power over lives, over what they would do, what they would say.

By five, she had worked her way through four chapters, adding paragraphs, more details, deleting sentences that didn't work, puzzling over sentences that didn't mean what she had wanted to say, wondering what it was that she *had* wanted to say.

Stretching, she rotated her shoulders and flexed her wrists.

She needed to stop and take a rest, maybe another mug of tea. But she was on a roll and she knew it. Her eyes flicked back to the screen, she typed another word, read back over the page, saw a change she needed to make. Her fingers moved almost despite herself, adding an adjective here, a noun there, deleting a comma, adding a semi-colon.

When the phone rang, she was startled to see it was almost eight. Reaching to answer it, her right hand finishing a sentence she had struggled for a few minutes to get right, she muttered a distracted 'Hello.'

'Hi Edel, it's Liz.'

Sorry she had answered, she swallowed a groan. 'Hi, Liz.'

'I was wondering if you were free to do a shift on Friday. Barbara has pulled a muscle or something and has had to pull out.'

Edel gripped the phone tightly. She wasn't going to be manoeuvred into this. 'I'm really not free, Liz. In fact, I was going to tell you at the meeting on Saturday, I want to stop volunteering. I don't think it's for me.'

A high-pitched squeal made her hold the phone away from her ear. 'You can't,' Liz said, 'so many depend on you. Mrs Roberts and Emma will be distraught. And Mrs Saunders. And Mrs Lee. Think of them.'

Annoyed at the guilt-trip Liz was putting on her, Edel took a deep breath. 'Emma Roberts' friends have made up a rota to be with her, and Mrs Roberts' sister has moved in to stay, so neither have need of me. I called to Mrs Saunders, and got the distinct impression she wanted to forget completely about what happened to young Max, she was almost rude, in fact, so I certainly won't be going back there. And I thought you knew, Mrs Lee's daughter has arranged a live-in carer for her, a Polish girl. So,' she finished, 'my presence is not required by anybody, and I think this would be a good time for me to say goodbye.'

The silence lasted a long time. Had Liz hung up? Just when she was about to follow suit, a voice thick with what sounded like tears, said, 'Oh goodness, we will miss you.' Liz coughed and cleared her throat noisily. 'But you will come to the meeting on Saturday, won't you? Viveka will be there, you know.'

It was, in fact, the only reason Edel wanted to go to the meeting. She hadn't met the Finnish woman again since her induction day, and was curious to see if the woman's charisma and magnetism still worked. 'Yes, I'll be there,' she answered, adding firmly, 'to say my goodbyes to everyone.'

'Oooh,' Liz said, 'we may persuade you to stay, Edel. Viveka can be very persuasive.'

'Oh, there's the doorbell,' Edel lied. 'Must go.' She hung up without waiting for a reply, more determined than ever to have nothing further to do with *Offer*. On second thoughts, she decided, she didn't really have to go to the meeting on Saturday. What was the point? They would be full of volunteer chat and would, perhaps, try to persuade her to stay.

Was she being selfish?

Volunteering with *Offer* had pulled her out of the doldrums, had given her the jump-start she had needed. But it wasn't for her. Perhaps it was selfish to leave but if it were, so be it. It was time to put herself first for a change. That thought alone told her how far she'd come. For the first time, in so long she couldn't remember, she was listening to the energising call of the future rather than the siren call of the past.

And if some of her new positive attitude was due to Mike West, well, that was okay too. A smile curved her lips, one that she guessed appeared every time she thought of him. It was a shame she'd had to turn him down for Saturday night. She'd wanted to explain, to tell him about the meeting, but remembered in time that he wasn't too keen on *Offer* and she hadn't wanted to spoil the moment.

Anyway, it wasn't good to be too available. But there was something about having a date on a Saturday. And conversely, there was something sad about sitting at home.

Especially, if she were sitting at home thinking about Mike West. Damn it, why had she turned him down? He probably had any number of female friends to take out, women who would be only too keen to oblige.

Anything would be better than sitting around feeling sorry for herself, wondering what Mike was doing on a Saturday night, and who he was doing it with. She'd go to the *Offer* meeting, meet the charismatic Viveka, give her thanks, regrets and goodbyes, and try very hard to avoid Liz Goodbody.

23

'Unfortunately,' West told the assembled team at the next morning's early briefing, 'any fingerprints that were on the paper were smudged beyond recovery. The page is a standard jotter page – the forensic guys say they *may* be able to match the page to the jotter if we find it.'

Edwards who was reading the note, snorted. 'Needles in haystacks springs to mind.'

West gave him a sharp look. 'I agree it's a very long shot, and I don't propose we waste any time chasing it up. I just want you to be aware of the fact. Add it to the information we have about the grater and liquidiser. Keep them in the back of your mind.'

'What's that?' Jarvis asked, looking puzzled.

'You're supposed to read the information on the case board, Jarvis.' Andrews looked at him severely. 'The lab rats say if we find a grater or liquidiser, they may be able to find a trace of the manihot stuff on it and match it to what was found in Gerard Roberts' stomach.'

'It's difficult to read the board,' Jarvis argued, annoyed at being pulled up in front of Edwards. 'It's way too small, all the reports are on top of one another.'

West had been asking for months for a bigger board or preferably a second one. 'Can you chase up requisitions,' he asked Andrews. 'Jarvis does have a point.'

'I'll ask for one again. But you know what they'll say.'

'Fine. I'll buy another one myself,' West snapped. 'Now, let's concentrate on solving one of our cases, eh?'

There was silence in the room, Edwards and Jarvis exchanged glances. A couple of uniformed gardaí raised their eyes to the ceiling. Foley shuffled his feet and looked down. Baxter, as usual, looked bored but as that was his default facial expression it was hard to know what he was thinking.

West, didn't care, he paced the floor ignoring them. He was frustrated. Annoyed with himself for being so; worse, for letting it show. That wasn't the way to lead an investigation. Or maybe it was the way others did, but it wasn't the way he operated. At least, not usually. He took a deep breath and let it out slowly. 'What *do* we have?' he asked, his voice once again even, controlled. 'Or, more to the point, what don't we have?'

'Motive,' Foley said, from the back of the room.

'Motive,' West agreed. 'Gerard Roberts is dead. All evidence points to an unknown woman having provided the poison and yet, not only can we not find this woman, we don't have a shred of information pointing toward a motive.'

Jarvis sat forward as if going to speak, and then obviously thought better of it, shrinking back down in his seat, self-deflated.

West caught the movement from the corner of his eye and turned to look at him. 'If you have something, Jarvis, spit it out. It can't be as stupid as some of the ideas we've come up with.'

Jarvis waved the copy of the Roberts' note. 'I've read this. It's just...' He hesitated. 'Maybe the woman didn't know... was just being nice and friendly. Maybe it was just an accident, and that's why we can't find a motive.'

Edwards joined in. 'Or maybe the death was an accident. Maybe she just wanted to make him sick, cause some trouble for the family?'

'But then we're back to motive.'

Edwards shrugged.

West wiped a weary hand over his face. 'We need to find this woman. We now think, based on the note, that she might be an older woman. Get back out there. I want every shop, café, super-market and pub in Foxrock canvassed.' He indicated the two uniformed gardaí. 'We have a little help today, so make the most of it, please. And before any of you say what you're thinking, I know it's a long shot. I know the vague description of a blonde, older lady who speaks funny may not get any hits. But it's all we have.'

There were a few shrugs but no vocal dissent. This was the way the work went. No epiphanies, no lightning bolts from the blue. Just the long hard trudge of mundane questioning, hoping against all odds for the slightest sliver of success.

'You don't really think we're going to get her this way, do you?' Andrews asked after the rest of the team had left in dribs and drabs, the lack of speed in their departure highlighting exactly what they thought of the idea.

Frustration writ clearly on his face, West said, 'Sadly, no. I don't. But at least we'll be seen to be out doing something, and that's important.' He ran a hand through his hair. 'To be honest, Pete, I just can't think of anything else to do.'

24

It wasn't an epiphany or lightning bolt that woke West the next morning, it was more like a light bulb switching on, a single moment's clarity in the early morning darkness.

He had come home weary from a day that had gone absolutely nowhere. He was out of ideas, frustrated, irritable, with the sense that he was missing something nagging at him. That just-on-the-edge-of-tongue sensation that wouldn't go away. A brief hello and cursory pat on the head were all he could spare for Tyler who, with animal instincts larger than his size, retreated to the bed near his automatic feeders rather than curling up on the sofa beside his adopted owner.

West, unaware of Tyler's quick read of his mood, dropped a slim folder onto the sofa. It hardly made a sound, not like other files he had brought home that had landed with a satisfying *splat*. Taking off his jacket, he draped it over the back of a chair, undid his tie and top button and sat heavily.

It was nice just to sit for a moment, head resting back, eyes focused on the ceiling and he wished he could just stay this way. Maybe have a couple of beers, a whiskey chaser, just chill and forget about everything. His long fingers rested on the file beside him. After a few minutes, they began to tap the cover and with a groan he forgot about beer and whiskey chasers and picked it up.

He read over everything again. It didn't take long. The bare bones of the case. Various reports. The list of people known to Roberts, their alibis. When he closed the file, he sat back and frowned. Again, the sense that there was something he was over-looking, nagged. What was it?

Whatever it was, it hovered irritatingly out of reach. He let his head rest back again, went over the day, flickered over conversations, situations. There *was* something, but he was damned if he knew what it was.

He was hungry but there was nothing in the fridge to eat. There were bananas, of course. Smiling, he went and grabbed a couple, peeled, munched them and tossed the skins into the bin. Then, dinner done, he went to an old oak cabinet he'd got for a song at a car boot sale several years before. He'd had it for several months before deciding it was perfect as a drinks' cabinet, filling its shelves with a collection of expensive whiskeys. But that was in his law days when he could afford such indulgences. Nowadays it held Jameson, and the odd bottle of luxurious stuff he'd been given as a gift that was used sparingly.

He poured a generous Jameson and, switching on the television, sat and listened to the news, sipping the whiskey slowly. Not too slowly, he noticed, the news over and the glass empty. 'I shouldn't,' he muttered, as he stood and refilled the glass. The second went down as smoothly as the first, and a mellow, warm feeling took over. Whatever it was he was trying to remember he certainly wouldn't remember it now. Grateful for the mental release, he took himself to bed, dropped clothes on the floor, climbed under the duvet and fell asleep without another thought.

It took that complete shutdown, for the niggling pieces of

information to emerge from the glut of facts and figures that cluttered up his brain. And in that quiet time, just before dawn, they consolidated and woke him with that brief, if blinding, flash of light.

He lay for a moment, eyes wide open, adjusting to the solid darkness of his room, trying to make sense of the idea that had pinged and woken him.

Could it be that simple?

Surely not.

It was a tenuous link at best, he argued, taking the Devil's advocate side. But it *was* a link. Something Edwards had said triggered a memory of what Andrews said when young Max went missing and returned unharmed; a similar remark to one Foley had made when Mrs Lee had her house broken into and nothing was damaged or stolen.

Edwards, Andrews and Foley had all made remarks to the effect that it looked like someone had deliberately set out to cause trouble. And if the manihot esculenta had been better cooked, Gerard Roberts may have had some mild form of paralysis, would probably have been very sick, definitely hospitalised. But not dead. But perhaps the woman who bought the manihot esculenta wasn't aware it was a different type; wasn't aware it could kill.

And if Roberts hadn't died, it would just have been another troublesome case. Another motiveless case. Except it wasn't. That was the light bulb moment. There was a motive for each of these cases. They all caused an element of trouble – and they had all needed the services of *Offer*.

Once West had switched that light on, it wouldn't go off. It all made sense now. This group appears, doesn't make much inroad, is deemed surplus to requirement, dismissed by all and sundry. And then suddenly, within the space of several days they become indispensable. It had all been orchestrated.

'It makes sense,' West murmured. 'Orchestrated. But by whom?' And then, in the way one idea will often trigger another, he sat bold upright. 'Oh, for goodness sake, of course. She speaks with a foreign accent. Pat's lady who speaks funny. Viveka Larsson.'

Throwing back the duvet, West almost leapt from the bed, energised for the first time in days. He was right. Dammit, he was right. Now he just needed to put it together. Proof, not conjecture. Pulling back the heavy curtains, he saw that the dawn had put out the streetlight and caught his breath as he watched an urban fox move with quick, light steps down the centre of the road, ears pricked, eyes scanning left and right. He released his breath on a half-laugh, the window fogging before him. 'Walk straight down the middle, keep your eyes and ears open. Got it. That's the way to go.'

He'd allowed himself to become befuddled with this case. But now he knew why. That subconscious feeling that all was not as it appeared. He'd never have thought of linking the three cases. And now. Well, now he knew.

It was still too early to start, but he was too wired to go back to sleep. Naked, he went downstairs to start a pot of coffee brewing. Sensing an improved mood, Tyler pattered over for some attention and was rewarded by being scooped up, fussed over for a few minutes before being plopped down in front of his food bowls.

West drank the first mug of strong coffee, still naked, leaning against the counter, staring into space. His brain was spinning, planning, organising. He checked the wall clock. Five. Time for a long shower. He drained the mug, left it on the counter for later and headed upstairs.

Originally a four-bedroomed house, West had reorganised the upstairs space. The old too-small bathroom was now an ensuite for his bedroom, while the smallest of the four rooms had been converted into a spacious, luxury bathroom. He had bought the best he could afford; a large shower with a powerful pump and a deep bath with a broad rim where you could balance a glass of wine while you soaked. The wash-hand basin was handmade, a beautiful piece of glass with a subtle concave, and discreet taps operated by a sensor.

West loved it and only used his ensuite when his sister came to stay. If he were having a bad day, he would stand beneath the powerful spray of the shower, the water cascading over his head, the positive energy of the flowing water chasing away the blues. Better than any drug. Almost as good as a neat whiskey. And on a good day it woke him up, washed away the sleep, readied him for whatever might come. He had time this morning, so he stood under the water a long time before squirting shower gel into his hand, the fresh smell of lemon filling the cubicle.

Getting out, dripping water everywhere, he grabbed a towel from the pile his housekeeper left folded so neatly every Monday, dried himself roughly, ran the towel through his hair and dropped the towel into the laundry basket.

Ten minutes later he was dressed, his dark grey suit complemented by a shirt a shade lighter, and a burgundy tie with a faint grey pattern. His hair was brushed severely back, but once dry it would fall artfully forward, just as his hairdresser had intended. He wasn't a vain man; good dress sense came naturally. He'd had the money to spend on clothes when he was in law, expensive clothes, made to last. His mother added to his wardrobe. Birthdays and Christmas, regular as clockwork, some new item of clothing would appear. He wore them because they were there, that and the fact his mother had extremely good taste and the money to indulge it.

Another mug of coffee, and he was ready to go. Arriving in the station, he ignored the startled looks of the night shift as easily as he ignored the relaxed uniform code, the vague whiff of cigarette smoke, the general air of untidiness. It would all be sorted over the next hour leaving no trace for the beady, all-seeing eye of Sergeant Blunt.

It took him thirty minutes to gather the files and information he wanted. He needed to display it carefully in order to make his point. He regarded the case board with disfavour. Of course, he hadn't got around to buying another, not that he had the slightest idea where to buy a damn board anyway. Requisitions were such a pain in the ass. He looked around the general office for inspiration.

Notices had gone out to everyone after the station had been redecorated the previous year. The use of Blu-Tack, Sellotape or any generic forms of the same were now strictly forbidden. So far, the walls had remained pristine.

One of the walls of the general office had windows, two had doors but one was a big clear space. Perfect, West thought with a shrug. If they wouldn't provide what he wanted, he'd have to improvise. It took fifteen minutes, and a large packet of Blu-Tack he found in a drawer, to fix all the relevant data on the wall, setting out the information on the three cases side by side. It was like finding the right piece of the jigsaw puzzle, everything was clicking into place. Now all they had to do was find the proof.

He made a pot of coffee and drank a mug while he perused the wall, moving pieces of information around, trying to make the pattern that was obvious to him, look clearer. It would make sense to call Mother Morrison down to see it. Then he remembered with a grimace, that the inspector was a patron, of sorts, of this Larsson woman. He'd certainly promoted the use of *Offer* and, by all accounts, had been extremely friendly and helpful to her. It was an added complication he could have done without. Standing back, he was convinced he was on the right track. Lack of motive was the common denominator.

A rattle and clatter announced the first of the team to arrive, and West turned to see Andrews framed in the doorway, the look of surprise on his face changing to wonderment when he saw West's wall.

'Mother Morrison is going to have a head-fit,' he said, dropping his jacket carelessly on the back of a chair.

'I'm sure it's him who tells requisitions to cut back on supplies. They wouldn't give us another damn board, would they? And I needed to put this information together. What do you think?'

'I think I need a drink.'

'Look at it with an open mind,' West said, as Andrews poured coffee, ladled in sugar and came back to stand beside him.

Andrews slurped his sugary brew and said nothing. After a few minutes' silence he moved to the left, his eyes scanning, processing. Just when West thought he had done, he moved to the right, moved some notes to read others pinned underneath. Then he moved back to stand beside him once more.

'Well?' West bit out finally.

'Let me see if I have this straight,' Andrews said. 'You think these three cases are linked because the common element is that there was no motive for each of the crimes?'

'*Offer,*' West said, and waited for a look of enlightenment to appear on Andrews' face.

Instead, Andrews' eyebrows raised almost as far as his hairline.

West ran his hands through his hair in mute desperation before letting out a groan. 'I'm not explaining this very well, am I? I thought it would be clear... Okay, let me start again. It was something Edwards said yesterday.' He perched on the side of a desk. 'Do you remember he said, what if it were someone just out to make trouble? Well, I'm suggesting that he was absolutely right. *Offer* was a group that was going nowhere and it was suddenly galvanised into action by these three cases. And the group is led by a foreign blonde lady.'

Andrews' sceptical expression didn't change.

'Pat, from The Vegetable Shop, mentioned the woman spoke strangely. Well, Viveka Larsson is Finnish,' West persevered. 'I bet she speaks with an accent. Wouldn't that be speaking strangely?'

'Pat said she spoke *funny*,' Andrews corrected him and then gave a half-hearted shrug. 'I suppose, at a push, an accent might fit.'

'You're thinking it's all a bit...' West searched for a word, discarding the more scatological that came to mind, settling on, 'far-fetched. Then let's bring it down to basics. We have three recent unsolved cases, all unusual, all motiveless, with one connection... *Offer*.'

'We don't have anything else,' Andrews said, his tone of voice telling West clearly he wasn't convinced. 'We may as well look into this Larsson woman. But I'm guessing you haven't broached this with the inspector yet?'

Footsteps, doors opening and closing, greetings and ribald comments, the general hullaballoo of more of the team arriving, halted conversation between the two men. But West guessed Andrews hadn't needed an answer to his question.

Jackets off, coffee in hand, the team stood and listened. West read their faces, saw healthy scepticism waver as he pointed out the links, and used his oratorical skills to swing them to his way of thinking. At the end, even Andrews' doubt had softened to a wary acceptance.

'This is what we're going to do,' West said. 'Edwards, find a photograph of Viveka Larsson. *Offer* has posters and flyers; she's bound to be in one of them. Take it around to The Vegetable

Shop, and see if Pat recognises her. It's a long shot but worth a try.'

Edwards turned to his desk; the computer powered up and fingers flew over his keyboard. Less than a minute later, he crossed to the printer and held his hand for the page as it trundled out.

He took it to West. 'It's a group shot of her with the original six volunteers,' he said handing it over. 'It's a good shot, the faces are clear, not the usual grainy photographs often used in cheap flyers. There was money spent on these.'

West looked at the image of Viveka Larsson, turbaned, exotic and looking larger than life. 'It's a good one. Let's hope Pat recognises her.'

'What about taking one around to the young Saunders' lad?' Baxter asked.

'No, the Saunders want to put it behind them. I'm not sure they'd agree. Anyway, it sounded like she kept herself well covered with a scarf when she was with him, so we'd be wasting our time. Let's concentrate on getting information on this Larsson woman. I want to know everything there is to know. Contact the Garda Vetting Unit, see if everything is in order with them. I want to know exactly where she came from. She's supposed to have run a similar group in Finland; find out where, does it still exist, why she left. I want to know what she had for breakfast. Okay?'

Nods all around, and then everyone was moving together, hitting phones and keyboards, gathering information from a wide and varied network of sources.

West went to his office to prepare for his conversation with the inspector. He was putting it off for as long as possible. It would be so much easier if they had something a little more concrete. Despite his rousing oration of earlier, he was under no illusion. Everything they had was circumstantial. Conjecture.

Morrison wasn't keen on the first. And downright hated the second.

'Anything you want me to chase up, Mike?' Andrews asked coming in, leaning against the doorframe. 'The lads are beating down every door getting the info on Larsson.'

West stretched and rolled his shoulders. 'I'm spending far too much time sitting at a desk these days.'

'A nice walk upstairs to talk to Inspector Morrison will sort you out.'

'Thanks. And yes, there is something you can chase up. It just came to me; I should have remembered earlier. When I spoke to Sergeant Blunt last week about *Offer,* he mentioned they were fairly redundant at first, and then they had a number of cases with, to quote Blunt, "needy victims". Check with him, and pull up those cases. See if they match our three. Maybe the pattern started with those, and not ours.'

The sceptical look had returned, but West ignored it. He had more on his plate. It was time he bit the bullet and told Morrison what they were up to. Better he heard it from him than from one of his many sources, better known to the rest of the team as the sneaky ass-lickers who listened in on conversations and reported to Morrison, currying favour for God-knew-what. Yes, far better he heard it from him. Reluctantly, he got to his feet. He'd given up the idea of bringing him down to see the wall of information. If he hadn't managed to convince Andrews, who would have been more than willing to be convinced, he certainly wasn't going to convince the inspector who, as soon as he mentioned they were investigating Viveka Larsson, would probably go ballistic.

The initial response was more catatonic than ballistic. Morrison sat and stared at him, mouth slightly agape, eyes almost cartoon-like, protruding from his rather thin face. His hands were on the desk in front of him, fingers slightly clawed.

Holding on for dear life, or getting ready to spring and scratch his eyes out, West wondered, shifting uncomfortably under the inspector's scrutiny.

Finally, Inspector Morrison managed four words. Each bitten out, self-contained. 'You. Are. Doing. What?'

The man was bloody intimidating, but West was made of tough stuff. He listened as the inspector ranted and let the words *circumstantial, conjecture, idiotic, jumped-up, far-fetched* and even *nonsensical* go right over his head, waiting till he ran out of steam to make his case again.

'Call your team back,' Morrison said. 'Cancel any of these daft plans you have put into motion. I don't want to hear about this nonsense again. Is that understood, Sergeant West?'

'It may be conjecture, supposition and circumstantial, sir. But that is often the way an investigation starts. Then we find the facts to confirm what we had conjectured, and our circumstantial evidence becomes firm proof of a crime. My team are looking now, sir. Give me to the end of the day. If we find nothing, well, then we have lost nothing except a few hours. And Ms Larsson will be none the wiser.'

Inspector Morrison sat frowning; his hands still clawed on the desk. Then they splayed out, middle fingers tapping the desk in a slow rhythm. 'This sounds like both a wild goose chase and a fishing exercise, Sergeant West, but...' He hesitated, before sighing loudly, then continued, '... you are right. And you have enough belief in your convictions to continue to stand there after one of the best rants I have given in quite a long time. So, okay, go with it. But I want to hear from you before close of day. Now, go away.'

West didn't need to be told twice. Amusement battled with surprise at the inspector's unexpected remark. *One of the best rants!* With a chuckle, he returned to the detective's office, still smiling as he pushed open the doors, the smile dying quickly when he saw the clock. Where had the morning gone?

He needed coffee after his meeting with the inspector. Filling a mug, he took it into his office, and was just about to take a sip when Andrews all but bounced into his office.

'I think maybe you're right,' he said with a grin.

25

West looked at the handful of slim files that were dropped on the desk in front of him, and lifted his eyes to meet Andrews' expectant gaze.

'We'd never have guessed, Mike,' he said, pulling up a chair. 'We'd never have linked these cases together with ours. They weren't even serious enough to interest us, the uniformed guys dealt with them all.'

The office filled with a tense silence as West opened the first file.

'It's all petty, small stuff,' Andrews commented. 'Troublesome though. Upset people. A lot of crying and hysterics. But, like our break-in and Max's abduction, nobody was hurt. No real damage.'

Still no comment from West, as he worked his way through the five files. He read the final one, closed it, lifted all five and tapped them on the desk, lining up the edges. 'She's got a good imagination, I'll give her that,' he said quietly.

'Blunt is annoyed with himself for not spotting the connection,' Andrews said. 'He wants those *Offer* volunteers barred from the station.'

'We can't do anything without proof,' West said, shaking his head. 'Blunt knows that. It's still all circumstantial and conjecture. Just eight odd cases instead of three. I mean look at this,' he said, opening the first file again. 'This poor woman finds all her underwear gone from her washing line, and the next day it's posted through her letterbox with the crotch cut from each one. A lady from *Offer* sat with her in the waiting room, because she was too hysterical to speak to any of the male gardaí; there's been no similar incident since. And this one' – he opened the next file – 'a face peeping in through the windows of that residential home in the village. Put the wind up some of the old dears. The gardaí who responded didn't see anyone, some of the residents were so upset, they rang the station and an *Offer* volunteer went and stayed all night. She didn't see anyone. There've been no reports since.' West slammed the bundle of files down on his desk. 'The same with every one of them. Irritating and troublesome, but no real damage. And *Offer* involved, every time.'

Andrews crossed his arms. 'She was clever too. If she'd used the same ruse each time, Blunt would have noticed and brought it to our attention.'

'But then she did something stupid and Gerard Roberts died. She crossed a line there, Peter, she can't come back.' West tapped his fingers on the stack of files, his face grim. 'She made a quick progression from petty misdemeanours to serious crime, didn't she? Even without Gerard Roberts' death, the other two cases are more serious; they have caused more pain, more grief. Max's parents will take a long time to recover, and Mrs Lee's life has been devastated.'

'Maybe she's got a taste for it now. And we both know how this kind of appetite develops.'

'She'll kill again,' Andrews agreed. 'Deliberately or by accident.'

West tapped the files again and bit his lip. 'I think she will. We need to stop her. But we need something more than a series of bizarre cases to get a warrant for her arrest. We need proof.'

The door opened and Edwards popped his head through the gap. 'You busy?'

'You should knock,' Andrews said sharply.

Edwards closed the door, knocked and opened it again. 'Better?' he asked.

'Nobody likes a smart-arse, Mark,' West said quickly, forestalling the remark Andrews had on the tip of his tongue which would have led to another from Mark, and another from Andrews. They'd probably have got funnier, Edwards being the joker in the team, but today, he wasn't in the mood. 'Tell us what happened.'

'I showed Pat the photograph. She thinks it's the same woman. But she was pretty vague. I don't think her testimony would stand up.'

West wasn't surprised. 'It was always going to be a long shot. We'll put it together with all the rest anyway. In combination, it might be enough to get us a search warrant.' It was approaching four o'clock. If he didn't contact the inspector soon, Morrison would no doubt contact him, and he wouldn't be happy. He needed something to give him.

Heading into the general office, he raised his voice. 'Okay, everyone,' he said, lowering the volume when he had their attention. 'Finish what you're doing, and let's put it together. I need to let the inspector know what's happening.'

It took a few minutes for calls to finish, notes to be gathered from desks and printers. Jarvis rolled his head, loosening muscles cramped from holding the phone. Baxter stretched and yawned, stood and walked a turn around the room. All filled a mug of coffee before assembling in front of what they had taken to referring to as The Wall, its capitalisation in their heads ensuring it would last long after this case had ended. Why bother with a board after all, when there was a perfectly suitable wall, standing bare, doing nothing?

'Okay,' West said, quietening their chatter. 'Before we start, listen up to what we've got from Sergeant Blunt.' He quickly filled them in on the five cases that had first brought *Offer* into the spotlight.

'None of these five cases were serious enough to involve the detective division, but then we had the murder of Gerard Roberts. The next two cases, the Lee break-in and the Saunders' abduction were also more serious. No physical harm in either case, true, but a lot of people have had their lives turned upside down.'

He looked around the room, saw Allen was bursting with news and, wanting to get the salient points from the off just in case Mother Morrison beat him to the phone, nodded at him. 'Tell us what's bubbling away in that head of yours.'

Allen picked up a sheaf of papers from the desk beside him. He was a stocky, ginger-haired, freckle-faced man who looked like he'd stepped straight from the farm which, in fact, is exactly what he had done a few years before, straight from his father's farm in Tipperary to the training college in Templemore, just a mile down the road. 'It took a while to get through to our counterparts in Finland,' he said. 'And then there was a lot of toing and froing before they gave me the information I wanted. Once I mentioned Viveka Larsson's name, it went a bit more smoothly and, eventually, I ended up chatting to someone who knew her well.' He stopped and looked around, and West knew that he'd got something he could use. Something to satisfy Mother Morrison and keep him off his back. Maybe even enough for a search warrant.

Certain he had their undivided attention, Allen continued. 'An officer by the name of' – he stopped and read directly from the page – 'Eetu Laakkonen. He's with their Vice Squad and knows Viveka Larsson very well indeed. She did run a group in Helsinki, and it *was* called the Finnish name for offer which is *Tarjous*. But, it's not the same as *Offer* here. *Tarjous* is, or rather was, since it closed down about a year ago, a brothel.'

Men inured to criminality in all its many and varied forms can still be surprised, and whereas there weren't gasps, there were certainly a few *well, well, wells* among the older and *bloody hells* among the younger men.

West's reaction was a more restrained 'yes' muttered softly. This would certainly get him off the hook with Morrison. 'How on earth did she get through Vetting?' he asked, puzzled. Garda Vetting wasn't foolproof, but something as glaringly obvious as this should surely have rung a few bells.

Allen smiled his slow smile. 'Well, our Madam Larsson is quite clever. She is the founder of *Offer*, but she doesn't actually work as a volunteer so...'

'But surely she had to register with someone?' Edwards asked. 'Don't you have to register as a charity?'

They all looked to West, who they knew would have the answer. He did and proceeded to explain. 'The term *registered charity,* despite what most people think, doesn't actually exist in Ireland. Instead, charities are governed by a statute going back to the seventeenth century. I'm guessing, and it's a very complicated area, that *Offer* would be classified as a charity *beneficial to the community* and the Office of the Revenue Commissioners would view it as that.'

'Why did the brothel close down?' Andrews asked, getting back to the point. 'Or was it closed down?'

Allen grinned. 'This is Finland. They have a different view of these things. No, the brothel was a legitimate, taxpaying, and, according to my new best pal in Finland, Eetu, a very high-end, lucrative business. He doesn't know why she suddenly shut it down, but she did. Closed it completely, and vanished off their radar.'

West stood, two hands palm-together, fingertips softly tapping, brain spinning new facts, adding them to the mix. They needed more. 'Personal data, anyone?'

Jarvis held up a hand. 'There's not much available, I'm afraid. Viveka Larsson was born in Stockholm in 1955. She doesn't seem to have married. No children. No financial problems reported, but obviously I couldn't get access to her bank accounts. She moved to Helsinki in 1985 and has lived there ever since. There is no indication as to why she came to Ireland.' He looked up from the notes he was reading. 'Actually, there is surprisingly little written about her, personally. Any reference to her though, is invariably accompanied by the words *charming* or *charismatic*.'

'She wouldn't be the first murderer to be described in either of those terms,' Baxter pointed out.

'Let's not jump the gun,' West said sharply. 'She is still just a suspect, a person of interest. Let's keep our language appropriate, okay?' Ignoring Baxter's embarrassed nod, he continued. 'Anything else?'

Edwards raised a hand. 'She's not on any social network that I could see. In fact, she's not anywhere. *Offer* have a very basic website but apart from mentioning that Larsson is the founder, there is no other information. However,' he said with a smirk, 'I contacted the people who made their advertising flyers and managed to get the billing address from them. It's an apartment on Nutley Lane. I checked with the Property Register; it hasn't been sold recently so I contacted a friend who works for a property maintenance company. He gave me the name of the company that manages the apartment complex, and they were happy to tell me that she lives there alone in a two-bedroom apartment. She has been there almost eight months. There have been no problems. No complaints.' Edwards finished and relaxed back.

'Nutley Lane, eh?' Andrews muttered. 'Posh area. Is she running a brothel from there, d'y'think?'

Edwards picked up the phone. 'I'll check with Vice. See if they've heard anything.' A minute later, he hung up. 'Nothing to report,' he said. 'Vice don't have any record of a problem there, but they said they may not have heard, if she were being very discreet.'

West paced the room. 'None of this makes sense. Why would she move from running a successful brothel in Finland to a discreet, small-time affair here? And why on earth has she started this *Offer* group?'

He wasn't surprised to see blank faces staring back. Even Andrews, who could normally be relied on to come up with some vague theory, looked stumped.

'Right,' he said. 'I'm going to go to the inspector with this, see if I can convince him we have enough for a search warrant. If we can find a grater or liquidiser in her apartment, and the lab can find a trace of manihot esculenta on them then we have her. We can also search for a match to that jotter page.'

It all hinged on Morrison. If West could convince him. They were all thinking the same thing: Mother Morrison would either be so incensed at being taken for a fool he would want to go after her, guns blazing, or be so embarrassed that he'd want to cover the whole thing up and dismiss all their work as circumstantial conjecture. Being an ex-brothel owner, after all, didn't make Larsson a murderer. They were still missing that essential element.

Proof.

26

E del didn't leave the house on Thursday. Following her breakfast at eight, she sat in front of her computer and worked through till five with just a break, every now and then, for coffee. She resisted the sudden and unusual need to vacuum the house, the unexpected desire to sort through her clothes, divide them into dump, keep and charity. She even resisted the temptation to go to the new coffee shop in the village and eat cake. Facing each distraction down, she forced herself to sit and keep writing.

By five, she had edited the first ten chapters and was happy with what she had done. She stood and stretched, feeling shoulder and back muscles groan. Of course, she had planned to stand and stretch every hour, but it hadn't happened and now she regretted her long immobility. Five minutes stretching made a difference, and she hummed happily as she went down the stairs. She'd skipped lunch and her stomach was growling. There was a lasagne in the fridge that she'd bought from the village deli earlier in the week, and when it was heated through, she took it and a glass of red wine through to the sitting room.

She switched on the television, and channel-hopped with

little enthusiasm before reaching a music channel playing the mellow notes of a blues band that suited her mood. She felt very relaxed. Maybe it was the satisfying day's work. Being busy was good. Putting her past behind her was better. She finished the lasagne, put the plate on the floor and sat back with her wine.

Her thoughts switched to the undeniably sexy garda sergeant. Had they a future together? She wasn't ready to admit, even to herself, that she hoped so. There was something so reassuring about him, and after all she'd been through, that beat sexy and handsome any day.

Another glass of wine and then, because for the first time in a long time, she hadn't dissolved into tears after drinking, she had another, feeling very chilled indeed. She stood, wine in hand, and swayed to the beat of the music that played, wondering if Mike were a good dancer. She hoped so. Was there anything in the world as good as being in the arms of a man, feeling something connect as the music started and took you over. Sublime. She twirled a bit, drank a bit and then a bit more.

In the morning, her first thought was, *I'm never drinking again.* Her second was, *Oh God, my head.*

She should have drunk lots of water before going to sleep. That was the trick. Or maybe, she admonished herself, the trick was to stop after a glass or even two. She sat up and swung her feet to the floor in one swift, but less than smooth motion, and stayed sitting on the edge of the bed waiting for the world to stop spinning. She'd not undressed, she realised then, just kicked off her shoes and collapsed on the bed.

It had been a very long time since she'd drunk so much. And it would be a hell of a long time before she'd do it again. In the bathroom, she filled a glass with water, drained it, and instantly felt sick. When the sensation passed, she went back to her bed, lay down and, despite the hammering inside her skull, drifted into a light sleep.

The ring of the phone startled her bolt upright, a hand going immediately to her pounding head. To stop the noise, she reached out to answer it, her 'hello' less than cordial.

'Edel?'

Why had she answered? What had she done to deserve this? Was this her punishment for getting wasted? Maybe she could just hang up, leave the phone off the hook, invent a story about a problem with her phone line. Instead, hiding the groan, she said, 'Hi, Liz.'

'Oh Edel, I'm so pleased I caught you in,' Liz said.

And I'm so sorry you did. She wanted to hang up, but couldn't bring herself to be rude.

'We need every volunteer we can get hold of,' Liz said. 'Please, get over here as soon as possible.'

Despite her hangover, and her reluctance to volunteer once again, Edel wasn't immune to the urgency and distress in the woman's voice. 'What on earth has happened?' she asked.

'It's the primary school in Cabinteely,' she said, naming a suburb adjacent to Foxrock, 'there's been an explosion.'

Shocked, Edel sat up, her hangover forgotten. 'What? Where? I'll be there as soon as I can.'

Liz gave her the address and hung up.

Quickly, Edel stripped and stood under the shower, the water virtually cold, the chill driving away the last vestiges of her hangover. She dried herself, tied her wet hair back in a tail and pulled on jeans, shirt and a warm jacket. With her keys in her hand, she was out of the house ten minutes after the call.

There didn't seem any point in taking the car; an explosion would close off roads. Instead, she half ran, half speedwalked the mile to Hollybank Primary School and arrived at a scene of chaos. Parents, already alerted in a variety of ways, had started arriving on foot, cars were abandoned as the drivers joined the throng who were shouting, crying and grabbing hold of one another. Uniformed gardaí had erected a cordon and were effectively keeping everyone from entering school grounds, ignoring shouted pleas to be told what was happening, where their children were, if they were safe.

Two fire engines and three ambulances filled the car park to the front of the school. There was no sign of the fire crew, but the ambulance crew were standing around with folded arms and grim faces.

Edel squeezed through the anxious crowd to speak to a garda and explain who she was. He looked puzzled, but she was saved from having to elaborate by Liz Goodbody who, coming around the side of the fire engine, spotted her and waved. With a nod from the garda, Edel quickly ducked under the cordon and hurried to her side.

'Thank God you've come,' Liz said, putting her arm around her shoulders and giving her a comradely squeeze. 'They're leading the children out now. They'll need someone to hold their hands till their parents come.'

'Of course, whatever I can do to help,' Edel said. 'But what happened? There's ambulances, have there been injuries?'

Liz shook her head, curls bobbing against her cheeks. 'Helen was in the garda station, doing her shift,' she said, 'when a call came through that there'd been an explosion and the school was on fire. Knowing we'd be needed, she rang me to alert everyone, and I got here as fast as I could. The teachers followed their emergency evacuation procedure and brought all the students to the assembly hall. It's a separate building, so they were safe from whatever was going on in the school. They stayed there while the emergency services arrived.'

'So, nobody was hurt?' Edel asked, wanting to be sure of what she was facing.

Another emphatic head shake. 'Thank God, no. The ambulances weren't needed. We were lucky.'

Edel looked around, puzzled. There was no obvious damage, no smoke billowing from the building. 'Was the fire put out?'

Instead of answering, Liz grabbed her arm and pointed to where a teacher had appeared leading a line of children. Firemen and gardaí walked alongside, helping to keep the line intact as the children spotted the frantic faces of their parents in the crowd that now surged forward. Some of the adults leading the children were *Offer* volunteers, Edel realised, and seeing one child begin to cry, she moved forward to catch her hand and lead her on.

There was more need for vigilance when the surging crowd broke through the hastily erected cordon and pushed forward, frantic parents searching, grabbing and pushing, desperate to find their children.

'Careful,' Edel pleaded, as one adult pushed through and almost knocked her off her feet. Afraid the child was going to be hurt, she picked her up and held her close, searching for an exit from the crush.

'Stand back.' A loud, authoritative voice silenced the cries and shouts and stopped everybody in their tracks. West moved into view. 'Right, now listen to me. All of the children are safe. All of them.' He looked around, meeting the eyes of the more anxious in the crowd. 'To ensure they stay safe, I want everyone to move back. Now,' he said loudly when nobody moved.

Slowly, muttering quietly, people did as they were asked. The school head rushed forward into the silence and, with a look of gratitude for West, took charge. Within minutes, the parents who were present were reunited with their children. They were encouraged to leave at once, the head promising a full account of what had happened at a later date. On the street outside the school, gardaí directed traffic; arriving cars with anxious parents directed one way, reunited families directed another. Ambulances and fire engines, happily redundant, squeezed through and departed.

Edel handed her small charge to a relieved mother and held the hand of another who waited. She saw four volunteers from *Offer* making themselves useful, holding a child's hand, chatting to them, keeping them occupied until someone came to pick them up. Liz, she noticed, had her arm around a distressed teacher. She was glad she'd been free to come and help.

West had spotted Edel in the crowd, but hadn't had an opportunity to speak to her. He wasn't sure he would get the chance. It had been a hell of a morning.

He had arrived in the station that morning full of expectation. Inspector Morrison had been very supportive the previous evening. He'd listened to West's report, his mouth tightening and the furrow that separated one hairy brow from the other deepening, as he was told about the Finnish brothel.

'What do you expect to find with a search warrant, Sergeant West?' he'd asked, his voice even, giving nothing away that his face hadn't already.

'The lab boys say they might be able to find a trace of the manihot esculenta that poisoned Roberts on a grater or food processor, so we'll be looking for either of those items. We'll also look for a match to that page the recipe was written on – that's a longer bet, to be honest, but a possibility we won't discount.'

The inspector had nodded and without another word, picked up the phone. It didn't take long, and West left with the promise that the warrant would be ready early the next morning.

Now, instead of picking up that warrant, he was stuck here in this fiasco.

A frantic 999 call from the school, talking about an explosion, brought the full range of emergency services, including all available gardaí.

West arrived at the same time as the fire brigade, their sirens deafening and adding to the overall sense of chaos. Smoke was pouring from the school. A thick grey carpet sneaking from under the doors, spirals escaping from air vents. Smoke, but no fire.

It was quickly established that all the pupils and staff were safe; West sent uniformed gardaí to the assembly hall to reassure them, and to ensure they stayed put. More gardaí were sent to cordon off the front gate with instructions to keep everyone, including parents, at a safe distance.

There was nothing else for him to do until the fire officer and his team came out. To his surprise, they were out within minutes. The fire officer was a man he'd met before. 'Hi David,' he said, approaching him. 'That was quick work.'

David Quinn glanced back to the school. 'The smoke has almost dispersed, they can return whenever they want.' He held out a bulging evidence bag. 'It was smoke bombs,' he said, 'and what the staff thought were explosions, were firecrackers. Somebody lobbed a couple of each through two open windows at the side, and a couple more through the letterbox at the front. Plenty of smoke, lots of noise. Would have lasted' – he rocked his head side to side – 'about a minute each, I'd guess. Somebody lit them and threw them in. The distance from the windows to the letterbox is short so they'd have gone off fairly simultaneously.'

'None at the back?' West asked, looking at the remnants of the devices in the see-through evidence bag.

'Nope, they had a clear path to the assembly hall through a back door. Looks as though they were pushed that way, doesn't it? It meant nobody was hurt.'

'Frightened. But no, not hurt,' West agreed, his face grim.

'What kind of sick bastard would have done this?' Quinn sighed, as if knowing the answer to the question. He held up the evidence bag. 'I'll send this to the forensic people, maybe we'll get lucky.' And with a wave, he was gone.

West headed to where Andrews was speaking to the obviously exhausted school head.

'My thanks to you and your men for responding so quickly,' she said, her voice trembling.

'That's our job, Ms Cosgrave,' West replied. 'I've just been speaking to the fire officer. It was a particularly nasty prank, I'm afraid. Smoke bombs and firecrackers. Thrown through two open windows and the letterbox.'

Frances Cosgrave's face was a mixture of relief and puzzlement. 'I heard explosions. There was so much noise, and it seemed to be coming from different places. It was disorientating. And then I saw the smoke.' She screwed up her face, making a conscious effort not to cry. 'I didn't know what was happening. It was really quite frightening.' She took a deep breath. 'Who would have done such a thing? And why?'

West tried to keep an open mind. He knew the danger of jumping to conclusions. The possibility of it being another in the series of troublesome, but inherently harmless crimes was a strong one – still he had to follow procedure. He had to investigate this as a stand-alone crime.

'You've had no trouble with anyone recently? No parents causing you grief?' he asked.

She managed a smile. 'Parents are always causing me grief, Sergeant. But no, nothing out of the ordinary. And certainly, I can't think of anyone who would be capable of an act like this.'

'Any of your children absent today?'

She thought a moment before shrugging her regret. 'I'm sorry, I really can't remember. Maisie, the admin, usually tells me in the morning, but generally, to be honest, the names go in one ear and out the other. It only becomes a problem if the absence is continuous or frequent. Those names I get at the end of the month. I can check, it will just take a minute.'

'If you wouldn't mind. The fire officer says it's okay to go back inside.'

She hurried off back into the building she had exited in such confusion hours before.

'What do you think?' Andrews asked. 'Our troublemaker again?'

'It looks very much like it doesn't it? But let's look into it before we jump to that conclusion.'

The head bustled back. 'All present and accounted for today, gentlemen,' she said. 'Actually, we have a very low absence rate. It's something we're quite proud of.'

'Okay,' West said. 'Obviously, we will be investigating this matter. I notice you have CCTV cameras in the school, but none in the grounds. It might be worth having a system installed to take in the grounds as well. And your windows–'

'They only open three inches,' she interrupted, 'we thought that was considered a safe gap.'

'This isn't a criticism, Ms Cosgrave,' West reassured the woman. 'Unfortunately, there are people who will take advantage. I'm just advising. A grill to cover that three-inch gap will prevent a recurrence.'

She wrapped her arms across her body protectively. 'I remember my mother used to say, "what's the world coming to?" a lot when I was younger. Now I know what she meant. What is the world coming to, when we can't leave a window open for a breath of air without some crazy fool seeing it as a way of having his version of fun?' Her voice caught. She put a well-manicured hand to her mouth and shaking her head, turned and went back into the school.

'Poor thing,' Andrews said with quick sympathy.

'The fire officer is sending all the devices to the lab. Let's hope they can manage to lift fingerprints off them. Meanwhile, have some of the lads do a house-to-house. See if anyone saw anybody lurking around. We better be seen to be keeping an open mind. After all, it may not be another one of our cases.'

But they both knew it was. It was just too similar to be a coincidence.

West checked his watch. It was almost two. He'd still have time to exercise that warrant. Damn sure he would, this had to stop.

His eyes scanned the area to look for Edel, hoping to have a quick word with her, but she wasn't among the groups of people who lingered, oohing and aahing over the morning's events. Damn it, he'd missed her. Still, he consoled himself, Sunday was only two days away.

Andrews finished taking a statement from the last of the teachers and joined him. 'We off?' he asked.

'Yes, we're done. Let's get back to the station and pick up the warrant. We'll brief the team and head to Nutley Lane. It's time to get this stopped.'

27

E del had also hoped to have a word with West before she left. But every time she looked his way, he was deep in conversation with someone. He looked worried. She watched him surreptitiously while tending to one child after the other. Then the children were gone, and Liz was there fussing, thanking the volunteers for having come so quickly.

The others made their excuses and left. Edel, whose hangover headache had come throbbing back, tried to get a word in edgeways, but Liz wittered on without a pause. 'I must go,' she said finally, interrupting whatever it was she was saying.

'Come and have lunch with me,' Liz insisted, linking her arm through Edel's, guiding her toward the road, refusing to listen to her excuses. 'We need to talk the morning through, you know. Debrief. You'll feel better for it. Honestly.'

Edel tried to insist she felt fine. That she didn't need *debriefing*. For goodness sake, she hadn't just finished a mission for the CIA. She just wanted to go home, take something for her headache, have something to eat, and get back to her writing, but her words fell on deaf ears.

'I'm just down here,' Liz said ten minutes later, as they turned down a narrower road and stopped outside a tidy-looking house. 'This is me.' She smiled, released Edel's arm and fished in her coat pocket for a key to open the front door.

Edel followed her into the small hallway, waited while she wiped her feet several times on the mat inside the door and took the not very subtle hint to follow suit.

'We can sit in here,' Liz said, opening a door that led into the front room, 'we'll be nice and cosy. Tea or coffee?'

'Tea would be lovely,' Edel answered with a forced smile.

'Make yourself comfortable, I won't be long.'

If Edel had been asked to put a name to Liz's decorative style she would have gone for kitsch. There was a hideous, garish picture over the fireplace, of a boy with an impossibly sparkling tear on his chubby cheek. China cats sat in a variety of poses on virtually every surface, and the uncomfortable-looking sofa was piled with cushions all bearing some pithy cat-related epigram.

'Please, sit down, sit down,' Liz fussed, coming back into the room. 'Just move the cushions. I have far too many, I know.'

Edel lifted one, holding it on her lap as she sat back against the rest of the pile. Despite the cushions, the sofa was just as uncomfortable as it looked. 'You have cats,' she said, for want of anything better to say.

To her surprise, Liz shook her head. 'Allergic, unfortunately. I come out in a terrible rash and sneeze my head off. It's such a shame because I do adore them. I collect cat-related items instead. As a consolation, I suppose.'

Edel couldn't see the logic herself, but was unable to think of anything to say.

'Would you like ham or cheese sandwiches?' Liz asked, clasping her hands together, looking for all the world as if she were going to give her the greatest treat.

'Ham would be fine, thank you. Can't I come and help?'

'Goodness me, no, you're my guest. Sit and relax. I won't be long.'

With that, she went away, leaving Edel to sit, twiddle her thumbs and look around the room with a critical eye. The sofa was covered in a bright floral fabric. Unfortunately, it clashed badly with a loudly-patterned carpet that was almost, but not quite, hidden by the biggest coffee table Edel had ever seen. Brown velvet curtains, with sun-faded pale stripes, finished off the room. But not in a good way. 'Enough to give anyone a migraine,' she muttered, checking her watch, giving an exasperated grunt when she saw it was almost two. She really should have been firm and refused the invitation. Then she was hit by guilt. Liz had only ever been kind to her; she was probably lonely. Maybe, too, she needed to talk about the stressful morning. She sighed. If only she weren't quite so irritating.

Every now and then, Liz's voice sang out, "won't be long now," but it was fifteen minutes before the door opened and she appeared with a large tray clasped between her hands. With a beaming smile on her face, she placed it gently on the coffee table.

Despite having specified ham, Edel saw there was a selection of ham, egg and cress and cheese sandwiches on a large and pretty china plate. All were neatly cut into tiny crustless triangles. Another plate held slices of cake; a rich yellow colour, the tangy smell of lemon drifting toward her. Lemon drizzle cake, her favourite. Maybe she was glad she had stayed. Maybe.

Liz passed her a cup and saucer, and a small plate. All pretty, fine china. Edel put the plate down on the table in front of her, and held out the cup and saucer as Liz lifted a matching china teapot and proceeded to pour. It was all very civilized, and Edel started to relax. To even enjoy it.

She took a ham sandwich when Liz held the plate forward. It was good, but tiny, no more than a bite really. She waited to be offered another. And waited. But Liz was busy chatting about the morning's drama. If Edel were hungry before, she was starving now, the tiny sandwich having served to whet her appetite and, if the plate had been within reach, she'd have tossed etiquette aside, and helped herself. But it was on the other side of the huge table.

Her stomach growled, a loud gurgle she passed off with a quick laugh and the excuse, 'I missed breakfast. My stomach is having a moan.' But if she hoped Liz would take the hint and pass the plate in her direction, she was disappointed.

'I'll just wrap these up so they won't go stale,' Liz said, standing and taking the plate away to the kitchen.

Left alone once more, Edel wasn't sure whether to laugh or cry, and settled for giggling softly. *Oh well, at least there's cake.* She eyed it, her mouth responding with a flush of anticipatory saliva, and was tempted to take a slice and gobble it down before Liz got back, but she knew... she just *knew*... that she'd take a bite, the door would open and she'd choke and spray lemony crumbs all over the dreadful carpet.

On the cusp of the thought, the door did open and Liz bustled back, her face wreathed in smiles. 'More tea?' she asked, sitting and lifting the pot, pouring carefully when Edel held her cup out. 'And would you like a little cake?'

'Yes, please.'

She waited for Liz to hold the plate out to her but, instead, she took a knife, cut the top slice of cake into narrow fingers and then, using tongs, lifted a finger and dropped it onto the plate that Edel hastily held out. She bit her lower lip to stop the giggle she knew was waiting, the stomach pain focusing her temporarily. If she could just gain control, she could swallow the cake, drink her tea, and escape. A minute later, she was finished. She put the cup and saucer on the plate and, stretching, placed the lot carefully on the table. 'Thank you,' she said, preparing to stand and leave.

She was stopped in her tracks as Liz suddenly spoke with a level of urgency. 'You see how valuable we are. You will stay now, won't you?'

Why had she allowed herself to be persuaded to come? She should have guessed this would happen. Frustrated, she decided she'd agree to anything, just to get away, and as quickly she reconsidered. She wasn't willing to lie. There'd been enough lies told in her life. 'No,' she said, without qualifying her answer, or prettying the word up. 'I don't want to continue as a volunteer. You know I'd already decided that. I was happy to oblige today, but that's the final time. Please, don't ask me again. I would like to come along to the meeting tomorrow to say goodbye to everyone, and to meet Viveka again, if you think that would be okay.'

Liz clasped one of her hands in the other. She held them up to her mouth, as her eyes filled with tears, one spilling to trickle down her cheek

Horrified, Edel stared at her.

With a snuffle, Liz stood and moved to sit on the sofa beside her. 'Won't you reconsider? Can't you see how vital we are to the community? Please, tell me you'll at least think about it?'

What Edel wanted to do, was to push the older woman out of the way and run out of the house as fast as she could. Instead, she took a deep breath and did what was often done, even by someone who was determined not to embark on a series of lies: she fudged the truth. 'I will give it some thought, I promise.' To her discomfort, Liz threw her arms around her. Perhaps her fudging had been too subtle? 'I'll just give it some thought,' she reiterated, 'I'm not making any promises.'

'Oh, you,' Liz said and hugged her again. 'We knew you'd change your mind after today.'

Edel half opened her mouth to relieve her of that delusion, and then closed it again. That was it. She was finished with *Offer*. Not even the prospect of meeting Viveka Larsson could tempt her into spending one more minute in Liz's company.

28

W est had gone immediately to Inspector Morrison on his return to the station. He needed to bring him up to date on the situation with the school, but more importantly he wanted to collect the warrant the inspector had promised him.

Morrison looked grim as West filled him in. 'We were lucky there were no injuries. You think this is our woman again?'

West, refusing to stand like a naughty schoolboy in front of the inspector's desk, but never invited to sit, leaned against the wall. 'It's of a type,' he said, deliberately vague. 'It caused a lot of annoyance, involved a lot of people including volunteers from _Offer,_ but didn't cause injury to anyone or to property.'

'It's all a bit bizarre, isn't it?'

West guessed the question to be rhetorical and waited for him to say more.

The inspector picked up a pen, held it between his middle and index fingers and rocked it backward and forward, stopping now and then to adjust its position before continuing. 'Why set up _Offer_ in the first place? Why not a brothel? Why not stick to what she knew?'

Rhetorical questions again. But West had asked himself the

same questions, had given them a lot of thought, mulled them over and finally came up with what might be the answer. 'Reparation,' he said now, putting forward his suggestion.

Morrison stopped his pen twirling and gave him a sharp look. 'Reparation?'

West nodded and pushed himself away from the wall. 'Running a brothel for years, seeing the seedy side of life, contributing to it. Maybe she took advantage of people, young women especially; or those who were in trouble. Desperate, vulnerable people who she lured into a life of vice, with vague promises of money, and God alone knows what else. Maybe, eventually, she had enough, had seen too much. A Damascene moment of some sort.' He shrugged and leaned back against the wall. 'I'm just guessing, of course, but if she were trying to make amends, what better way than to start a group to support people in need.

'And if she really wanted it to work, if *Offer* was to be her salvation, her atonement, it might have pushed her into ensuring its success.'

Morrison leaned back in his chair and gazed up at him. 'You know,' he said, 'that's the kind of far-fetched nonsense that just might be true.' Taking a key from his pocket, he opened a desk drawer. 'Here's your warrant. Let's hope you come back with something concrete.' He handed the document over.

Experience had taught West to check paperwork immediately. If that meant Mother Morrison thought he was checking up on him, so be it. It was good practice. And as he read the warrant, he bit back the oath he wanted to spit across the table to catch the inspector smack bang in the middle of his supercilious face. 'They've put the wrong apartment number, sir,' he said carefully. 'She doesn't live at number six; she lives at number nine. It will have to be reissued.'

Inspector Morrison snapped the document from his hand,

and read it as if West must have made a mistake. 'That bloody idiot, Dempsey, I always doubted he could count beyond five.'

As if they read each other's minds, they both looked at their watches. Friday afternoon. The likelihood of getting someone to sign a warrant on a Friday afternoon was about as likely as the inspector staying in his office after four the same day. Wasn't going to happen.

'It will have to be Monday,' Morrison said grimly.

There was no point in railing at something that couldn't be changed, at a system that insisted on a Monday to Friday response to a seven day a week need. But that didn't stop West clenching his fists and his jaw.

'I should have checked the damned thing when it arrived,' Morrison continued to his surprise. 'If I had, I might have been able to do something. Damn it.'

The same thought had crossed West's mind, but now he just shrugged. Blame games were never a useful exercise.

'We may have more to go on by Monday anyway, sir,' he said. 'The remnants of the smoke bombs and firecrackers are with forensics; they're being checked for fingerprints. We should have the results later today. If they find any, we could get the next warrant to include taking Ms Larsson's fingerprints.'

The inspector nodded. 'We need to get this case done and dusted. I don't like it. We've been lucky, so far.'

'I doubt Mrs Roberts would agree, Inspector,' West said quickly. 'But, yes, you're right. We've been bloody lucky so far. But this woman's ideas are getting more unstable.'

Inspector Morrison chewed his lower lip and tapped his index finger on the desk. 'We don't have the budget for this, but I think we need to run surveillance on her,' he said. 'Liaise with Sergeant Blunt, he'll organise some uniforms to do it. We can't afford to let another situation like this morning happen again.'

Back in his own office, West put a call through to Blunt. He filled him in on the situation and had surveillance arranged in the space of a few minutes. Appreciating the brevity of the call, he hung up and sat with a smile just as Andrews came in waving what he knew to be a laboratory report.

'Fingerprint results?' he asked, hoping something was going to go his way today.

Andrews' smile gave the game away before he said the words. 'We got prints. On one of them. A little smudged, but good enough for a comparison. The rest were clean. She probably took one out to have a look at it after she bought them, and then put it back with the rest. She knew to wear gloves when she threw them into the school, but forgot about the one she'd already handled. We can pick up something with her prints when we're there, can't we? Get the comparison done before the end of the day. The lab guys said they'd stay late if needed.'

West hadn't seen him so enthusiastic for a long time. It seemed a shame to burst his bubble, so he waited and watched.

It didn't take long. Andrews stopped speaking and perched on the edge of West's desk. 'You should be dancing for joy at my news. What's happened?'

He quickly explained, watching Andrews' face cloud over as he did so.

'Monday?'

'You know the way things are. Anyway, it's good news about the prints. We can get the warrant to cover taking her fingerprints. And the other good news is that Inspector Morrison suggested surveillance.'

Andrews' eyes bugged. 'Mother Morrison is allowing surveillance?'

'He suggested it.' West smiled. 'I didn't think about asking, to be honest. Never thought we'd have been allowed.'

'Just as well,' Andrews said sagely. 'If you had, he'd probably have shot down the idea. But his idea. Well, that warrants the expense.'

West yawned, two hands covering his face and rubbing his eyes. 'At least we'll have an eye on her over the weekend. No more crazy escapades. We've been lucky. Well, apart from Gerard Roberts,' he hastened to add, almost making the same blunder that Inspector Morrison had made.

There was nothing more to be done, so after some chit-chat and some outstanding paperwork, West decided to call it a day. It had been a long time since he'd finished work so early, and he felt mildly guilty for no reason he could think of. He sat in his car, turned the key in the ignition and let the engine idle while he wondered what to do with himself on a Friday evening.

He supposed he could go visit his parents. Long overdue. Or he could go visit his sister. Also, long overdue. He could do some shopping, get some beer, some food and flake out in front of the television. Nothing appealed to him. Perhaps he should have stayed in the office, found something to do there. Maybe, he should double-check with Blunt about the surveillance. But he didn't move.

For one thing, Sergeant Blunt would take it very badly that he thought he'd need to check. And for another, he knew exactly what he wanted to do, but didn't want to admit it.

He smiled. *Damn it, why not?*

29

Ten minutes later, West was pulling up on the road outside Edel's house. Twilight faded to darkness as he sat and stared at it, seeing the lights in the windows, feeling a sense of contentment that she wasn't too far away. Or was it relief that she wasn't out somewhere with someone? When it came to her, he questioned every thought. It was unsettling.

He was concerned too about her connection with *Offer*. Perhaps he should tell her their suspicions about them. She was tougher than she looked. He knew that. But he also knew she had found it hard to come to terms with the months of lies her bigamous marriage had exposed her to.

Now here she was, once more involved in something that wasn't what it seemed.

He needed to tell her.

Unofficially, of course.

A yawn stretched his jaw. He was tired; he should just go home. It was completely against the rules to tell her anything about an ongoing investigation. Completely. But the idea still niggled.

Finally, bored with procrastinating, he opened the car door and climbed out. He'd just get some fresh air with a walk to the church gate. The same padlock and chain were in place. Reaching for them, he felt the weight before letting them drop with a clunk. He peered through the gate at the church and the gravestones. What was it now? Six months? Lights, high on the church walls, lit up some of the graves, but the one where they'd found the body was set too far back and was shrouded in darkness. Simon Johnson. He wondered vaguely how his sister was coping.

Walking back, he kicked fallen pine cones along the road, but instead of stopping at his car, he walked to the gateway of her house and stared in. He was behaving like a schoolboy with a crush. Picking up a pine cone, he tossed it from hand to hand, before firing it across the road where it hit a stone wall with a dull thud. It was a shard of light in the corner of his eye that made him turn back to the house, his breath catching to see Edel standing in the half-open doorway. Her face, pale in the bright light, looked puzzled.

'Mike?'

Feeling caught out, he smiled ruefully as he approached. 'I'm sorry, I was passing, thought I'd call in and then... well, then I thought maybe I shouldn't.' West hoped it sounded less lame to her than it did to him. How could he possibly be passing when she lived in a damn cul-de-sac? He stopped a few feet away. 'I didn't mean to intrude.'

She opened the door wider, and tilted her head in invitation. 'You'd better come in,' she said, waiting as he did so and closing the door behind them both.

He'd been in her house before, of course, all those months ago. Automatically, he went into the room they'd been in then, pushing open the door into the kitchen and reaching blindly for a light switch. He stood back as she passed through, catching her scent, watching as she moved directly to the phone, picked it up and dialled a number.

'My neighbour, across the way,' she explained to him briefly, and then spoke into the phone. 'Bill, it's Edel. Did you ring the guards? Okay, no, don't bother. It's a friend of mine. No, that's okay. Honestly. No, that's unnecessary. Thank you. Yes, thanks. Goodnight.'

She put the phone down and smiled at West. 'He rang a few minutes ago to tell me there was a car parked outside and somebody acting suspiciously. He was going to ring the guards. I don't know why, but it crossed my mind that it might be you. That's why I went out. Bill wanted to come over to check I wasn't being forced to say that, that I wasn't being held hostage. I'd say he reads too many bad detective novels, but he does know my story so maybe he was being understandably nervous.'

'Mr Nosy Neighbour,' West said, returning her smile. 'Andrews had some dealing with him.'

'Bill told me all about that. Told me he'd been asked to keep surveillance on me.' She tried to look annoyed, but couldn't quite manage it. 'I think he really enjoyed himself.'

'Peter enjoyed winding him up. He has a strange sense of humour.'

Edel moved to put the kettle on, stopping with her hand on the handle to ask, 'Cup of tea or something stronger? I've got some nice wine chilling in the fridge.'

'Wine would be nice.' He rested a shoulder against the door frame, watching as she took two wine glasses from a cupboard, and opened the fridge for the wine. Her movements were unhurried and relaxed, and he felt the stresses of the day easing just looking at her.

The room had certainly improved since his last visit. He'd thought, six months ago, that it was a remarkably pretty room, but it had been incredibly untidy, even dirty, with piles of papers, smeared plates and cups. Every surface had been over-flowing with paraphernalia. Now the worktops gleamed, the cinnamon-coloured tiles on the floor shone, and the cushions on the old church pew in the alcove sat up straight, their edges perfectly aligned.

Edel put the glasses down on the oak table he had admired even when it was covered in rubbish. 'Please, sit down,' she said, pouring the wine and handing him a glass.

He took it and sat, not at the table where she probably expected him to sit, but on the pew in the alcove, pushing cushions out of his way. 'This is nice,' he said, taking a sip and putting the glass on the low table in front of him.

Edel took a seat at the table, crossing her arms in front of her, balancing the wine glass on the crook of her arm. She took a sip and then looked at him quizzically.

He gave a short laugh, took another quick sip of his wine and cleared his throat, surprised to find himself nervous. It was tempting to knock the wine back. Instead, he put it down and gazed across to where she sat, looking impossibly calm, and incredibly beautiful. Would things ever be simple between them?

He sighed, the sound loud in the quiet room.

'You've had a rough day.' It was a statement, not a question, so he said nothing. 'Did you find the person, or people, who caused the explosion in the school?' she asked, and then imme-diately gave an embarrassed laugh. 'Gosh, I'm sorry. Of course, you can't discuss your work. I know that. Anyway,' she continued with a half-smile, 'you probably didn't come here to talk about that.' She looked at him quizzically again, her nose crinkling. 'Why did you come? You haven't changed your mind about Sunday, have you?'

He debated lying to her, telling her he just wanted to see her, didn't want to wait until Sunday. He pictured her response. But she'd had a husband who lied. He didn't want to follow that trend.

'No, of course I haven't changed my mind,' he said quickly. Then he hesitated and chose his words carefully. 'It has been a rough day, I'll admit. But then, you've had part of that too. *Offer* were there quickly. Lending a hand,' he added, not wanting her to think he was being critical.

'What is it, Mike?'

He smiled. 'Reading my mind, are you?'

'You have a good poker face,' she said, lifting her glass, 'but even so, I can tell there's something bothering you.'

He picked up the glass, toyed with it for a moment, took the minutest of sips and put it carefully down again. Sitting in the pew was a stupid mistake; he should have sat at the table. Getting to his feet, he moved to the seat opposite her. 'Listen,' he said, keeping his eyes fixed on hers. 'I had to come, there's something you should know.' He ran a hand through his hair, his default gesture of frustration, anxiety. 'This group *Offer*–'

Edel held up her hand to stop him. 'I know you don't like them,' she said. 'You haven't from the beginning. All they do is try to help people, and they've had nothing but derision and criticism. But you have to admit, they did help this morning. Really, you should be grateful.'

'Grateful,' he said, annoyed. 'I–'

'Yes, grateful,' she said, interrupting him again. 'If you only came to criticise *Offer*, I'm sorry you came, and I think you should go.'

'Now, just hang on a minute,' he said, horrified by the way the conversation was going. 'If you'll just let me explain. Honestly, Edel, you have the wrong end of the stick.'

'So, you haven't come to complain about them?' she asked, standing to look down on him.

'No, of course I haven't,' he replied quickly, trying to put what he had come to do in words she would accept. 'Not complain about exactly. More...' He hesitated, searching for the right word. 'More to warn you about them. We think they may be involved in engineering some of the episodes, where the volunteers subsequently appeared to help.' He wasn't sure he had made it clear, but he'd said it.

'What?' Edel said, her face creasing in dismay.

Maybe he hadn't made it clear enough; he tried again. 'We think that someone in *Offer* is orchestrating these accidents, events, whatever you'd like to call them. And then the volunteers appear like knights in shining armour to save the day.'

'That's ridiculous,' she said, shaking her head. She turned away from him and walked to the window. 'You think a volunteer planted the explosives in the school this morning?'

West stood and crossed the room to stand behind her. 'There weren't any explosives. Someone threw smoke bombs and firecrackers into a couple of windows and the letterbox. It was smoke and noise. No injuries, no damage. We've had a number of cases with a similar MO.' If only he'd stopped there, he thought later, if he had left it at that, and given her time to think about it. But, unfortunately, he decided to elaborate. 'We've been looking into *Offer* for a couple of days, specifically Viveka Larsson.'

She turned to face him with fire in her eyes. 'Absolutely no way,' she said, her voice like flint. 'What rubbish. I've met her; she's the most amazing, charismatic lady. You've got it wrong, Sergeant West.'

It was back to *Sergeant West*. He shouldn't have come; it was a situation he couldn't possibly win. If he'd left her to find out about *Offer* from somebody else, she'd have been annoyed he hadn't told her. It was a case of damned if he didn't, and from the closed-off look on her face, it was certainly a case of damned when he did.

When she finds out he'd told her the truth would it make a difference? Was he being a fool? She'd been a suspect in a murder inquiry, a victim in the same one, and he was the garda who had pursued her. Now she was connected, however loosely, to this case and he was, once again, the investigating officer. When the case was solved, she would, as before, stop being a victim or suspect, and her connection to the case would dissolve like candyfloss, but he would always be a garda.

He could get past that. He just wasn't sure she could.

'I'd better go,' he said quietly.

'Well, fine,' she said, her voice rising to a shout. 'Get out.' She turned her back on him, crossed her arms and stared out the window, her breath coming in short, gusty puffs.

He stood and watched her. Even in her reflection, he could see the dislike. Without another word, he turned and left.

30

She listened as the front door closed. Not slammed, she noticed, and this irritated her further. He had closed it gently, as if he weren't bothered by the whole situation. She was still standing as he had left her, arms wrapped around herself, protective, excluding everyone, including Mr Officious Garda Sergeant West.

When she heard the sound of a car engine, she wanted to go out and shout at him some more. How could he? He knew she had been through a lot. Didn't he see that helping out with *Offer* was her way of getting back into the swing of things? Contrarily, it didn't matter that she had decided to leave. After all, he didn't know that.

She didn't give a moment's credence to what he had told her. She had met Viveka. The woman wasn't capable of what he was suggesting. Why on earth did they suspect her? It was absolute nonsense. That terrible desk sergeant, Blunt. He'd always disliked *Offer*. She'd bet it was his idea.

So much for the relaxing evening she'd planned. Now she couldn't stay still, angry energy fizzing and making her restless. She had to do something. Going for a walk and getting some cool fresh air sounded like a plan. She took a warm fleece from the coat pegs in the hallway and picked up her keys. Normally, she left the lights on if she went out, reluctant to return to a dark house. But tonight, just in case West returned with an apology, or an excuse tripping from his lips, she switched them off.

Heading down Wilton Road onto the busier street that ran through Foxrock Village, she kept walking without any conscious sense of direction. *How could he? Unforgiveable.* The words kept whirling though her head. It wasn't until she'd been walking for a while that irritation faded to the sad resignation that she and Mike just weren't meant to be.

And then she realised where her feet had taken her. Holly-bank school. She stood for a moment, staring through the gates. How could they think *Offer* could be responsible for doing such a wicked thing? Her throat clogged with unshed tears that still came far easier than they used to. Resting her head against the cold metal of the gate, she gulped and turned to lean back tiredly against it, realising how far she had travelled. She had a long walk home.

A thought crossed her mind. If she'd been upset to hear the gardaí were accusing *Offer* of wrongdoing, how much more upset would Liz be? The woman lived for the group, and worshipped the ground that Viveka walked on. She'd be devastated. Edel owed it to her to warn her; Liz might be incredibly irritating, but she was kind. Wearily, she pushed away from the school gate, and headed in the direction of her house. Liz would spit feathers when she found out, if a woman of her calm demeanour could ever do anything so fierce. Ten minutes later, she was at her front door, hoping that the light shining through the glass panels was a good indicator she was home.

Edel looked for a bell, didn't see one and reached instead for a heavy door knocker that sat dead centre on the door. It fell with a resounding bang that surely must have been heard in every room, and possibly next door as well. She eyed the other half of the semi warily, as if the answer to her knock would come from there. Reluctant to knock again, she waited, shuffling from foot to foot, wondering if she should leave. She risked peering through a glass panel and was about to give up when a dark blob appeared in the light of the hallway. It grew larger, consolidating into a woman shape before she heard the noise of latches being drawn, locks being unlocked. A lot of security for a small house. She shivered; it would be difficult to get out in a hurry.

Finally, the door opened, the security chain still attached, and Liz peered through the opening. 'Edel?' she cried, managing to fit puzzlement, curiosity and a minute amount of irritation into that one word.

Edel expected her to open the door, once she had identified her as not being a threat to her safety, dignity or, at a stretch, her chastity. But, no, Liz continued to stand, staring at her through the gap.

'Can I come in?' she asked. This wasn't a conversation to have on the doorstep.

With just a moment's hesitation, the door was shut, the safety chain removed with a sliding rattle and it was opened. Liz stood in the entrance, with her head tilted bird-like in question, before she stepped back to let Edel in.

They went through to the same room they had sat in earlier, Liz moving to switch on a lamp in the corner. 'The main light's blown,' she explained, looking up at the old-fashioned fringed shade that surrounded the dead bulb hanging from the ceiling. 'I don't use this room much at night, you know. I usually sit next door, it's warmer.'

Edel hadn't noticed earlier, but there was a distinct lack of warmth in the room. She was glad of her fleece. She didn't wonder why Liz hadn't brought her into the other room. It was a division the older generation took more seriously; guests being brought into what would have been classified as the *good room*. Her mother had done much the same, would never have dreamt of bringing a stranger into the family room that was shabbily comfortable and warm. Instead strangers, guests, anyone *not* family, sat in cold splendour among the bric-a-brac and furniture that was considered *good*.

'Please, sit down,' Liz said, indicating the sofa she had sat in earlier. 'Now, what brings you here again, so late in the evening?' Sitting beside her, she looked at her expectantly and then leaned forward abruptly, startling Edel who moved back in response. 'Oh, you've reconsidered. You're going to stay as a volunteer. I'm so pleased. And how kind of you to come to tell me in person.' She clapped her hands together. 'This is wonderful. Viveka will be so pleased.'

Flustered by the woman's obvious excitement, Edel held up her hands, palms out in an unconscious *stop* gesture. But Liz either didn't notice, or chose to ignore it as she stood and did what almost amounted to a pirouette, saying in her breathy voice, 'Wonderful, wonderful news.'

Edel stood. This was too much. What on earth had possessed her to come? Honestly, she needed her damn head examined. 'Liz,' she said firmly, 'I'm afraid you've got the wrong end of the stick. That's not why I've come.'

Had she been in the mood to laugh, had she found any of this day remotely funny, she would have laughed as the woman's face went from radiant excitement to deep despair in a matter of seconds. Like one of those dolls she'd had as a child; it had a sad, tearful face, but turn it upside down, and instead of feet under its long skirt, there was another body, another face, this one grinning from ear to ear. She'd never liked it. It gave her the shivers. And as she looked at Liz's face, she felt the same sensation.

'I'm so sorry,' she said gently, seeing the woman was

genuinely upset, tears sparkling her eyes. 'I shouldn't have come. I'd gone for a walk, and found myself near the school.' She put a hand out, laid it tentatively on the older woman's hand, felt a slight tremor, and the instant guilt that comes when you know, through no fault of your own, you've caused another person pain. 'I should go,' she said, moving away. 'I'm sorry to have upset you.'

Liz snuffled, but put her hand out and caught Edel's arm. 'No, stay. Please. Tell me why you did come.'

Should she? Edel wavered. Perhaps it would be better if she kept her mouth shut? Wait and see what happened? She looked at Liz, her big eyes all concern. She'd be devastated, if it were true. But it wasn't... it couldn't be. But the fact remained, *Offer* was being investigated.

Telling someone the truth wasn't easy. Suddenly, with a piercing pain, she wondered if she'd done Mike an injustice. Wasn't he just looking out for her? As he had so many times before? She closed her eyes, trying to close out the memory of her behaviour, and his unrelenting calm. And if she did tell Liz, was she breaking a confidence? Because, it came to her suddenly, he probably wasn't supposed to have told her the details of an active investigation. As before, he'd put himself out to protect her.

But she couldn't not tell Liz – the woman had been kind to her. Being forewarned would ease the trauma of the situation.

Taking a deep breath, she said, 'I had Sergeant West round at my house earlier. That's why I went walking, to be honest. I was upset.'

'Oh, my dear,' Liz said, patting her arm kindly, 'sit down please.' She waited while Edel sat, before sitting herself. 'Honestly,' she said, 'why was he around upsetting you? I think I will go and have a long, hard talk with Inspector Morrison about Sergeant West and Sergeant Blunt. Classic bullies. Both of them.' Her voice took on a conspiratorial tone. 'Perhaps we should go together. Make a formal complaint about their manner, and their obstructiveness. The Inspector is a firm friend to *Offer*. He recognises our worth.'

If Edel had had a brick in her hand, she would have hit herself over the head with it. Why on earth had she come? 'I don't think that's really necessary, Liz,' she said quietly. 'I think Sergeant West was trying to be kind, actually.' She hesitated, and with a sigh carried on. 'He knows I am involved with *Offer*. He wanted to let me know... please, don't be upset... he wanted to let me know that *Offer* is under investigation. They have this crazy idea that someone may have deliberately caused some of the incidents that have occurred recently.'

The silence was deafening. Liz seemed to freeze, with her eyes fixed and focused on her face.

Unnerved, Edel broke her gaze and looked around the room. The lamp had thrown eerie shadows on the walls, and forced darkness into the edges. A notion crossed her mind that she found hard to dismiss; for some unaccountable reason she found the darkness threatening. She tried to dismiss it as melo-dramatic whimsy, tried to laugh. But the laugh wouldn't come, and the feeling remained to send a shiver down her back that had nothing to do with the increasing coldness of the room.

Finally, just when she was about to get up to leave, Liz spoke. 'Evil.'

Edel thought she must have misheard. 'Sorry?'

Liz fixed her with a cold stare. 'That man, Sergeant West. He is evil. All *Offer* has done is support the needy, the deserving.'

'Please,' Edel tried to calm the situation, 'don't get upset. It's not *Offer* as such that's the problem. I think they're looking at Viveka Larsson.'

If she thought this would be an improvement, she quickly learnt her mistake. Liz's nostrils flared and her eyes flashed. 'Our foundress? Viveka is an angel. Above reproach. A kinder, more philanthropic woman doesn't exist.' She stopped and took a deep breath. 'We are being vilified, hounded. Evil, I tell you.' She reached for Edel's hand, caught it tightly, ignoring her wince of pain. 'We will go to the press,' she said, spittle forming at the corner of her mouth, 'and tell them of their infamy. Expose them for their corruption. To think that Viveka could be involved. The sheer and utter stupidity.'

'They're just investigating, Liz,' Edel said, desperately trying to downgrade the issue. 'But you have to admit, there have been some very odd incidents. Like this morning's, for instance – there weren't any explosions, you know, just smoke bombs and firecrackers.' A terrible thought flashed through her mind. Liz had said that Viveka hoped she'd change her mind after this morning. She stood, took two steps, and then turned to face Liz again, wringing her hands together. 'This might sound crazy, but is it possible that Viveka engineered the whole thing to persuade me to stay?' She saw a strange look flit across Liz's face, and gasped. 'You think she did! You do, I can see it in your face. Oh, my God. We have to go to the guards. I have to tell Mike he was right; she is involved.'

Liz was the calm one now, reaching out to lay a hand on Edel's arm. 'Let's have a cup of tea,' she said, 'we'll sit and discuss what to do.'

The last thing Edel wanted was a cup of tea, but she needed some time to digest the idea that had come barrelling into her head. Liz had obviously been suspicious too; she'd seen the shadow of truth on her face. Were they right? Could the charismatic Viveka really be to blame?

From the kitchen, she heard the opening and closing of cupboard doors, the sound of the kettle coming to the boil, the clink of cups. She wished she had the courage to get up, shout a goodbye and leave. Then she remembered the long walk home;

it would be better to phone for a taxi. She felt in her pocket and swore under her breath. In her haste to leave the house she'd forgotten her mobile. Fine, she'd have the damn tea, her head would stop spinning and she'd ask Liz to ring for a taxi.

Tomorrow she would ring Mike, apologise, tell him what Liz had said about Viveka and leave it at that. He was the detective. She'd let him do his job and keep out of it. The last thing she wanted was to be embroiled in anything like this.

It occurred to her that the house had gone silent. She was just about to stand when she heard footsteps coming down the stairs. Lost in her thoughts, she hadn't heard them going up.

'I'll just be a moment,' Liz sang out, passing the doorway on her way back into the kitchen. There was more clinking before she appeared carrying a tray with a teapot, two cups of tea, and the lemon cake from earlier.

'I thought, perhaps, I could ring for a taxi,' Edel said, as Liz placed the tray down on the coffee table, and handed her one of the cups.

'Have your tea, we can talk about the situation, and I'll run you home,' Liz said with a smile.

Frustrated, but unable to argue in the face of kindness, Edel did as she was bid, realising she was thirsty anyway, and drained her cup. Before she could stop her, Liz lifted the teapot, stretched across and poured her another.

'Long walks can be so dehydrating, can't they?'

Edel gave a weak smile of thanks, but when she put the empty cup down again, she kept her hand over it when the teapot was held forward. 'No more, honestly, I've had enough.'

'Some cake?'

She shook her head, and then regretted doing so. Her head spun. Curiously, when she stopped shaking her head, it still spun. Or was it the room that was spinning? She opened her mouth to tell Liz she felt strange, but couldn't seem to put the words together. All she could manage was a little laugh, as she felt her body slump back in the chair. She closed her eyes, opening them quickly when she heard something.

Liz was so close that she could feel her warm breath brush her face. She tried to tell her again that she felt very strange, but her tongue was thick in her mouth and she couldn't speak.

The last thing she saw was a strange smile twisting Liz's lips.

Then she didn't see anything.

31

West hadn't planned to go into the station on Saturday morning. There was nothing outstanding, and not a thing he could do about *Offer* until the warrant to search Viveka Larsson's apartment was issued. Monday at the earliest. It was frustrating to be confined by bureaucracy, but railing against it did nothing except give him a headache. And his head ached enough as it was.

When he'd arrived home the previous night, cross and irritated, he'd poured a Jameson and then another. He wasn't sure how many he'd had in the end, but enough to make him swear never again when he opened his eyes this morning. Enough to make his brain bang painfully inside his skull at each movement, and keep him lying where he was for way too long, going over and over the conversation of the evening before. When he finally decided to crawl out of bed, it was in surrender. He'd never be able to figure out women.

Regrets were a waste of time, an exercise in futility, but still he had them. He wasn't sure what he regretted the most. That he'd gone to Edel's in the first place, that he'd told her they were investigating *Offer* and the Larsson woman in particular, or that he'd been relegated to being just a garda, when he felt he was becoming much more. Stupid. It was all so damned stupid.

Refusing to waste a rare free Saturday – nothing to do and all day to do it – he showered and dressed in casual jeans and a soft cotton shirt. Thanking whatever gods there were for the wonderful Beth who freed him from the chains of housework, he thought about doing a bit of tidying in the garden.

He got as far as looking out the window before deciding that mucking about in the garden wasn't going to keep his mind off Edel. It needed something more mentally challenging. Visiting his parents might do the trick; his mother was mentally challenging enough. But she'd see right through him; would take one look and know there was something bothering him, and then wheedle the details out with a few pointed questions.

Work was his usual hideaway. Romantic entanglements were forgotten about as soon as he went through the station door. Truth be told, often before that, and he wouldn't think of them again until he was in the mood for company. Then, he'd call and, if they were free, he'd bring them out for dinner, spend the night and head away in the early hours without a backward glance. If the first woman he called wasn't free, there were other numbers, other women.

Casually promiscuous, his sister called it. He didn't argue, nor did he point out that the women he spent time with were more than happy with the situation the way it was, and would have run a mile if he'd suggested anything more committed. He also didn't tell his sister that it had been several months since he'd been interested enough to ring any of these women, or that the only woman he wanted to spend time with was one of the most annoying he had ever met.

Okay. That was it. He had to get out of the house and think of something besides her. He decided to go to the station and take advantage of the peace and quiet to go over all the data again, and make sure he wasn't missing something. Edel's attack on him, her certainty that Viveka Larsson couldn't be involved, niggled.

Grabbing a jacket and car keys, he headed out, and twenty minutes later was swinging into the car park that surrounded the station. He had a designated parking space, but ignored it today, not keen on advertising his presence. Too many people would be happy to take advantage of a spare pair of hands, and ask him to do work allocated to others. And he'd be damned if he was doing any of Sergeant Clark's mountain of neglected paperwork.

Sergeant Blunt worked Monday to Friday and there was a young garda manning the desk that he didn't know. More irritatingly, he didn't know West, who, unfortunately, had forgotten to bring his identification. He couldn't criticise the garda for adhering to regulations. He had to hang around while he made a phone call, and wait a further ten minutes until a very surprised Garda Foley arrived to verify he was who he claimed to be.

A further five minutes was spent reassuring the desk officer that he had done the correct thing, that it wouldn't be held against him. That West would, in fact, commend his diligence to Sergeant Blunt when he saw him.

Finally, with a grinning Declan Foley beside him, he headed to his office.

'He's conscientious,' Foley said of the young desk officer.

'It was my fault; I should have had my ID on me. How are things in Robbery? Any word on Sergeant Clark's return?'

Foley snorted. 'No fear, he'll be off a few more weeks. We've just the usual petty robberies, a couple of break-ins. Nothing we can't handle.'

'How's Mrs Lee doing? You know we're looking at *Offer* for that, don't you?'

Foley stopped, and looked at him with a downturned mouth. 'Yes, I heard. Pretty nasty carry-on, if you ask me. Mrs Lee has moved in with her daughter. She couldn't cope with staying there after the break-in, even with the live-in carer. She'll be pleased to know who it was, but shocked to find out it was the very people who were helping her. And those people, those volunteers, they're still coming in. Can't we stop them?'

'Until we find some proof, Declan, it's just conjecture, so our hands are tied. As to the volunteers, some are genuine and want to help but, when the truth gets out, I think the group will die a natural death.'

'Won't be soon enough for me,' Foley said. 'Well, I'd better get back to work. Inspector Morrison saw the state of Sergeant Clark's in tray yesterday. He told me it's to be sorted by Monday. Some of the stuff has been there since January, and is pertaining to cases he dealt with personally. I haven't a clue what to do with it.'

West heard and ignored the hint of a plea in Foley's voice, but as he turned to go into his office, he had a change of heart. 'Tell you what, Declan,' he said. 'Anything you can't sort out, put it on the bottom of Sergeant Blunt's in tray. On the bottom, mind you. He gets a mountain of stuff added every day, by the time he gets to it, Clark should be back. Blunt will just dump it back in his in tray, regardless.'

He left the younger man with a relieved grin on his face and entered his office, firmly shutting the door behind him. He was tempted to turn the lock but decided that was taking privacy a step too far.

As it happened, nobody did interrupt him, and he spent the greater part of the morning going over every scrap of information, lab reports, timelines, alibis and personal histories of the various characters. He went out to the wall in the general office which was Mary Celeste quiet with the couple of detectives on duty out on a call. Computer screens were blank and the coffee percolator silent.

He could have done with some coffee. The canteen coffee was passable, but he knew if he went there, he'd bump into someone, and that would be the end of his peace. Instead, he stood and stared at the wall and read more information that had been added since he left on Friday. The brand of the smoke bombs had been identified from what little they'd found. But it was a common variety, easily obtained over the internet if you knew what you were looking for. So, no help there.

Some of the loose ends had been tied up. Edwards had taken the photograph of the *Offer* group to show to the staff in the amusement arcade in Bray. It was a no-go. Unsurprising, but one of those things that had to be ruled out.

He read the data on the area canvass of the route Gerard Roberts may have taken that fateful morning. As they had all guessed, there wasn't a positive sighting anywhere.

All the hours of time. All the manpower. Yet they knew, each of them, this was what they had to do. Leads didn't come out of thin air. They were dug up, slowly, with meticulous care, dusted down, examined and then sometimes tossed for the rubbish they were. Leads rarely came on an intuitive leap. And when they did, sometimes they too were discounted as utter tosh. As his yet might be.

But he didn't think so. He just knew he was right about this. And it fitted, when he looked at it all. It bloody well fitted.

Back in his office, he sat and did a little paperwork, but there wasn't much. Unlike Clark, he tried to keep on top of it, loathed it, but also hated sitting in front of a full in-tray. It was empty now and there was no reason to hang around any longer.

Still he sat. Tilting his chair back, he put his hands behind his head and gave in to thoughts he had been avoiding all morning, ones he wished he could continue to avoid, but knew he would have to face sooner or later.

Was she still willing to meet him tomorrow?

A twinge of annoyance shot through him that he had been reduced to thinking and behaving like a schoolboy. What he should be asking himself was, did he still want to spend time with her. Except that would be a waste of time. He knew the answer to that, and it was a resounding *yes*.

His sister would be delighted that for a change he didn't have the upper hand in a relationship. But then his sister was never going to find out; he had a hard enough time from her without giving her more ammunition. Reluctant to spend the next twenty-four hours wondering about tomorrow, he reached for the phone and dialled Edel's home phone number from memory. As it rang, he planned what to say, the tone to take. Justified, but apologetic would cover the bases without admission of guilt or wrongdoing.

He took a deep breath, but after four rings an answer machine switched on, a computer-generated voice inviting him to leave a message after the beep. Muttering a series of oaths under his breath, he hung up. Like most people, he hated leaving messages and only did so if absolutely necessary. He certainly wasn't leaving something as complex as this message to be played and replayed.

He'd try again later.

He did. As soon as he got home, he tried again. Still no answer. *Damn it.* He knew she was going out somewhere that night. Wondered, yet again, where she was going, who she was going with, and cursed himself for being an idiot.

Restless, unable to settle to doing anything, he headed into the garden. There was a bush he had wanted to cut down for months, it took up far too much room in an area of the garden that got the sun all day, an area he had earmarked for maybe a deck and barbeque area. Chopping and tearing things down suited his mood.

It was dark by the time he'd finished, and in the darkness he could see the space he'd made was bigger than expected. Pleased with his work, he locked away the tools he'd used, and then, hot and sticky, headed to the shower. Throwing on sweatpants and T-shirt, he headed back to the kitchen, checking that Tyler had enough food, and ignoring pleading eyes that begged for doggy treats. 'You'll get fat and won't fit through the cat-flap,' he told the chihuahua before heading to the fridge. Hadn't he shopped recently? How come there was nothing to eat? He rummaged a while, threw out some food that was way past its best before date and, taking out a beer, closed the fridge so vigorously that the rest of the beer bottles clinked in applause. Beer was something he never seemed to run out of. He supposed he had his priorities right.

He could go out for something to eat, or ring someone to keep him company. Maybe he should go home; his mother would be delighted to feed him. The options didn't appeal. But he was hungry. Settling for a takeaway, it took him several minutes to find the menus he knew he had, finally thinking to check the bookshelf in the living room. And there they were. Beth, with her inimitable logic, had slipped them between the only two cookery books he possessed.

A quick phone call to a local Indian restaurant, and thirty minutes later he was enjoying a starter of chicken chotpoti, with a lamb vindaloo keeping warm in the oven. He tried Edel's number again while he ate. This time, knowing she'd be out, he caved in and left a brief message asking her to call him. He kept the phone nearby in case she came back early from wherever she was and, finishing his starter, took out the vindaloo and rice and opened another beer. It wasn't a relaxing meal; all the time he was waiting for the damn phone to do its thing, knowing it wouldn't, hoping all the same.

His mouth buzzing from the vindaloo, he opened another beer to quench the flames and finished off with a Jameson. Between the vindaloo and the whiskey, he guessed there'd be little left of his stomach lining.

Satiated and mellow, he sat back on the sofa, whiskey glass in hand, and switched on the television. Flicking from channel to channel, he settled on a rerun of Frasier. Even as he chuckled at lines he had heard several times before, his mind was elsewhere.

Frasier was doing the usual verbal sparring with his brother when he fell asleep, the empty whiskey glass flopping onto the sofa from his sleep-loosened hand. When he woke, the TV had gone into standby mode. He peered at his watch. One o'clock. It was unlikely that he'd slept through the phone, but he checked to be certain and heard a disembodied voice telling him that there were no new messages.

She hadn't rung. Maybe she hadn't heard his message. Too busy with whoever it was she was out with. And when she'd returned? Too busy doing the horizontal mambo? The thought infuriated him. He felt for one dangerous moment betrayed.

Until he saw how ridiculous he was being. She had every right to do what she wanted, with whomever she wanted. She owed him nothing. And if he felt betrayed? Well, that was his problem; he'd have to deal with it.

Resisting the temptation to have another Jameson, by dint of remembering his hangover of the morning, he took himself to bed where he spent most of the night tossing and turning and trying not to imagine Edel, naked, in some other man's arms.

And he still didn't know the situation about Dun Laoghaire. She'd surely listen to her messages in the morning and contact him. Wouldn't she?

Sunday started bright and sunny. It was an ideal day to walk the pier and might even be warm enough to stop at Teddy's for an ice cream. He refused to entertain the idea that she wouldn't go with him, and waited for her to ring. At twelve, seething with a combination of irritation and frustration, he rang her number. Again, there was no answer and he slammed his phone on the table.

That was it, he wasn't hanging about any longer. Grabbing his keys, he got into his car and drove to Wilton Road. He didn't hang about this time, went straight to her door and rang the bell, keeping his finger on it for slightly longer than was polite or necessary.

Her car was in the drive, but that didn't mean she was at home. Perhaps she had stayed over with whomever she had been out with the previous night. Maybe she, like he, preferred to indulge in casual sexual pleasures in someone else's bed.

Or maybe she'd just gone to the shops.

He sat back into his car and waited, trying not to let his thoughts run wild. Or wilder, anyway. He had a mobile number for her, but knew it was an old one, he'd not thought to get her new number. But if she didn't want to speak to him, it didn't matter anyway.

Still, it wasn't like her to be so unreasonable. Stubborn, perhaps, but not unreasonable. He checked his watch. One. The news came on the radio, claiming his attention for a few minutes, and then he just waited, drumming his fingers on the steering wheel.

It was nearly two before he called it a day. He tried her doorbell again, keeping his finger on it until it went numb. When he tried her phone number, he heard the faint sound of it ringing inside, and the click as the answer machine took over, and he hung up.

Frustrated, angry with himself and with her, he got back into his car and drove away, driving far too fast, coming to a halt with a screech of breaks at the first traffic lights in the village, drawing looks of condemnation from more law-abiding members of the community who stuck to the *twenty is plenty* speed restriction in the village.

'Damn her,' he said, taking off again at a more sedate speed.

At home, he rang her number once more, and this time left the message he'd rehearsed all the way home. 'Edel. Hi, it's Mike. I've tried to get you a few times. I know we hadn't set a time for meeting up today, and I hope you're not waiting for me to come pick you up. As I said, I have tried to get you because, unfortunately, I have to cancel. Work, I'm afraid. Something I can't get out of. Maybe another time. I'll be in touch. Bye.' And then he hung up.

Pride was restored.

32

West's pride was the least of Edel's worries. She woke in pain, head thumping, limbs cramped, neck aching. And opened her eyes to total darkness.

She felt the instant sharp bite of panic.

Fear kept her still, and panic kept her quiet, but slowly she got to grips with them. After all, she was well acquainted with both. She stretched out a cramped leg and hit something solid. Under her hand, she felt the roughness of carpet and stretching it out as far as she could, she hit something solid again. And then the other arm reached out, fingers tentatively searching, and finding the same.

A coffin, was her first terrified thought, reaching her hand upwards, half expecting to feel a hard surface just above, her hand shooting into air, finding nothing within reach. Not a coffin then, and relief helped soothe the terror. She sat, waited for her head to stop swimming, and then tried to stand, banging her forehead on something solid, swearing softly as more pain added to the blinding pain behind her eyes. Confused and muddled, she lay down again, her head throbbing so badly it triggered a wave of nausea that swept over her and left her limp.

Curling up into a ball, she tried the relaxation technique the counsellor she had seen for a few months had advised. 'Simple deep breaths, in through your nose, out through your mouth,' he'd said, and she had laughed that something so simple could have the slightest effect. To her surprise, it did. 'People hold their breaths,' he'd explained, 'and when they do, everything tenses, becoming uncomfortable and more difficult. So, when you are upset, stressed or panicked... breathe. It doesn't make problems go away, but it allows you to deal with them.'

He'd been right. She had tried it and had been pleased with how effective it was. And of course, he had also been right in that it didn't make her life any more straightforward, but it did allow her to see it more clearly. And to deal with it.

She lay curled up in her foetal ball, took long, slow, deep breaths in, and let them out slowly. And fell asleep.

When she woke again, her head had stopped throbbing, only a faint thump reminding her of the previous pain. She uncurled, stretched as much as she could to release the kinks and cramps, and allowed her eyes to adjust to the darkness. Using her hands to judge where there was height, so as not to bang her head again, she stood up, reached out and, hand by hand felt the surface of the enclosure she was in. It was wedge-shaped. Three walls and a sloping ceiling. One wall held a door; she could feel a slight draught, fingers teasing out the edges. Definitely a door, but no handle. She put her ear to it and listened for a long time for any sound. Nothing. Spreading her hands flat on the door, she pushed, gently at first, and then with her whole weight behind it, putting her shoulder to it as if her life depended on it – but there wasn't the slightest movement.

She slid down onto the floor, and did what she had wanted to do since she'd opened her eyes – she cried. It was an indulgence she allowed herself for a few minutes before she wiped her eyes and nose on her sleeve, and sat up straighter to take stock of the situation.

She was in a small dark room. Maybe an attic, she considered, thinking of the shape. But it didn't really fit; it was too small for an attic. Then she gave a bark of laughter. Harry Potter. The room under the stairs; a wedge-shaped room with a door. It made sense. At least the dimensions of the room did. But why she was locked under someone's stairway, didn't make any sense whatsoever.

The last thing she remembered was having tea with Liz. Liz? She had drugged her? It was the only logical explanation, but it didn't make sense. Why on earth would she do such a thing? Was it because she'd told Liz that she would tell the police what Viveka had said? She'd been drugged and locked up to protect Viveka Larsson. It was unbelievable, but it was the only explanation that made sense.

Fear was replaced by anger. Much healthier. Anger would get her out. She wasn't going to stay there, waiting for something to be done to her, the proverbial sitting duck. If there was one thing she had learned about herself over the last year, she was a survivor. She felt around the floor, hands searching for anything that could be of use. Finding nothing, she felt the walls again, looking for a weak spot, something she could work loose, but they were perfectly smooth. She tapped them, and discovered that the wall around the door wasn't solid, maybe she could kick a hole in it. Unfortunately, she was wearing trainers, but that didn't stop her aiming several futile kicks at the wall and at the door.

Exhausted, she sat on the floor, cross-legged, telling herself not to cry. Then, with a sinking feeling, she realised she had another problem, she needed to pee. She banged on the door, calling Liz's name, shouting until her voice became ragged.

She couldn't just leave her there, could she? A year ago, Edel would have said a definite no, but events had conspired to teach her a hard lesson. It would be easy to say nothing surprised her anymore, but she had to be honest, she'd never have dreamt Viveka Larsson was responsible for all the appalling incidents that caused so much stress to so many people. And she was certainly surprised at being drugged and locked up by Liz Goodbody. Not so aptly named now, was she?

Hearing a noise, she scrambled to her feet, and put her cheek against the door. 'Hello!' she shouted. 'Please, can you hear me? Please, let me out.'

'Stand back from the door, move to the wall, and turn around. Do as you are told, and you will come to no harm.'

'Liz? Why are you doing this? Please, let me go.' Her ear was pressed to the door as she strained to hear.

'Do you know what a taser is?'

Of course Edel knew. She trembled. Maybe she was wrong, maybe it wasn't Liz.

'Do you?' the voice came again, cold enough to send shivers down her spine.

'Yes, I know.'

'Well, do as I say, and I won't need to use it. I have food and drink.'

Desperate now, Edel dropped her voice to a pleading whisper. 'Please, I need to go to the toilet. I've wanted to go for hours, I'm not sure how much longer I can hold it.'

This time the silence lasted longer. Edel heard movement, shuffling and the distant sound of a door slamming.

A few minutes passed before she heard the voice again. 'Stand back from the door, move to the wall and turn around. I've brought something you can use as a toilet. You can use it and pass it out. Then I'll give you food and drink. Don't forget I have a taser. I will use it if I have to.'

Desperate, Edel did what she was told, moving to the back wall and turning around. She heard the sound of a key turning in a lock, the rough slide of a bolt, and the creak as the door was slowly opened, the small room flooding with light. She risked a glance right and left, confirming the contours of the room, searching for a weakness, seeing none, all the while conscious of a rustling behind, then a faster creak as the door was shut, and she was once again in darkness.

Turning, she squatted down, hands searching and finding what felt like a plastic basin. More searching found a roll of toilet paper. She unzipped her jeans, squatted over the basin and with a sigh of relief emptied her bladder.

Finished, she knocked on the door. 'I'm done,' she shouted.

'Move back to the wall, turn around, don't move till I tell you,' the voice came immediately.

Doing as she was told, Edel moved back to the wall. The space was small; she could almost feel the other woman behind, removing the basin and replacing it with something else. More shuffling, a creak as the door was shut, and the rattle and clunk as it was locked and bolted. Turning around in the darkness, she heard a faint shuffling noise, and then silence.

Fumbling around with her hands, Edel hoped she'd find something she could adapt as a weapon or a tool, something she could use to work on the door, or to use as a chisel on the walls. She'd seen *The Shawshank Redemption*; she knew how it was done.

But all she found was a paper plate of food, and a plastic beaker of lukewarm tea. Cross-legged, she sat and ate, her hand picking up whatever was on the plate, guiding it to her face where she could just about make it out before biting, chewing and swallowing. She didn't want it, but knew she had to eat, had to stay strong. Then she bit into something she recognised. That blasted lemon cake.

Sugar had been added to the tea. It wasn't the way she took it, but she forced herself to drink, remembering something she had read once about dehydration. If you were thirsty you were already dehydrated. And she was very thirsty. Within minutes, she knew she'd made a mistake. Her head felt light, eyes heavy, head nodding, body swaying to someone else's beat.

She'd been drugged again.

When she woke, she had no idea if she'd been out for an hour or a day. There was a banging drum where her head should be, and a sick feeling in her stomach. She'd curled up, unconsciously protective, now she rolled onto her back, straightened her legs and lay still, trying to ride the wave of pain.

The food, or more likely that awful tea, had been drugged. She wouldn't eat or drink anything she was given again. But she was already thirsty. How long could she go without food or drink? From the cache of bizarre facts she'd acquired over the years, she came up with the statistics. Three days without water, three weeks without food.

But she wouldn't be here that long. Would she?

If it were Sunday, Mike would be looking for her. She clutched at that thought. He would have wondered if she was still mad at him, would have rung to see if she still wanted to walk the pier. *Walking the pier.* What a gloriously normal thing to do. They'd have walked the length of it, and stood at the end looking out to sea. Then they'd have gone for something to eat. And who knows what would have happened next.

When he couldn't contact her, he'd look for her. Wouldn't he? Or would he? She had been mad with him. Had been furious, in fact. But now her argument seemed futile, juvenile and so wrong, everything now judged against her current predicament. If he went to the house, he'd see her car. Would he think she was in, and wasn't bothering to answer the door to him? Would he go away and forget about her?

He'd come to her rescue before, she desperately hoped he'd do so again. As tears trickled down her cheeks, words she'd learned by rote in school came back to her, and she recited a childish prayer to a god she didn't believe in, promising to be good forevermore if He would grant this one wish.

Then she remembered doing the same when her husband had vanished. She had prayed so hard for his return.

And look how that had turned out.

33

When West hadn't heard from Edel by Monday morning, he decided he'd blown his chances with her, and was determined to put her out of his head. Anyway, there was way too much at stake today to allow his personal life to interfere.

The warrant came through just before eleven. Most of the team were present, and as soon as the paperwork was ready, they headed out to Viveka Larsson's apartment, taking two cars, West driving his own, Edwards, Baxter and Jarvis going with Andrews.

Warned to be discreet, they parked nearby and walked over to the apartment complex. West rang the doorbell and they waited quietly until a voice answered on the intercom with a soft 'hello.'

'Ms Larsson, my name is Detective Garda Sergeant West. I am here with some of my colleagues. May we come in and have a word?' He hoped she'd either come down, or let them in. An argument on the doorstep about her rights definitely didn't come under the heading of discreet.

There was no delay; they immediately heard the buzz that

announced she had opened the entrance door. They went up as quietly as it was possible for five grown men to be. At the apartment door, West signalled the three younger officers to take a few steps back, knowing how intimidating they would look massed together in the small corridor.

There wasn't a doorbell; he rapped his knuckles on the pale wood and it was opened almost immediately by an attractive woman who stood in the entrance with a smile of welcome. Her eyes drifted over West and Andrews and lingered on the three who stood in the wings. With dramatic flair, she said, 'How lovely, five handsome men to join me for morning coffee.' She stood back and waved them in.

The lounge was a big room with windows on two sides providing light. Pale wooden floors, white woodwork, and pastel shades on the soft furnishings made it a bright but restful space. 'Please, sit down,' she fluttered, waving them to a selection of chairs dotted about the room, most looking as if they would barely take her weight let alone any of the men. 'I'll make coffee,' she said, smiling sweetly. 'Unless you'd prefer tea?'

'I'm afraid this isn't a social call, Ms Larsson,' West said quietly.

'It's not? How you disappoint me, Sergeant,' she said softly, her large eyes fixed on his, regret the only emotion he could read there.

He took a breath. 'We have a warrant to search your apartment, Ms Larsson,' he said, holding it out as he spoke, waiting until she took it with a bemused look on her face. 'The items we are searching for are listed on the warrant. It also covers your computer and gives us the right to take your fingerprints.'

'What fun,' she said, causing all the ten eyes focused on her to narrow in surprise. She smiled at them. 'I'm sure you have your reasons, but perhaps you could tell me why?'

'If my team can get on with the search, Ms Larsson, perhaps we could have a seat and we can discuss the situation.'

She shrugged her acceptance of this order of service, and took a seat on the sofa, patting the space beside her with an arch smile.

West left the organisational aspect of the search to Andrews. Ignoring her invitation, he pulled up one of the sturdier chairs and sat at an angle to her. Surprised, and slightly unsettled by her calm demeanour, he took out a notebook and pen. 'Before we start, I need to read you your rights,' he said, and proceeded to do so. 'Do you understand?'

'Perfectly, Sergeant West,' she said calmly, but with a puzzled look on her face. 'Well, I understand that anything I say can be used in evidence against me, but I don't understand what I could say that would be of the slightest interest to the police.'

'You are the founder of a group called *Offer*?'

Her puzzled look increased. 'That's correct. And common knowledge.'

'And you ran a group in Finland. Called *Tarjous*.'

Her rather thin, pale face went a shade paler. Then she smiled again, but the smile was sad. 'Correct.'

'Is it not true that *Tarjous* was a brothel, Ms Larsson, and you were the owner of this brothel?'

She reached her small hand across and laid it on his arm. 'You are trying to hide the condemnation in your voice,' she said, her voice quiet, 'but not doing a very good job, I'm afraid. *Tarjous* wasn't all about sex. We did provide a service for lonely men.'

'And charged for it?'

She looked sharply at him. 'You should know by now, Sergeant, that very little comes for nothing. There is always someone who pays.'

'Even with *Offer*,' he said quickly.

She sank back against the sofa and sighed. 'Even with it.' She turned and caught his gaze. 'Shall I tell you why I started *Offer*? Why I came to Ireland?'

He listened to the background sound of his team turning her apartment inside out. It wasn't a big place, it wouldn't take long, but he had time to listen to her story.

She let her head rest against the back of the sofa. 'I ran *Tarjous* for many years,' she said, not looking at him. 'I made a good living, ran a nice place. My girls were clean, they worked for me willingly. I had no time for those who liked their plea-sures perverted; these people went elsewhere, were more than well catered for in other establishments. Then my attention slipped and I...' She turned her head to look at him. 'What is the expression you use... I took my eye off...?'

'The ball,' West supplied, and she inclined her head in thanks, and returned her gaze to the window.

'Yes, I took my eye off the ball. A new customer came and took one of my girls.' She stopped, bit her lower lip, eyes losing focus as she remembered.

'We spoke to someone in Finland, in Vice. They didn't mention an incident,' he said.

'Oh, Anneli didn't die. No. She had to have surgery. It was partially successful; she'll have ongoing problems, and will never be able to have children, but she's alive.' She sighed sadly. 'All I could do for her was to give her money, so I sold up and, except for enough to live on for a while, I gave her the rest. It will help.'

'Why didn't you go to the police?' West asked sharply. 'He shouldn't have been allowed to get away with that.'

She looked at him and tilted her head. 'You don't survive in my line of work without being able to take care of things. He didn't get away with it. Believe me, he'll never hurt another woman.'

West was horrified at the fate of the young woman, but he was a policeman to the core. 'You had him killed?'

'You really are an innocent, aren't you?' she said, and patted his arm. 'There are far worse things than death, my sweet man. There is life without what men hold most dear, there is life without fingers to scratch with, without a tongue to call a young, working woman a whore.'

He swallowed. If he'd heard right, she'd had the man's penis and fingers cut off, and his tongue cut out. He wondered where he was now, how he'd survived. Then he thought of the young woman and shrugged. Maybe not quite an eye for an eye, but close enough.

He looked at the woman sitting beside him with renewed interest. 'What brought you to Dublin?'

'The reason I took my eye off the ball. I was diagnosed with cancer last year. It has spread, and is inoperable. My doctor moved here earlier this year and has a consultancy across the road in St Vincent's Hospital. I didn't want anyone else to look after me in my last days, so I followed him.'

West saw her pallor now for what it was, and felt a dart of compassion. It looked like his far-fetched idea that she'd set up *Offer* as an act of reparation had been right on the money. 'You started *Offer* as an attempt at making amends?'

She looked at him now without smiling, her eyes dropping to her clenched hands. 'You make it sound wrong. Pathetic, even. But when I sat in the hospital with Anneli, day in and day out, I would have loved for someone to come and sit with me, not to speak but just to be there. When I came here to live, I thought of that time and decided to start this volunteer group. There are many people who have time to spare, and many who would benefit from that time.'

West had one of his light-bulb moments. 'And when you become unwell, there will be someone there to hold your hand?'

Not just an act of reparation, an insurance against dying alone. She didn't answer, and he let it go. 'What about this payment you mentioned?'

She looked at him, confused. 'Payment?'

'You said there was always someone who pays.'

'Yes, I remember.'

Her eyes closed for a moment, and he saw that her eyelids were translucent. He wondered how long she had been given.

As if she read his mind, she opened her eyes and caught his gaze. 'My time is measured in weeks, maybe only days. When I started *Offer*, I thought I would do a little advertising, get a few people on board, and it would run itself.' She stopped, her breathing rapid and shallow.

'But it didn't?' West said, guessing.

'I go for the first meeting of each new intake of volunteers, say hello, make a little motivating speech. But as you can see, it is difficult for me now. There is morphine for when the pain becomes unbearable. I keep it here, and inject it myself when the pain becomes impossible. There will come a time when I will not be able, when I will need help even to do that but, for now, it is okay. But I will admit, it is getting more difficult.

'Some of the volunteers have left, more are talking about leaving. My second-in-command, as Liz calls herself, asked if I would come and give another rousing, motivational speech last night. So of course, I felt obliged. Payment, Sergeant West.'

'Did it work?' he asked, curious.

She smiled. 'She seemed to think it helped. But a woman I expected to see, didn't come, a young woman who, Liz assured me, was more motivated after helping out at the school explosion. Liz said she had rung to say she couldn't come. It was disappointing.'

West's attention was caught by her reference to the school. She'd referred to the incident as an explosion. He filed the fact away for future examination. But for the moment he was curious about something else. 'Are you referring to Edel Johnson?'

'Yes, that's her name. I noticed her at her induction evening. She had such a sad smile; I thought it must have a story attached. Liz... Liz Goodbody, you know her?' At West's nod she continued. 'She told me about her husband, and the scandal. It explained the sad smile. I was sorry not to have met her again.'

West could hear the background shuffle of his men at work, the sounds had got nearer. They must be almost finished. Putting Edel forcibly out of his head, he asked, 'This making reparation is important to you?'

Her smile was sad and weary. 'It was little that I did, but perhaps it will be my legacy. Far better than the memories of *Tarjous*.'

West saw his opportunity. 'But it wasn't doing too well, was it? There was no real need for this group, and volunteers were leaving. There would be nobody to sit with you at the end, and no legacy. Until you began to create the need, and engineered some incidents to show your group in a good light. *Offer* riding to the rescue every time. Just one little mistake when Gerard Roberts died, but never mind, carry on and create a bit more mayhem to ensure the group's survival.'

Viveka Larsson rose with an element of difficulty, her face a mask of outrage, eyes glinting. 'Are you absolutely mad?'

And for the first time since arriving, West acknowledged that her English was as good as his; perhaps, in her careful enunciation and precise diction, it was better. It certainly wouldn't be said that she spoke *funny*. If he were honest with himself, he'd known he was wrong as soon as she opened the door. She was too short, too slight to be the woman in the CCTV footage from *Bang Bang!* The kaftan that enveloped her, was hung on a frame that was disease-thin. She could have padded herself out, but the hand and arm that had reached out for young Max was strong and firm. Not the hand and arm that extended like pipe cleaners from Viveka's sleeves.

'You must be mad,' she said again, her voice shriller, 'there can be no justification for this treatment. I assumed it was to do with your discovery of my past. That you were ensuring I was not running some kind of brothel here. But this...'

Luckily for West, she appeared lost for words. 'I'm sorry, Ms Larsson. We are just following the leads we have. Acting on information we have gathered. It is not our intention to upset or discommode you, but we are obliged to follow these leads.'

Her strength already ebbing, she sat and said something quietly in what West assumed was Swedish, or maybe Finnish. He didn't understand the words, but the tone was clearly not complimentary. She switched back to English. 'These things you look for, they will prove I am innocent?'

'If we find what we're looking for, we'll take it away to be examined and see if it matches our information. Only if it matches, will it be classified as evidence and be used in any subsequent trial.' If it came to that. Looking down at this frail woman, he didn't think she would be around for any trial that could take at least a year, if not more, to go to court. 'If we don't find what we're looking for, we will keep investigating. If we find it, and there isn't a match, we will keep looking but probably in a different direction.'

'This all seems very irregular. It seems to be, to be... what do you call it...' She clicked her fingers as she sought for the correct word. 'A fishing trip.'

'Exercise,' West corrected automatically.

She gave a slight smile. 'A fishing exercise. Yes, am I right?'

West, suffering from a rapid change of mind, was more blunt than usual. 'Absolutely not, that's not the way we operate.' Seeing her pallor, he relented. 'Ms Larsson, we have two concrete things we are looking for. Both of these are itemised on the warrant.'

A few minutes later, the search was finished and they had nothing. They took her fingerprints because they had the warrant to do so, but they all knew they were wasting their time.

Viveka Larsson may not be innocent, but she was certainly innocent of any wrongdoing in Foxrock.

34

Edel didn't know how long she had been held captive. She'd tried banging on the walls, but using hands or her soft shoes, it wasn't making much of an impact. There wasn't any point in banging on the walls into the house; whoever was out there was responsible, so she concentrated her banging on the party wall with next door, knowing it was pretty futile since it was probably the wall under their stairs. But maybe, just maybe, they had done as many do and converted it into a downstairs loo, and maybe someone would go to use it, hear the banging and call to investigate.

Okay, it was a slim chance, but she didn't have many choices.

Her ears pricked up when she heard a rustling, dragging sound from outside. And then Liz's irritating whisper. 'I've brought more food. Move back against the wall; keep your face to it. Remember, I have a taser and won't hesitate to use it.'

She didn't have a choice. As before, when the door opened, light came from the hallway. Desperate to find out something, even if it were only the time of day, she risked moving her head, just a little, straining her eyes to see what she could.

Nothing but shades of grey and black. But then... there at the very edge of her vision she saw the blurry outline of Liz, bent over. An opportunity? She couldn't let it pass, couldn't continue being a victim. In a fleeting second, she made a choice and turned, adrenaline pumping for fight or flight. But that second, fleeting or not, was too long.

Liz straightened, a hand shot out, and all Edel felt was pain, the worst wasp sting, an elephant-sized sting. Every muscle went into spasm, and she fell, banging her head on the sloped ceiling as she went down. She was gone before urine spread around her in a puddle, the pungent smell merging with the metallic smell of blood that trickled from the gash on her head. She was well gone before the door was closed and locked.

Edel retreated to an area deep inside. A place visited before. The sanctuary of victims.

Claiming asylum, she felt nothing more.

35

W est swung into the station car park so quickly he heard the tyres squeal a complaint. He needed to calm down before he had to face Inspector Morrison.

But he didn't get the chance. No sooner had he slammed the office door behind him, then it opened and the inspector stood there, frown lines cutting deeply. 'Please tell me you got something.'

West sat heavily into his chair and rubbed his face with his hand. 'Nothing. We searched every inch of the apartment. No jotter to match to Gerard Roberts' note, even easier, no jotters at all. And the woman never cooks, so doesn't possess a grater or liquidiser. The only equipment she uses in her kitchen is the kettle.

'Her explanation for leaving Finland, for closing *Tarjous*, and starting *Offer* is believable. I'll have her story checked, of course, but...' He filled the inspector in on Viveka Larsson's health prognosis, deciding he may as well make a clean breast of it while he was at it. Morrison could only get angry once.

It was enough. The inspector was steaming, almost incandescent with rage. 'Are you telling me, Sergeant West, that not only have we unjustly accused an innocent woman, the founder of a very helpful volunteer group, but we have accused a woman who is dying, who is trying to make restitution for any wrong choices she may have made?'

'I'm not sure you could classify running a very successful and lucrative brothel as a "wrong choice" and there is no "may" about it. She admits to it. Didn't seem a bit fazed about it, actually.' He held his hands up as Morrison started sputtering with rage. 'I know. That's not the point. And I'm sorry. It was apparent, fairly early that she wasn't the woman we were looking for. Her build,' he explained, 'it just doesn't fit with the footage we have. I know that's useless for identification purposes, but what it does give is an idea of height and weight, and Ms Larsson is a slight, petite woman. She doesn't fit.'

'Your whole idea that *Offer* was manipulating the situation for its own end has been blown out of the water. And we have nothing.' Morrison grimaced. 'The press is going to have a field day. And if you tell me they won't find out, you need your head examined.'

West wasn't going to be so foolish. There was no way the lid would stay on this particular pot. He knew the way it worked. No matter how discreet they had tried to be. Someone would know, and if they knew, that meant they'd sell. Where there was a juicy story and money to be made, there was always someone who would.

A juicy story, showing the Garda Síochána as insensitive bullies who accused a sick woman of nefarious crimes. Well, he could see the headlines now. Three inches high and unforgiving.

He rubbed his face again. His instincts may have been wrong about Viveka Larsson but there was still the connection between the cases and *Offer*. That can't have been just a coincidence. He put that to the inspector, who puffed his chest out and looked at him as if he'd just crawled out from under a stone, and a pretty grubby one at that.

'Get me proof. Something concrete I can take to the superintendent when he calls me in for a bollocking. As I have no doubt he will, when the shit hits the bloody fan.' The inspector's voice had risen incrementally, the final words heard by the rest of the team as they returned, having driven from the apartment at a more sedate pace than West.

They sat at desks trying to look busy, keeping eyes down, or anywhere else apart from the doorway, as the inspector turned and with anger in every step, left the office. A collective exhale of breath followed his departure, eyes immediately swivelling towards West.

'Sounds like the inspector isn't too happy with us,' Edwards said with the fine art of understatement.

'What now?' Jarvis asked, standing and moving to The Wall. 'Maybe we weren't right about the Larsson woman,' he said, 'but if we don't believe in coincidence, there is too much linking these cases for it to be accidental. If it isn't Larsson, it has to be someone else. Doesn't it?' he added as West joined him. 'Maybe we were just looking at the wrong person? Just because Larsson founded it, doesn't mean she is the only one with a vested interest in keeping it going, does it?'

'Okay,' West said, crossing his arms. 'If it wasn't Viveka Larsson, who the hell was it?'

They gathered in front of The Wall, each of them thinking back over the last few days, trying to pinpoint something that would indicate a direction to go. Edwards took a piece of information and started to read, quickly followed by Baxter and Andrews. Silently, without discussion, they moved back to their desks to deal with whatever had struck them as being important.

West didn't interfere. He knew his team. Quick, intelligent men, they'd look at everything. And, if by chance two of them were looking at the same thing, well, he would guarantee they were both looking from a different angle. And that's where success lay. Looking into those different angles.

But at the end of the day, having looked into all of them, they'd found nothing.

'I double-checked with Foley,' Edwards said, sticking the information on the break-in back on The Wall, 'to make sure he'd done a search on both Mrs Lee's daughter and the daughter's husband. Just to check they didn't need the old dear's house sold to bail them out of difficulty. But you know Declan; he'd already crossed every t.'

Andrews looked at him approvingly. 'Always safer to check. You were lucky it was Foley. He's good. But it could have been Sergeant Clark.'

There was a ripple of amusement. West tried to look severe, but ruined it with a grin. 'I'm sure Sergeant Clark has his strengths.'

'How to get out of doing as much as he can, you mean?'

The ripple became guffaws. They knew the truth of the matter only too well.

West let them have their moment of amusement. He remembered the inspector's earlier criticism. There wasn't much else to laugh about today.

Putting that to the back of his head, he asked Edwards, 'You don't believe the cases are linked then. You think the break-in is a separate case?'

Edwards looked embarrassed. 'No, sir. I was just ruling that aspect out. The possible, you know? You've always said, sarge, when you rule out the possible, and are only left with the impossible, then the impossible is it.'

West had said something along those lines many a time.

'I was on the same wavelength,' Jarvis said with a grin. 'I double-checked the school finances, made sure it wasn't intended to be some kind of insurance claim. Perhaps planning a fire, rather than lots of smoke and noise. But there isn't a problem. They've an extraordinarily healthy bank balance.' He grinned at Edwards. 'Another possible ruled out.'

'A lot of ruling out,' West commented. 'All very well and good, but did anyone rule anything in?'

'Not me, I'm afraid,' Baxter said. 'I did manage,' he said, and looked sideways at West, 'to access Viveka Larsson's medical records.'

West glanced at Andrews who shrugged. 'I suppose we are already up shit creek,' he said to Baxter, 'what did you find out?'

'Just what she told us. Her doctor moved here several months ago. She came the month after, and registered with the hospital. She's had several appointments. Most importantly, she had inpatient treatment over a few days this month. She was admitted on the Thursday, was supposed to be let out on the Friday, but due to complications was kept in until Monday.' He looked up from his notebook. 'It was the weekend young Max was taken.'

They'd known. But this information solidified the situation. Viveka Larsson wasn't the instigator. But they were no nearer to knowing who was.

West ran his fingers through his hair. 'Okay, we need to look at the rest of the *Offer* volunteers.'

Andrews waved an A4 page. 'I got the list of names from Sergeant Blunt.' He smiled as he felt West look at him, and turned with a wink. 'We are starting to think so alike, it's scary.'

West gave a short laugh and shook his head. 'How many?'

'Twelve volunteers of which eight are women. Some are more active than others. They're all volunteers, of course, and some may have other employment that requires their time. We have the clearance forms for them all. None have criminal records. But...'

'It could just mean she hasn't been caught,' Jarvis said quietly.

'A very, very clever woman,' Edwards muttered.

'Or a lucky one?' Baxter chipped in.

'She'll know we're on to her when she hears about Viveka Larsson, and will guess we'll be looking into everyone else. She might make a run for it. So,' West said, looking around, 'we need to gather as much information on these eight women as we can, as quickly as possible.' He added, 'I'm going to keep this from Inspector Morrison for the moment. I think his faith in my intuition has taken a bit of a beating.'

He waited until the expected laughter died. 'Go do your thing. If you're using methods that would turn my hair grey, don't tell me. Just remember discretion is the keyword. Okay?'

Nods all around, and they headed back to desks and computers. Baxter, the computer wizard of the team, had a quick word with Edwards whose fingers moved almost of their own volition across the keys. He might not have been as good as Baxter, but he was only marginally behind. Both West and Andrews were rather in awe of the younger men's computer skills, but were happy to set them loose on their keyboards and await the outcome.

Two hours later they had it, and it didn't make them happy.

36

'Nothing?' West said, trying unsuccessfully to hide his dismay.

'The lads looked everywhere they could,' Andrews said. 'There was nothing special about any of the eight. One of them spent time in Africa, I don't know–'

The phone rang, interrupting him. West swore loudly. 'If this is Mother looking for results, I am going to go and ring the bloody man's neck.' He picked up the handset. 'Sergeant West,' he said, his voice not quite a snarl, but close. He listened, his face changing from annoyed, to resigned, to outright puzzled. 'We'll be there in fifteen minutes.' Hanging up, he sat back in his chair, and smiled. 'Well, well,' he said. 'You will never guess who that was, Peter.'

'Probably not going to even try,' Andrews replied with a yawn.

'Bernard Beans. Our friend from The Vegetable Shop.' West stood and picked up his car keys. 'Let's go. He's expecting us. Tell Edwards to come, and take his group photo of *Offer*.' He gripped Andrews' arm. 'Someone tried to buy manihot esculenta a couple of hours ago. Pat says it was the same woman.'

They took West's car and barrelled through the traffic. None of them spoke, but all three thought *maybe*.

Arriving outside The Vegetable Shop less than fifteen minutes later, West parked immediately outside, half on, half off the pavement. Once more the shop was empty. He didn't hang about this time, went to the door at the back, knocked loudly, opened it and shouted, 'Mr Beans.'

He appeared within seconds, all business-like hustle and bustle. 'Here you are again then,' he said, peevishly, as if he had not rung and volunteered information just fifteen minutes before.

West cut to the chase. 'We need to know more about the woman who came in to buy the manihot esculenta,' he said. 'You're sure it was the same woman?'

Mr Beans shrugged a bony shoulder, looking like a tatty puppet on strings. 'Pat said it was. I never met the woman, if you remember.'

West and Andrews exchanged glances. Pat wasn't the most reliable of witnesses. 'Did she mention buying it here the last time?' he asked, hoping to link the two visits together with a stronger witness than Pat.

'She didn't say anything. I told her we didn't sell it anymore, and that we wouldn't be stocking it in future. She didn't say another word, or buy anything else,' he added, aggrieved, 'she just turned and left.'

'You said Pat thought it was the same woman. Is she here?'

Without turning round, Beans let out a yell. 'Pat. Get yourself out here. Now.'

They weren't waiting long. A shuffle sounded from the back of the premises, gradually growing louder until Pat sailed into view.

'Hello,' she said, the broad smile across her rosy cheeks growing broader when she saw Edwards. 'You're back.'

'Hello, Pat,' West said, and her eyes focused on him with a slight dimming of the smile. 'You remember we were here before, trying to find the woman who bought those funny vegetables. We hear she was in again today, wanting to buy more.'

'She's got pretty hair. But she speaks funny.'

West looked at Beans for clarification. 'Speaks funny? An accent?'

'I didn't notice an accent,' Beans said. 'She did speak in a breathy kind of whisper. Irritating, I found it, not in the slightest bit funny.'

West closed his eyes briefly, and gave himself a mental kick. He'd made an assumption, and it was wrong. He looked across at Edwards who reached into his jacket pocket for the group photograph he had shown Pat before.

'Pat, you told Garda Edwards that the lady who bought those funny vegetables was in this photograph. Can you look at it again? Just to be sure.'

Pat took the photograph into her grubby hands and peered at it, holding it so closely that West wondered if she usually wore glasses. He was just about to ask, when she beamed a smile. 'Yep. That's her.'

Knowing it couldn't be Viveka Larsson, West looked grimly at Edwards. 'Did Pat identify Viveka by pointing her out, or did she just say she was in the photograph?'

Edwards swallowed hard. He'd made a rookie mistake. Pat had said the woman she'd seen was in the photograph. Because they were looking at Viveka Larsson, he'd jumped to the convenient and erroneous conclusion she meant her. He met West's gaze. 'She just said she was in the photo. My fault.'

More assumptions. No point in blaming Edwards.

'Okay, Pat,' he said, keeping his voice gentle. 'Will you put your finger on the woman who bought the funny vegetables? The woman who came back today.'

They waited.

Pat, all eagerness to please, placed her index finger firmly on the face of one of the women in the photograph.

'You're sure?'

When she nodded, he handed the photo to Beans. 'Mr Beans, can you indicate the woman who was here in your shop today.'

Beans took the photograph and studied it before looking up. 'There is no doubt in my mind,' he said, and the three men let out breath they didn't know they were holding. 'It's a very good likeness. Pat was right, it was this woman here.'

West took the photograph back. He didn't need to read the name underneath to identify the woman they had picked out. 'Thank you both. Your assistance has been invaluable.'

'Well, I hope that's it now,' said the irascible Mr Beans, who promptly turned on his heel and went through the door.

Pat still smiled sunnily. 'I hope you do come back again,' she said, her eyes slanting to Edwards.

They headed to their car in silence. The doors had barely shut before Edwards, sitting in the back, poked his head forward, turtle-like between the two men. 'So,' he said eagerly, 'who is it then?'

'Liz Goodbody.'

'No way,' Edwards said, eyes widening. 'I've met her. She's a mouse, wouldn't hurt a fly. You mean to tell me, she killed Gerard Roberts?'

Andrews grunted. 'Remember I was telling you that one of the eight women we were looking into had spent time in Africa? It was Liz Goodbody.'

'I suppose she'd have come across that manihot stuff there, wouldn't she?' Edwards said. 'Still, Liz Goodbody!'

West started the car, indicated and pulled out into the traffic that stopped and started on its way through Foxrock Village.

'How're you going to play this?' Andrews asked. 'Trying for another warrant might be difficult, you know.'

West knew only too well. They'd have heard about the fiasco of the first, and would be very reluctant to issue another for the same items.

'We'll invite her in to assist us in our enquiries,' he said. 'If Beans had seen her the first time she went to the shop, I'd go for a warrant, but Pat just isn't a strong enough witness. A solicitor would demolish her in two seconds flat. And all Beans can testify to, is that she went in to buy some of that damned vegetable. Not a crime. Unfortunately for us, she didn't mention to him that she'd bought it there before.'

'When we get back, Mark, do some digging. Try and find out what she was doing in Africa. How long she was there. Anything.'

'Will do,' Edwards said. 'Still can't believe it's her. She was so helpful at the school on Friday morning. The last time I saw her, she was walking off, arm in arm, with Edel Johnson.'

West brought the car to a sudden halt, the car behind stopping with a screech of breaks and a prolonged blast of his horn.

'Bloody hell,' said Edwards who, still sitting forward to chat, was thrown back against the seat.

'You should have had your seat belt on. It's compulsory, you know,' Andrews said, looking back with a grin that faded quickly when he saw the worried look on West's face. 'What is it?' he asked.

'I should have known there was something wrong. It wasn't like her. I knew it.' He waved an apologetic hand to the driver behind and drove on. 'We were supposed to go out Sunday afternoon for a walk along the pier.' He shot Andrews a look. 'I called round to her house on Friday evening to warn her we were looking into *Offer*. She wasn't happy about it.' He gave a half-smile. 'She tore strips off me. Anyway, I left. Tried to ring her on Saturday, several times. Tried to ring her Sunday. Hell, I even went round, her car was there, but there was no answer. She'd said she had something on Saturday night. I made the assumption it was another man; thought maybe she'd stayed out.

'Then today, Viveka Larsson said Edel was supposed to be at an *Offer* meeting on Saturday night, but Liz said she'd rung to say she couldn't make it. I haven't heard from her. And it isn't like her. You know Edel, Peter, she's up front, tells it like it is. She wouldn't ignore the phone ringing, or somebody banging on the door.'

Andrews gave him a sharp look. 'You warned her about *Offer*.'

'Yes, yes, I know, very unprofessional of me.'

'It's not that,' Andrews said grimly. 'Didn't you know? It was Liz Goodbody who introduced her to the group.'

West's lips narrowed. If anything happened to her... 'Viveka Larsson said Edel had rung Liz to tell her she wasn't attending the meeting on Saturday night. That means the last person to speak to Edel, was Liz.'

'Maybe Edel felt she owed it to her to warn her about the investigation?' Andrews said worriedly.

West pressed a little harder on the accelerator. 'Just what she would have done, I bet.' He took the turn into Wilton Road without slowing down, causing both his passengers to draw a sharp breath and, seconds later, pulled up outside Edel's house.

Her car was parked in the same place. West looked at it closely; he'd swear it hadn't moved since he last saw it. Leaves from a huge walnut tree in her neighbour's garden had built up around the tyres. Hell, this car hadn't been moved in days.

The three men got out and approached the front door, West slightly ahead. It was almost dark, but there wasn't a light to be seen. He pressed the doorbell, keeping his finger on it even as they heard the sound reverberating through the house. 'Try the windows; see if you can see anything.' He kept his finger on the bell as the two men headed off, Andrews directing Edwards to go left while he went to the right. They were back in less than a minute.

'Can't see a thing. Windows are shuttered on this side,' Edwards said.

'Only the kitchen window on my side,' Andrews said. 'Nothing to be seen.'

West took his finger off the bell; the sudden silence uncomfortably heavy. 'Bill,' he said, startling both men.

'Who?' Andrews said, puzzled.

'Nosy neighbour. Come on.'

Andrews filled Edwards in, on his history with Mr Nosy Neighbour, as they raced up his drive, seconds later hearing his bell ring as West pressed, and then pressed again.

The man opened the door with a look of alarm on his face. 'What on earth?' he said, relaxing as he recognised two of the men standing on his doorstep. 'Oh, it's you lot,' he said, eagerly. 'I suppose you're here about my complaints. It's taken you long enough, I must say.'

Slightly taken aback to be expected, even if for the wrong reason, West was momentarily confused, 'No, Mr...'

'Munroe. For goodness sake, how can you be handling my complaints if you can't even remember my name?'

West tried to keep a rein on his mounting impatience and rising temper. 'Mr Munroe, we are not here about any complaints. We are here,' he continued, speaking over the man who was bristling and babbling about his rights, 'because we are concerned about Ms Johnson.'

Bill Munroe threw his hands up in the air, and made a sound of exasperation. 'Well, isn't this just typical. Are the Garda

Síochána in business just to serve Edel Johnson's needs? Is she the only one that has problems, I ask myself, and do you know what I answer myself?'

'Mr Munroe,' West said, 'I promise, I will assign a garda to look into your complaints tomorrow. In fact,' he turned, and with a wave indicated Edwards and sacrificed him, 'this officer, Detective Garda Edwards, will be at your disposal, all day tomorrow. Okay?'

'All day?' Munroe asked, the wind taken out of his sails.

'All day,' West promised, ignoring the groans coming from Edwards. 'Now I need you to tell me when you saw Edel last.'

'I'm not her keeper, you know,' he started, 'but it just so happens, I saw her going out on Friday evening, not very long after you left. She didn't take her car, so I assume she wasn't going far. And she was just carrying her keys. No bag.'

'And after that?'

He shrugged. 'Haven't seen her since. Which is very unusual. I normally see her once or twice a day.'

'Maybe she came back late on Friday?'

Munroe shook his head. 'No, she didn't. My living room and bedroom are on this side of the house, you see, and if she'd come back, I'd have noted the security lights coming on and checked.' He pointed up to his bedroom. 'Never close my curtains, so I always know what's happening.'

West thanked the man and reiterated his promise of Edwards' help the following day and walked back to the car, Andrews and Edwards a step behind.

West leaned against his car and looked back at the house. 'She was mad at me. She'd have walked rather than driven for that reason.'

Knowing Edel, Andrews nodded in agreement. 'What's our plan?'

'Liz tried to buy that damned vegetable today. If we're right, and she killed Gerard Roberts, why would she want to buy more, if not to use on someone else?'

'But why would she want to kill Edel?' Edwards said.

'If Edel went to warn her about the investigation into *Offer*, maybe Liz gave herself away. Edel is no fool and, if you remember, she's had some experience in dealing with nasty customers. Okay,' West decided, sitting into the car and waiting till the others had followed suit, 'we're going to go around to Liz Goodbody's. We don't need a warrant to speak to her. We can tell her we're making inquiries.'

'The houses where she lives are standard three-bedded semis. Not many places to keep an adult hidden away. If she's there, we'll find her, Mike.'

'We have to. If we're right, Liz's plan was to kill her the same way she did Gerard Roberts, and that plan has failed. She'll be desperate. And desperate people do stupid things. We have to find Edel before anything happens to her.'

37

Liz Goodbody's house was identical to the others on the quiet suburban street. They stopped outside, switched off the engine, and surveyed the area – the quiet and unassuming semi-detached homes and well-tended gardens. A place where children could play outside and be safe, their parents unaware that a murderer lived within reach.

'Let's go,' West said, opening the car door, and then the garden gate, peering in the windows as he approached the house. Nothing out of the ordinary. Just what they expected. Normal. Dull even.

With Andrews and Edwards close behind, he looked for a doorbell. Finding none, he lifted the heavy door knocker and smacked it smartly. They weren't kept waiting long. It was opened moments later by a smiling, seemingly unconcerned Liz Goodbody.

'Hello,' she said, 'this *is* a surprise. What can I do for the Garda Síochána today? It's not my day to volunteer, you know. Marion O'Grady is on call today.'

'Actually, we're here to ask you a few questions about *Offer*,'

West said, calmly. 'If we could come in, it'll only take a few minutes.'

'Oh dear, I'm so terribly sorry to be unhelpful, but I was just heading out.' Liz looked at her watch. 'In fact, I'm already late. Perhaps if you had rung and let me know you were coming. Maybe, I could come into the station tomorrow.'

Frustrated, West stood his ground, but he had no warrant, no proof that Edel was being held. Short of pushing the woman out of the way, there was nothing he could do. He was about to admit defeat when a whimpering sound from behind made him turn.

Edwards was swaying and holding his head in his hand. 'I think I'm going to faint,' he said, swaying alarmingly toward West who grabbed him just as he fell, staggering to hold his weight.

'I think he's having a heart attack,' Andrews said, looking closely at Edwards' face. 'We better get him lying down. If you get him under the shoulders, I'll grab his legs.'

There was a scuffle as they struggled between them. 'Where can we put him, Liz?' West said, grunting as he shifted the weight. 'We need to call an ambulance.'

'Oh dear,' Liz cried, 'it really isn't convenient, you know, but I suppose you'd better come in.'

'Where to?' West said, moving backwards, as Andrews, with an arm under each of Edwards' knees, wheelbarrowed him forward.

'Oh dear,' she said again, and then opened the door into the sitting room. 'You'd better put him in here.'

Puffing, they manoeuvred Edwards' long frame onto the sofa. He made a mewling sound as his head flopped onto a cushion. 'Oh,' he said, eyes fluttering open. 'I fainted.'

'Andrews thinks you may have had a heart attack,' West said

to him. 'Stay still, we're going to call an ambulance. How do you feel?'

'Dreadful,' Edwards said. 'My mouth is very dry. Would it be possible to have a drink of water?'

West looked across to where Liz was hovering in the doorway, irritation written in the creases of her forehead. 'He'd like a drink of water, would that be possible?' Just then, Edwards gave another, louder whimper and with a look of annoyance, she vanished into the kitchen.

Edwards took the opportunity to grin and give a thumbs-up sign. West patted him on the shoulder. Okay, they were in. Now they just had to see if there was any sign of Edel.

Liz returned quickly with the glass of water, slopping it onto the floor in her haste. 'Here you are,' she said, almost throwing it at him. 'Have you called for an ambulance?' she asked, looking first at West, and then over to where Andrews stood at the window.

'I can't get a signal in here,' he muttered, waggling his phone. 'I'll go outside.'

'It needs to be here as quickly as possible, please. I need to leave.'

'If you want, you could go, and we'd close the door after us,' West suggested. 'You can trust us, we are gardaí, after all.'

If West hadn't been looking directly at her, he would have missed the look of absolute hatred that crossed her face. A microsecond later, it was gone, replaced by her usual bland look.

'Oh, I couldn't do that, Sergeant West,' she said, wringing her hands.

Andrews came back in the front door and, without stopping, headed up the stairs. 'I'm just using your facilities, Liz,' he called out.

She was out the door in a flash, looking after him.

Aha, she's up there. West stayed beside Edwards; his ears

pricked for Andrews' call.

Liz came back in, her lips a flat line of annoyance. 'Honestly, he might have had the manners to ask.'

Her expression was annoyed but there was something else in her eyes. *Satisfaction*. West felt his gut squeeze. He was wrong, Edel wasn't being held upstairs.

Andrews' grim look when he returned confirmed it; meeting West's gaze, he gave a subtle shake of his head.

Edwards tried to sit up, groaning as he did so. 'I hate to be a nuisance,' he said, with a forced tremble in his voice, 'but I really need to go to the toilet myself. Do you have a downstairs one I could use?'

Liz looked pained. 'Honestly, can't you wait? The ambulance should be here any minute.'

'I don't think I can wait.' Edwards twisted his mouth in a grimace. 'I'm sorry. Perhaps if you help me,' he said looking at West, 'I might make it up the stairs.'

Liz was almost jumping from foot to foot, peering out the window every few seconds, expecting an ambulance to sail into view. She sighed loudly and in a voice laced with exasperation, said, 'There's a toilet in the utility room. Off the kitchen. You can use that. If you must.'

Edwards made a big performance of getting to his feet, ad libbing with a whimper when he stood, and a groan when he walked. He leaned heavily on West's arm, swaying dramatically as they squeezed past a lovely old Welsh dresser in the hallway.

Neither the kitchen not the utility room held any surprises. Edwards closed the door into the small utility/downstairs toilet, seconds later flushing and turning on taps before coming out to join West, who had taken the opportunity to scrutinise the back garden. A shed or garage would be the ideal spot for concealment. But the rectangular, walled garden had neither.

They were out of options. Edel wasn't there.

38

'Let's get out of here,' West whispered to Edwards.

They met Liz in the hallway. 'Edwards is feeling a bit better now, Miss Goodbody, so I think since the ambulance hasn't turned up, I'll take him to the hospital in my car. We'll phone the emergency services and cancel them.' West offered her a conciliatory smile. 'I hope we haven't made you too late for your appointment.'

'Well, you have,' she replied, not in the least bit mollified. 'I'm not happy about this. I'll be having a word with Inspector Morrison.'

'Perhaps, if you come into the station tomorrow,' West suggested, 'around ten? We could ask those questions we wanted to ask, and you could speak to the inspector. Two birds with one stone and all that.'

'Perhaps,' she conceded frostily. And she closed the front door without further ado.

Back in West's car, the three men sat staring at the house. 'She's not rushing out, is she?' he said. 'I thought we'd made her late?'

Just then the door opened and Liz appeared, still bristling, chin up and back ramrod straight. If she was aware of their car, she didn't show it, walking away with quick determined steps, arms swinging by her side.

West watched till she vanished around the corner before starting the engine.

'What now?' Edwards asked from the back seat.

'Firstly,' West said, twisting round to look at him, 'well done, with the amateur dramatics.'

He laughed. 'It just came to me. Would have been great if we'd found Mrs Johnson. You still think Liz is responsible?'

Did he? It felt right. But if she were holding Edel captive somewhere, where was it?

'Maybe I should follow her and see where she's going,' Andrews said, and then with a glance at West, he took a cap from his pocket and pulled it on. 'My disguise.' He smiled, then got out of the car and walked briskly down the road.

Back in the station, West debated going directly to Morrison. Deciding he couldn't face it quite yet, he headed into the main office with Edwards a step behind. Leaving him to update the other members of the team, he headed into his office, closed the door and sat heavily onto his chair. He held his face in his hands for a few seconds before rubbing the tiredness away and sitting back. Where the hell was she?

He needed to focus on the case.

On Liz Goodbody. Circumstantial. All of it. That's what they'd say.

Especially after the fiasco with Viveka Larsson. They wouldn't forget that in a hurry. Damn it, they were right too. It was all circumstantial. All they had was the word of a woman, even the most politically correct advocate would have deemed not quite the full shilling.

They were back to no motive, no proof. No damned case.

And all he could think about was Edel. He was sure he was right about Liz. But, as Morrison would point out, he'd been sure he was right about Viveka Larsson as well.

It was becoming a muddle, a tangle he couldn't seem to unravel. He really needed to step back, try and get it all into focus.

He was still sitting trying to do just that, going over his notes yet again, and getting absolutely nowhere, when there was a quick rap on the door. He didn't have time to reply, to tell whoever it was to go away and leave him in peace, before the door opened and Edwards' face popped into view.

'Just had a call from Andrews,' he said. 'Liz Goodbody has just gone back to her house. I'm going down to pick him up.'

'Right,' he said, and Edwards left, leaving the door ajar. It had only been ninety minutes; wherever Liz had gone, she hadn't gone far.

Fifteen minutes later, Andrews' head appeared round the door.

'Coffee?' he asked, not waiting for an answer, throwing his coat over a chair and turning to go back into the general office, returning moments later with two mugs.

'Thanks,' West said when the mug was placed carefully in front of him and then, unable to wait any longer, asked, 'Well, where did she go?'

'She walked to the bus stop,' Andrews said, sipping his coffee. 'Luckily, there were a few people waiting, so she didn't notice me hanging around, and when she hopped on a 46A, I was able to slip on behind. At Nutley Lane, she got off, walked to Viveka Larsson's and stayed there about five minutes. She wasn't carrying anything going in, but she was carrying a small package when she came out.'

West frowned. 'And then?'

'She walked back to the main road and waited at the bus stop. I couldn't get too close, but got lucky again, two 46A buses came together, she got on the first, I got on the second. She went home again, Mike.'

'We need to find out what was in the package,' West said.

Andrews sipped his coffee. 'I suppose we could call on Viveka Larsson and just ask her.'

Running a hand through his hair, West grunted a negative. 'She wasn't happy with us this morning, Peter. I'm not sure she'd take too kindly to being asked questions about what she gave to Liz Goodbody. It may be something totally innocent to do with *Offer* or something else innocuous. She'd be under no obligation to tell us anyway.'

Just then, Sam Jarvis' handsome face appeared in the doorway looking, as usual, as if he would be more at home on the cover of a fashion magazine. He looked from one to the other, a serious look on his face. 'Am I interrupting? It's just something I wanted to mention.'

'Come in, Sam,' West said, waving him to a chair. 'What is it?'

Jarvis sat and drew a quick breath. 'Mark filled me in on what happened earlier. With Liz Goodbody. He told me about his clever plan to get you all into the house, but that you didn't find any trace of Ms Johnson.'

When he hesitated, Andrews used the toe of his shoe to give him a nudge and muttered, 'Get on with it, Sam.'

Sam flushed and took another deep breath. 'Mark says you searched everywhere, even the attic. But... what about under the stairs? A lot of people converted them into downstairs cloakrooms.'

West shut his eyes and swore.

Jarvis flushed a deeper shade of red. 'Sorry,' he said. 'Of course, you've thought of that.'

'No, Sam, I didn't. Goddamn it, she has a Welsh dresser in the hallway. It never entered my head that it would be covering something. But something did strike me as being strange. It's the kind of dresser you would put plates and pottery on, and yet the shelves were empty.'

'Because she needs to move it,' Andrews said, looking at Sam with approval. 'Good thinking.'

'Yes, well done,' West added and then said slowly, 'We need to get a look in there. The same trick won't work, unfortunately.'

'Wouldn't Ms Johnson have called out?' Jarvis asked. 'She'd have heard you outside. From what Mark has said, you were all making enough noise.'

'Unless she wasn't able to,' West said quietly, the frown marks between his eyes deepening.

'She could have been gagged or anything,' Andrews said calmly. 'No point in trying to outguess ourselves. Can't we try for a warrant?'

West didn't answer for a few minutes. Jarvis shuffled, anxious to be doing something. Andrews, his eyes focused on West, waited patiently.

'We'll never get a warrant with what we have. We've nothing concrete. Hell, Edel hasn't even been reported missing. After all,' he added, with a trace of a smile, 'she has been known to disappear. Remember?'

'She certainly led us a merry dance,' Andrews replied, 'but this isn't the same.'

'No, I think she's in trouble. But we have to go by the book. If we're right, this inappropriately named Goodbody woman murdered Gerard Roberts. We don't want her getting off on a technicality. Come on, I think we should visit Ms Larsson and plead for her help. Jarvis,' he added, answering the unsaid plea in the younger man's eyes, 'you might as well come along too.'

West drove and they arrived in Nutley Lane thirty minutes later, traffic conspiring against them all the way.

'We're going to play this quietly and cautiously,' he said, parking outside. 'She's not best pleased with us; hasn't any obligation to tell us what Liz took away with her. But she had a connection to Edel, felt sorry for her. I'm going to play on that.'

They waited for a long time after ringing the intercom bell before a quavering tinny voice asked what they wanted.

'Ms Larsson, it's Garda Sergeant Mike West again. We hate to disturb you, but is it possible to have a word?'

Static greeted his request and then the distinct buzz as the catch was released and they quickly pushed open the door as they had done several hours earlier.

They reached her apartment door as it opened, Viveka Larsson waving them in. It had only been a matter of hours since they had last seen her, but West thought she looked frailer, weaker. There was an air of finality about her that hadn't been there that morning. A knowledge that time was now measured in hours, not days, and that she had done all she could do to ensure safe passage.

'I didn't think to see you again, Sergeant West, or,' she said with a sideways look at Andrews and Jarvis, 'your satellites.'

She waved them to chairs, and moved slowly to sit in a small winged chair that faced the window, lowering herself carefully, but unable to hide the wince of pain that flitted across her face. 'I was admiring the view,' she said eventually. 'I was born in the mountains, Sergeant West. It is nice to see them again, now that I am dying.'

There was no quest for sympathy in her words, just a measure of acceptance. West moved a chair to sit near her, leaving Andrews and Jarvis hovering near the doorway.

'Is there someone who could come and stay with you?' he asked gently.

Dragging her eyes from the view, she looked at him and smiled. 'A volunteer from *Offer*, maybe? No, Sergeant West, you were wrong about that. It was never my intention.' Her smile widened and her eyes sparkled, and in that instant West saw the charismatic woman she had been. Then her eyes dulled, the smile faded and she moved her gaze back to the view. 'I have all I need here.'

West glanced back to where the others stood. Andrews raised his open hands and nodded, encouraging him to ask the questions he needed to.

They had no choice. Liz had killed before. There was nothing to stop her killing again. West hesitated, searching for the right words, needing to stir up some empathy for Edel.

'Ms Larsson,' he started hesitantly, 'you mentioned that you'd met Edel Johnson, the woman whose husband was murdered earlier this year. You had hoped to see her again.'

It was a minute, at least, before Viveka Larsson nodded, lost as she was in the business of dying. Without turning her head, her voice a shade quieter, she said, 'She didn't turn up.'

'No, she didn't. In fact, she hasn't been seen for a few days. We're looking for her. She had appointments she didn't keep; neighbours haven't seen her, and her car is parked outside her house.'

A look of sadness crossed Viveka's face and, this time, she turned to look at West. 'Something has happened to her?'

'Yes, we believe so.' He sighed and continued, 'You know we've been looking into *Offer*, Ms Larsson. We found a connection and erroneously thought you were involved.'

Frail, and unwell as she was, Viveka Larsson was not a fool. 'And I am not, as you know. But it seems to me that, perhaps, you have found another connection. Not, I hope, this woman?'

'No, not Edel. But we think she may have gone to warn

someone else that we were looking into the group. Someone, we have reason to believe, *is* connected.'

If it was possible to look paler and frailer, Viveka Larsson managed it. 'Somebody I know? You think it is one of my volunteers, and that they have hurt Edel too?'

'We have no evidence, just our suspicions,' he said, trying to feel his way to bring Liz Goodbody into the conversation.

'I had hoped *Offer* would be my swan song,' Viveka said, and for the first time a note of desolation sounded in her voice. She coughed then, a sad rattle of a sound. 'Tell me who this person is, I insist.'

'We think this person has Edel,' West said, ignoring her request, 'and means to do her harm.'

'But you know, it is not I. Why then are you here?'

It was time. 'Liz Goodbody called to see you a while ago, and stayed for a short time. When she left, she was carrying something. What was it?'

There was a palpable silence as West watched an array of emotions cross Viveka's face. 'You think Liz Goodbody is responsible? Impossible,' she said, her voiced laced in disbelief. 'She has been my second-in-command, the person who has done the most to keep *Offer* going. In the beginning, when it seemed it might fail, it was she who encouraged me; she stood by me, and had belief in what I was trying to achieve.' She finished on a high note, her voice frail but euphoric.

'In fact, she would do anything for you, Ms Larsson. Anything to keep *Offer* going for your sake.'

Viveka Larsson looked appalled as the truth hit home. 'Surely not... no, no this cannot be true!'

'Why did she come here today?' West persevered.

'She just came to see if I needed anything. Nothing more.'

'Does she do this regularly?'

She shrugged, and winced, needing to wait for the pain to subside before saying, 'Not really. But it is not too unusual.'

There had to be some reason she came today. West knew he was right. 'What did she take away with her? She was carrying something small in her hand when she left.'

'I gave her nothing,' Viveka said. 'Honestly. She stayed only a few minutes before leaving.'

Frustrated, West tried again. 'Are you sure? There was nothing she could have taken? Think, please, Edel's life may depend on it.'

The woman shook her head and sighed, her head slumping, the very effort of holding it up becoming too much of a feat. Raising her eyes, she whispered, 'I'm sorry, I cannot help you, or Edel. There is nothing more I can tell y...' She stopped mid-word, looking at West in dawning horror. 'Oh, my goodness,' she said, holding a thin, bony hand to her mouth as if to prevent the words, the thoughts escaping. A sob edged its way around her fingers, quickly followed by another.

'What is it?' West asked, sitting forward. 'What?'

Her face a picture of desolation, Viveka took her hand away and on the back of a sob, whispered, 'She asked to use the bathroom before she left. The bathroom cabinet. It's where I keep my morphine.'

Without a word, West got to his feet, taking a pair of latex gloves from his pocket and pulling them on, Andrews and Edwards following on his heels. The cabinet over the wash-hand basin was unlocked. Inside, it was packed with medication of all sorts, one shelf holding syringes and needles. Seeing what he was looking for, he took out the boxes, opened and counted the supply and returned them to the cabinet shelf. If they were right, they'd have the door fingerprinted and collect the hard evidence they needed.

'There are two boxes, with five ampoules of morphine in

each,' he said, returning to the sitting room. He looked to Viveka for confirmation, watching with a sinking feeling as her face contorted and tears appeared.

'There were three boxes. Oh my God, there were three.'

West pushed down the leap of fear and swung into action. 'Jarvis, I'm leaving you to organise having everything checked for fingerprints. We need to get this pinned down.' He wasn't going to risk compromising the case; he owed it to the Roberts' family to make sure Liz Goodbody was put away for Gerard Roberts' murder. Edel couldn't be the only person he considered. 'Peter, get on to the inspector, fill him in, he can get them to issue a warrant based on this theft. Tell him we're going straight to Goodbody's house. There is a strong possibility the morphine is for Edel.'

Jarvis and Andrews started on the phone calls, leaving West to console Viveka Larsson who had been overcome with grief at the outcome of something that had been designed to be her atonement. 'It was no fault of yours, Ms Larsson. You just wanted to do something worthy. You should know from all your experience with people, it's impossible to tell the good from the bad.'

'You will save Edel?' she said, her voice muffled with tears.

West's face looked grim. 'Yes,' he said. 'I promise.'

39

Leaving a reluctant Jarvis behind to advise the fingerprint techs when they arrived, West and Andrews took off at speed, hoping the warrant would be issued before they arrived at Goodbody's house. Andrews drove, West acknowledging with a nod the other man's faster driving skills. Anyway, it left him free to speak to Morrison when he rang five minutes later with news that the warrant had been granted.

'Thank you, Inspector,' he said, 'we're on our way there now.'

'Garda Baxter will meet you there with it. I hope you've done everything by the book.' Morrison's voice was sharp. 'We don't want this case compromised.'

'I have, sir and I've left Jarvis at the Larsson apartment; he'll monitor the situation there. The case against Liz Goodbody will hold.' West didn't tell him they'd inveigled their way into Liz's house earlier. That was most definitely on a need-to-know basis and, hopefully, the inspector would never need to know.

Traffic was heavy, and conscious that it had been more than two hours since Liz went home with enough morphine in her possession to kill, West pressed the switch that activated the strobe lighting on his front and back window and sent the siren wailing. Traffic moved out of their way, and Andrews put his foot to the floor.

They switched off the lights and siren as they pulled into Liz's road. There was no point in forewarning her. It didn't take long to cause grievous bodily harm. Even less time armed with a syringe filled with morphine. Pulling up directly outside, they stared grimly at the ordinary suburban house in front of them. There was no hint as to what was going on inside.

They reached the front door together. West reached for the door knocker and slammed it down smartly, waiting a second to see if there was a reply, before hammering it down again and again.

Andrews peered in the downstairs window. 'Nothing in view, Mike.'

They'd never kick the door in – it was old-school; heavy and dependable. There were two small panes of glass, set at eye level, too small to be of any use. 'Let's try plan B,' he said, and turned to scan the garden.

'What's plan B?' Andrews said, giving up on the window and trying to see through the small panes of glass in the door.

West picked up a heavy garden ornament – a weather-worn stone tortoise – and waved it in Andrews' direction. 'This is,' he said, moving to the front window and drawing his hand back to throw it through the glass.

Just then, Andrews saw movement inside. 'Hold it, she's coming.'

There was the distinct sound of a key in the lock and bolts being drawn. The door opened slowly and Liz Goodbody stood in the gap, one hand holding the door, an uncertain smile on her lips that faded quickly when she saw the tortoise in West's hand.

'What on earth?' she spluttered, closing the door, fiddling with the safety-chain and opening the door wide. 'What are you doing with that?'

West dropped the tortoise unceremoniously and brushed the dirt from his fingers, his eyes focused on her face. He expected a trace of anxiety, some outward sign of her guilt, but her face was a bland, blank mask of unconcern.

'Ms Goodbody,' he said, his voice firm, 'you are under arrest for the theft of morphine from the home of Viveka Larsson. We have a warrant to search your house to locate and confiscate the stolen items.'

'This is ridiculous,' she blustered, her free hand going to rest on the doorframe as if to bar their entrance.

Time didn't allow for gentle persuasion. Andrews moved in, firmly removed one hand after the other, and led her into the house just as a car pulled up. Turning, West saw Baxter and Edwards climb out and hurry up the path.

'We have the warrant,' Baxter said, waving it.

Andrews could be heard reading Liz Goodbody her rights. 'We got her then?' Edwards asked.

'We need to find the morphine she stole, and locate Edel before we can celebrate.' In the hallway, West stood in front of the tall dresser. Telltale marks on the carpet in front of it told him it had been recently moved. He gripped the edge and pulled, the dresser sliding easily to reveal the door behind. There was a small key in the lock and bolts to the top and bottom.

'Edel,' he called, fumbling with the metalware before wrenching the door open. They were immediately hit with the offensive smell of body waste and a cloying, metallic smell of stale blood. West looked down in disbelief at the body lying prone in the small space. Baxter squeezing in front of him, bent and picked up the wrist that lay almost at his feet.

He looked up; his mouth set in a grim line. 'I can't get a pulse.'

West couldn't move. He saw Andrews push the others out of

the way and bark an order at Edwards to stay with Liz before he gently turned Edel, his fingers moving over her neck. 'There's a pulse. But it's faint. She has a wound on her head. It looks like she might have banged her head on the sloped wall. There's blood there.' He pointed, and West, following his finger to the dark stain, felt his stomach lurch.

Baxter moved, took out his phone and called for an ambulance. 'Possible morphine overdose,' he added, knowing that the faster they administered an antidote the better the outcome would be.

'We need to make sure,' West said, tearing his eyes away from the motionless body. He couldn't stay there watching her die. 'Seamus, see if you can find the empty vials.' With a swift glance at Edel, he turned to Andrews. 'Stay with her, Pete. I'll go and find out what I can from Liz.'

In the sitting room, Liz sat looking unperturbed, while Edwards stood in the doorway, one eye on her, one eye on what was happening outside.

West brushed past him and sat in the chair opposite her. 'We've found Edel, Ms Goodbody.'

He was interrupted by the return of Baxter. 'I've got them all, Sergeant West,' he said, his mouth twisting as he opened his gloved hand to show five empty morphine vials and a syringe and needle.

West swallowed. Five empty vials. His eyes were bleak when he looked back to where Liz sat comfortably relaxed. 'You injected her with all the morphine you stole from Ms Larsson?'

Liz looked at him calmly. 'She tried to escape. I had to do something.'

West could hear Andrews speaking softly to Edel, murmuring words of reassurance. As he listened to Goodbody's attempt to justify her actions, he resisted the temptation to shout at her, waiting for her to say more.

'I did warn her,' she said, as if this vindicated her next action. 'I gave her clear warning that if she tried anything, I'd use my taser.'

Shocked, West looked at Baxter who immediately moved on the quest for the weapon.

'You used a taser?'

'She tried to escape. It's very effective; she hadn't regained consciousness by the time I returned, so it was easy to inject her with the morphine. I wasn't sure how much to use, but it seemed a shame to waste it, so I used it all.'

West heard the faint sound of a siren. They'd be here soon; Edel would be safe and this monster would go away for a long time. Looking at her, he didn't bother trying to hide the contempt in his eyes. 'Why did you do it?'

Liz's face wore the fervent look of the fanatic, and her eyes sparked with the flame of the zealot. 'For Viveka, of course,' she cried. '*Offer* has to be a success. It is going to be her legacy. And it was working. Everything was going to plan. You needed us.

'But Edel thought Viveka was to blame for the incidents. She was going to tell you. If she had, you'd have questioned Viveka and realised she wasn't responsible, and... well, the game would have been up, I suppose.'

'So, you decided to kill her, just as you had killed Gerard Roberts.'

A puzzled look fluttered across her face. 'Who?'

West could see no guile in her face, she'd really forgotten. 'Gerard Roberts. The man you poisoned with the manihot esculenta.'

'Oh, him,' she said, as if they were discussing someone she'd once met socially. 'Well, I'm sure you realise, that was an accident. He wasn't supposed to die.'

'But it wouldn't have been an accident with Edel,' West said. 'It would have been premeditated murder.'

Her smile was unpleasant. 'It may still be, Sergeant West. She hit her head quite hard when she went down, you know, and it was quite a lot of morphine. Strange,' she said, looking at him with a quizzical tilt of her head, 'I was a little upset when I heard that man died. It's much easier second time around.'

40

W est went with Edel in the ambulance, leaving Andrews, Baxter and Edwards to deal with Liz. He really couldn't spend any more time in her company without attempting murder himself. She was mad, he decided. No other excuse.

Thanks to Baxter's quick thinking in providing the information about the morphine, the ambulance crew had the antidote ready to administer, the intravenous drip already set up when they wheeled the gurney onto the ambulance.

Desperately wanting to ask if they were in time, if she'd be okay, West bit his tongue. He knew they were doing all they could.

The ambulance pulled up outside the A&E department of St Vincent's Hospital. The doors were opened, a ramp lowered and West followed as the gurney was wheeled at speed through the mass of people who swarmed about the entrance.

A young nurse attempted to stop West from following into the cubicle. 'Garda Síochána,' he said quietly, 'I have to keep her in my sight at all times.' The nurse looked at Edel, unconscious on the trolley, and at West with a raised eyebrow, but as she was about to remonstrate, a call came for her assistance in another cubicle. With a sigh, she gave him strict instructions to keep out of the way and headed off.

A very efficient doctor in a green scrub suit listened as the ambulance crew gave a rundown on what they knew, what they'd done. She nodded, dismissing them and turning to give Edel the once over before checking and adjusting the flow of the intravenous infusion. With a small torch, she shone a light into her eyes. West watched, feeling tension release a notch when she seemed to be satisfied with what she saw.

Without raising her voice she gave instructions to the staff, her tone a measure of calm in the hectic unit. Within minutes, monitors were attached, the slow steady beep from them reassuring. Surely that augured well. West released and stretched fingers that had been clenched tightly since they left the house.

He stood, at a distance, not getting in the way, but close enough to see Edel's pale face behind the oxygen mask. Close enough to see a worried look appear on the very efficient A&E doctor who immediately rapped out a new set of instructions.

Moments later, in the answer to a phone call West hadn't seen made, another older man entered the cubicle. Wearing an expensive suit, crisp white shirt and striped tie, he looked as if he had wandered into the cubicle by accident straight from the nearest law office.

But West caught the faint look of relief on the face of the A&E doctor as she moved to greet him, handing him the clipboard she carried. She pointed out some figures; he muttered something and moved closer to Edel, the other staff pulling back out of his way without a word being said. Taking a tiny pencil torch from his inside pocket, he shone the light into Edel's eyes, repeating the action twice before switching off the torch and nodding.

'I agree, Dr Salmon,' he said, addressing the A&E doctor.

'Let's get a CT scan done stat and we'll go from there.' He turned to leave and found West blocking his way.

Quickly, West identified himself. 'It was my team who found Ms Johnson. Can you tell me what's happening?'

The man looked at him severely. 'Dr Salmon tells me the lady was tasered.'

West looked horrified. 'Not by the gardaí, I assure you Dr... Mr...'

'Mr Noonan, I'm a neurosurgeon,' he said, the severe look softening a fraction. Seeing something in West's face, he asked more kindly, 'Ms Johnson is a friend?' He waited for the nod before continuing. 'We are going to take her for a CT scan to see the extent of the damage. If, as we think is the case from our examination so far, there is a cerebral bleed, we may proceed to do what we refer to as burr holes – these are small holes drilled in the skull to release pressure. If this is successful, we may keep her in the coma she is in, to allow the brain to recover.'

West felt himself go pale. 'There are a lot of *ifs* and *mays* there, Mr Noonan.'

The neurosurgeon smiled briefly. 'They may treat me like God,' he said, 'but I'm afraid my skills, though exceptionally good, are not divine.' He drew West out of the way as staff readied Edel's trolley and moved her slowly from the A&E department. 'You can follow if you like,' the neurosurgeon said, his mind already elsewhere, 'there's a waiting room. You can get a cup of appalling coffee, if you need sustenance.' He rejoined the medical team surrounding Edel's trolley as it made its slow progress up two floors to where the CT scanner was situated.

West followed and found the waiting room. He spent two euro on a cup of coffee, and gave a brief smile at the first sip, hoping Noonan was as skilled a neurosurgeon as he was a judge of coffee; it was truly appalling. He sipped it anyway – he'd need the caffeine fix for what was probably going to be a long night.

He'd no worries about what was happening back at the station. Andrews was as dependable as they came. And even Morrison, when he knew the score, would pull out all stops to make sure things went as they should. They'd give him all the time he needed here.

Draining the disposable cup, he sat and held it, folded it in half, in quarters, then folded it again. There was a bin alongside the vending machine; he took aim and fired the wadded cup. Bullseye. Then there was nothing else to do. No magazines. No papers. Nobody else waiting to watch, weigh up, or exchange the time of day with. Just four walls, several very uncomfortable seats, and thoughts he didn't want to think.

It couldn't end like this. Not after all she had been through. They hadn't even had a chance to get together, not really. Never had that walk along the pier, never held hands, never kissed, never made love. All the *nevers*.

He sat, linked his hands on his head and dropped it back so that he was looking at the ceiling. Thoughts he didn't bother trying to untangle jumbled about, butterfly-flitting from one to the other, the only common denominator being Edel. Times they'd met. Things she'd said. Her face. Her body. A look. A smile. Too few memories. Too many regrets.

And then, after he didn't know how long, the door opened and he saw the neurosurgeon in the doorway, dressed now in scrubs he wore with the same air of authority as his expensive suit. He turned back as somebody outside called him, and West heard him answer abruptly. 'No, tell them I'll be there in a moment. They don't need me here anymore.'

West's hands dropped to his lap. Had he not been sitting, he would have fallen to the floor, all the strings of his meaningless existence cut. How would he stand? How could he carry on?

She was dead.

He'd met death before. In Glasnevin. A colleague, a mother,

her children. Had seen it all, he'd thought. Had felt the pain, the loss. Up close and personal. He knew nothing. Hadn't had a clue. Hadn't known about the hole it made, the huge sense of loss, a deep relentless void, a bottomless pit of sorrow.

Andrews appeared in the doorway beside the neurosurgeon who was still in conversation with someone out of view. He moved by him and catching sight of West, the look of misery on his face, he went quickly to his side, grabbed a chair and sat opposite him.

'Mike,' he said, reaching a hand out to take the other man's arm. 'Don't tell me...'

West couldn't say a word, couldn't seem to remember how. He met Andrews' eyes and knew he didn't have to.

'She's dead?' Andrews whispered in disbelief. 'Oh Mike, I don't know what to say.'

There was nothing to say. In death, there was no hope. West knew that only too well.

41

John Noonan had seen Andrews enter the room, so when he finished his conversation and turned, he assumed West had been brought bad news. He'd seen that expression too often not to recognise it, that awful look of loss, of desolation tinged with disbelief. For a change it was someone else giving bad news.

He checked his watch. There was never enough time, he needed to get on.

He approached the two men.

When he saw him, West stood unsteadily, his face pale. 'She didn't make it. I heard,' he said. 'I'm sure you did your best, thank you.'

The neurosurgeon looked confused. 'Who didn't make it?'

It was West's turn to look puzzled. 'Edel Johnson,' he said, feeling the first whisper of hope. 'I heard you tell someone you wouldn't be needed anymore.'

'Misinformation and miscommunication,' Noonan said. 'The bane of my life. Let me be very clear. I won't be needed, Sergeant

West, because the CT scan was clear; there was no indication whatsoever of any damage. No damage equals no surgery required.' He spread his hands and smiled. 'No surgery required, equals no surgeon required. I've transferred Mrs Johnson's care to the medical team.'

The whisper of hope turned into a jubilant roar and West grabbed his arm. 'She's not dead?'

'She's most definitely not dead,' Mr Noonan said, patting his hand. 'She'll be sent down to a ward and kept under observation. My colleague, a Dr Barbara Mitford, will be in charge of her care. Rest assured, she's top of her field.' He looked at both men and then, with a shrug, said, 'Dr Mitford won't mind my anticipating her diagnosis, but it is my opinion that Ms Johnson is suffering from a serious concussion that was exacerbated by the taser blast and the morphine overdose. I estimate she'll come around in the next couple of hours, and be back to her old self within a day or so.'

As it turned out, Mr Noonan was out by a couple of hours. By the time Edel had been transferred into a bed, in the private room West had insisted upon, she had opened her eyes and asked in a very faint voice, 'Where am I?'

The nurse who was adjusting the monitors and intravenous infusion, heard and came to her side. 'Hello there,' she said gently. 'Everything is okay. You're in St Vincent's. You're quite safe.'

'What happened?'

The nurse made a final adjustment to a monitor, and smiled down at Edel's anxious face. 'Well now, if you hang on there a minute, there are a few people who will be able to fill you in. A little anyway.'

She went away and Edel closed her eyes. When she opened

them again, she guessed she'd fallen asleep because sitting in a chair beside the bed, his eyes closed, sat Mike West. He needed a shave and his tie was undone, but Edel thought she'd never seen a better sight.

'Hello,' she tried, the sound frail and weedy. She tried again, 'Hello.'

Immediately his eyes opened. 'Edel.'

'How long have I been here?'

West moved closer, reached for her free hand and held it. 'About six hours now. How do you feel?'

Edel thought a moment. She wasn't sure. 'I ache a bit,' she admitted finally, 'my head.' She looked down at her arm with the intravenous infusion. 'And this.'

'You're going to be fine,' West reassured her. 'There's no damage. The doctors have done a cluster of tests. Everything is okay.'

'Good,' she said, shutting her eyes. She would have liked to have slept again, but she needed to know what had happened. 'Liz drugged me. And locked me under the stairs. And then, there was a terrible pain. I don't remember any more.' Then she did remember something and she turned her hand and grabbed his. 'Liz is protecting Viveka Larsson. I don't think she wanted to hurt me; she was just afraid I'd tell you about what Viveka had said.'

When she opened her eyes again, it was to see two nurses disconnecting the monitors that had been beep-beeping a lullaby. 'Hello,' she said and they stopped and came over to her. 'Hi there,' the taller of the two said with a smile. 'How are you this morning?'

Actually, to her surprise, she felt fine. Her head was still a little sore, her arm ached. But otherwise she felt good. 'I don't know what you're pumping in to me,' she told them, 'but it's working. I feel good.'

'Would you like to try some breakfast?' one of the nurses asked, as the other wheeled the monitors from the room. 'The doctor will be around in about an hour. If you're eating and drinking well, they'll probably take the drip down.'

Even without the added incentive, Edel would have agreed to breakfast. She was starving and when it did arrive, looking decidedly lacklustre, she tucked in as though it were Michelin star quality and was draining the teapot when Dr Mitford came in surrounded by a bevy of younger doctors.

'How are you feeling?' she asked, opening the file she held before casting a knowing eye over her. 'Head still aching?'

Edel smiled. 'Not so bad now.'

The doctor took a torch from her pocket and looked into her eyes. 'Fine,' she said, 'everything looks good. Your bloods have come back. No problems there. The Narcan infusion reversed any lingering effects from the morphine you were injected with. And the ECG showed there were no side effects from the taser blast.'

'What?' Edel said, looking confused. 'I thought I had been drugged and banged my head. A taser blast?' Suddenly, she remembered the terrible stinging sensation and closed her eyes. 'Yes, she threatened me with it. I remember now. And the terrible sting when it hit.' Her eyes opened, shining with tears she refused to let fall. 'Where did the morphine come into it?'

Dr Mitford looked embarrassed. 'I was told you had been informed of the circumstances. My apologies, Ms Johnson. It's a little complicated, I'm afraid.' She drew a sigh of relief, when a knock on the door was followed by the entrance of Sergeant West whom she'd met the night before. 'Come in, Sergeant,' she said, 'I think your arrival is timely. Ms Johnson has questions I feel it best to leave to you to answer.' Looking back at Edel, she said, 'I'll have the intravenous infusion removed. See how you feel, but as far as I'm concerned you are free to go this afternoon.' With a smile, and a nod to West, she made her exit.

West closed the door with one hand. His other hand, hidden behind his back, was brought forward and Edel smiled at the huge bouquet of red tulips, each trimmed with a frill of yellow, the petals flopping open to show a matching yellow centre.

'Tulips,' she exclaimed in pleasure, taking the flowers, holding them to her face to hide emotions she knew were too fully on display. 'They're so beautiful,' she whispered, 'where on earth did you get tulips at this time of the year?'

West took the chair he had sat in some hours earlier. 'Anything is possible when you want it badly enough,' he said, hoping she realised he wasn't speaking only about the flowers, and then deciding it possibly wasn't the right moment. 'You look much better. And you're eating. Always a good sign.'

'I feel much better,' Edel said, putting the tulips down on the table in front of her. She looked at West. 'You need to tell me the truth. What happened to me? The doctor said something about morphine. I know I was drugged, and she used that taser on me.' Reaching to her head she felt the row of small stitches. 'And I banged my head.' She looked at him suspiciously. 'Or did someone knock me out?'

West laughed. 'No, that's one thing that didn't happen to you.'

'Well, that's a relief,' she said, leaning heavily on sarcasm. 'Now tell me what did happen to me.'

And he did, leaving nothing out, and Edel's eyes grew rounder, her face paler. 'And that's the whole story,' he finished.

She said nothing for a few minutes, just lay there trying to take it all in. There were probably questions she should ask, but for the life of her she couldn't think of one. All she managed to say, with heavy disbelief, was, 'Liz Goodbody.'

They sat in silence for a moment.

'I'm sorry I shouted at you,' Edel said quietly. 'I realised later that you'd been trying to protect me.'

West reached for her hand and held it tightly. 'If I hadn't told you, you'd never have gone there. It's all my fault. A few minutes later, and you would have died.'

'I was drugged, tasered, banged my head and given an overdose of morphine. I reckon I'm virtually indestructible.' An attempt at a smile failed, her eyes filling. 'Liz Goodbody,' she said with a tinge of bitterness. 'I really do have a great knack for judging people, don't I? She tried to kill me. Killed Gerard Roberts. Terrified so many people. And all of it done for Viveka?'

West rubbed a weary hand over his face; it had been a long week. 'She knew Viveka was dying,' he said slowly, remembering the frail woman he had left behind in the apartment. 'And she believed that *Offer* was to be her legacy to the community.' He smiled ruefully. 'Viveka led everyone to think that she ran a similar set-up in Finland, but she didn't, she ran a brothel. A well-run one, by all accounts, but there had been a problem and one of the young women was badly injured. Viveka was trying to make amends before she died.'

Edel laughed uncertainly. 'A brothel? Does Liz know?'

'Not yet, we're interviewing her in about' – he checked his watch – 'three hours. She'll probably find out then.'

'The pedestal she built for Viveka will come crashing down, won't it?' Edel didn't bother trying to hide her satisfaction.

'I don't know,' West replied honestly. 'It may go higher. A sinner repenting and all that. It could elevate Viveka to sainthood in Liz's eyes. What will devastate her, is that *Offer* will come tumbling down. It won't be able to survive this. Liz will be charged with murder, attempted murder, kidnapping, assault, theft, and several other charges arising from all the events she'd orchestrated over the last few months. She won't see daylight for a long time.'

The silence was broken by one of the staff coming to remove Edel's breakfast tray. 'Would you like me to put your flowers in water?'

'No, thanks,' Edel said with a smile. 'I'll be going home soon; I'd like to take them with me.'

When they were alone again, Edel pulled her hand away. 'I'm indestructible, but also very grubby. I need to find my clothes, have a shower, and get dressed.'

'I think they had to cut your clothes away to put the intravenous line in and attach the monitors.' He grabbed her hand back, holding it tightly when she tried to pull away. 'I have your keys; I'm going to go and fetch you some fresh clothes. And before you start arguing, I think I'm capable of finding suitable garments for a woman to wear.

'What?' he asked, when she muttered something under her breath.

'I said I have no doubt. But that doesn't mean I like the idea of you rummaging in my knicker drawer.'

'If I promise not to rummage?' he said with a grin, watching a smile grow on her face. 'Have a long shower; I'll be back as quickly as I can. And then you have a choice.'

'A choice about what?' she said, suspecting she wasn't going to like what she heard next.

He held her hand in both of his, and looked her straight in the eye. 'Think about it until I come back. Either I stay in your house, in your spare room, of course. Or you come home with me, stay in a spare room in mine.' He stood, bent down and kissed her on the forehead. 'The choice is yours. I can drop you in either place before going back to the station.'

She was about to say *absolutely not* when he kissed her again. This time full on the lips. Gently, softly, lingering, his fingers brushing her cheek. And with no conscious thought, she reached a hand up to his.

They broke apart, reluctance on both sides.

'I've dreamt about kissing you for a long time,' he said, his eyes grey velvet. 'I'd hoped for a more romantic setting than this.'

She felt giddy. Maybe the after-effects of the morphine. Maybe not. 'I don't know, it seems wonderfully romantic to me.'

He chuckled, and checked his watch. 'I'd better go. You decide where you want me to take you, and I'll be back in about forty-five minutes.' On that note he turned and left with a wave of his hand.

She smiled, took a deep breath and settled back against the pillows.

Which choice to make. His house? Her house?

It didn't matter. Not really.

Or did it? She remembered the excitement when she and Simon had bought the house in Wilton Road, how much in love they were, how happy. It was the first time she had remembered the good times, and she was glad. And it made the choice easy. The house was beautiful. But it was filled with memories, good and bad, that belonged to her past.

Mike was her future. She'd go home with him.

And, for the moment, she'd sleep in his spare room.

ACKNOWLEDGEMENTS

A huge thanks to Bloodhound Books for publishing No Obvious Cause which was first self-published as Close Ranks. The new title and brilliant cover do it far more justice.

I'd also like to thank all the readers, reviewers and bloggers who have been so supportive over the years – reviews, comments, even criticism, help to focus my writing.

As usual, I couldn't keep writing without the support of my friends and family – the ones who read and encourage, the ones who keep me supplied with cake and other essentials and who don't complain when I obsess about edits. A special thank you, as ever, to writing buddies, Jenny O'Brien and Leslie Bratspis.

No Obvious Cause is the second book in this series; the next, No Past Forgiven, is due out in March, followed by No Memory Lost, in April. Hopefully, the as yet unnamed fifth in the series will be published later in the year.

If you'd like to contact me – and I love to hear from readers – you can find me here:

facebook.com/valeriekeoghnovels

Twitter: @ValerieKeogh1

Instagram: valeriekeogh2
https://www.amazon.co.uk/-/e/BooLKoNMB8
https://www.amazon.co.uk/-/e/BooLKoNMB8
https://www.amazon.co.uk/-/e/BooLKoNMB8

Made in the USA
Coppell, TX
10 November 2020